THE CORPORATE WORLD JUST TOOK A TURN FOR THE WORSE

THE
DEMON
IN
BUSINESS
CLASS

THE CORPORATE WORLD JUST TOOK A TURN FOR THE WORSE

THE
DEMON
IN
BUSINESS
CLASS

ANTHONY DOBRANSKI

To Matt —

Bon Voyage!

WordFire Press
Colorado Springs, Colorado

A. Dobranski

THE DEMON IN BUSINESS CLASS
Copyright © 2016 Anthony Dobranski

ISBN: 978-1-61475-474-9

Cover design by Duong Covers

Edited by Vivian Trask

Kevin J. Anderson, Art Director

Book Design by RuneWright, LLC
www.RuneWright.com

Published by
WordFire Press, an imprint of
WordFire, Inc.
PO Box 1840
Monument CO 80132

Kevin J. Anderson & Rebecca Moesta, Publishers

WordFire Press Trade Paperback Edition November 2016
Printed in the USA
wordfirepress.com

CONTENTS

November 2009

December 2009

October 2010

DEDICATION

for Jackie

ACKNOWLEDGEMENTS

I've wanted to write fiction since childhood, but after college I knew I had to see the world first. I traveled, and worked, at odd jobs and good jobs. The best job, and the only one that matters to this book, was at a wonderful, intense, and explosively successful company called America Online, later AOL. To my many AOL friends, colleagues, bosses, and business partners, in Northern Virginia, Hamburg, London, Paris, Tokyo, Sydney, and Hong Kong, who taught me so much and helped me see how big this world is—who gave me something to write about—thank you all.

The idea for this book fell small yet whole into a letter (on AOL Japan stationery) to my dear friend and collaborator Erik Bennett. No one else could have made me comfortable enough to bring this fragile whimsy out into the light.

This book went through a lot of changes and hit many dead ends in the writing. Without the support, encouragement, and advice of these people, I would have done much worse. Thanks to Erik Bennett, Adrian Bryant, Maren Pyenson, Masi Denison, Luke Christopher, David Guimbellot, Geoffrey Kabaservice, Lars Sorgenfrey, Kendra Harpster, Jennifer Russ, Kathryn Johnson, Cindy Sommer, Frank Sommer, John Mahshie, Jennifer Brinn, Melissa Cox, Jennifer Azantian, Wayland Smith, James

Artimus Owen, Joshua Essoe, Laila Sultan, Jessica Epperson-Lusty, Kate Yonkers, and Jacqueline Dobranski.

This book benefited greatly from workshops, at The Writer's Center in Bethesda, Maryland, and at Aspen Words (formerly Aspen Writers' Foundation) in Aspen, Colorado, led by writers Fenton Johnson, John Beckman, Robert Bausch, Pam Houston, Leslie Pietrzyk, T. Greenwood, and Kathryn Johnson.

The Cat Vacuuming Society of Northern Virginia is a tough bunch of literary critics, and nurturing too. Superstars Writing Seminars is brutally honest about the publishing business, and nurturing too.

My editor Vivian Trask reads deeply and with exquisite sensitivity. It's hard enough to find the weak parts; she also finds the missing parts. I am blessed to have worked with her.

APRIL 2009

CHAPTER ONE

Washington, DC

In the fake-oak-paneled conference room, Zarabeth Battrie found a dozen others standing. All looked wilted and worn, with bunched shirts and bowing ankles. The plastic tables were gone, the plastic chairs stacked in the corner. More people arrived but no one unstacked the chairs. A herd instinct, Zarabeth decided, to keep a clear path for fleeing.

A natty beige man in a crisp blue plaid suit came in, pushing a low gray plastic cart with stacks of documents. If the standing people surprised him, he didn't show it. With practiced ease he lowered the room's screen, plugged in his power strip. Someone passed the documents around but no one spoke. In the silence, Zarabeth felt anxieties around her, about money, status, children, groping her like fevered predictable hands. Too intimate, these people's worries in her skin when she didn't know their names, or want to. She shook them off, pushed through to the front so as not to stare at men's backs all meeting.

Projector light bleached the natty man while he talked through slides of sunsets and bullet points, with the real news a seeming afterthought. Her office and two others were merging with Optimized Deployments, in Boston. A great move. Efficiency for all. The animated org-chart realigned over and over, three squares gone and Optimized's no bigger. Reorganized like a stomach does food.

People asked tired questions, their hot worry now clammy hope. The natty man smiled no matter what he said. Yes, redundancies. Jobs would move, details to work out. All would be well and better.

He left to spread his joy. The room lights rose.

Zarabeth's boss, Aleksei Medev, slouched in the corner like someone had whacked his head with lumber. His unshaven olive skin hung gray and limp. With all eyes on him, he straightened.

"A very challenging time," he said. "We're sending reports to justify—to guide the transition. Client work is secondary."

Zarabeth was in no hurry to fill out Aleksei's useless reports. Nothing she had done in the last two months justified keeping her employed, she knew that. She went out the broken fire exit to a stand of pine trees behind the parking lot. She lit a cigarette, paced in the shade.

Once, Zarabeth Battrie had traveled the country as an Inspiration Manager, connecting the best people at Straightforward Consulting to an in-house knowledge network. She had good instincts which managers to flatter, which to cow, which to sneak past. It surprised her how much she understood when she finally got her quarry to talk their special arcana, over morning jogs, lobster lunches, steak dinners, midnight hookahs with shots of tequila. Later, on airplanes, she'd think of those and other conversations, watching the pieces fit together in this strange unity and balloon, her world growing with a drug-like jolt. To let her do that, week in, week out—taking off, landing, on the move, on her feet—had been the greatest praise.

On Valentine's Day, it had evaporated without explanation. Zarabeth had been reassigned to Reston, in the Virginia suburbs, to do public-relations grunt-work for industry trade groups. Aleksei Medev, still shiny then, had put his feet on her new desk and spun a great tale, core knowledge toward a turnkey marketing solution, select team deep study. At least she got an office with a door.

Zarabeth had visited Boston twice in her old job. Optimized had smart people and kept them by being greedy. They would suck the money from her division like marrow from bone. Everyone fired, no matter how they danced.

Doubt ate through her like some parasite come to lay its eggs. She pinched the cigarette's cherry to burn it off with pain. Six years at this firm would not end this week.

* * *

Zarabeth sublet a furnished apartment in Foggy Bottom, facing west and the Potomac River. She had chosen it for the balcony view and the location near the highway, but she didn't like the place much. The heavy dark furniture and metallic abstract art looked good at night, but menacing in morning shadow and grim in afternoon sun. Some days Zarabeth fantasized trashing it, taking a sledgehammer to the whole gloomy aquarium. This was a good day for that.

But Missy Devereaux was there, watching TV, in new red hair, her dirty bare feet on the coffee table.

"Hey, sugar," Missy said, in her perky Kentucky accent. "Want some wine?"

"Get your bow legs off my table," Zarabeth said. "When did you go ginger?"

"Do you love it?" Missy muted the sound. "I love it. Gramma hates it. Do you love it?"

A year ago, Missy Devereaux had been a straightforward legislative liaison, frost-blonde hair and pricey suits, working her congressman daddy's contact list. Now on the ground floor of Missy's Georgetown mansion, her grandmother died slowly of bone cancer. Missy came to Zarabeth's place as a retreat, a chance to smoke without blowing up the oxygen tanks. In return Missy watered the plants and filled the wine rack. It was a good arrangement, most days.

"It's great." Zarabeth went to her bedroom. She wiped off her makeup, washed her face with cold water. Her copper skin looked flushed. Small zits on her forehead. Twenty-seven, and she still broke out. She turned from the mirror so as not to smash it.

Missy came with a glass of white. "Three hours 'til the nurse leaves. You want dinner?"

Zarabeth shook with fury. "I so don't deserve this."

"I know, sugar-pea. I know."

"The fuck you know, witch?"

Missy's eyes flashed, from blue to bright green. Like the unlocking of a cage.

Zarabeth backed down. She checked herself by punching her palm repeatedly. "Fuck me! Fucking fuck."

"You just *relax*," Missy said. Maybe to herself too. Her eyes blue again, at least. She pulled a joint from behind her ear. "Drink and smoke. I'm ordering food. Lamb kebab with fries, right?" She closed the door.

Zarabeth struggled to light the joint with her smarting hands. She took small drags of the sweet smoke. The pain in her hands faded. Clearly Missy already knew about the re-org. Maybe she had known in advance, not that it would have done Zarabeth good to know sooner. Still, it was fine to pretend they were just two gals in the city, but one was an heiress and more.

That Missy came from old money, or close enough by American reckoning, Zarabeth had known from the start, but they both looked good, worked hard, and closed down bars too. Six months earlier, at a warehouse nightclub in Northeast, Zarabeth had lost track of Missy. Noises on the phone when Zarabeth called, rustle of a hand hanging up. A man's hand. She had felt his sweaty soft skin through the phone.

"A white guy dosed my friend and they're here," she had told the bouncers. The bouncers had known which private room to try. A dark crowded party, Missy in the back on a couch, waving like a broken doll, a fat preppy fuck in seersucker kneeling between her legs, his own belt undone. Zarabeth took his open-mouthed fat preppy picture and dragged Missy out until her own walking took over.

The next night Missy had come over, without makeup, not in crisp linen but in the hippie disarray that soon became her general uniform.

"Thank you for saving me," Missy had said. "I'm leaving the firm. Going back to the family business."

"Stop. What was that?" Zarabeth had asked. "On the phone?"

Missy hadn't tried to pretend. "I didn't think we had become so close. Let me tell you a story. May, 1593. King James was burning witches, and more who weren't, on Edinburgh stakes. But in the Highlands, the widow Cullodena McCauley walked into the forest, and was not seen from new moon to new moon.

"Cullodena returned with a compact from Queen Mab, signed in blood; a proof of her new arts, which is not discussed; and, though it was only found out later, pregnant. So our old books say. Six families followed Cullodena from Scotland to Ireland. Their daughters studied the old ways, and charmed the men learning the new ways. A century later, they came to America as one coven, ruled by Cullodena's female descendants. I'm fourteenth in that unbroken line. Soon, my grandmother will die. My mother will rise to advise the coven. I will be the Brigid, both queen and high priestess, of a coven of hundreds—a secret matriarchy, hiding in plain sight."

Missy had stood. "Know what else? We really are witches."

Missy had risen in the air, eyes glowing hot green, arms shaking as if they bore her weight and more. "Go ahead," Missy had grunted. "Check."

A jet-engine on Zarabeth's sensitive skin, either Missy or the weight she bore. "I'm good. That's a neat trick."

"One of many. But they have rules." Missy had somersaulted backward, landed standing on the floor, dying green light in her eyes. "You know this is secret, right? So shut up. We kill from a distance." A last flash of green, a smile less mirth than hunger. "Thanks for that picture, by the way."

Heiress and witch. One thing Zarabeth had learned, neither liked to owe. Sometimes Zarabeth wondered if that wasn't why Missy had told her, not to bring them closer but to bind her with fatal threat. It made their friendship a little sharp.

Heiress and witch. This evening the witch was close to the surface. Maybe Missy wasn't having a good day either.

Zarabeth changed into yoga clothes. She found Missy lighting a glass pipe on the apartment's small balcony. "Sorry."

"Sugar, please," Missy said. "Don't even. Bad day at Straightforward. Three digits, I hear tell. Maybe four."

"You've been gone a year and you have a better network than I do." Zarabeth slumped in her chair. The high relaxed her too much, weighing on her limbs like Christmas ornaments.

"Boys always talk to pretty girls," Missy said. "You should try that sometime. Have you seen my babies?" Missy grew seedlings on the balcony to amuse herself on her visits. "Here's wormwood, coneflower. Brings butterflies. Valerian, bloodroot, and that whole row is tansy. Pretty flowers but itchy leaves. Some is for you. Keeps away cops."

"Nice of you." Zarabeth refilled their wines. "Four digits? I'm out on my ass."

"I still don't see how you're in Reston. What happened to, uh, Execution Exemplary?"

"Executive Exemplars." Zarabeth shook her head. "No one ever said. Four hours in Anchorage and they made me fly back. The next day the server was locked. So was my office."

"You know Boston staff. They'll see your worth."

"I never met Magda Crane herself. Have you?"

"Couple times. She acts a bit dotty, but she knows her stuff. Not a nice person."

"I don't need nice. Do you miss working?" Zarabeth asked. "I mean, corporate life."

"It was a good time," Missy said. "Work was like college. I knew it would end."

Zarabeth bobbed in her high. She could play with Missy, until Missy moved back to Kentucky to assume her throne. Zarabeth didn't want to play. The firm had taken her seriously. It hurt when they stopped.

The food came cold but they didn't bother heating it up. They said little, less eating than refueling. Missy seemed antsy, getting up for more wine, for hot sauce, for water.

"I'm afraid Gramma doesn't trust me," Missy finally said. She looked around as if for eavesdroppers, a reflex that amused

Zarabeth, though Zarabeth didn't smile. Missy rarely discussed her family. Maybe the wine, maybe her own bad luck. Zarabeth paid a snake's attention.

"Why would you even think that?" she asked.

"Without our arts," Missy said, "Gramma would have—and her pain—but she hangs on. I don't know how to prove myself."

Zarabeth swallowed so as not to chuckle. "Maybe it's not you? Your kind are all circle-of-life, but dying sucks. When my dad died, he was so angry, he could barely see me. Maybe she's angry. Maybe she's scared. Sometimes on planes, in turbulence, I think—if we crashed, would this be enough life?"

"No," Missy said.

"Fuck no. Maybe it's even harder when you're older."

Zarabeth cleared the wrappers and refilled the filtered water pitcher. Missy sat in the living room, under a lamp of metal thorns, idly fan-shuffling Zarabeth's tarot cards with a stage magician's flair.

"You still read the cards?" Missy asked.

"They don't say much," Zarabeth said. "My days are all the same." Zarabeth had bought the cards at Missy's prompting, last of a display in a stationery store. Missy had offered to teach her, and she had, three serious evenings when Zarabeth had expected a ten-minute lark. In retrospect, maybe Missy had done it as groundwork, to see how Zarabeth handled woo-woo, but it had felt like girlish friendship.

"Mind if I try? If you don't mind spoilers, I'm curious."

"If you're offering," Zarabeth said carefully.

Missy grinned, tapped her nose. "Of course. Re-org special. Can you turn down these lights?"

Levitation was the only impossible thing Missy had ever done in front of Zarabeth, but a card reading was enough to bring out Missy's gifts. Zarabeth refilled her glass and dimmed the lights. All the while she watched Missy, who sat motionless, eyes closed, hands crossed over her chest. Zarabeth felt a long cold drip down her spine, sensed big furry moth wings beating the air. Behold the great witch Artemis McCauley Devereaux, robed in dark

9

power, sipping the future from the goddesshead. Zarabeth pulled up a chair to face it.

Missy fanned the deck across the table. "Plus-minus," she said. "Choose your proxy."

Zarabeth drew Brand 7, a picture of a messy supermarket shelf, boxes and cans with bright quick-sale tags. Discards and leftovers.

"A humble card," Missy said. "Stuck, paralyzed by choices, out of time. Sure?"

Zarabeth shrugged and put down the card.

Missy drew a weeping man in a sleeveless shirt and placed it on top of Zarabeth's card. "Bankruptcy confronts you. Failure and ruin." She turned the next card sideways, a smiling natty man with lists of black X marks. "Reorganization challenges you."

She placed the next card below the first three, a shifty low-life walking away from a rotting city. "Money 4, under you. Greed whetted by poverty. Past experience you draw on, for good or ill." To the left, undressed people in a room strewn with bottles. "Brand 3, behind you. Overindulgence and mistakes." Above, a mini-skirted woman with a wolf's grin. "Marketing crowns you. That's good. She creates the image. Gets people to buy." A long-chinned man with an armful of trophies completed the plus sign. "Well, well. Brand 9, living large in your future. That's the plus. Now the minus."

A woman in the shadow of a lamppost. "Inside you, Product 3 upside-down. The traitor's card. You know your own moral limits are elastic." White roses on a white pedestal. "Outside you, Brand Ace. The marriage card."

"Let's just hope it means I'll get laid," Zarabeth said.

Factory workers in a long line. "On your journey, Money 5. Downsizing, unemployment, limited opportunity. The ugly dark old economy. And where you arrive—"

Silver airplanes flying over green fields. "Product 8," Zarabeth said. "That's success?"

"I would say freedom," Missy said. "A fresh start. But a good card." The spell of her presence had lifted. Missy looked tired.

"Nothing bad. Professionally successful. Whatever happens this week, you'll be working this summer, but it's complicated. You'll meet a guy, might be rocky. And, you're going to be lying to people. A lot. So say the cards."

"Fantastic!" The reading delighted Zarabeth, more basic than belief, the pleasure of winning the game. "Couldn't ask for more. Best fortune-teller ever."

"Queen of woo-woo." Missy turned on the light. "More ice cream? Or a nightcap?"

"Just water." Zarabeth gathered the cards. She yawned. "I still have a job."

"Be glad it doesn't involve bedpans," Missy said.

* * *

Thursday morning in the office, the overhead lights were off. Aleksei's door locked, many cubicles empty. Had the layoffs begun already? Or were the missing ones safe?

Her voicemail light blinked. "This is Jill Carson of Optimized," a woman with a heavy Boston accent said. "Magda Crane will be calling you at two-thirty. Please be available."

Zarabeth hissed. At least it wasn't a summons to Human Resources.

In her in-box, more forms from Aleksei. She ignored them. She worked out her annoyance trolling news sites for a bankers' association, posting nonsense invective against mortgage reform. For lunch she ate a Greek salad at the Korean deli while surfing job sites on her phone. Consulting jobs, spec jobs. Work now, salary later. Nothing with health care.

No call at two-thirty, not at three. In the western distance out her window, gray clouds glinted silver-white with lightning. The office phone wouldn't forward calls. She was stuck. She went through her files to see what was worth saving.

The storm broke at four, heavy downpour drumming the window. It took her a moment to notice the knocking through it.

"Are you Zarabeth Battrie?" The woman in her open doorway had a drawn, pale face under stringy gray hair. Her voice was clear and nasal, a Northeast boarding-school hauteur. She wore a red pantsuit and carried a slim brown briefcase. In flat shoes, she was taller than Zarabeth in heels. She got the name right.

Zarabeth's heart beat faster. "You're Magda Crane."

"I am. I planned to call, but things came up. And this rain. Does it always rain this hard here? So I came to find you." She cocked her head, raised her thinned eyebrows. "Here you are."

Everything the woman said was false. Another day, Zarabeth might have enjoyed it.

"I didn't know you were in town, Ms. Crane. Come in. Sorry about the mess." Zarabeth put her box of saved files under her desk, closed open drawers. "The chair's clean."

"Thank you. You don't care to be idle, do you, Ms. Battrie?"

"Zarabeth, please. No, Ms. Crane, I don't."

"Better ways of being the devil's tool, yes? Call me Magda." She perched on the edge of the chair, twitchy like a squirrel, her voice tipsy on sherry. She placed the briefcase on the floor between her legs, as if it held valuables.

"I'm so excited to meet you," Magda said. "My people mentioned you. Mention-itis. You're a little thing but you make an impression. Of course, we studied up on you. Did a search, as they say. You came so far, in so little time. It's remarkable, really. Especially since you didn't go to college."

Zarabeth was too surprised to lie. Her heart, even faster.

"Don't look so glum," Magda said. "You did well, fooling the Philadelphia office, and once you're in, no one looks twice. But, we did. You're from the school of hard knocks, as we used to say. I'm curious. When you sit in meetings, with people who went decades into debt to earn what you assumed with a forged transcript, what do you think about them?"

Zarabeth fought to unclench her teeth. "Sometimes, they have jokes," she said. "One says something, like from a book, and others laugh." She thrust her shoulders out. "I laugh too."

"I understand. They can laugh someplace else."

Zarabeth felt jerked upwards, as if her parachute opened. "You're not laying me off?"

"I'm offering you a new job. My personal representative, in certain unusual matters." Magda patted her chest below the notch of her collarbone. "Of course we'll give you a title. Director of Special Projects?"

Director was a salary raise. "Yes. Great. I accept."

"You do? Don't you want to hear more about it?"

"Sure. But it must be better than this. I'll take it. Why me?"

Magda laughed in high titters, coughed hard with paper-bag sounds, laughed again. "You're a card, you are. A card. Why you? A few reasons. For one, people talk about you. I know people. Those people?" Magda waved behind her. "Worthless. Couldn't pour me coffee. You're a tough cookie."

Magda bent over and took a black envelope the size of a greeting card out of her case. "Also, because you've had a singular education. For example, you know what this is."

Taking the envelope made Zarabeth uneasy. She used a letter opener. Inside was a slip of parchment, the real kind made with animal skin, greasy and cool to touch. On it, a messy five-pointed star, in a circle, drawn in dried blood.

It was a magic spell, embedded in an object. If Zarabeth burned it, something would happen, most likely something nasty.

"I've never seen a charm before," Zarabeth said.

"Then you should know this one is quite expensive, and hard to come by. How do you know what this is? Your witch friend?"

So much for secrecy. "Missy can't tell me much unless I worship her." Zarabeth slid the charm back inside the envelope, handed it back to Magda. "When I was a kid, I could find things. Anything. I'd pretend I had seen it earlier, but I hadn't. In high school, if I danced at parties, sometimes—something would come over me. If I wanted something then, I got it. Money, a bike, a necklace. It hurt though, and I never had them long. I shoplifted books from stores and tried to do their spells, but they never worked. I do magic. I just can't control it."

"This is more than your witch friend knows, isn't it?"

Zarabeth nodded.

"Just as well," Magda said. "You'll never do magic like she

13

does. Wildness like yours can't be tamed, just harnessed for a while. Which is fine. I don't demand worship," Magda said. "But I do demand honesty. You know there's more going on with this firm than just consulting."

"I find hidden things," Zarabeth said. "In Houston, this drunk engineer told me about our occult work for the CIA. Janice Goldman in Los Angeles doesn't age, and no one talks about it."

"No one ages in LA," Magda said. "Hide in plain sight."

Zarabeth smiled politely. "What is all this?"

"You'll have to play the game to learn the rules, I'm afraid. I do think you're a natural. For now, you'll just poke around. There are things I'm curious about."

"You mean I'll be a spy?" Zarabeth asked.

"You're clever, they said so. Clever spy. First up, there's a client we have in London. Telecoms firm. Doesn't add up to me. You'll tell me everything. What people say in the kitchen, at the pubs. Oddities in your tarot cards. Think you can do it?"

Cards. *You're a card. Bankruptcy confronts you.*

"Executive Exemplars," Zarabeth said. "You killed my project."

Magda's left eye narrowed grossly, like a mask had fallen off. "Killed 'my' project. Well." She frowned. "It was nonsense like that which got us to this reorganization. But I liked you. So I tucked you away. Time to blow your dust off."

Zarabeth felt ashamed of her own self-doubt. If she had only known—but anger now would get her less. "OK," Zarabeth said. "I'm your spy. I'll be a good one."

"Of that, I'm sure. And now, back to work. These people won't lay off themselves. It's been a pleasure meeting you, dear." She stood, so Zarabeth stood. "With a little luck, together we might even start a war."

Zarabeth took Magda's hand.

A shock and a dread sang through her, as if Magda were a garbage disposal. The moment before the pain.

Done on purpose.

Zarabeth jerked back her hand. Magda smiled nastily and

walked off. Zarabeth rubbed her hand on her thigh until Magda was out of sight.

A beatdown to establish dominance. Fine. At least she had a job. An executive had watched her career. And fucked with it. At least she had a job. She closed her door and sat.

On her desk, the black envelope, not by itself but in an odd pile. Under it, a folded printout of a flight itinerary. On top of it, an orange silicone wristband with the firm's three-arrow logo and the tagline: *Straightforward Consulting—The Devil You Know.*

All without Zarabeth seeing.

"That's a neat trick," Zarabeth said aloud. She picked up the wristband. Stink of packaging, feel of goo. Just a wristband. She put it on her right wrist.

She shook the parchment out onto the desk, rotated it with a pencil eraser. The star and circle were drawn in a continuous, splattered line, as if squeezed from a body part. When she touched the parchment, its clammy feel moved up her arm. She put her hand above the blood, but wouldn't touch it.

Magda wouldn't let her just *accept.*

Zarabeth slowed her breaths, made them full. The charm could make her a monster. It could make her a slave. It could be—awful.

As awful as sneaking around the edges, a grifter of magic with no one to teach her or even believe her, and not taking the chance to trade places? Who had fallen for her to rise? Whoever had bled onto the charm, for sure.

She could walk. Take a package, move to a cheaper city, get a desk job. Her brush with the uncanny, a story in a journal no one would ever read.

Twelve good years since she had left Pittsburgh, each one better than the one before. Six at Straightforward, and after each, money and respect. She could take that elsewhere, but never get anything like this for it.

Zarabeth emptied her candy jar and knelt on the floor. Her heartbeat shook her chest, her hands.

Zarabeth held the clammy charm by the corner and lit it with her cigarette lighter.

The charm burned fast, with red hissing flames. She dropped it into the jar, her fingers smarting. Oily white smoke spilled out. Zarabeth inhaled it, coughed hard. She inhaled again, pressed her hands to her mouth to hold it in. It itched like bugs in her lungs. When she exhaled the smoke was gone. The jar was still warm.

She leaned back against the desk. Her arms fell asleep. She felt a newness in her mind, an idea with no meaning.

The phone rang. She clambered onto her chair, keying the speaker.

"This is Endre," the caller said. "Optimized, Internal Support. We shipped you a device. Any problems with it? Sorry we sent no documentation." Something odd in his voice.

"No," Zarabeth said. "I think I did it right. Am I—waiting for something?"

"It sounds as if everything worked," Endre said. "I also wanted to give you our phone number here in case you have questions later."

She keyed the number into her phone's contact list. Something odd. His accent. His numbers. His words. "Endre? Am I—we're speaking Hungarian, right?"

"Igen, mi magyarul beszéltek." Through the strange-familiar words, Endre sounded pleased, the same gotcha Magda had also enjoyed. These people liked to fuck with you.

She filed that for later. "Wow. Cool. So it just—"

"It just works." Endre switched to English, with a thick accent. "The Polyglot begins with standard speech, and adapts to your current region. You can brush up before you go with webcasts or movies. Call if you have questions. We staff this desk twenty-four-seven."

"Köszönöm szépen, Endre."

"Szívesen, Szarabet. Look forward to working with you."

Zarabeth laughed with joy and relief. Wait until she told Missy, in her own coven's old Gaelic.

CHAPTER TWO

Lake Tahoe

The sunset over the Sierra Nevada lit the cocktail party through the tall chalet windows, washing out the men's light sport coats and sparkling the women's silk skirts. Among the forty-odd people, three middle-aged couples stood out, colorfast and non-combustible in sagging cotton, as if pasted from a yacht-club newsletter.

At the catering bar Gabriel Archer asked for a ginger ale and a bourbon with ice. His friend Walt Wisniewski, the party host, stood by the windows, his untucked pink oxford shirt hazy in the light, his face dark and sour. Gabriel gave Walt the bourbon.

"Thanks. Cheers," Walt said. Walt was taller than Gabriel and robustly overweight, his shaved head tanned to cork. "You cleaned up well."

"You might have warned me you were hosting a party," Gabriel said.

"Most people enjoy parties." Walt winced at the drink. "Fucking caterers. They never stock bourbon, just Tennessee whiskey and hope you don't notice. I should have told Laurie." Laurie was Walt's current girlfriend, a leggy bottle-blonde whom Gabriel had only met in passing. "It's her party, of course. I just forgot, to be honest, until the caterers rolled up. It's not even a

party. You've noticed the distinction between mosquito and target?"

"The targets are wearing bug spray. Selling real estate?"

"They bought the real estate. Now they need additions and retaining walls, or so we hope to convince them. 'Meet your new hometown,' Laurie says. The contractors know the properties and try to size up the owners. They offer Laurie a kickback. Best kickbacks get the work. At least, her staff has cuties. Your car should help with that."

For the drive from San Francisco, Gabriel had rented a luxurious Italian four-seater GT, six hundred horsepower, long red hood, grinning black grille.

"I only got it for the mountain roads," Gabriel said.

"Yes. People asked about it, of course. I said something about hedge funds." Walt rattled his ice at the crowd, at Gabriel. "My shamanic benediction. Go get laid."

The car, alas, attracted the targets, who took Gabriel as one of their own. Somehow he became a pretend rich person at a pretend party, talking about British and Italian styling, racing clubs, and storage fees. Walt rescued him, inviting Laurie's staff for phone pictures in the driver's seat. Many came to egg them on, but few lingered in the chilly night air.

Gabriel went for a rag to clean a spilled daiquiri. When he returned, he found a curvy auburn-haired white woman, her gentle hand on the side mirror.

"Can I see the engine?" She smiled big crooked teeth. "I'm Tammy."

They spent a half-hour on the car, starting it with the hood up, revving the engine, Tammy kneeling on the cleanup rag to inspect the chassis. "Please can I drive it?" she asked.

"Only sober," Gabriel said.

"Not tonight then."

As the caterers packed up, the remaining dozen took over the rear deck. Tammy and Gabriel sat close together by the fire pit, looking over dark woods and a distant sliver of gleaming lake. "Walt said you used to live here?" Tammy asked.

"One season," Gabriel said. "Worked the chairlifts. Took a year off during college."

"Clearly it didn't hurt your career," she said. "I'm finishing my associate's. Or I was. I dropped a class. Mom was pissed, but it was the best season in years. My last chance for good snow." She ashed her cigarette in her empty bottle, reached behind her for a fresh beer. "You should have come up sooner."

"Better late than never," he said. Seven months ago, a drunk driver had killed Gabriel's brother. Walt had invited him many times, but the late-spring storm had finally inspired him to accept. He opened her bottle, a small gallantry for a big smile. He held her hand to look at the Tibetan script on her pinky ring. "*Om Mani Peme Hung?*" he guessed.

Tammy squeezed his fingers. "Are you a Buddhist?"

"I tried it, for a while. 'The diamond in the lotus.' The mantra of compassion."

She frowned. "If you say it seven times a day, Buddha blesses you?"

"I'm sure he would," Gabriel said. "There's a story about it. A guru assigned two disciples to say it, a million times each. The first disciple stayed in the temple, saying it every minute, day after day. The second disciple went out into world to help others. Ten years passed. Word spread that the first disciple was almost finished. So the second disciple climbed a hill to meditate. He thought of all he'd seen and done. He imagined the whole wide world, everyone, everything, filled by compassion, down to the smallest atom. In a moment he was done."

"Sucks to be the first guy," Tammy said.

"That's the point. It has to come from the heart."

A red flare in Tammy's eyes. She glanced away and pulled her hand from his. "You're gonna make my beer warm."

* * *

The snowpack at the base of the mountain had nearly melted, but higher trails stubbornly held spring snow, crystalline from daily melting and freezing. Gabriel hadn't skied in years, but after

19

a few runs, he could match Walt's speed. Together they drew long helixes down the sparkling oatmeal-brown trails. His head floated like a fat cloud, while his thighs sparked like jumper cables. He had forgotten just how good he could feel.

On the canyon lift, Gabriel took off his helmet. "Sun is nice. In Russia, I got so little sunlight I was afraid I'd get rickets."

"Careful you don't burn, my pasty friend," Walt said. He clapped Gabriel's shoulder. "Good to have you here. Feeling your wasted youth?"

"Feeling more alive than usual, at least."

"That's a start. What are you doing now?"

"Market research. It's lame. First open position I qualified for."

"I thought you came back early because of—" Walt hesitated. "Of your brother."

"I was supposed to go back to Moscow after the funeral," Gabriel said. "But I think they're corrupt, and they thought I was a stuck-up prick cutting into their good arrangements."

"And you don't drink," Walt said.

"Ha. Our clients thought commodity futures were as dependable as bonds. I told them to save, to restructure, to invest. They complained to my bosses. My bosses made me do accounts. I didn't even have to try to find the skimming, it was obvious. I filed reports, highlighted issues. My office nickname was *Inakomysluchnik*. Dissident Archer."

Walt laughed. "Dissident is not a good word in Russia."

"It's not funny. Russia's a mess. It's a Potemkin economy, shipping its wealth to London behind branded façades. Meanwhile, I had nightmares. I couldn't sleep. The directors threw me on pro bono work. That was even worse. Outside the cities, life expectancy is forty. The only people who work are Tajiks, and the white Russians would kill them if they weren't drunk all the time. In ten years, Russia will be like a nuclear-armed Myanmar."

"That's a bold statement," Walt said.

"When we were kids, women in Kabul wore skirts above the knee. Things change fast. My firm Empyrean Group isn't helping. At best it's enabling." Gabriel felt hot with shame. "So I used Jeremy's death as my excuse."

"Smart move," Walt said. "No value in getting fired. Now, you need to go where your skills are worth something. They speak Russian in Tallinn and Riga and Tbilisi and even Berlin. Don't just drink chai lattes in Frisco and crunch numbers. You're what, thirty? Jesus died at thirty-three. Get cracking." Walt raised the safety bar. "Let's ride."

They took a shady trail of big moguls. Walt nimbly hopped between the tops of the bumps, his snowboard shaving icy curls. Gabriel struggled to follow. "Think of them as shortcuts," Walt coached. "Like warped space. Down in the troughs, that's the long way." Walt fell forward lazily, popped two feet high off a bump, yelling with glee as he rode into the trees.

Hard-packed snow paths dotted with needles and broken cones banked around drought-thinned pines. After the trails' bright light and crisp sounds, the glade's dim hum unnerved Gabriel. He scraped behind, side-slipping through tight turns, the confidence of his last runs gone. He crouched, hoping for control, but shot over the bank. Hard cruddy snow held his legs but lucky momentum carried him down to another hard path. Too fast. He spun across it, threw himself down to hit a tree with both feet. Pain in his knees as the impact traveled up.

"Not fun!" Gabriel yelled, dry needles raining on him.

Walt stood waving below him, his orange jacket buzzing. As Gabriel made his way down, Walt pointed to the right. "Quickest way out," he called.

Gabriel went through scrub to find sudden air, over the edge of a steep drop. He landed on two feet, whipped by stripped saplings, but lost balance and rolled out of his bindings.

Walt shot out of the trees below him, stopped hard and dropped to his knees. "Did you take that drop? How did I miss that all season?" He drummed his hands on his helmet. "How high was that?"

"Ten feet?" Gabriel's eyes stung from sweat-run sunscreen.

"Twelve at least. Fucking bit my tongue." Walt spat red on the snow. Even the color seemed like bragging.

"Listen," Walt said. "I didn't mean to sound unsympathetic. We all get dealt bad hands. Just figure out your head. Feel more alive and do what stokes that feeling."

Gabriel nodded so as not to speak. In the light and salt and sting and the cold blood smell, he felt impatient, imminent, nearly complete. A formed but still transparent wasp, about to be marked and unleashed. He felt not yet but soon. Not just yet.

* * *

After skiing they went to the Keys for happy hour, en route to meet Laurie and Tammy for dinner. As they drove past the high-rise casinos, Walt made dorky hand-signs at jaywalking tourists ogling the car.

"Bitches," Walt said. "Keep spending money. That's why Nevada's got no income tax."

"I thought it was a libertarian thing."

"Libertarians are bad at paving desert roads, yo," Walt said. "Tourists pay casinos, casinos pay taxes. Bitches want to be players. I want to be the house."

"But you have to live in Nevada," Gabriel said.

"At least we don't have earthquakes. Good luck when Frisco falls into the sea."

Tahoe Keys was a pricey subdivision on the California side of the lake, with homes in nautical blues and whites. At the oak and brass marina bar, they took a table inlaid with backgammon and played for the bar tab, to five points. Gabriel won in two games.

"You lectured *me* on business," Gabriel said, resetting checkers. "Backgammon's all about business. I can slow you down but I can't stay still. Russians like chess for strategy, Americans like cards for odds and luck. Both are zero-sum. Backgammon's tactics, on the fly."

"I play pool and I golf," Walt said.

"That's why you take checkers too quickly and you don't drop doubles. It's not just a hunt. You have to bring it home."

"Interesting. Next match to see who buys dinner?"

"I thought you weren't a gambler," Gabriel said.

"I'll put your ideas into practice. After I pee."

Gabriel waited, sipping the dregs of his ginger ale. A couple came into the bar, blonde brassy woman, gray man. The woman had a good build under a sad, sun-dried face. The man's shiny white belly pushed out of his gray jacket like it was his bodyguard. A bitter taste like coffee grounds rose up Gabriel's throat.

Walt had returned, and stared at him warily. "Do you know those people?" he asked.

"No." Gabriel took a deep breath. "No. Let's play."

*　*　*

To kill time before the nightclubs opened, Walt staked the women a hundred each on blackjack. Tammy lost hers quickly, too distracted by Gabriel to pay attention. Laurie gave her winnings to Tammy to keep playing until they both lost it all.

"Tammy Tammy wallet whammy." Walt was lit on free bourbon. "You're bad luck."

They retreated to the lounge to read the entertainment calendars. The casino concerts were cover bands and one-hit wonders. Walt suggested a nearby sports bar, really a dive.

"That's not someplace you *go*, Walt," Laurie said. "It's just someplace you end up."

"Ha. I'm done gambling," Walt said. "Clubs aren't open. Let's go."

The dive was a noisy windowless box lit by video poker and sports channels, the bar dividing diner from game room. Sullen men, in sports-team hoodies or plaid shirts, shuffled around the bar and the game tables.

"See?" Walt said. "All the nightclub people come here."

The women drank cocktails at the bar while Walt and Gabriel threw miniature free-throws. Gabriel smelled a sharp gas, like from a dumpster in the heat. At the bar, Tammy talked with a sandy-blond white man in sagging clothes, his face spiteful.

"Problem?" Gabriel asked.

"I believe that is Tammy's ex," Walt said. "Nate something. Loser."

"Should we go over?" Gabriel said, coughing.

"We'll just raise the temperature," Walt said. "Last game?"

"Fine." Gabriel coughed again. "What is that smell?"

"What smell?" Walt put coins in the machine.

"The really bad smell?" Gabriel's ball bounced off the rim. The women had left. "Walt?"

Walt looked around. "By the door."

On the other side of the bar, the smell was worse, like shit from a street drunk. At the door, Laurie faced down Tammy.

"Tammy, don't go outside," Laurie said. "Talk to him here."

"She can come outside," Nate said, loud and lisping. "I'm all right."

"I don't want a scene." Tammy looked sad and stupid, a clown in makeup. "A minute."

"Don't go outside," Laurie said, grabbing her arm.

"Let go of her," Nate rumbled. "She can come if she wants."

Gabriel's eyes watered. Smells now, all foul: shit and rot and hot and *thwarted*. He stumbled forward, caught himself on Walt's shoulder.

The sight of the men angered Nate. "Who the fuck are you?" Nate said. "Fuck off!"

"He just wants to talk," Tammy said.

"No he doesn't," Gabriel growled. He felt gleefully angry, ready to burst.

Nate sneered. "This your new man? Or is he paying you?"

Gabriel's head jerked sideways. Hot salt in his mouth. Nate had hit him. It was funny.

Nate swung again, comically slow. Gabriel blocked the punch, twisted Nate's arm high behind his back. Nate lowed like a slaughterhouse cow, tried to kick out. Gabriel pinned him against a video poker table, bashed his greasy head down. Again, again, again, again, a silver shiver in his arm, a smell of blood. A chant in his head, *exult excise excite exult excise excite.*

A long blink. He stood outside the car, shivering. The others were running after him.

Walt grabbed the key from Gabriel's hand and unlocked the doors. "Laurie, ride shotgun. Let's go," he said, getting behind the wheel.

"I need to throw up," Gabriel said.

"Do it in California. Cops are coming, Gabriel," Walt said. "Get the fuck in the car."

Another long blink. They were on the Al Tahoe beach road, a few miles from the casinos. Walt pulled over. Gabriel got out, walked a few paces, and threw up.

Walt came out and gave him a handkerchief. "You all right?"

"I could use some water." When had he eaten? He didn't remember. The smell made him feel sick again. They walked back to the car. "How are the women?"

"Laurie's worried about her business. As if the bar will call the Chamber of Commerce. Tammy's weirded out. Hell, I'm weirded out. You were someone else back there."

"I don't know. I—" He remembered an odd tingle, like a happy sore tooth, small in his dark head. In the cold wind from the lake, smells of lake weeds and pine resin. His stomach turned again. He held his breath until the feeling passed.

"Go home to San Francisco," Walt said. "Nate's a piss-ant. No one will get involved."

"You think he'll bother Tammy again?"

"Be a while before he can, I know that. Get going. We'll call a cab."

The women got out. Laurie marched up the road without a second look.

Tammy's soft touch stung his face. "Sorry," she said. "Thanks for sticking up for me." She hugged him awkwardly, and kissed his other cheek. She shivered. He held her tighter but she squirmed away. "I'll see you around."

Walt clasped Gabriel's shoulder. "You should have done some of that in Russia. Ladybug, ladybug. Fly away home." Walt jogged after the women.

Gabriel spat. He looked at the red car in the bright night. Fly away home. He wanted to drive, not to flee but to move. Speed, endless acceleration, a way to never stand still again.

He had missed fighting even more than skiing.
He should never have come back to Tahoe.

CHAPTER THREE

London

From Holborn Tube it was a short walk to the Mercurex building, a ten-storey glass box fitted with spiked armor beams. Zarabeth too had dressed severely—hair up, charcoal skirt-suit, fat briefcase, swank black high-heels. Through glass lift doors, she saw grey cubes in grey spaces, each floor's carpeting colour-coded to staff badges. The top floor grey on grey, in disarray, cubes listing, cables dangling from the ceiling. A plaque with the Straightforward logo sat on the floor.

"A hasty job, but, couldn't be helped." Kath Boyle's Estuary voice squeaked like bent steel. The chartered accountant was Zarabeth's minder for the hour. "The focus was areas we now can't visit. Control rooms, data centres. But, a functioning business in three months."

"Truly excellent work," Zarabeth said. "I'm sure it will be interesting reading."

"If I knew more about what you were looking for?"

"Everything. As you said, a hasty job. I'm here to find inefficiencies before solicitors deem them problems."

Solicitors. Minder. Hasty. Lift. Paracetamol. Fortnight. Whilst. Words Zarabeth never used now came unbidden, along with

Anthony Dobranski

dangling helping verbs and a low news presenter's voice, less accent than air. Even her spelling had changed. Two days on and it still felt strange-not-strange, like a helmet worn all day.

Kath led her two rows past the last occupied one. In the middle, a lone light. The farthest spot from anywhere. "The bound volumes are in the front closet." Kath smiled.

Petty. Zarabeth could handle petty. Endre had opened all the network server ports for her.

Mercurex provided high-bandwidth wireless data using high-altitude dirigibles, cheaper than satellites. Formerly a defence programme for secure communications, its engineers had contracted with Straightforward to build a business around the technology. Hire a company like a car, a new service model. Optimized was curious. As one of the re-org's winners, it could ask, and Zarabeth was its question.

Zarabeth read spreadsheets, studied contracts, checked billing codes. She also smoked every hour, in a nasty corner by the loading dock, trading duty-free cigarettes for chat and gossip across the company. Over two days, she formed a basic picture: a high burn-rate, bad cash flow, but no fraud; an unhappy workplace, teams not talking, defence-sector secrecy hard to shed. Zarabeth wrote reports at night in Indian restaurants, allowing herself a beer.

Magda said nothing.

Wednesday afternoon in the smoker's ghetto, she happened alone on Rex, an ash-white grey-haired Scot with a wireless-signal icon tattooed behind his right ear. She took a chance. "An auditor's life is a tedious one," she said. "Numbers here, words in the hotel. It would be immensely more pleasant with marijuana."

"Ah-ha. Not for me to judge your filthy hippie pleasures." Rex had a pretty voice, a lively Glaswegian tenor. "I take it you're not part of the random urinalysis. All I can do now is club drugs. Out of the system in a day. You're wanting solid?"

"I prefer real herb, but beggars won't choose."

"No drug beggars in London," Rex said. "You're at Green Park, aye? Where they put all the visitors. Tell me your room and

28

when my friend should come by." Rex flicked the fag filter in the ashcan. "I don't know if we really introduced. Rex Densmore. What is it you do here?"

"Zarabeth Battrie. Forensic accountant. I ensure Mercurex got what it paid for."

"Most considerate of you. Sorry your lot is so grim."

"At least I have weekend shopping to look forward to."

"Oh, aye? Might do a bit myself. My man's out of town. Care for some company? I also know Soho boutiques, or the ones still left us as the chain coffee conquest continues."

"It sounds delightful. Shall we start with lunch?"

They exchanged cards. His read, *Director, Signal Encryption.* Her new best friend.

Zarabeth smoked another cigarette, working out a hunch. If Magda were displeased or if something interested her, she'd have said so. Magda wanted Zarabeth to find it on her own.

Rex Densmore's social page was public and proud: firsts in maths, models of disaster relief, letters to journals in English and German (the long words woke the Polyglot, stinging her eyes like smoke). Holiday snaps of Austrian skiing, Sydney Mardi Gras.

If Magda wanted her to find him, why not just tell her?

* * *

Saturday morning Zarabeth played with her look, hoping for London-ness. Hair straighter, red nail polish to clear, light top, black skirt, low heels. It would do.

She shuffled her tarot deck and dealt three cards. Data 7, theft or treachery. Strategic Planning upside-down, missing the forest for the trees. Brand 3, the morning-after card Missy had seen. Troubles of her own making, despite the cards' warning.

Best go make them.

The Malaysian restaurant Rex suggested had tall palms under grow lights, ridiculous in wet cold London. Rex was waiting. His skin looked sallow and flabby.

"You look bloody awful," Zarabeth said. "Did he respect you in the morning?"

Rex smiled. "I should hope not. You look bloody hot."

Over fish laksa they talked shop. "They're sticking me with web app security," Rex said. "Hardly my bailiwick. I'm the signalman, not the guard."

Zarabeth knew fuck-all about trains. "Outsource it. My firm already does half your code."

"Your firm does spreadsheets and custodial work," Rex snapped. "Code is my product."

"As you like," Zarabeth said, hiding behind her Ipoh coffee. "Writing a developer's kit will cut into your clubbing." Mercurex didn't sell encryption; it was merely their way to control access. What did Rex think she already knew?

After lunch she stood outside under Rex's umbrella and smoked a hasty spliff, Rex's discomfort as amusing as the high. They cabbed to Soho and wandered tiny streets, Rex nattering away about where so-and-so bought such-and-such. She bought versatile pieces: embroidered blue jeans, a navy blazer with wide white pinstripes, a beaded yellow baby-doll top. Her high helped in the stores, good for flipping through hangers, this or that, A or B, like lenses at the oculist. Two new looks, an edgy red skirt-suit and an African-print sundress in turquoise and brown. Two pairs of shoes. Three. By teatime, she had more than her suitcase would fit.

They walked in fog, past an old black water pump surrounded by black posts, to a gay bar with chrome rails and studded leather stools. Rex ordered shandies. Not her favourite, but she didn't protest. "To your expense account," Rex toasted.

"Cheers. Outside, the black pump? What was that?"

Rex gave her a curious smile, both satisfied and hungry. "That is the birthplace of epidemiology," Rex said. "Seriously. Two centuries ago, this was a low and filthy district. A local surgeon named John Snow traced a cholera outbreak to that one well, and stopped the outbreak when he convinced the city to close it. A science was born."

"You even know his name," Zarabeth said. "Nerd heroes. How sweet."

"I admire seekers after knowledge. My current hobby is the early occultists. Crowley, Spare, the Golden Dawn. Good fun—

sigils and patterns, binding demons. Even do a bit myself."

Of course. What Magda wanted her to discover. "You're having me on," Zarabeth said.

"Why not? Throw a bladder of air up in the sky, bounce invisible light off it so the box in your pocket can talk, how is that not magic?" Rex laughed. "Maybe the occultists were onto something. First pass at a new technology. Like alchemy, mostly wrong and full of crap, but it got us to chemistry. I don't usually mention this stuff to sexy friends."

"Perhaps you should. It's so sexy."

"Pity you're not my type," Rex said. "But, if you're curious, I'm seeing some mates later tonight. Like-minded, in these matters."

"A magic club?" The mistake she needed to make. "Good I've something to wear."

*　*　*

Zarabeth arrived an hour late, her high fading in Soho's crowded streets. Her clothes, all new: pinstripe coat, black collared shirt, embroidered jeans, leopard-skin kitten-heel ankle boots. The unwashed clothes itchy, shoes destined to blister. She looked good.

The basement club had exposed brick walls and a low plaster ceiling. A small band played on a platform, a bouncy tempo like a children's song. Beefy old men in dark jackets with bright waistcoats sat with frail old women in frilled dresses and small hats. On the packed dance floor, middle-aged men, in browns and denim blues, danced spastic waltzes with sturdy cross-dressers in tall wigs and tight sequined dresses. The longer Zarabeth looked, the dreamier it got. In for a penny.

Rex wore a tight black t-shirt and pink pleather pants. "You're late. We're drinking tequila." He led her to a back table, with three white people and many glasses. "Everyone," Rex said, "behold the splendid forensic accountant Zarabeth Battrie. Ta-da."

The three raised glasses to salute her. The nearest to her, an old ruddy bald man with a paisley ascot and broken blood vessels in his mushroom nose, offered his hand.

"Thomas Underwood, my dear," he said, in a raspy clipped voice. "Welcome."

"That's Polly and Hugh," Rex said. Both were slim and pale with wide eyes, in black clothes and silver jewellery. Polly gave her a horsey smile of large teeth. Rex poured her a shot of white tequila. "Tonight's word is *Salud.*"

"OK. *Salud.*" They drank. She took a wedge of lemon from a bowl and sucked it.

Underwood fanned a deck of playing cards. "Will you take a card?" he asked.

"A magic trick? Do I look?" She drew Jack of Spades. He cut the deck. She placed the card in the middle. When she did, he tapped the deck with his forefinger, one two three, and flipped the top card. Jack of Spades.

"Oh, that's good," she said, golf-clapping.

Underwood gave a little bow. He poured shots for her and himself, his hand steady. "*Salud.*" They drank. "You have a Latin look. Are you of Mexican heritage?"

"Brazilian." Her eye-bone itched. Other than the toast she was sure they spoke English.

"I lived in Mexico after the war," Underwood said. "The start of these studies."

"You mean sleight-of-hand or the occult?"

"Both. Magic is a way to shape reality, but often all that's needed is to shape perception."

Hugh sloppily poured around the table. It looked slow. The band now sounded far away.

"You don't curse people, just make them feel cursed?" she asked. "That's advertising."

"A fine comparison. Like any force, magic is best applied toward imbalance. The tipping point. You understand this better than Rex realised. I've heard of your mistress Magda Crane."

"You mean my boss," Zarabeth said. "I don't know you."

"She does. Do not interfere with me."

Zarabeth felt woozy, as if breathing thick smoke, but not drugged beyond the tequila.

In the club, the crowd had thinned. Underwood made excuses to leave. Polly and Hugh helped Underwood stand and made to go with him. For a handshake, Polly gave Zarabeth's fingers a hard squeeze. Something animal in her large eyes, threat or fear. They left.

Rex gave her a quizzical look. "Y'right?" he asked.

"Fine. Bit tipsy." She sat. The strange feeling had passed.

"Tipsy's good." He filled Zarabeth's glass to the top. "What say we get pissed?"

*　*　*

The chirp of a text message woke Zarabeth at eleven. The room was a mess, piled covers and full ashtrays, the minibar fridge door open. She felt sick and worn out.

Flashes of the evening: More bad tequila and its wormy smell. A cross-dresser, Deirdre, fit and sweet. Dancing. A cab ride. Lines of ching off a minibar plate. Deirdre submissive, more fun for Rex. Rex holding a strand of Zarabeth's hair during his blowjob, with a creepy smile.

She washed her face and brewed coffee. The message was from Missy, to a large list: *My gramma died Sun morning. Love you all, but no time now. In touch soon. PS please no flowers.*

Zarabeth Battrie, naked and raw, while her friend Missy laid claim to the world and everything. Business class and still a loser. Squeeze harder and she would shatter the phone.

Instead, Zarabeth texted Magda: *Thomas Underwood threatened me. Now what?*

Still no idea why Magda sent her here.

CHAPTER FOUR

San Francisco

Empyrean Group's Tactical Models division sat in the SoMa district below San Francisco's hills, in the offices of a failed dot-com. Empyrean had left the old firm's décor, dated islands of cubicles in faded pop colors, quaint and grim like an empty playroom.

At his cubicle, an intimidating Empyrean security officer in black and blue uniform stood by Gabriel's chair. The man drew himself up. He recognized Gabriel.

"Gabriel." Jeff Prender, Gabriel's boss, came up behind. Jeff wore a green sport coat, buttoned tight, his ruddy-white head half-extended like a turtle's. "Follow me, son."

Gabriel followed Jeff. The guard stayed behind. The only reason for this—couldn't be.

Jeff's office had a cluttered desk and a cleared table with a coffee service. At the table sat a dark black man with a long chin, in an olive-brown suit. The coffee smelled delicious, with spicy oils and almond.

"This is Bill Thorn," Jeff said. "Executive Investigations."

Bill Thorn stood to offer his hand. "Very nice to meet you, Gabe." Thorn spoke in a northwestern singsong, with low rounded vowels. His use of a nickname sounded forced and false, a ploy to get a rise out of Gabriel.

"Hello, Bill. I go by Gabriel. Jeff, what's going on?"

"This is my meeting," Thorn said with cool authority. "Sit down. Coffee?"

Gabriel shook his head. After the nickname his guard was up. Jeff backed away to stand by his desk. It felt like a video game. Gabriel sat.

Thorn filled a mug and added sweetener. "Nathaniel Coleman. He goes by Nate."

"If you know about it," Gabriel said, "you know he swung at me first."

"You swung back," Thorn said. "Three broken bones in his face and a fractured wrist."

"It just happened."

"No, it didn't. And if it did—it was exceptionally violent. Can you explain why?"

"No." Gabriel's thighs twitched, ready to run. "No, I can't."

"Gabriel Archer," Jeff said from behind him. "Your employment at Empyrean Group is terminated, for unbecoming conduct. Human Resources will send a packet. I'm sorry."

"Can you do that?" Gabriel asked. "I wasn't arrested or anything."

"You've admitted to it," Jeff said. "Your employment contract has a morals clause. We can enforce it at—at the firm's option."

"And we so option," Thorn said. "We can also share your name with Nevada police. But we won't. You're fired, that's it." He turned to Jeff. "If you would leave us alone?"

Jeff grew red as if insulted. Thorn straightened. Jeff walked out, slamming the door.

"That wasn't about me," Gabriel said.

"I think it was. But Jeff and I have a history." Thorn settled back, crossed his legs. "You saw the guard at your desk. But he'll wait. Have a coffee. It's good. Real brew, not the pods."

"What is this?"

"This is recruiting. Executive Investigations does background checks on senior staff. Meticulous work. Not exciting." Thorn smiled. "I've a hunch you'd be a natural."

"You just fired me," Gabriel said.

"I did. You are welcome to leave." Thorn closed his eyes, arms slack as if to meditate.

"What is this? An exit debriefing?"

"I told you. I'm recruiting." Thorn opened his eyes. "To be clear, no one else at this firm will hire you. Tell me what happened."

Gabriel winced. "He hit me first. He was bothering my date." Gabriel remembered anger but also joy, the satisfaction of being necessary. "She was drunk, he was shouting. He hit me."

"You broke his face." Thorn leaned close. "You wanted to."

"I was fighting. You fight to win."

"That's true. Did you feel justified?" Thorn spoke slowly, sympathetically. "Did it feel proper? Did he deserve punishment? Or did you just like hurting him?"

"I should leave now," Gabriel said.

Thorn poured a mug of coffee and handed it to Gabriel. "Good luck then."

Gabriel drank. It was strong coffee, bitter and nutty. He must have had it daily, but he had never noticed it being this good. The gray mug sported the Empyrean logo, a simple motif of nine floating gray steps. Ascension, progress. Now it looked rickety, unfinished.

Thorn wanted something specific from Gabriel. Maybe still a game. If Gabriel could figure it out.

"What would I have to do?" Gabriel said.

"I take you for a drive," Thorn said. "To Oakland. A public street, outdoors."

"Why?"

"I can't tell you. Come for a drive with me or go home."

"What's in it for me?" Gabriel asked.

"Maybe a job, which is good these days. Also, it might be what you're looking for."

"Looking for how?"

"In your life. Do you like your life? Does it make sense? Or do you lie to everyone about it so you don't have to try to explain? This might be part of that." Thorn stood. "I'm going now. Come with me. C'mon."

Gabriel felt like when Walt had steered him down a cliff. Look what had happened after that.

* * *

Bill Thorn drove a long gold American convertible, with cream leather and burled wood trim. Even with the top down it stank of detailing, a sharp chemical citrus.

"Where are you from?" Thorn asked at the garage exit.

"That's not in my file?" Gabriel asked.

"Wasn't the part that interested me."

"Ha. I grew up in Madison, Wisconsin."

"Good town. What did your father do?"

"After the Navy he was a power-plant engineer. My mom teaches Russian. We all learned it from her. As a toddler I had Cyrillic blocks." He felt a snap of fear, as if Thorn's gold boat would steal his childhood. "I shouldn't have come."

"It's a half-mile to the freeway. If you're going to leap to freedom, do it soon." Thorn turned on upbeat swing jazz. Gabriel wondered if this was part of the interview, would he stay or run, why it felt stupider to run than to go someplace he didn't know.

On the Bay Bridge, Gabriel smelled salt, rust, and exhaust, curdled like cheese. He closed his eyes to focus on the smell. Even the sun moved but the Bay didn't move. An odd thought.

When he opened his eyes, Thorn's sedan aimed at the Oakland port's great cranes. "Where are we going?" Gabriel asked.

"Not far now. It's an old industrial park. Just a couple more miles."

They exited onto narrow streets of old warehouses, parking lots fenced and topped with razor wire. He saw vans and trucks but no people. With the top down Gabriel felt more aware but also exposed. The Bay air hard to smell through wire rust.

"If I said to take me back, would you?"

Thorn glanced at him. "You need to be more decisive."

"You're an asshole."

"That's right," Thorn said. "Besides, we're here."

Thorn turned down an alley of old uneven brick. The car rattled past crumbling buildings, boarded windows, rust-eaten dumpsters. No salt smell. Gabriel should have paid more attention. He could run. Was Thorn armed?

Thorn pulled up to a chain-link gate and turned off the engine. "Let's go."

Gabriel followed him, past a door stoop littered with cigarette butts. Acrid stenches, sewage and chemical. "This is nasty," Gabriel said. He backed away, coughing. "I'm not going there." He coughed in spasms. "My God, what is this?"

Thorn pointed at the barred windows on the building's top floor. "There."

A lava of odors poured down on Gabriel. Blood, shit, acid, copper, flame. He felt a horrid layered buzz in his nose, like a hive of pain and shame. Gabriel threw up but it was just a drop in the filth. In his head, a siren's shrieking: *bad habanero bad habanero bad habanero.*

* * *

Gabriel woke in Bill Thorn's sedan, his arms under the seat belt, his jacket draped over him like a blanket. He freed himself. They sat in the parking lot of a gray-white strip mall. Coffee house, drugstore, framing, salon. The car's top was up. His phone had service. Gabriel leaned back into his body's smells, sour-sweet vomit, vinegar sweat. "Where are we?"

"San Bruno," Thorn said, looking at the sky. "It's foggy. We'll wait out rush hour." Thorn's suit was rumpled and dirty. "Let's get coffee. You can freshen up."

The coffee house looked unfinished, with empty green-white walls and few tables. The restroom had no mirror. Gabriel rinsed his mouth, washed his face, brushed off what dirt he could.

Thorn was waiting for him at a rear table, with a large mug of coffee, two bottled waters, and a bottled iced tea. "Take your pick," Thorn said. "I like them all."

Gabriel drank a water in one go. "Please just tell me what's going on."

"You're psychic," Thorn said.

Gabriel felt he had walked into a window. "Again?"

"Psychic. Though, 'sensitive' is more in vogue. You have a supernatural awareness of people's emotional and volitional states." Thorn took the coffee and sipped it.

Gabriel pushed his chair back. "That's ridiculous."

"I don't think so. My sensitivity emerged in my late teens. With the hormones. Bad dreams, hallucinations, total certainty about bizarre courses of action. Some make it on their own. Some meet up with others. The Internet's helped. Others become addicts, or diagnosed as schizophrenic. You repressed it."

Gabriel waited for an outrage that never came. Instead, he felt a curious unfurling, like a dry sponge soaking water. "Convince me," he said.

"You work hard to be good," Thorn said. "People do that when they used to be jerks."

Gabriel nodded. "My dad was a hard-ass. I never measured up. It rolls downhill. I liked getting in people's faces. My mom pulled strings to get me into college but I cared less than she did. I left with two friends to be a ski-bum in Tahoe, working for lift passes and beer. But some nights, I looked for trouble. I'd go alone to different towns around the lake, strange bars. My specialty was macho assholes with self-hating girlfriends. I could smell them. Literally. Like burned coffee. Once I found one, it didn't take much. In a minute we'd be outside."

"You win?"

"Usually. I was more prepared. By springtime, I was working a second job, and—I don't know. Like it was out of my system. One night there was this big house party, out by the airport. Didn't really know anyone, friend-of-a-friend thing. I walked into the woods to take a piss. Found this couple. She was drunk, he was kissing her. She didn't like it. I hauled off on him. Face, gut,

gut again, knee to his face." Even now, he felt the satisfaction. "She tried to stop me. When I pushed her off I felt her nose break. That woke me. I ran until I collapsed. I don't know how I got home. Next morning, I left my share of the rent and drove to San Francisco. I quit drinking, got my head straight, got a scholarship. I haven't been in a fight since, until Saturday."

"In the woods," Thorn asked, "why did you look for the couple?"

"I didn't—" The question stung him sharply behind his ear. He had been chatting up a pretty brunette in black, with a New York look to her. He had left to give her space. Outside, the stars had shimmered like sparks above South Shore's blue-white glow. He had ducked behind a tree. Above the smell of his own piss, a stench of sweat and come.

"I smelled them," Gabriel said. "I smelled the sex."

"They weren't having sex."

"That's right. I—" Another sting. It made him shiver. "I smelled his plan."

"Drink the tea," Thorn said. "Then tell me about Saturday."

He drank the tea like water until its strange scents stopped him. Plum, prune really, a jammy viscous sweetness. He put down the bottle. All day, he'd been distracted, his hassles sidelined by the world. By smell. "Nate smelled horrible," Gabriel said. "Like sewage. I smelled him from far away. He caused the scene. He hit me—it wasn't even a good punch. But something took over. I liked when it did."

"The vigilante is justice's proud bitch," Thorn said. "Maybe Nate had evil in mind. But Nate hit you. If you stood down, they'd have thrown him out."

"So I should have just—"

"Not hospitalized a person," Thorn said. "What about today?"

"Slave labor. Kidnapped immigrants." Now Gabriel could parse it: bitter sadness, coals of anger smoldering under damp shame. Fooled, fleeced, harnessed like donkeys, chained and crapping in buckets. "You pretended you didn't smell it."

"I don't smell," Thorn said. "What I *saw* was as ugly.

Sensitivity uses dominant senses. I have perfect vision, so I see—colors, auras, distortions. You have a great sense of smell."

"No, I don't," Gabriel said. "Not for years. Lately I smell a lot."

"You repressed it. Now it's back. That will be tough. Smell is immediate and evocative. Smell is why moths die in candle flames."

"I thought—wait, the sweatshop? How did you know? Are we going to do something?"

"I knew, how you know. Authorities have been notified. But I figured I'd use it."

"That's cold." Gabriel panted. "We have to do something."

"Ha. You can't even stand up near that place. Be glad it can be fixed, Gabriel. We're not the ones to fix it. You understand?" Thorn shook his finger, opened his hand. "You can't just react. You have to handle it. I'll try to help you. It would be easier if you worked for me."

"Why can't I just keep my job?" Gabriel asked.

"Did you like it all that much?"

"That's not the point."

"Do you know Empyrean Group is a devout workplace?" Thorn asked. "We have the same diversity of belief as most white-collar businesses. But from executive to custodial staff, we are more devout. High rates of church attendance, involvement, tithing. Even our atheists volunteer more and attend spiritual discussion groups. Such people have a sense of order, of community, of rules. You and I are *witchy*. We violate the rules. Remember how Jeff Prender behaved this morning? He's not alone. The Russian office hated you. Even in a machine translation, it seemed all out of line. They had you put under surveillance when you came back, for corporate espionage."

"You're joking."

"No, we're paranoid. Obviously you weren't spying. They just wanted to get you fired. Luckily for you, Jeff Prender doesn't like Russians. But that's over. There are few places people like us can work at Empyrean. We're gargoyles. Protect the church but no communion."

"You don't really do background checks," Gabriel said.

"Oh, I do, but as a cover."

"Cover for what?"

"I can't tell you until you accept," Thorn said.

"What if I don't like it? What if I want out?"

"I don't know, Gabriel. I do know you need help. The world is going to drown you. I can help you swim."

"And I don't have a choice."

"You can quit," Thorn said. "It might be the best option. I'm a very tense fellow. I go to church twice a week, and the shooting range more."

"You're not much of a salesman," Gabriel said.

"Thank you. If you say no, I'll get you a good package. What I said, about our community, I'll help with that too."

A sudden panic gripped Gabriel. He imagined wires in his brain, screams and pain, guns and laughter. Against his fears, this one dour man, strangely calming. He was real. The tea was real. The place was real. His breathing slowed.

"I'm in," Gabriel said.

"May I ask why?"

"Because your crazy is better than my crazy. My crazy, I'm alone and hallucinating this. Your crazy makes sense. Not just now, but before. My childhood."

"That's a start, Gabriel. We should probably head back."

Fog glowed around the parking lot lights. Thorn looked around as if satisfied. He took off his jacket. They drove a mile not talking, listening to a jazzy guitar.

"Some call us witchy," Thorn said. "Others call us blessed. They call your crazy smells a gift from God, with righteous ends."

"That's stupid," Gabriel said.

"Who did you fight? Date-rapists. Jerks. You could have targeted weak women. I won't insist on our holiness. But some believe we are here for good reasons." His face shone brightly in the freeway light. "Our CEO, Luther Koenig, has dreams. Specific dreams, in advance, about real people. People who can do good they're not doing, or people who need to stop doing harm."

"Koenig is psychic?"

"Not like us. We know what is. He knows what will be. He is a prophet. The people he dreams of are real. We try to change their fates. I don't know why, and if Mr. Koenig does, he's not telling. But it's real, and it's our firm's biggest secret.

"Three weeks ago, Gabriel, Koenig had a dream about you. I was in Tahoe this weekend, Gabriel, in that same bar. I stole the security recording. I kept the police from finding you."

Dry pressure in his throat, as if Thorn had fed him balloons. "Why didn't you stop me?" Gabriel asked.

"We didn't know what you would do," Thorn said. "We only know time and place."

"Did you see me fight?"

"I did. You were fast."

A great fatigue came on Gabriel. "Is it in my file?"

"The recording? If it were, would you want to see it?"

"I see it fine in my head." Gabriel closed his eyes. "But it's slow."

"Look on the bright side," Thorn said. "Now that you know you're psychic, you can start drinking again."

CHAPTER FIVE

London

onday morning Zarabeth woke shivering and sick to her stomach. She knelt in the bathtub, drinking greedily from cupped hands. Some germ from that horrid club.

She came late to the morning review, which made her a target for the senior manager, a skinny toff named Harold Bourke with a prize rooster's hair and temperament. "I'm sure you have so much to tell us after your week's audit," Harold said.

"Happy to discuss it," she said, in her flattest Yank accent. "I feel good, overall. Excellent service, good return. And, great job keeping the meetings short."

"That's all?" Harold said. "Optimized flew you from Boston just to pat our backs?"

Territorial pissing? Or Underwood? "More to ensure there aren't any risks to the firm, Harold. Our role here is unusual. More responsibility than a consultancy contract."

"I'm not sure what you're implying."

"Mercurex bleeds money. As their finance division, how have we advised them?"

Harold drew himself up, but his swimmy eyes betrayed him.

"We shared our concerns," Harold said, "but it wasn't for us to underline the issue."

"Even to put it in writing?" Zarabeth asked.

Harold strained to smile. "Even to put it in writing." He looked away as if to banish her.

She sent Magda a quick message and went to the kitchen. Petra, a tiny blonde network engineer and frequent smoker, was getting coffee.

"Aren't you on the wrong floor?" Zarabeth asked.

"Our machine is broken," Petra said, in her breathy Bavarian accent. "So I hacked the badge reader." She poured Zarabeth a cup. "Don't tell?"

"Mum's the word," Zarabeth said. "Good weekend?"

"No weekend. Spent it here, installing new servers to speed decryption."

"I thought the network centre was in Birmingham?"

"Just the dirigible pilots. The network is here. Come on, I'll show you."

Petra led her four flights down the fire stairway to a thick metal door. The network centre was a dim blue-lit cavern with rows of workstations, staffed by people on headsets.

Above and behind them, a square of sixteen large screens displayed a giant outline of Great Britain, covered by a lopsided chevron of pulsing lines. Purple, blue, cyan, a rare flash of orange. "That's usage on the ground," Petra explained. "Cool colours are lower traffic. Distracting, yes? I am glad I don't work here."

Zarabeth nodded. Hard to speak while watching it, as if the lines were a language the Polyglot didn't yet know. She made herself look away. On other walls, lesser Britains, different patterns but similar colours. "They're all cool colours."

"I guess we don't have a lot of traffic yet," Petra said. "Not really my department."

"Nor mine." Zarabeth took out her phone.

"The room is shielded. No mobile signals."

"Just checking when my next meeting is." Really she keyed a video, to send to Magda.

Back at her desk, her copies of Mercurex spreadsheets wouldn't update. Open ports shut. Her spat with Harold had improved security. Maybe she could ask Petra to hack it for her.

She went for a walk instead. Around her, the bustle of the City, the financial district, high-priced people in high-priced suits. A skilled pickpocket would have a field day.

Or not. Any pickpocket preying on City folk would be caught soon enough. Most people paid with credit cards, not purses of gold. A good thief today was a hacker, not a bandit. Mercurex seemed to answer that problem, but really it didn't. Businesses hiding their information needed secure databases and encrypted transmissions. Secure comms were for soldiers and spooks. Mercurex was a business with one customer, who had moved on.

She felt herself tiring like an old woman. She bought a take-away sandwich in a tiny café near a tony square of white townhomes. Unwrapped, it looked too daunting to eat whole. She picked out the meat while she called Endre in Internal Support.

"Tally-ho, old chap," he joked. "Everything ship-shape?"

"Stop kidding around," she said in Hungarian. "I need perspective." She laid it all out: Rex's occult connections, Underwood's threat, Straightforward letting Mercurex bankrupt itself. "Why build a giant network with no revenue?"

"You don't know there's no revenue," Endre said. "Just no traffic."

"Traffic is revenue. Those dirigibles aren't routing any data."

"No client data. The network still exists. Signals, time checks, tests, reports."

"Interesting," Zarabeth said. "Is all that encrypted too?"

"Don't want your competition to see your traffic logs."

First pass at a new technology, Rex had said. "Can a network be charmed?" she asked. "It's all Rex's code. What if it writes a spell at the same time?"

"I don't know," Endre said. "It's a clever thought. Good that you're technical. Your predecessor Sasha was a people person, but helpless with gear."

Not an accidental mention. "Thanks for saying so. I never did meet her. Sasha."

"People change jobs. Got to go."

She searched the company directory. Two Sashas, both in Midwest offices, one clerical, one industrial. Her predecessor had left the firm. Endre wanted her to know about it. Why?

* * *

Zarabeth woke. She felt nothing but knew there was a damage inside her. Something in her dream had told her more.

It was four-thirty. She made coffee and turned on the TV. In a news report on tensions in Iraq, a gray-haired Kurdish politician spoke around his bristly black mustache. She couldn't understand him before the translation. Meaningless scribbles on the walls. She changed channels. German business, French drama, Russian news. All foreign again. Her demon was gone.

Rex's smile. How had she missed it? She ran to the toilet, vomited yellow bile.

She called Missy. Missy answered. She retold the weekend in a breathless babble.

"You careless slut," Missy said. "Rex is eating your life. But for your Polyglot you'd most like be dead. Sigil magic. Bet he's an Osman Spare type, doesn't come during sex. Sweetie, nothing good in sperm except X chromosomes."

"What*ever*. I think I need help."

"We'll break his connection. Got a pen?" Missy dictated a simple spell. "Around the star, center to close. You know the drill."

"Not really."

"Learn by doing. You gotta perform it. Singsongy. A bit boo. The powers like a show." She added another line. "If you want to hurt him, use that for the close, if you can stand it."

"Stand what?"

"You thought this wouldn't hurt? But you'll hurt him too. Get to work. Good luck."

"Thanks," Zarabeth said. "I guess I owe you."

"I reckon we're even," Missy said. "And, we're friends. See you soon, I hope."

Zarabeth had no time to reflect on Missy's generosity. She had never done anything like this, and had it work. This, or dying.

She traveled with tea light candles, in case she smoked in hotels with sealed windows. Two fresh bars of soap on the vanity. She pushed the bed back and rolled up the rug. Enough space for her body, barely.

She hammered a safety pin into the floor with her shoe, and tied a length of dental floss to it as a compass. Using soap, she drew the circle, marked even points for the star, and used pin and floss to draw straight soap lines.

Blue light seeped up the eastern sky. Zarabeth showered in cold water, put up her hair with hotel pencils. On the bed, she rehearsed Missy's spell. Not getting it. Easy for drama queen Missy. Zarabeth had no talent for performance.

She spread her bathrobe on the floor outside the circle, sat cross-legged, breathed deeply. She raised her abs into downward-dog pose. If she had to put on a show, better yoga than singing.

She lit the candles and stepped into the star in the circle. She stood in tree pose, left foot flat against right thigh, arms raised and thumbs linked. The spell was chanted once from the center, four times at each point, five more at the center. No water, no rest: endurance was part of the cost. Cross the circle, or break the soap lines—worse than what she fought.

Zarabeth chanted, her voice rough and plaintive:

"I want this to be over now, I want him to be gone.

"He steals my life to feed his youth, he sucks me dry to bone.

"I will sever his connection, he can no more hold on.

"I want this to be over now, I want him to be gone."

She stepped out, pivoted, held out her arms to warrior pose. She repeated the spell, eyes on the tips of her fingers, on the edge of the circle. Her arms a sword of light.

She dropped her hips, raised her arms, high crescent lunge pose. Her hips lower, lower. Her left knee hurt to take the weight. She chanted in hard breaths. She touched the ground, rolled sideways, grabbed her toe with her free hand, side plank pose. She fell over, raised her hips and straightened her limbs, downward dog. Clean lines, perfect lines. Zarabeth had girders

49

for sinews. Let earth be impressed how she holds up the sky.

She stepped counter-clockwise into warrior at the second point of the star. The candles burned painfully white and a foot tall. Her voice, already a whisper, but her poses felt strong.

At the third point, fatigue walloped her. Wavering warrior, wobbling lunge, her side plank floppy, a cow sitting on her dog. She pushed back against it as if to throw it in the air. The candle flames shed little floating spheres of white fire.

At the fourth point of the star, the powers poked her, prodded her, resisted her. The floor like nails in her palm, her knee about to crack, bloody bone out her skin. The fire spheres turned orange and burst like seed pods. Each shard a tiny burn and she unable to squirm.

"I want him to be gone," she spat.

At the fifth point she gasped between verses, through flurries of hot pain. A stream of sweat ran down her spine, maybe enough to rinse a break in the soap-lines. In her head, the Polyglot egged her on in Sanskrit: *Virabhadrasana! Chandrasana! Vasisthasana! Adhomukha svanasana!*

She returned to the center. The votive flames burned blood red now, the color of the pain eating through her. She folded her body down, touched her palms to the ground. Her calf muscle ripped. She dared not cry out. She had one shot. She clasped her hands together, straightened her back, her bellybutton opening wide. Headstand, legs in the air, toes pointed high. She grunted:

"I want this to be over now, I want him to be gone.

"He steals my life to feed his youth, he sucks me dry to bone.

"I will sever his connection, he can no more hold on.

"I cannot let this deep wound close 'til our pain pays all debts."

She pushed her arms up, from headstand to handstand, chanted again. Red-hot needles twisted inside her, keening like birdcalls: *kiri kiri kiri, kiri kiri kiri.*

Again. Hot coals rained on the soles of her feet, on her legs. She chanted through clenched teeth while her elbows crack-crackety-cracked with each word.

Another voice in her head now, buttery and elegant. *Take a break,* it said. *Stop now.*

"'Til our pain pays all debts!" she shrieked.

A volcano's breath of sand and ash, she would fall she would fall. *Twenty-five is plenty,* the buttery voice said. *Enough as good as a feast. Stop now.*

One more if it killed her. She chanted louder than the voice:

"I want this to be over now *lava rain each* I want him to be gone *drop a blister* He steals my life to feed his youth *smoking charred* He sucks me dry to bone *pockmark skin* I will sever his connection *devil piss strip* He can no more hold on *flesh like acid* I want this to be over now *well-done food* I want him to be GONE *fine you win.*"

A ball of semen in her throat, big as an egg. She retched it out. Gone and never been there. Cold wind blew out the candles. She fell into the dark.

*   *   *

That morning Zarabeth felt fantastic, not merely recovered but healthy, though her arms were sore from scrubbing the soap off the floorboards. She wore new shoes, pointed brown patent leather with a saddle-strip. Rex had called them Governess Fetish.

Rex. Smoke breaks would be awkward. More awkward for him.

At ten, she sat with Durjaya, a scrawny code manager with a rubbery face and a thick Yorkshire accent, as he showed off his archiving system. She felt back in form, back in her old job, a good memory on this wonderful day. She even took notes.

The mail icon on Durjaya's screen flashed. A moment later Zarabeth's phone buzzed. The same message, from Kath Boyle. Zarabeth read over Durjaya's shoulder:

With great sadness, we inform you of the untimely death of our Mercurex colleague, Mr. Rex Densmore, from a heart attack this morning. In respect of their grief, the encryption team will take the afternoon off.

She stopped reading, sat back so Durjaya couldn't hear her excited heartbeat. Zarabeth had never broken the sixth commandment before. It was thrilling.

"My word," Durjaya said. "Did you know him?"

"Yes. Both smokers."

They sat saying nothing, unsure how long to accord the dead respect. In the silence her mood soured. Magda had wanted them to swallow her up, both worm and hook. That Zarabeth had survived it was her own good fortune, not Magda's plan. All Magda had wanted was for her to cause some damage.

"Durjaya," she said. "I mean your name. Means 'hard to beat,' right?"

He raised a thick eyebrow. "I suppose that's the translation, yes. Impregnable really, difficult to conquer." He drew himself up. "Hard to beat. I like that."

"Me too." She would have to like it. From now on, it was the only way to live.

CHAPTER SIX

San Francisco

Executive Investigations sat at the end of a dim windowless hallway on the thirteenth floor of the corporate headquarters, behind a door Gabriel's badge couldn't yet open. His new office was a six-foot square with a standing-height desk and a rack of coat hooks. Two computer screens, no chair.

"I'm afraid it's a bit spartan," Bill Thorn said.

"Better than a cubicle," Gabriel said.

"New meat!" A gray-haired white man, deep lines in his tough ugly face, stood in a cloud of tobacco stink. Despite the paunch pushing out his blue Hawaiian shirt, Gabriel immediately knew him for an elite soldier, the kind Gabriel's father had bowed his head to at VFW barbecues.

"This is Del Murphy," Thorn said. "He's our admin."

"Nice to meet ya," Del said. Gabriel shook his hard heavy hand. Del's brightly lit office screamed with flair: surfing photos, war photos, motorcycle photos, a poster of handgun history from flintlocks to automatics.

"You have a chair," Gabriel said. "Do I get a chair?"

"I have a drafting stool," Del said. "I'm an old fart. No chair for you, you'd fall asleep. Last office is my assistant Thi Tam.

She's a peach. Makes great coffee. Pretty, too."

The last office was empty even of furniture. "Where is she?" Gabriel asked.

"Boss keeps forgetting to hire her. Hot-cha! So I get my own coffee. You want a coffee?"

"One sugar, thanks." Gabriel followed Thorn into his office, the mirror of Gabriel's but for a glass bowl of Japanese gummy candies. He smelled their fake-fruit aromas through the wrapping. "Does Del know about our—our whatever thing?"

"Some Del knows, some Del doesn't. This, Del doesn't." Thorn wrote a number on the back of his business card. "These people run an online forum. Fax them a copy of your driver's license. From a public location, a copy shop, not from here. Shred the card when you're done."

"Maybe I should eat it," Gabriel said. "To be safest."

"If you like," Thorn said. "Oh, that was sarcasm? We discussed this. There's Empyrean and there's people like us. The Venn diagram is a thin sliver. Respect their paranoia. Candy?"

"No thanks."

"Then we're done. I have meetings." Thorn left.

When Del returned he explained the work, reviewing background checks on applicants for executive positions in North American offices. Reports ran from seventy to a hundred pages, including interviews, financial statements, and summaries. Just going through the checklist took until lunch. In the afternoon Del walked him through a completed file, but Gabriel could barely focus. He felt woozy and his nose ran buckets. After his bus ride home he went straight to bed.

Wednesday he found three tissue boxes on his desk. "I pulled strings for that," Del said.

"You just got them from the supply closet. If you really want to help, stop smoking."

"That'll happen. I set you up two practice files. Should keep you busy until lunch."

Gabriel sneezed. "This is all busy work anyway, right?"

Del clacked his tongue. "Clean a toilet with a toothbrush, that's busy work. Get to it."

By lunch Gabriel hadn't finished the first one. "I'm really behind," he told Del. "Sorry."

"You're not behind," Del said. "If you had done more, we'd know you were skimming."

"Ha. Is everything here a test?"

"Until you pass them."

At lunch Gabriel bought a turkey sandwich in the lobby cafeteria. He unwrapped the cellophane and sneezed a dozen times. His handkerchief had blood on it. He wobbled back to the elevator, throwing the sandwich in the trash. Del sent him home.

Thursday morning Del's office was dark but Thorn was in. "Del's surfing North Ocean Beach," Thorn said. "He told me you're doing well. Not that it's challenging for an MBA."

"It'd be easier if I didn't have this cold."

"It's not a cold," Thorn said. "It's like an allergy. Your brain suffers what it used to repress. To protect itself, it's stuffing your nose. Notice how you get worse through the day?"

"Did you have a mind allergy too?" Gabriel asked.

"I was blinded. Two weeks, full moon to new moon. I was eighteen. And I've heard of worse onsets than mine." Thorn squinted disapprovingly. "Do you know anything about smell? Do you know how it works?"

"I breathe in through my nose. Then—I don't know how it works."

"But it rules your life. I think you have homework," Thorn said. "After you take these." He gave Gabriel a box of antihistamines. "And more busy work."

* * *

Antihistamines cleared Gabriel's nose, but clarity was worse in the poison world: chemicals for drink and food, bile and smoke for air, store shelves of bright new trash to stink up his home en route to the landfill. For breakfasts he ate yogurt and honey; for dinner, fish and chicken, baked unseasoned or with rosemary. He fell asleep to recorded nature sounds, wearing a swimmer's nose plug. He woke tired from frantic dreams.

Web encyclopedias and science sites gave him a little resolve. The olfactory bulb was part of the brain itself. Smell was the most intimate sense, the closest a person let the world invade. Gabriel had lost that, and regained it.

He tried a journal but he was no writer, and besides there were no words for the orders of sensation he perceived. Constellations of sweaty feet and blue cheese, of peanut butter and brown rice. The Internet had no spectrum of smells, no table explaining bases and combinations. Reviews of perfumes and food were florid and imagistic, like fanciful names for paint colors. Gabriel read them like a new language, flashes of recognition in a blizzard of nonsense.

* * *

Welcome ritegard! Posts since your last login:
—BEGIN DIGEST—
[bathouse] [thread: support] [yesterday 22:54]
The helicopters thunder over the house to the base nearby. I hear them approaching and plug my ears but they take so long, I hear them after they go. I can't afford to move.
——
[oeri2319] [thread: support] [yesterday 23:21]
> I can't afford to move.
Can you insulate a room? Basement is best. Did they just start? Maybe they'll stop soon.
——
[ritegard] [thread: What are we?] [today 02:09]
> clear the sensitive nature is a superior connection to the noosphere
clear the witch is in deeper league with the prince of lies? A theory isn't just saying. It has to be right a lot of the time. I know what I feel but no one can explain it. I don't know if it's damage with a neat side effect. I just want to live with it.
——
[trigrfin] [thread: What are we?] [today 08:53]
> I just want to live with it.

So do we all. I don't want to be mean brother but this is not a place to ape normality. People come to reflect on their hidden natures and yes to whine a bit too. Try a little tenderness.

—

[oldpinok] [thread: What are we?] [today 12:37]
> not a place to ape normality
I ape normality in a nursing home with dusty vents. I'm the doddering simpleton. This is where I can be honest but unafraid. Good luck in your real world ritegard. Never did much for me.
—END DIGEST—

* * *

Saturday morning, two weeks after Tahoe, Gabriel woke in clammy sheets. Dust swirled in the bright sunlight. He turned on the ceiling fan while he stretched. Pipes in the ceiling knocked slowly. Eleven-thirty, late for Gabriel. But he felt all right.

Gabriel rented a second-floor room with bath from Denise Tong, a craft potter who got the house in her divorce but couldn't afford it alone. Downstairs, Denise was watching television in stained work clothes. She had a wiry build, with a long face and hollow cheeks like a forensic reconstruction. "How was the open mike night?" she asked, pausing the TV.

"Patricia's brother needs to practice his guitar," Gabriel said. "I met this woman, Gita Tiwari. Cute face, sharp tongue. Didn't get a number. You went shopping."

"Do they smell good?" Denise accepted Gabriel's recovered senses easily, as the spiritual upgrade due to all San Franciscans. "I was at Ferry Plaza. I decided to splurge for tonight's dinner party." She unpaused the TV. "Find that woman online. You need to get out more."

In the kitchen, food spread across the counter like a giant toy xylophone. Mottled orange heirloom tomatoes, red bell peppers, purple and jade baby lettuces, wrist-thick teal leeks, fist-sized magenta eggplant. Sprigs of ruffled basil, yellow oregano, purslane. He felt the wet and waxy skins, opened tubs of goat cheese and tofu. Smells draped the world in help balloons, informative but quickly fading. He had learned to take an extra breath.

A narrow loaf of pumpernickel sat in the breadbox. Sweet aromas, dough and salt and caramel. He ate a slice. Fine foam like a head of beer, salt crystals dissolving in puffs, yeast and coffee to balance the sugars. Another slice, a third. It was heavenly.

Denise came into the kitchen. "Must escape evil TV— Gabriel, what the fuck?"

He'd eaten half the loaf. "I'm sorry," he said, his mouth full. He brushed dark crumbs off his shirt. "I don't know, it just smelled so good. I couldn't stop. I'll replace it."

"Then get going." She gave him directions to her bakery's stand. "They're the only ones with pumpernickel." She menaced him with celery. "Pray they still have it."

By bicycle to Ferry Plaza, he took the same route as his work commute, east through tidy Russian Hill, then south and downhill. His tires hummed past stately homes and tired apartments a century younger. His phone shuffled fast loud songs: a ribald chantey, a pouty punk dismissing a lover. On bright bleached Columbus, a hip-hop remix of a folk song wove him through parking tourist cars. He raced past Embarcadero Center, trying not to breathe the heat-lamp air. Blocks later he coasted through a park, gasping for cool Bay breeze.

In Ferry Plaza, hundreds of people shuffled between white canvas tents. Gabriel smelled a dozen kinds of skin, stale sweat and fresh bacteria, suntan oil and vinyl and leather.

He stopped for samples at orchard stands, sweet pears and apples, acidic yellow tomato. He pricked a leaf of purple basil with his thumbnail and inhaled the licorice oil. Dizzying scents came from vegetables in pine crates: spice and bitter, cream and sugar, rust and glass. Fat and thin hot peppers, long spiny cucumbers, baby squash, string beans, turnips, radishes. He felt like Abel, suffused with awe and delight at the profusion of the earth. He stood and breathed through his jittery rush, as if he'd just made the last flight home.

MAY 2009

CHAPTER SEVEN

Rome

In the days since her London assault, Zarabeth had eaten huge meals to regain her strength and perhaps also the demon's. On her arrival in Rome the night before, she had checked every box on the breakfast card. Room service brought most of it, on a chrome cart with curlicue handles: toast, butter and jam, yogurt, sliced fruit, muesli, espresso. They had only given her grapefruit juice alas, and no meat. Still, enough to fill her.

She went onto the balcony to smoke. Zarabeth's hotel sat east of the great Villa Borghese park. She saw green space and painting-blue sky, the downtown's gritty bustle just a distant brown desert. The view from inside the mirage. Better than hiding in her London hotel, afraid of Underwood's retribution.

Better but still secretive. When Jill sent Zarabeth to Rome, she would only say it involved a meeting, outdoors. Her cover was as an Italian-speaking staffer, on loan to help with Straightforward-Roma's *Simposio della realizzazione di Intelligenza Artificiale* (hosted in English despite the title).

The lectures mixed theory and practice in artificial intelligence, from technical primers to venture panels, a chance for the firm to pick nerd brains over salad, for information to sell executives over steak. A fun room to work, no doubt, if tame after London—and after London, tame would do.

A cloud moved. Hot sun pressed on her. She took her cigarette inside. The cool chrome and tan furnishings soothed her after days in dark baroque Green Park. She unwrapped her Tarot cards and dealt. Product 4 upside-down, Product 10, Bankruptcy upside-down. A nervous survivor in a stagnant place. Did the cards mean her hotel room or her life?

At nine, she was the first to arrive on the lower level. She had made her face but dressed to move chairs and boxes, in black and pink London trainers, a pleated black skirt, and a white manga-cat top. In the fluorescent light the conference room looked stark and grainy, like its own phone selfie. Beige metal chairs sat stacked on carts by the wall. Even on tiptoe she couldn't lift the topmost clear. She smiled at her own frustration. Too cool to move chairs in Reston. One demon later, a team player.

From the elevator came a gaunt white brunette in a gauzy black skirt and platform stilettos. Behind her, a bellman pulled a baggage cart loaded with boxes.

"Signora Piacitelli?" Zarabeth asked.

"Fabiana Moretti. You're the American." Fabiana pointed the bellman ahead, offered a limp handshake while looking Zarabeth up and down. "Cute shirt. The others are coming."

Bottle-blonde Teresa and real-blonde Renata also led bellmen with carts. Also stimulant-slender, not dressed to sweat. Fabiana got chairs unloaded while the others unpacked boxes of journals and conference swag. The Polyglot soaked up their girlish slang.

At ten, the local director Minerva Piacitelli swept in, with air kisses for staff and waves to bell captains. She drew up before Zarabeth. She had brushed her chestnut hair high, like a bulwark against flood. Cool violet eyes glinted in her well-made ivory face.

"Good of you to help with our little conference," she said in Italian.

"Optimized is delighted my skills are of use to the Rome office," Zarabeth said floridly. "Plus I get a vacation."

Minerva smiled, rubbed her temple. "Enjoying Rome?"

"What little I've seen. Last night I turned in early to read up on the conference speakers." Really Zarabeth had watched frenzied tabloid news wearing a warm gel mask, eating gelato. "Technical for me, but the venture panel looks interesting."

"Very professional. Special Projects sounds more exciting than event planning."

"I've done many trade shows," Zarabeth said. "I'm here to help."

"Of course. What wonderful Italian! Many conferees only use English in email." Minerva brushed her fingers through her hair. "Do you speak any other languages?" A trap in Minerva's voice, as if to give Zarabeth some shit-work no one else wanted.

Zarabeth copied the staff's curt mean wit. "I've picked up some Spanish from my maid," she said. "But not so technical."

Minerva laughed. "You'll fit right in." Workmen arrived with platforms to build the stage. Minerva led her around, explaining registration and the buffet. "A sponsor is donating wireless. We have to monitor the server."

"Good. What can I do?"

"When the caterers come, supervise refreshments. After that—you plan to change clothes, yes?"

"Of course."

Minerva crinkled her nose. "With Americans you never know."

* * *

Roman taxis were white German sedans, smaller than London's cabs but better than the rust buckets plying Washington's streets. Zarabeth's driver took them smoothly around sharp curves, only minutes away to a sooty-white mansion north of Piazza del Popolo. Zarabeth wore her African-print sundress and the Governess pumps, both tighter since she had bought them.

The old concierge hurried her in, as if it were cold out. "Come, child, come come." In the light she saw he was dreadfully mutilated with burn scars, as if to cow the uninvited.

She looked at him squarely. "Signora Piacitelli?"

He didn't care whether she looked. "Yes yes. The third floor." She followed him into a tall plaster silo with wide marble stairs rising clockwise, the central shaft filled by the tarnished brass grillwork cage of an antique wood elevator. He closed the elevator door behind her with a scarred three-fingered hand. "You're in luck, they just fixed it."

When she got out, a fit gray-haired olive-white man with big brown eyes waited with a glass of sparkling wine. "You are Zarabeth," he said in thick English, the end of her name an F. "I'm Fabrizio." He kissed her cheeks as if friends forever, gave her a glass. On her stem was a gold charm of a leaping cat.

The apartment had cork-yellow walls with colorful prints of old advertising posters. Minerva wore an apron over a tank top and jeans, and was sweaty from the kitchen. "So pretty," she said, inspecting Zarabeth's dress. "Soho? I love it."

Another man joined them, Zarabeth's height and twice her weight, in a white guayabera, his long thinning hair brushed back. "Good to see you again," he said. "Alessio Taglieri."

"That's right," Zarabeth said. "You were at registration." A puppy playing with a ball for his wine charm. "Are you with Straightforward?"

"Alessio works for our sponsor," Minerva said. "And Fabrizio is a civilian. Agricultural lobbying. Cincin." They clinked glasses. Minerva's wine charm was a rooster.

"So are we speaking English tonight?" Zarabeth asked.

"Minerva decided she needs practice," Alessio said.

"You were fine," Zarabeth said. "She was fine."

"You are sweet. Come see what we're having for dinner." She led Zarabeth into the kitchen. On the cutting board sat chicken filets and piles of chopped vegetables. Minerva handed her a tobacco-hashish joint. "Do you cook?"

"Only with a microwave." The joint had gritty smoke like bus exhaust.

"Americans. Go entertain the men," Minerva said. "I have to watch the sauce. I really love your outfit, it goes so well with your color. Those shoes? Also London? Fantastic."

Alessio stood in the doorway. "Where's the prosecco?"

"In the, in the—" Minerva pointed.

"Refrigerator," Alessio said, as Zarabeth said, "Fridge."

"'Fridge'? I like that better," Minerva said. "It's in the fridge. Pour for me too."

In the living room Fabrizio paged through streaming stations. Alessio put a light hand on Zarabeth's shoulder. "Fabrizio's English isn't good," he whispered. "Not sure he'll manage the first course." His hand uncommonly cold, his soft British voice squirmy in her ear.

"Your English is excellent," she said.

"I use it a lot. Minerva says your Italian is a wonder."

"She's kind."

"Only when she wants something."

"Ha. Why is a sunglasses firm sponsoring an AI conference?"

"Interfaces," Alessio said. "As machines get smarter, the interface must change. Speech is for commands, not directions. Imagine if your car told you everything instead of showing it in lights. People need a virtual desktop, natural and unobtrusive."

"Like sunglasses," Zarabeth said. "Neat. And well-rehearsed."

"Thank you. But AI is a bigger opportunity. Italians excel at bespoke heavy manufacturing. We build trains and ski lifts all over the world. Future systems will need to react faster, and more fluidly, than a human operator. AI is the twenty-first century gearbox."

"Sounds like you're lobbying for government money."

Alessio raised an eyebrow. "Really? Perhaps we should host this in Rome. Oh, wait."

Dinner was long, the Italians slow and appreciative eaters. Between her high and the Polyglot's appetite, Zarabeth's stomach burned. She paced herself to Alessio, clearly the foodie of the group, but he was also the storyteller, with gossip about politicians. Too slow.

Explaining his job in agricultural policy exhausted Fabrizio's English, but in Italian he was hardly more interesting. Soon Alessio picked a cool fight with him over protectionism. "You lobbyists are alarmist," he said. "What's so bad about competition and mass production? The South needs capital investment. Foreign firms, cross-border mergers, even a joint venture with, I don't know,

Norwegians. You would make that impossible."

"The Norwegians don't let the Chinese farm their herring," Fabrizio said, English abandoned. "You can't compete with shit just on price. Shit is always cheaper."

"Now you're just spouting slogans," Alessio said. "All those well-fed boys in Palermo die from bullets. The Mezzogiorno soon goes the same way."

"I've been told I speak Italian," Zarabeth interrupted, "but I have no idea what you're talking about."

"Agreed. Enough!" Minerva said. "Or no dessert. Fabrizio, help me in the kitchen."

Alessio snorted, shook his head. Zarabeth looked over at him, willing to engage him out of boredom, but he stared at the kitchen. Did he want to fuck Minerva or Fabrizio? She dragged her finger through ricotta-flecked Marsala sauce, snuck a lick.

Peace came with strawberries in cream, sweet wine, and a fresh joint. They set on Zarabeth like stylists. "We're bored with ourselves," Minerva said. "Tell us everything."

"How is it you speak such fine Italian?" Fabrizio asked.

"I dated this guy," Zarabeth said unthinkingly. "In high school." She remembered a boy a year ahead of her, only as Italian as college pizza, but pretty. "His parents were from Naples."

"I'm envious," Alessio said. "No one ever learned a language for me."

"Was he handsome?" Minerva said. "Was it passionate? It must have been love."

"Very handsome. I was sixteen, so of course it was passionate."

"To your lover," Alessio toasted, "with all our gratitude."

Zarabeth blushed with pride at her lie.

After thick creamy coffee Minerva ended the night abruptly, insisting she and Zarabeth had work to do. Drunk Fabrizio pawed Minerva sullenly. Alessio took Zarabeth's hand in his cold one and kissed her cheeks. Minerva closed the door and sighed.

"Sorry about Fabrizio," she said in English. "He drank too much."

"I wish I had men fighting over me. What work do we have?"

"None. It was either you or Fabrizio staying, and he can't help with my English."

Over glasses of grappa they talked about hometowns. Minerva had grown up in Bolzano, at the base of the Dolomite Mountains, where Austria and Italy bled into each other. "It was heavy industry, now it's banking and tourism," she said. "It helped when they got the Iceman."

"Iceman?"

"This guy they found frozen in a glacier. Five thousand years old. The Austrians claimed him, but they analyzed the food in his—" she patted her belly.

"Stomach?"

"Yes. They found pollen from Alto Adige, so Bolzano got the museum. Of course, they make him Italian because of food." Her phone buzzed. "Fabrizio. He still wants sex tonight."

"Is he your only or just a regular?"

"He's good company. I barely have regulars. The life of the businesswoman."

"Beats squeezing out kids like a sow in the suburbs."

"Sow?"

"Scrofa." Also troia, which was a pun. Zarabeth shook her head. Fucking Polyglot. "It sounds like women have it tougher here, being taken seriously."

"Easier in America," Minerva said. "Here, too much expecting the woman run the house. Partly because we still have houses, still have family meals. It's better than it was."

"Is that why you only have women working for you?"

"Ha. Like Amazons? No. Marketing, communications …" Minerva waved lazily.

"It skews girly," Zarabeth agreed.

Minerva laughed. "You have so many good words. 'Skews girly.' This I think is the poetry of English, these weird sounds. Like a guitar."

"You mean twangy?"

"Exactly. Twangy and skews and fridge." She stared intently at Zarabeth, enraptured and high. "Wonderful words." She emptied the bottle into her glass. "There's more in the kitchen."

"I'll get it," Zarabeth said, taking the empty.

"Bringen Sie etwas Wasser," Minerva said. "Es ist in den Kühlschrank stellen."

"Wasser, natürlich." Zarabeth was in the kitchen before she realized. High and drunk she had missed the change to German.

Minerva watched her over the back of the sofa, eyes wide. "You have a Polyglot."

Zarabeth clenched her teeth and gripped the bottle tighter. Club her and run.

"Oh, just tell me," Minerva said. "Americans, so uptight. Your Italian was too perfect. And Optimized offering anything for free, ridiculous. What is this? An internal audit?"

"I don't even have a badge for the Rome office," Zarabeth said. "How can I audit you? I'm just here to help with the conference. After that, vacation."

"So, something at the conference. Poaching talent? Or just using us as cover."

They sat nervously still, candy pop music stupid in the air. Minerva's phone rang. "Fabrizio again. Don't go away." She went to the kitchen to talk, just out of earshot.

Zarabeth stood by the open window. City noises, squat buildings and lights, empty streets. She spread her fingers, imagined herself a vengeful goddess, leveling buildings with a wave. Explosions, glowing orange sky, howling, death.

Nothing. Not a goddess, just a rube.

Minerva came back, phone still to her ear. "Of course I miss you," she cooed in Italian. "I have a job. No, listen, good night." Minerva closed her phone. "Sorry."

"It's fine. I should go."

"Look, I have to—" Minerva smiled. "Another good word. Turf. This is my turf."

"I get it. Thanks for dinner. See you tomorrow."

Zarabeth took off her shoes and walked down the cold worn marble stairs circling the old elevator, unsteady on her sore feet. In the lobby the scarred man was gone.

She put on her shoes. Splintering chicken bones in her swollen feet. She panted through the pain. She should walk to the hotel in them, penance for her fuck-up.

Ten minutes waiting for a taxi. Penance enough.

* * *

In the morning, Zarabeth was shuffling her cards when Magda called. It was the first time they'd talked since they had met.

"I thought you learned your lesson about partying with the locals," Magda said.

"Slow learner. You're up late," Zarabeth said.

"I don't sleep much. Now don't say anything. I'm sure they bugged the room."

"Really?"

"I would," Magda said. "So. They know you have a Polyglot. Three questions. How? I know what Minerva said. I don't buy it."

A long pause. Zarabeth had to talk, without saying anything. "Your friend?"

"Underwood? Such ghastly queers. Like Plato mixed with both Francis Bacons. Spunk, meat, blood, Latin. For the best really. Imagine if men could do magic? I tell you. Anyway, they didn't talk to Underwood, that would be far too interesting. Second question, can you guess?"

"Why say it?"

"Exactly! Put you on guard and learned nothing. Not wise for a Minerva. She might have meant to warn you, but that's not our corporate culture. What's third?"

"Who," Zarabeth said.

"I don't understand?"

"You said 'they didn't talk.' Who are 'they'?"

"I did," Magda said. "Funny, that wasn't my question. Expense a foot massage. Ta-ta!"

The cards wouldn't tell her Magda's question. She wrapped them up and went to dress.

* * *

A mess, to start, with the wireless out. The conferees, all fat in ill-fitting suits, complained with curt whines, as if the staffers were their mothers. Minerva went onstage and read the schedule aloud until the audience wandered in.

The keynote speaker was a retired Interpol secretary general, an old gray man in an old gray suit but his voice a robust Flemish bass. "No one questions that we design shoes and keyboards for our bodies, to be comfortable. Imagine a highway so safe you let your children play alongside it. How do we build one?"

Zarabeth ducked out. The morning pastries had been cleared, but they had left an urn of coffee and bottles of water. She filled a mug and took a bottle to Fabiana, on server duty. The storeroom for the server was a janitor's closet, shelves of paper and bottled cleaners. Fabiana read a fashion magazine in a cloud of smoke. She took out her earbuds.

"Is it safe to smoke in here?" Zarabeth asked, offering the drinks.

"I don't care," Fabiana said, taking the water. "Why do I have to stay here? All I can do is page the technician." She drank half the bottle. "How's it going?"

"They're seated. The speaker is some old fart who wants robot friends."

"Do they still have food out there?"

"No." Zarabeth lit a cigarette.

"Shit. No signal in here so bring music. Check this out." Fabiana keyed to another program. The screen slowly filled with images: graphs, advertisements, news photos, website buttons. "It samples server traffic and randomly selects images. Each picture is on a web page opened by someone here." Corporate banners, social-network headshots, a gaudy gold and diamond bracelet, a skinny white girl in a string bikini. "Watch out!"

Zarabeth's cigarette had grown a long ash. When she moved her hand it fell. "Sorry."

"Whatever. It's a fucking closet." Fabiana flicked her own ash on the floor and put in her earbuds. "Thanks for the water."

Zarabeth walked through the rear doors out to the fish-smelling loading dock. She lit another cigarette, wondering if the firm sampled more than web images from the conferees, but nothing here seemed so glamorous as that. She had left the hash she palmed from Minerva's cake in her cigarette pack. Tempting, but it would make her hungrier.

She called Jill Carson and got voicemail. "Hi. It's ten, ten-thirty, here. Shit, you're not even at work yet. Sorry. Anyway. Just ... let me know."

Inside, Renata put her on billing errors from registration. When those were done, she caught half of a presentation on solving shipping routes using virtual ants without central control, and the implications for cognitive structure. *Our skulls, each a big ant farm,* said the speaker. She could see the audience shiver. It made perfect sense to Zarabeth. She was never just one thing.

At lunch she chatted with two young imaging programmers dressed as twins, in gray-stripe suits and plain black t-shirts, curlicue hair.

The taller looked over the crowd with disdain. "Old fogies. All theorists. There's nothing in Rome," he said, more to his colleague. "We should be in Milan."

"Training code in virtual worlds was fascinating," the shorter said to her. "It puts the Turing Test on its head."

Across the room Alessio, in a blue suit, chatted with a slender brunette. Zarabeth felt oddly jealous. She left the coders.

Minerva and Fabiana intercepted her. "Everything going well?" Minerva asked.

"People liked the virtual worlds lecture. I'm on the server at one."

"We can't smoke in there anymore," Fabiana said. "The janitor has asthma."

Zarabeth shrugged. "Anything I can do until then?"

"If you're mingling," Minerva said, "that's a big help."

"They just stare," Fabiana said. "Like I'm from Mars. What do you talk to them about?"

"I just let them talk," Zarabeth said.

Alessio had vanished. A group had formed by the coffee service around an older white man in a blue blazer, wearing a speaker's badge. "What amazed me in Japan is their devotion to interaction," he said in Brooklyn English. "They don't mind if it doesn't look human, so long as it knows how to *act* human. Even the way it nods. You should see the gestural subroutines."

"Do they write them or evolve them?" a frail man with brushed white hair asked, also with a speaker's badge, an air of picking a fight.

"Sorry, that's under my non-disclosure agreement." The crowd smiled at the dodge. "My point was how we researchers will have to think. Gestures impart meaning, or respect—so are they part of language? We get caught up in our own categories. Evolve, design, body, word. With AI it's a big blender."

Zarabeth's phone buzzed. Jill Carson. She stepped away to take the call.

"We've narrowed it down," Jill said. "Wednesday, sunrise to sunset. Just be ready to walk out the door of your hotel at quarter to six your time."

"To do what? Work clothes?"

"Casual. Like you would go shopping in."

"That's not so casual here."

"Are they dressy?" Jill asked. "I've never been."

"My toes are bleeding from high heels." Zarabeth yawned loudly.

"Late night out?" Jill asked.

"And an early morning." Zarabeth had a thought. "I'm sure it was tough on Sasha, too."

"Oh!" Jill yelped. "Oh. Yes. Of course Sasha worked here longer. I should run."

Sasha was not a welcome subject.

* * *

At the evening sponsor party in the white-on-white hotel bar, investors swam around the nerds like dolphins, sounding for money. German, Swiss, French, neat and clipped. The Polyglot recognized accents and wanted to use the language. It was tripping her up.

She found Alessio. Air-kisses. "The virtual-ant stuff seemed good for your gearbox."

"Way over my head," he said.

"So you're just here for the women? I saw that little girl you were talking to."

"She's a city planner in Sorrento."

"Did she like your sunglasses pitch? See the future in the monitors of tomorrow."

"Oh, I like that," Alessio said. "I'm stealing it. No credit but I'll buy you a drink."

"The drinks are free. Buy me lunch. Thursday's good."

"Thursday it is. Noon?"

"Have your sunglasses call my sunglasses," she said.

In her room she changed to yoga clothes and made a hash/tobacco joint. While she wrote her report, she watched an insect documentary in Canadian English with French subtitles. A black spider, her hairy abdomen mottled purple like a scrotum, dug a burrow in sandy dirt. When an ant walked by, the spider leapt out, too fast to see even in slow motion. Swarm cognition versus brutal patient predation. Code that.

Over her weak phone signal she logged into an onion network and searched for *Sasha Blackwell*. She found no one who could be Magda's Sasha. She searched *Magda Crane* and found obvious links, press materials and investor packets, dating to the seventies. In a yellowed group shot of junior staff she was the only one to look at twice. Blond helmet of hair, big white earrings, dress tight on her slim build. A hottie in the days of free love.

On the next page, a link to a New York society rag:

... *offered by Magda Crane*, née *van Brugh, who debuted at the 100th Anniversary Ball forty years ago this night*

Zarabeth felt sick like after her night with Rex. The day Missy texted. Everyone else with more money and no mother to drink it away. She wiped her sour mouth and keyed *Magda van Brugh*.

A social register traced the name to Dutch settlers of Albany County in the 1600s. Magda's birth announcement, daughter of

George and Alma, no siblings. An equestrian site listed steeplechase victories, a boarding school listed honors in debate and oratory. No wedding announcement, but John Crane's obituary, a CIA analyst hit by an unknown car. Magda had been twenty-six. She could have remarried, or lived off her family, but she went to work.

Magda was the Amazon. Minerva was something else.

*　*　*

Tuesday morning started with a prototype of a robot eel, dropped in segments in a glass aquarium. The segments found each other in less than a minute. The screen above them became a camera view, ghostly hints of the audience beyond the glass, to huge applause.

Zarabeth ducked out to raid the remains of the buffet. The meat was gone but there were fruits and pastries. She sat behind the audio/video board to eat. On stage now was the frail man from yesterday's lunch discussion, discussing Bayesian decision-making. Unlike most presenters he used an overhead projector, with a transparent sheet of printed equations. Zarabeth admired the retro spirit. He wore a white polo shirt and light gray pants. With his wispy build he looked like a bare dandelion head.

A pause grew long. The man stared ahead, frozen. In the monitor his face sagged, drool from the side of his mouth. "Cut his mike," she told the tech. "Turn it all off."

She jogged up the side aisle. Minerva and a hotel manager met her at the stage. The frail man shivered, his left hand curled. "Microphone's off," Zarabeth said.

Minerva nodded. "Excuse me," she shouted in Italian, "we have a medical issue. Please stay in your seats for a moment." She repeated herself in English while unclipping the microphone from his shirt. "Can you take him someplace?" she asked the manager.

The manager was wary. "What's wrong with him?"

"A seizure, obviously. He won't bite."

The manager tried to steer the frail man by pushing on his

shoulders, hugged him awkwardly to heft him offstage. In the break area the manager stood the frail man against the wall. "Can you watch him?" he asked Zarabeth, backing away. "I have to call the ambulance."

The man was drooling again, now onto his shirt. Let him drool.

A new voice from the conference room. They had continued the lectures. She scanned her e-mail. Invoices from her bank. Another party invite, $10 Light Beer Buckets. The start of Washington summer.

The frail man made quick nods like a start-up screen. Rebooting.

She found the Mercurex network video and held it up to him.

"Look at this," she commanded in Italian. "What is this?"

He kept nodding but his eyes focused on the phone. "Protein. Signal protein. Antigen." He stopped nodding. A bone in his neck cracked. She hid her phone.

"I was speaking ..." He smiled sheepishly at Zarabeth. "I see. When I'm nervous. How long?"

"Not long. An ambulance is coming."

He frowned. "I hope I can finish my talk," he said.

* * *

Wednesday, Zarabeth dressed to move, black pants and blouse, black and pink London trainers. Eyeliner and lipstick, just in case. The cloudy sky flickered like a tube light. She did light yoga to morning television, hosted by opiate-slow anchorwomen in shiny mermaid green, string-music segues and sea-blue sets. Wired at night and zoned by day. Land of stabbed Caesars and poisoning Borgias, of the Camorra and the 'Ndrangheta and the Mafia. Good for fun, good for crime, bad for business.

She dealt her cards: Data 5, Money 2, Product Director. Careful work brings success despite the caprices of the powerful. A strangely optimistic reading. She could lighten up. Maybe it would be an adventure.

At nine, a text message came from a blocked number: *Go sightseeing in the Foro Romano*. Like a card from a board game. Zarabeth looked it up. Ruins of the center of the Roman Empire, two kilometers south. She grabbed her blazer.

The Foro sat below street level, excavated from the buildup of centuries around it. Stones, pillars, walls, bleached and yellowed, shaky Latin carved and half-erased. Zarabeth had seen collapsed barns in New England, but nothing like this ancient devastation, a thousand-year ruin of a thousand-year civilization. Crumbs of empire, scrubbed clean by time of the last human desires, soothed her skin. She changed direction randomly, doubling back on paths, looking for someone too often in her field of view. No one. Less tradecraft than playacting.

She took off her blazer and smoked in shade near the Temple of Vesta. Skinny school kids ran giddily past her. Girls climbed up the headless female statues. When their heads assumed the curvy bodies, the boys hooted and took pictures. People from her school had gone on such trips, cheap tour packages with free tickets for teachers. Zarabeth's mom paid for loser men and a different vodka at each meal.

Zarabeth was here now. Better late than never. *Here now, you worthless cow.* She sang it in her head.

Maybe she was a decoy.

As if to answer her, a new text: *Piazza del Risorgimento*. West of the city, across the Tiber River. She left by the southeast exit, near Circo Massimo. In the crazed city driving she fixed her lipstick.

The empty, brown Piazza del Risorgimento seemed less a town square than an abandoned lot. Her skin itched furiously. Behind her sat the Vatican, its sanctity burning the Polyglot. As she paid the cab, a third text came: *Walk up Via Cola di Rienzo, north side. Window-shop, go in stores but not food market. Turn off your phone and put it away.*

Via Cola di Rienzo had sleek boutiques, jewelry and clothes and clever housewares. The sun was high and hot but her itch was gone. In a shop she saw her new sunglasses, made by Alessio's firm, bronze frames with large gold lenses. They changed the set of her chin and swept her cheeks higher. Catalyst for her new Roman self. In the shop mirror, she brushed her hair with her fingers, back and out like a cobra's hood.

She dawdled up the street, catching the eyes and flirts from young well-dressed men with slicked dark hair and sharp faces, not a case of Asperger's among them. She studied shop windows, idled at newsstands and screens of headlines. Just a bored girl, shopping, again.

In the distance she saw the forbidden food market, a huge white arcade amidst traffic and bustle. She thought about Fabrizio at Minerva's dinner, defending fresh food. Less crazy here than it had sounded. She paused by a wedding dress in a tiny storefront, white silk with concentric circles of gold thread, austere and stately, like a soldier of virginity.

Saliva ran in Zarabeth's mouth. This dress she would never wear. No suburban sow, no minivan, no kids. She was shaking now like the frail man. Men wanted her sleek strong surface. Deeper, where it was scarred and barren, they didn't want that. No one stays in a big empty room. *Here now, you worthless cow.* She turned away, hotter than the Polyglot had been.

"Signorina!" In the dressmaker's door a shrunken old woman in dreary black smiled sycophantically. "You forgot your package." She offered a white paper shopping bag.

"I'm sorry," Zarabeth stammered, "this isn't—"

The woman hooked the handles on her outstretched hand. "It will look lovely on you." She retreated into her burrow.

The bag weighed little. Inside was a white box, with a small envelope taped to the top. *Find a public phone*, it read. English words, Italian penmanship. She palmed the envelope.

She found a phone across the street, a chrome box like a robot head. The yellowed plastic privacy afro obscured the sidewalk and made her feel less safe. She clamped her calves around the bag, opened the envelope and took out a red phone card. On the inside flap of the envelope was a phone number, country code 241. *Eat me*, it read. Her fingers fought her. Fuck

Magda and her mind-games. She made a fist, beat the phone once, twice. The pain cleared her head. She dialed. When she heard the first ring she tore the flap in strips and started chewing. The paper tasted bitter. Maybe it was poisoned.

A machine answered with a rapid handshake tone, a lower pitch than a fax machine. A second series of high-pitched louder tones. Behind them faint noise, or maybe the real message. She closed her eyes, envisioned a figure eight of moving red lines, drawing and redrawing itself. Could the Polyglot graph code?

The phone spat out the card with a loud clunk that startled her. She hailed a cab back to the hotel. She turned on her phone, searched country codes. 241, Gabon. She had never heard of it and didn't care to look it up. She left the card on the cab floor. No one had said not to.

Her room, already clean. In the box, a gorgeous black halter-top woven with silver thread. It raised her breasts and slimmed her. Not virgin, not wife. Bauble. She stripped naked, curled up in the bedcovers. She wanted to gnaw on something.

* * *

Alessio chose a restaurant on Esquilino, near Termini Station. The dining room faced a small sunlit garden. Alessio wore blue gabardine, silver pin through his striped green tie. By the table, a bottle of white already open.

"I did not mean to be early. You're on time like a good American," he said, air-kissing her. "Red flatters you." They sat. "The wine's all right. I like the sunglasses."

"I bought them in your honor yesterday." It was a good seat but bright. She kept the sunglasses on. "Via Cola di Rienzo."

"You went shopping?"

"My vacation begins," she said. "I got these and a top. Also some sightseeing."

The server came to pour her wine.

"Do you like oysters?" Alessio asked.

"I thought you didn't eat them in months without an R?"

"That was before refrigeration. How are they?" he asked the

server.

"They're all right," the server said.

"Like the wine. A big plate of oysters." Alessio's eyes were smaller and harder than she recalled. Topaz eyes, set in dark circles. He smiled regretfully, put on frameless sunglasses with black lenses. Creepier than his eyes.

"Sparkling water," she added. The server left. "I've been thinking about our dinner party." She chewed dry chalky breadstick. "When we were at dinner, what Fabrizio was saying about imports."

"Fabrizio is an idiot."

"He's an Italian kind of idiot," she said. "You pay a premium to keep food close-at-hand. Your milk cartons advertise they came from local family farms. Americans wouldn't care if our milk came from mutant cows eating sewage. Local production and purity are costs you're willing to bear." She felt trapped in the deep cushioned armchair.

"That's too much credit," Alessio said. "If Fabrizio cared about our food, he wouldn't lobby for olive oil corporations selling us Moroccan leavings." He smiled with fury.

"You don't work in sunglasses, do you?"

The server put a plate of oysters between them. Alessio took a shell, a slice of lemon. "I have an interest in Straightforward," he said.

"Interest. If I ask our security about your interest? I thought so." She took a shell, poked the ugly gray flesh with the end of her breadstick. "Why let me into your little club? I'm gone this weekend. What good am I to you?"

"You're not here for other meetings," he said. "You haven't met anyone. You speak magic Italian. A man died at the company you worked with in London."

She hissed. "Empyrean. What the hell do you want?"

He grabbed her wrist. "Calm down."

"Don't touch me!" she yelled. The other tables stared. He let go. Where he had touched her felt venom-cold. She stood. "Thanks for lunch."

She ran a block, until her wobbly shoes forced her to walk. She glanced behind her. No one followed. She was at a large busy piazza. Honks, squealing tires, men checking her out. She caught her breath, worked the shivers out of her wrist.

A huge yellow turd of a basilica squatted before her, dressed in clashing columns and crests as if scavenged from royal junkyards. Celebrity fashion victim, wearing whatever and too famous to care. Zarabeth hurried across the street. Her Polyglot squirmed in her stomach. Dull ache like a brick on her eye socket. "Suck it up," she told it.

Outside the basilica, a souvenir vendor blocked her path, holding out a strip of felt with silver coins. "Remember holy city!" he cried in la-la-English. "Mementos of Blessed Virgin!"

"The Virgin was a whore and so is your daughter," she said in Gypsy. When she walked away, she felt a ghost spitting on her back. She whirled around. "Make the evil eye at me? Fuck off now before I learn the names of your children." He backed away, waving epileptically.

In the basilica she felt hot steam from her skin. The basilica was dark below and bright above, gold walls hewn and buffed by slaves, commissioned by kings as addled as movie stars. Light lapped around the gold dome like water. If God were everywhere He could be upside down, the dome His golden hot tub. She could just about see Him there, fat filthy old God bathing above His whining worshipers, splashing as He soaped His balls and laughing, just *laughing*. Hate boiled her guts like microwaves.

She withdrew to a darker alcove with racks of small votary candles. The Polyglot chattered pedantically to relieve its pain (basilica, βασιλική, letters collapsing into neon red waveforms). She idly tried to touch a flame.

It bent away from her hand.

Zarabeth poked flame after flame. Each drew away, as if a little breeze blew from her skin. One doubled over, melting the candle rim, to protect the prayer inside it.

She squealed with delight. It echoed off the walls. She waved her hands above the candles. Flames flared and jumped, ducking out of her way. "Cattivi fiamme," she cooed. "Bad bad flames. You know which side I'm on." She scratched out beats in fear and fire. Hiss-hiss-hiss. "Move, clever flames, jump and run, you're so scared but I'm having fun." Hiss-hiss-hiss.

She stepped back. Fooling around and not thinking. Soon they'd bring out priests to wave crosses at her. No discipline.

She went outside and texted Magda: *Minerva's pal is Empyrean. Fucker touched me. I ran. What now?*

* * *

In the evening Jill sent a ticket. Discount shuttle to Dublin the next morning, puddle-jumper to Aberdeen. She called Jill. "Why Aberdeen?"

"Magda's en route to an executive retreat. She's spending the night there. Since you're nearby, relatively speaking, she wants to do your one-month review on your way home."

"For fuck's sake. What's wrong with a phone call?"

"Sorry. In person."

Zarabeth ordered carpaccio and salad. When it came she wasn't hungry.

Minerva called. "I'm sorry," she said in English. "I told Alessio it was a bad idea."

"What idea? That you're part of a corporate espionage scheme or you sent a wacko from Empyrean to tell me?"

"It's not what you think. Can we talk, face to face? The hotel bar. In an hour?"

"Fine." Probably a ploy so they could search her room. Let them search. Zarabeth primped and changed clothes. Embroidered jeans, a dark t-shirt, low black heels, striped hairband. She shuffled her cards but didn't deal them. She ate the meat.

Minerva was waiting when Zarabeth came down. White top, cream skirt and silver mules, sparkling wine. "Ciao, Zarabeth. You look sleek tonight."

Zarabeth smiled sweetly. "Thanks. Love the skirt." She ordered rum and chinotto in Italian. Minerva looked pained. "You feel the Polyglot, don't you?" Zarabeth asked in English.

"That's how you knew."

"It gives me headaches. Each time is worse. In my day we learned languages."

"When was this, before mobile phones?"

"Ha. Ours was a cold war. We were us, they were them, there was even a wall. But the Polish Pope freed his people. Meek apparatchiks became media-savvy free-market reformers. There has to be a different approach. Some don't see that."

"Are you talking about Straightforward?"

"I'm talking about Italy. The Church, the government, the criminal families. You know when they invade Muslim countries and they have to deal with warlords? It's like that here. It's not like America where companies already own everything. My country is a tourist destination, a nation of craftspeople in a mass-produced world. It's all so old. Without change, the modern economy will never take root. So we work together. Little initiatives. We may be rivals but it's the same game."

"You can't trust them," Zarabeth said. "They'll fuck you."

"Talking to you is pointless. You're a soldier. What will Crane do?"

It was a good question. "I guess she'll tell you," Zarabeth said. "You're hers now."

"What is that like?"

"Fun, so far." The sugary chinotto hurt her teeth. She stirred the ice with her finger. "At the conference this guy was talking about Japan, how the Japanese want machines to act human. Japan has a culture of movement. They bow, they kneel, they sit on tiny chairs, they have dancing video games. It's their thing. But the guy does cognition and language. He's Jewish. A lot of the language guys are Jewish."

"Jews tried bodies," Minerva said. "Rabbi Loew lost control of his monstrous Golem. They do minds now."

Zarabeth didn't know but she could search it later. "That's the point. Every culture has obsessions. Its own bit of humanity." Zarabeth finished her drink, winced. "Maybe we won't make a true artificial being until every culture offers subroutines. Until

Japanese teach it to bow, Jews to debate, West Africans to dress. You know what Italians will teach it? Duplicity. Having it both ways. You do it so much that you do it by reflex. Ambivalence is the rut you're stuck in."

She kissed Minerva on the cheek. Minerva's face hot like a new fever. "Ciao bella. Tell your little harem I said goodbye."

CHAPTER EIGHT

San Francisco

Gita Tiwari invited Gabriel to a Scotch tasting with buffet, on Thursday. Tasting wasn't drinking and he was eager for a date.

They met at a floridly nautical Fisherman's Wharf hotel, brass and wood railings, staff in puffed-sleeve shirts. Gita was a small woman with big hazel eyes and a cleft chin, her skin shiny brown like a beer bottle. She wore a short blue cocktail dress and gold heels. Her skin caramel and pepper, her cologne dark and bitter like almond liqueur. Cranberry and lime from her cocktail. Like a box of pricey chocolates. He inhaled deeply when he kissed her cheek. Maybe smells could be arranged, like clothing or furniture. Maybe some people had a knack for it.

It was a hard compliment to make. "You look fantastic," he said instead.

The buffet dinner was served outside the hotel ballroom, with a bar of soft drinks and beer but no tables. Oily spring rolls, dry shrimp, chicken in beige sauce. The crowd set desperately on new trays of vegetarian maki, their chopsticks like seagulls.

Gita complained about work. "New data service," she said. "Ohmigod. You can't get a signal in half the buildings. I screwed up three orders last week. I have to use my own phone."

"Maybe you can deduct your data bill as a business expense."

"That's smart. Sorry to talk work." She laughed nervously. "Trish said you do security?"

"White-collar background investigations. I ensure the people in corner offices don't have dark secrets. Mostly I just check bank statements. Some travel. And, handgun training."

Her eyes grew big as tangerines; a flare in her scent, salt with her pepper. He kept it light, explaining the video targets, the full-weight fake guns. She didn't offer the usual San Franciscan pacifist piety.

Staff opened the ballroom doors and called guests to table. Inside, large round tables were set with small plastic cups of Scotch at each chair. Gita slipped her arm around Gabriel's and led him to the table nearest the projector screen. "Do you mind? When I'm not vain, I wear glasses."

A man with port-wine hair and a light Scottish brogue cajoled people to sit. Gabriel studied the small pours. Maybe three shots total across eight glasses, and Gabriel didn't have to finish. The smells alone gave him a buzz, burned sugars and nuts like a trail mix. A group took the other seats at the table, introduced themselves around. Gabriel grinned too much.

The Scot picked up a microphone. "My name's Gerry, and I have the best job in the world." He clicked his remote. An image of a green river valley, stone and wood buildings, the tallest with a peaked roof like a pagoda. "This is the Spey, the only water in all our whisky."

Over a slideshow of landscapes and bulleted lists, Gerry explained single-malt and blended whiskies, had them smell and taste pairs of pours. The people at Gabriel's table clowned, those with large noses glorying in presumed skill. Gabriel loved the complex fragrances, how quickly they faded, like catching snowflakes.

Whisky had its own words for smells. What Gerry called malty reminded Gabriel of Denise's pumpernickel, a smoky sweetness like roasted marshmallow. The other looked the same but smelled like rotting fruit, leaving an oily taste in his mouth. "That has to be the fourteen-year," he told Gita, pleased with himself.

Gita stared vacantly at the table, her shoulders slumped. "Migraine," she told him. She took out a tin of blue pills, swallowed two dry, clutched his arm for rescue. "I need to go now."

Upstairs, Gabriel asked the bellman for a taxi. While he massaged her hands she dug her forehead hard into his shoulder. He could feel her clench and relax her teeth. Heat and pressure, the most intimate he had been in years.

The bellman waved them over. "You OK?" Gabriel asked.

"Shouldn't drink without food." Gita kissed his cheek. "You go back. I'll be fine," she said. "Let's try again, OK?"

In the ballroom the tasting was over. People sat with small wedges of cake and coffee. At his table sat a man and two women. "Your friend all right?" one woman asked.

He nodded. He felt cheated. He took Gita's fourteen-year and drank it down.

Flesh and meat tastes in the alcohol burn. He looked at the women, neither one as fine as Gita, and for an exultant moment knew the breadth of his urges. He would gladly spill blood to fuck them. It would make the fucking better. A wolfish moment, beauty become tool, like a jeweled candlestick used as a club. Gone, like the whisky. He regretted it and wanted it back.

One woman frowned at his staring. Gabriel looked away and took deep breaths.

* * *

On Tuesday, Thorn's office reeked of peppermint. In the candy bowl, blue wrappers with white Korean characters. Thorn was casual, a blue blazer over a golf shirt, and in good spirits.

"We have a project," he told Gabriel. "One of Mr. Koenig's visions. But we'll be working with another firm, a defense contractor. The target is being recruited to work for them. We make the offer. If he accepts they take over."

"Does the defense contractor know about our abilities?"

"Ha. They'd dissect us if they did. Read the file."

The file had police reports on a man named Efraín, his last name one of many things redacted with thick black marker. What

Gabriel could read was damning enough: assault, mutilation, extortion, murder. No defense contractor would hire this man.

An anonymous report in odd bureaucratic language detailed Efraín's tactical thinking. Gangs employed desperate people as drug couriers and decoys, fatally risky for the couriers but each one insignificant to the gang. Efraín had a knack for it, with more decoys killed by rivals than couriers. Dates in the tactical analysis matched arrests without evidence.

Gabriel went back to Thorn. "Soldiers aren't dope couriers. What is this?"

"When mass-production can be brought to bear," Thorn said, "drone planes and self-driving cars will be commonplace."

It took Gabriel a minute. "Because this guy treats people like expendable drones, he's going to program expendable drones? Can I talk to Mr. Koenig now please?"

"Mr. Koenig is probably busy," Thorn said. "Let's go for a walk."

"It's raining."

"We won't melt."

They said nothing through Security's corridors, in the elevator down. Gabriel brought his umbrella but the rain had turned into cold. They walked north along busy sidewalks, close together in the diaphanous crowd. They stopped in a grim concrete plaza with a drained fountain.

"To begin, I'm sorry," Thorn said. "I was not prepared for you. Luther Koenig is active and alert, but he's seventy-six. I never expected to train a successor."

"Thank you for saying," Gabriel said. "But it's not the issue. You said we would give people a second chance, not put thugs into military strategy."

"This one is special," Thorn said. "The important thing is to change people's futures, not judge their pasts. Do you think Nate's family feels justice was served in his case?"

Gabriel snorted. "I suppose not. Tell me how it works."

"Tomorrow—"

"No. The woo-woo part. Koenig's visions."

88

Thorn shook his head. "Koenig dreams he sits in a wooden chair in a long hallway. 'Like a schoolboy waiting to be disciplined,' he told me once. Someone—he never sees a face—drops a note in his lap. A name, a place, date and time."

"GPS coordinates?" Gabriel asked.

"No. But we get floor and room numbers. Koenig wakes and writes it down. It is always accurate. The named person is always there, then. We usually get a couple weeks' notice, enough time to figure out who they are, though in some cases, such as yours, we're not sure what it's about. This one tomorrow came months in advance. But we know where he will be at 6:45 AM tomorrow. It is certain."

"He'll probably be in bed."

"It's happened. Also, wherever it is, we can always get to. I once walked into the home of a counterfeiter. Big house, bolts and alarms. All doors were open for me."

"Why don't they call the police? Or shoot you?"

"They are—prepared, I guess you could say. In a way it's stranger than Koenig's visions. They have dreams too, just before we visit them. People sometimes mention them. They vary. Whatever that person needs to hear."

Even after weeks waiting for it, Gabriel had a hard time with it. "You said 'we.' Have you done this with others?"

"I was trained by Koenig's first assistant." He smiled regretfully. "Since he retired, I've been alone, save for Del. Koenig's had the dreams since he came to San Francisco in the late sixties. I'm well into my second decade. It is not easy work. Tomorrow we visit a drug dealer. A killer. We offer him a new life that will never thrill him like his current life. It will be dangerous and probably futile. But sometimes it's not. We only get one shot. Are you in or out?"

"I'm in," Gabriel said.

"All right," Thorn said. "Pick you up at six tomorrow. Go back. I have things to do."

Gabriel walked west. The fog made the street and the high-rise buildings look insubstantial, a stage set or a mirage. He slipped on the slick sidewalk and fell hard on his hip.

On the sidewalk was a round white sticker. *LOVED BY GOD*, in block lavender letters. Around the edge was a church name, an address in the Castro.

He bent down and peeled it off. *LOVED BY GOD* was good for an omen.

* * *

On Security's virtual range, the virtual shots popped like bubble wrap. Gabriel's arms burned from the authentic weight of the fake gun.

A camouflaged man with a machine gun appeared to his left. Gabriel's first shot hit the top of the heart. His second went wild, hitting the left shoulder. "Sorry."

"At least the first shot killed him," Del said. The target became translucent, his shot pulsing green in the cartoon aorta. "Spread your feet. Helps your recovery before the second shot."

"Give me a minute." Gabriel put the gun on the shelf. "You know why I'm here?"

Del grinned. "The woo-woo? Basically. Yeah."

"Nothing I've been doing involves the woo-woo."

"It will. Meantime, we gotta do something with you."

"How did you start working here?"

"Short version—I got banged up. As rehab I learned to type. Old school, manual typewriter. These hand problems people get now?" Del said. "Mushy computers. Nobody ever got carpal tunnel from a typewriter. When they discharged me I needed a job and I'm a little old to bodyguard. I started working for Ella Connors in Finance. We were a good team. She was tiny, and a paper pusher. When people saw me as her admin—"

"It changed the dynamic?"

"You and your phrases. Plus, it wasn't hard for me to get clearances. That's how I learned about programs like this one."

"There are others? I don't even know what this job is."

"Some jobs are like that. Gabriel, you may like being a numbers guy but you're tapped into something. You just gotta tame it." Del made a grim face. "Sometimes Bill plays things too close to the chest, you ask me."

"You think he won't tell me things I need to know?"

"You make up your own mind. Break's over."

* * *

At six the next morning, a white limousine stopped in front of Gabriel's house. The door opened. Smell of coffee and fake hazelnut, hot and sweet in the wet asphalt air. Inside, Thorn sat in a plain black suit. Across from him sat a young woman with gold-brown skin, in a navy suit, her brown hair in tight braids. Deep hollows in her cheeks.

"Yo, pimp daddy," Gabriel said. "We're going in this?"

"Just get in," Thorn said.

Gabriel sat next to him. The woman closed the door. The window tinting made the interior dark. The limousine drove off.

"There's another coffee if you like," Thorn said. "We're going to the Mission. It won't take long. Traffic's still light."

Gabriel offered the woman his hand. "I'm Gabriel Archer."

The woman studied his hand as if to look for weapons. She had an unappealing woodsy odor, moss and moist mushrooms.

"This is Keisha," Thorn said. "She's here to protect the car." Thorn passed Gabriel a black cloth drawstring bag. "Empty your pockets."

"The car should be fine," Gabriel said to Thorn. "What about us?"

"We'll be fine, or we won't." Thorn held up a large blue foil envelope, sealed on each end. "There may be a time I hand him this. It's a test. If he takes it, time him. Count seconds. One-steamboat, two-steamboat, you know. We make the offer. We don't enforce outcomes. We're not dragging him out."

"If he says yes?"

"Keisha takes him. We catch a cab home."

"If he says no?"

"Keisha takes us home."

"Assuming he doesn't shoot us."

Keisha gave Gabriel another hard look.

"Assuming that," Thorn said.

After that no one spoke. Gabriel sipped coffee, until he worried he would have to pee.

In the silent dim gray, the facing benches seemed less car than train. He remembered long rides in Russia, bundled up in the cold cheap seats. The memory grew immediate, the start of a dream he shook off. The limousine had stopped.

Gabriel followed Thorn out to face a bluer brighter sky above a boarded-up building that stank of urine and rat. The rest of the street looked like anyplace: market, laundry, nail salon, carry-out Chinese, bank. As they walked Gabriel orientated himself. Van Ness behind them. The bar where he'd met Gita was only a few blocks away. Gita would find all this exciting.

Thorn led him to the nail salon. "It's downstairs. All I know is we'll get in."

At the bottom of the stairs was a gray metal door, with a webcam stuck to the doorframe with duct tape. Thorn tried the doorknob. It was unlocked.

Inside, boxes and bright light and dust. Gabriel sneezed four times.

Ahead stood two men, one photographing the other. The model stood shirtless, muscular, his head and face shaven, in the hard white light of photographer's lamps clipped to ceiling joists, a silver screen behind him. Black tattoos on his chest, his arms, his forehead, crude work by San Francisco standards. In one hand he held the skull of a longhorn bull, in the other a 9mm pistol, pointed at Gabriel.

"You should try allergy pills, vato," the photographer said in a nasal voice. He wore a tank top shirt and jeans. He turned his back to them, showing a smaller gun tucked in the waistband. "Make yourselves at home. Wit' you in a minute."

Gabriel and Thorn sat on the floor. The shirtless man kept his gun on them. Behind him, a screen rotated webcam images: the door, the alley, two views of the limousine.

"You know," the photographer said, "with the gun, muy cool." He took a few rapid pictures, stepped back and squatted low to take more. He reviewed the camera's display screen, frowned. "Maybe." He turned to Thorn. "Like your ride, güero. Good for parties."

"Thank you," Thorn said. "Are you Efraín?"

Efraín whistled. "Está bien, Buenaventura. Baja el arma."

The model frowned at Efraín.

"OK. Baja la calavera."

The model put the skull on the floor. "Maldita policía," he said.

"My friend thinks you're cops," Efraín said, putting down his camera.

"Somos consultores," Gabriel said. "No tenemos armas."

"Consul—" Efraín laughed, a short ugly bark. "These guys are bagmen, B.V. I don't see no bag though." He moved fast, putting his gun inches from Gabriel's face. "You shouldn't know about this place. Who told you?"

Gabriel smelled powder from the barrel, smelled oil and lead and steel. He was jealous. All his guns were toys.

"This is our bag," Thorn said, holding up the envelope. "We're offering you a job."

Efraín stepped back. Gabriel looked away from the gun in quick glances. Unkempt black hair, sallow skin with red pimples on his face and upper arms. Wide narrow eyes. Tattoos poked past the edges of his shirt.

"Bagmen speaking college Spanish." Efraín spat on the floor. He tucked the gun away. "Always nice to find work. Buenaventura." Efraín passed the envelope to Buenaventura.

Buenaventura tore it open with his teeth. "Papeles," he said. To Gabriel they stank of vinegar.

"It's a test," Thorn said. "The center is the goal, held by your enemy. The black lines are buildings, same on every page. Blue squares are enemy soldiers. The colored dots are ways of setting up your people. Each page is different. Some use five men, some seven. Which is best?"

Efraín sat on a stool and studied it, wary at first but increasingly absorbed. At eighty-five seconds by Gabriel's count Efraín put down his camera. At one hundred forty seconds, he nodded his head, eyes vacant. At one hundred ninety he beamed. "Anaranjado. Orange. Seven men."

Thorn nodded. "Orange is the best. Gabriel, how long?"

"Three minutes twelve seconds."

Efraín rubbed the paper between his fingers, wrinkled his nose. He too noticed the smell. He let the papers fall to the floor. "That was fun. You got any more?"

"That's urban combat strategy," Thorn said. "Average time about twelve minutes. Less than half get it right. We have jobs that use your talents. Worth a lot of money and also not criminal. You'll have a new life."

Efraín put his fingertips to his eyes. "My sister Marisela came in a dream. All grown up, muy hermosa. Marisela got sick when she was nine and died. But this woman was Marisela. She read from a Bible. 'Llegaron, pues, los dos ángeles á Sodoma á la caída de la tarde.' So you angels, huh?" He held the gun at arm's length, pointed at Thorn. "You fuck with my mind? How the fuck you make me dream my sister?" Efraín was dripping sweat now. Gabriel smelled anger, fear, some smoked stimulant.

"Is that a digital camera?" Gabriel asked.

Efraín looked as if he would spit on Gabriel. "What?"

"The camera. It's nice. My brother took pictures. I have this one, big pink rhododendron with a bee in it. He used film though. He didn't like digital."

"He didn't develop on the move," Efraín said. "Digital's the best ever." He patted the camera. "Flowers, it's hard not to make them look boring. Why'd he stop? You said 'used.'"

"He died," Gabriel said. "Drunk driver hit him."

"Lo siento. So how you make me dream?"

"We don't know about that," Thorn said. "You want a job?"

"I'm listening."

"New identity. The works. Citizenship, relocation somewhere upper-middle-class. Intensive training: engineering, avionics, programming. Tattoos removed."

"You got dental? My teeth hurt a lot. Ha. You cabrones think I buy this bullshit?"

"I don't care," Thorn said. "We make the offer. At eight, our ride leaves. It never comes back. Either you are in it, or you're not."

"If I don't let you leave?"

"The limo drives away," Thorn said, "calling the cops as they go. They'll give the cops everything they have. No deportation this time. Just a needle."

"Maybe I tell the cops about your little test." He picked up the papers. They dissolved into threads and vinegar smell. "What the fuck?"

"Spy paper," Thorn said. "Light triggers an acid. Tell the cops it was a military intelligence exam. Say we drove a white limo and sent you dreams too."

"Fuck you. You think I just go? Get in the car and disappear? Like witness protection?"

"Efraín," Buenaventura said. "You do this. This is America. Only happens once. All we do, we just survive. You do this. Go away with them."

Efraín looked ashamed. He shook his head. Not anger but fear. It was over.

Thorn and Gabriel stood. "We'll leave now," Thorn said.

"I'll go," Buenaventura said. "Take me. I'm a good soldier."

"I'm sorry," Thorn said. "My client can't use you."

"I can't go?"

"You can't go with us. Goodbye."

In the sunlight Gabriel sneezed. When they approached, Keisha stepped out, gun in hand.

"He didn't take the job?" she asked tartly.

Thorn shrugged. The limousine drove off. Keisha passed back their bags.

Thorn nodded to Gabriel. "Thanks for distracting him."

"Glad I could help," Gabriel said. "That test wasn't real, was it?"

"I made it last night on my computer," Thorn said.

"It's all nonsense," Keisha said.

Gabriel sneezed.

* * *

That afternoon Gabriel rode to unwind. He ended up in SoMa, near his old office. He rode around the familiar streets, dodging cars and running lights like a messenger. On the long uphill return, he gasped for breath through gritted teeth. On Filbert he crested the hill and fell sideways, barely catching himself. He walked the bike the rest of the way.

Denise wasn't home. On the staircase landing sat a tall shelf of plants, watered recently. Gabriel smelled wet dirt and moist twigs. Smell of autumn. Smells had associations but often he didn't know how they had been formed. Dirt autumn evening water leaves. Maybe it was instinct.

In the bathroom mirror he saw the gun, in his face while most people ate breakfast. It was said near-death made one appreciate life, but Gabriel had nothing to appreciate, just the butt of whatever joke remade his nose. He wanted to own himself.

He called Thorn. "I want a vacation. I want to taste whisky in Scotland."

"You don't drink."

"I think it will help my nose."

"Sure. Fine. Not next week. I'll be away. After that. Set it up with Del."

"I'd want to go for a week. I don't quite have the leave."

"We can square that. Are you OK? Do you want to talk?"

"I'm good," Gabriel said. "See you tomorrow."

Affordable flights were hard to find, with multiple stops and long layovers. Even the shortest would mean more than a day in transit each way. He played with departure dates, tried other airports. Oakland to Los Angeles, non-stop to Glasgow, late morning. Fourteen hours. Coach was sold out. Eight thousand for business class.

His sister had miles. Michelle Archer, eleven years Gabriel's senior, traveled thirty weeks a year as an auditor for an engineering firm. The two had never been close and, since their brother's death, they hardly spoke. Gabriel called her.

"You want my miles?" she asked.

"You said they expired faster than you could use them."

"When did I say that?"

"Thanksgiving. Two years ago."

"I don't remember. Why are you going to Scotland?"

"I want to taste Scotch. They have distillery tours."

"Scotch? Since when are you drinking? Have you talked to Mom about this?"

"Michelle, I never ask you for *anything*. Now I ask you for miles you can't even use and you want me to talk to Mom?" His tantrum embarrassed him. "Sorry. I'll hang up now."

"Wait," she said. "Gabriel, I'm sorry. Absolutely. Have my miles. Just e-mail me the flight info. It's good to talk to you. You sure everything else is OK?"

"I changed jobs again," he said. "Still with Empyrean. Rocky at first, but it's all right."

CHAPTER NINE

Washington, DC

pretty black concierge with straightened hair in plastered waves escorted Walt to his suite. Big, boxy furniture in little rooms, paired televisions and a conference table.

"Anything less election-night?" he asked.

"Lovely view," she said, opening curtains. "There's the river." In the window glare she had a pert silhouette, shapely legs coming to a split point. Like a fountain-pen nib, to sign away his future for present satisfaction.

"Fine. Where do women as lovely as you go for happy hour?"

She forced a smile. "People go to the waterfront. Out the lobby, right and right. Walk until you reach the water."

He washed and changed clothes. Outside the sun seemed magnified by the thick humid air, but the walk was all downhill. On the short busy boardwalk, runners in shiny tight colors navigated through groups of ambling tourists and tie-loosened office workers out early. Gleaming white cabin cruisers tied to the pier hosted small parties. Downriver, past the boathouse, sat the white and gold Kennedy Center, framed by trees and water like a Japanese temple.

He took shade under the canvas roof of an outdoor bar. The bartender, setting up the bar, didn't notice him. As she loaded beer into coolers, her taut muscles flickered under her freckled skin. She looked like a sports car raced on dirt roads.

But he was thirsty. "Is this bar open yet?" he asked.

"Didn't even see you," she said. She had tall cheeks and a square jaw, bright blue eyes, short dark hair. "Mind's a million places today. What'll you have?"

"Bourbon on ice and a bottle of water. More ice for my forehead."

"Ha. What bourbon?" She held up the well bottle.

"Not the well. You sound like you know bourbon."

"This Kentucky daughter thanks you," she said. "Though I drink wine myself. If it's not that, it's this." She held up a better brand. "In a plastic cup. Unless you go inside."

"'This' is fine. In Kentucky they don't use plastic?"

"Mother tried crystal but Daddy insists on jars." She poured. "Where you from? Oregon?"

"You'll have to explain that."

"You said 'well,' not 'rail,' so Western. The shirt's too stylish for Mountain time. Pacific Northwest, Q.E.D." She drank water.

"Lake Tahoe, at your service." A boat awkwardly parallel parked across from them, engine revving loud wet bursts. "Do they reserve spots?" he asked.

"First come, first serve. Later arrivals tie up to the early ones, four or five deep."

"How do the outer ones come ashore for drinks?"

"I'd be pleased if they stayed aboard. Sometimes they run tabs," she stage whispered.

He watched Kentucky heft a cooler, biceps tight and corded. He could watch her all day. He looked over the water instead. A sudden deep breath took him. He had felt driven since the plane had touched ground, as if a secret reason for his coming here awaited him. No such thing, and a relief. Let the breath out, he was just nervous. He'd been out of circulation.

Kentucky returned, to chop limes. "You're not fussing with your phone," she said. "Washingtonians love to be connected. If you fuss with your phone, people might not notice the missing belt. Another round?"

"Next bourbon with water in it."

"Ice too? In Kentucky it's not assumed. Here on business?"

"Yes, ice. Yes, business. Also hoping to enjoy the change of scene."

"Let's hope," she said. The busboy called her away.

The bar filled quickly. His fellow patrons were a decade younger, willowy women in dark skirts, stripling men in striped Oxford shirts. Eager and in-place. It had been a while since he'd been in such a large crowd. Louder music, louder voices, hands reaching past him for drinks. Boat people came through, lumpy older men in faded sports shirts, ogling the young women. Low sun glinting yellow on the river. Pooling sweat at the small of his back.

Kentucky came to lift his mood. "Another?"

"Just a water if you don't mind."

She passed him a bottle with her right hand while she took orders. "What will you see on your change of scene?"

"Scientists in Bethesda. Alzheimer's research. There's also—"

Kentucky stood her full height to face down a wiry man in a manager's long pants. They argued in gestures. "Sorry," she said when he left. "It'll get busier."

"Good for tips."

"One hopes." She didn't leave. "So there's also?"

"Day care for children. In Highlands?"

"Washington Highlands?" She raised an eyebrow.

"Yes. Sent a proposal about child development. Caught my eye. A Hail Mary. Maybe."

"It's a tough part of town. They could use some good works. I have to—"

He handed her his card. "Close me out."

She took a long time to come back with his check. The crowd pressed steadily against him. She leaned close, raised her voice. "Enjoy your visit, Mr.—*Viz-nu-ski?*"

"*Wiz-neff-ski.* Walt. Kentucky, I'm only here two nights. Have dinner with me?"

"I work until ten," she said.

"That's fine."

"Falafel. By the gas station. Ask your hotel. Ten-thirty. Don't be late, I hate late."

"Ten-thirty, falafel, gas station. What's your name?"

"Missy." She winked. "See ya."

* * *

The stinking server's toilet was small as a coffin, its washbasin improvised from a plastic bucket, but it had a mirror. Missy decided to look as nice as one could in sweatpants and a vinyl shirt. She drew careful lines with her eyeliner. A little big, but better owl than pig.

On her way out Naveen the manager caught her. "Darren said a guy was bothering you tonight?" Darren had no doubt complained about her slacking, but Naveen wouldn't see that.

"Oh, sugar, not even." She rested a strong hand on Naveen's shoulder, personal but not coy. "Some hippie from Vermont, looking to score weed. I sent him on his way."

"You can call security. Or me." Naveen frowned, as if surprised by his own vehemence.

After her first hopeless interview, Missy had kept a lock of Naveen's thick black hair. The glamour got her the job but gave Naveen a weird crush, like a lovesick older brother. For now she acted stupid and hoped the spell would fade.

Missy gave a dopey smile. "Naveen, it's fine. I gotta go. I'm meeting some friends."

"You look nice," he said.

She jogged past House of Sweden's amber glass tiles, glad for loose clothes and sports shoes. Work was a workout, like tennis in heat, but the city re-energized her. Noise and motion, chatty tables at restaurants, pop music from convertibles. Dumpster air and exhaust in the warm breeze. She crossed the canal, a frolic inside her, a mad urge to run up the towpath, shucking her clothes, growing fur and long teeth.

She took a breath, held her hand before her, long fingers twitching. In coven lore only Moira McCauley O'Connell claimed lycanthropy, tales of running past tents of Union troops, in the same fields where now sat car factories. Until this sharp moment Missy never felt great interest. Nothing this feral—

She took a deep breath, let her heart settle, shook her arms out. This, after she'd thrown herself at Mr. Walt Wisniewski. A question in itself. He was hardly the first to ask, not the first passing through. Not the first truly single, not the handsomest. He was grand, though, his height and size, his stern face, his aquiline nose. A truth to offer Mother when next she pried. Still a question, but the answer might spoil the fun, and mostly she wanted fun.

At the Lebanese place Walt waited outside reading his phone, in a crisp black shirt with green and brown circles. He stood when he saw her, kissed her cheek, clasped her hand in both of his. He pointed across M Street at the clock tower. "Is that a nice place? I hate my hotel."

"It's quite fancy," she said. "I thought you were only here two nights?"

"I hate my hotel."

"If you complain maybe they'll give you a suite." Missy laughed. "You already have a suite, don't you? Perhaps I should have picked a better restaurant."

"Being with you is the best part of my day. And there's no Lebanese in Lake Tahoe."

Inside the three tables were full but the counter only had one customer. Sounds of frying, loud Spanish from the soccer game on the screen. She exchanged French pleasantries with the owner's nephew while he got sodas from the case.

Walt paid and led her back outside. "So you're a regular."

"Alumna, really. Time was I lived here on Saturday nights." She tilted her phone to check his reflection in the dark mirror of the sleeping screen. Nothing evil that eyes couldn't see. "After the clubs closed, diplomat kids came here. Sat in sleek clothes, smoking and chatting, a taste of home. After Kentucky it felt so cosmopolitan."

"You're slumming, aren't you?" Walt asked. "You tend bar for kicks."

She blew her annoyance out from rounded lips. "You put that together quick."

"I know from slumming," he said. "To slumming. Cheers." They clinked cans. "Why?"

"My grandmother just died," Missy said.

"My condolences."

"Thank you. I was her main caretaker. I stopped working. Now I'm studying. I needed something social to balance it, and a little exercise too. Beats paying for the gym. It's been an education. I used to work on the Hill, before Gramma. These customers I serve now, I used to be one. I've seen old co-workers not recognize me. Shit tips too."

"That sounds like penance."

"I don't even apologize, sugar. It's been an education, though. There's a few actors or wonks awaiting security clearances, but mostly the people who keep server jobs here can't afford to be unpaid interns. I've learned to bite my tongue, not to keep my job, but not to risk anyone else's. Maybe it will be useful going forward."

"You're rich," Walt said. "You're richer than I am. Hmm. A puzzle. I like puzzles."

The food came, falafel for her, two shawarmas for him. Walt took a bite and slapped the table. "Locals know the best places. What was your old job?"

"Legislative affairs for a consulting firm. I studied political science. My father's trade. Not that I could ever run for office. I'm better with deals in smoky rooms."

"That's sexy. Was he state or national?"

"One term here, a decade in Frankfort. He helped bring auto factories to Kentucky."

"And now, you're studying?"

"Cultural anthropology," Missy said. "Celtic and Pagan religious traditions." Her stock answer but tonight it sounded embarrassingly weak. Ridiculous. To tell her truth to a man she'd known for an hour was crazy, a wetness, not lube but nervous pee.

He had no idea. "If you already have money—"

"You're a stinker. Enough about me. You don't seem like a businessman."

"English major," Walt said, "I have a third of a bad novel somewhere. I had a knack for computers, and friends I trusted. Easier to make a company."

"Do you regret it?"

"No one has ever asked me that." He looked away. She waited him out, glad to have hit a nerve. He spread out his foil sandwich wrappers and folded them into neat compulsive squares. "In business I saw more and did more and earned more than any graduate student. But, it wasn't—once I made my money I got out. I graduated. You understand?"

"I do. There's a park nearby. Shall we stroll?"

He offered his arm with an easy smile, but his skin was hot. They walked uphill. After a block the streets grew dim and quiet. "Is it all residential up the hill?" he asked.

"Mostly. Here—" she pointed up "—one of our infamous gingko trees. Their berries stink like vomit in the autumn."

"People put up with that?"

"Georgetowners are impressed with their own stoicism, especially those with chauffeurs."

"You live here, don't you?"

"Six blocks away. Not the biggest mansion." They walked across the street to the long narrow park. "Below us is Rock Creek Parkway, which follows Rock Creek through the city."

"Nice to have green in the middle of the city. Are we going to the creek?"

"We are going to that picnic table to our left," Missy said, "being careful as we walk not to step in dog poo. May I ask you, what are your spiritual beliefs?"

Walt looked glum. "And it was going so well."

"Really? Do you worship serpents?"

He looked down. "Is there a lot of dog poo?"

"Some things are harder to avoid," Missy said. "But we can sit at that picnic table."

"Fine." Walt sat on the tabletop, his feet on the bench. Missy stood in front of him. "Since you ask. I'm a grim agnostic, or maybe that's a gnostic. I don't believe in the God of my fathers. There may be intelligences greater than ours. I think they act in their sphere, for their own reasons. If any greater being were to notice us, to guide us or punish us, I suspect it's not with our best interest at heart. I no more trust it than the rat should trust the researcher. When I die, I die. Not here, not anywhere. With luck, remembered by the living."

His eyes bright in the dimness like he expected a slap.

"I can work with that," Missy said.

"Oh. Good."

She took his hand and sat next to him. Lone cars passed on the parkway below.

"I love that sound," Walt said. "Cars on old roads. You know those albums of nature sounds for relaxation, rainstorms and waves and jungle birds? I want this. Cars on night roads. No honking, no rumbling, just—" He let the next passing car end the sentence.

"It is relaxing. I never noticed," Missy said. "Are you going to ask what I believe?"

"You'll tell me soon enough."

They sat a while, calm and quiet. She liked it past all telling.

* * *

The paved park trail led Walt and Missy northeast to a playground and tennis courts. They walked hand in hand. Missy talked about farmer's markets. "Wednesdays here, Sundays in Dupont. Fine meats, cheeses, fancy mushrooms. Great produce. I used to do brunches but the last thing I want is to serve people these days."

They took a stone bridge with old-fashioned metal lampposts, over the parkway and the creek. Missy leaned over the high stone railing. The creek ran fast below, glinting in the streetlights. "The park widens as you go north. Two miles up there's stables. Before Gramma, I owned a share of a horse. I'd ride trails three times a week. Now I walk, a couple hours every day. For my people, nature is the start and the end."

"Your people?" Had it come up? "Devereaux. Cajun?"

"You were doing so well. What does your girlfriend think about philanthropy?"

"My ex-girlfriend," Walt said, "considered it cheap marketing."

"Is that why she's your ex-girlfriend?"

"I liked her fine. She figured out I wasn't going to put a ring on her finger."

"Did you think you were going to?"

"She was good company."

"So no. I want coffee. Nice place up here."

They got iced coffees to go, and walked uphill past busy bars and restaurants. More people in a block than Walt saw in a day in Tahoe.

"I love this too," Missy said, as if she heard his thoughts. "Gramma and I were city mice. Last week I'm walking home and a block from my house two guys were having oral sex in a minivan. I love it. Do you like city or country?"

"I haven't made a lot of time for city life lately. Around Lake Tahoe it's all towns. But I know how to enjoy cities."

"Oh, that sounded so worldly." At the top of the hill a large traffic circle enclosed a park ringed with benches and trees. "Let's sit in the circle."

Sad-looking people on the benches, talking excitedly and laughing hoarsely. "Is it safe?" Walt asked.

"A little sketchy. But you're a big man." She led him at arm's length, wrist cocked up, like a dance. They sat at the gnarled base of a bushy tree, knees to knees. "Do you know why pumpkins are part of Halloween?" she asked.

"Because they're in season?"

"But, isn't that orange a little spooky? Like a tarantula, a dying fire. Where's your phone?" He handed it over. She walked through the settings and gave it back. She had turned the display color-negative, black for white, green for red, the sky-blue browser button now pumpkin orange. "The pumpkin inverts the sky. A primal understanding, a backstage pass beneath consciousness. I study the deep structure of our species. How to use it, how to hack it. The seat of dreams and the power of wishes. If you had a wish, what would it be?"

"Other than getting my phone restored?"

"Ha." She took it to reset. "What else?"

"The game is, if I could wish for something? Any wish?"

"I'd like to grant you a wish."

Streets and cars and fountain, hooting people sharing booze. The trees eerie in the stark white streetlights. Hands brushed the hairs he had shaved off his neck. "Are you a genie?"

"If I was?" She wasn't smiling. "Nothing about me specifically. No killing ancestral enemies. No world peace, and nothing you can just buy. Other than that—try me."

"What's it cost?"

"This time it's free. Special introductory offer. If I can do it."

"Does something bad happen for my wish to come true?"

"Depends on the wish."

It was a quirky game but clever. A long time since a woman had made him nervous. "I said I know from slumming," Walt said. "That letter to my foundation? It was a mirror. I used to make things. I'm out of practice. I'd love to skip the montage. I wish to feel my peak again. Not just caffeinated, but energized. Clear-headed and quick. Body and mind."

"That's a good wish. I will grant it. As thanks for the evening." She sprang to her feet. "Let's share a cab to your hotel."

"Am I inviting you up?"

"If you were to, I would decline. But thank you."

They rode an old rust-brown taxi down wide avenues of low buildings. She held his hand but looked out the window, smiling coyly.

"Give me your phone again," she said when they neared his hotel. She dialed a number. A buzz from her pocket. She hung up. "For your contacts. Devereaux ends in X."

"Sure I can't tempt you to come in?"

She shook her head. "Temptation's *my* job."

She pulled herself on his lap. They kissed in turns as if sharing air. She broke away with a gasp, a proud smile. Her eyes glinted green.

On the sidewalk, he felt as if he had leapt from a carnival ride. As if he were still falling.

* * *

The spell for Walt had been hard, the powers fighting her altruism like a skittish horse avoiding deep mud. Her tinny rhymes, her cracking voice, her pinprick doubts—but none of the foulness of a spell gone wrong, the hot wet feel of carrion failure. She sat lotus on her purple ottoman, meditating on giving, on sharing, joyous yang to the spell's dogged yin. Stillness, sounds of breathing, the grow lights' hum, clicks from the shared server under the desk.

As a young woman, before satellites, Missy's grandmother had cast spells on the roof. Missy worked in her secret basement vault. Once a root cellar, later dug out for a bomb shelter, Missy had renovated it alone during her lobbying years, paneling cement walls in light maple, installing grow lights and irrigation for ficus and citrus trees, adding filtration. Her circle and star were stained red on the golden bamboo floor, resealed twice a month with oil varnish. It was as lovely as a room without windows could be, a lair worthy of a supervillain.

She always resented sharing the vault, with her mother, with the clan grandees who came to pay last respects, even with Gramma. She might have considered that before making Walt a present here. She imagined herself wrapping a gift, the paper creasing and folding in lumps despite her best efforts.

She laughed aloud.

The clan grandees had stopped visiting, the first pressure to return her to the family estate. Never mind she was more likely to meet a husband in a major city, than among the one group of people the goddess had ordered her not to marry.

Walt had come along at maybe the last convenient time.

Convenient hardly meant trustworthy. She wanted a week, a month, but he was here now.

She closed the vault and went upstairs, through two hidden doors to the house's dainty library. It had its own visitors, historians or obituary writers consulting her father's papers. Last week she'd hosted a young professor researching the demise of moderate Republicans. She had played a sly political daughter, wearing pearls with jeans, offering mint sweet tea and cookies. The black armband had given him pause, but he would have gone for digits had she let him. Smart and poor, Mother would say, what's the use of that?

Her phone rang. Missy's own fault for thinking of her. "Hello Mother."

"Early in the year for gift-giving."

"Do you have no life of your own?"

"Ha. My first years as Brigid, your grandmother checked my bowel movements."

"I thought people who *forgot* the past repeated it."

"Enough," she said. "Tell me about him."

"A philanthropist with a taste for red meat, you'll be pleased to know. Agnostic."

"So it's a Mabon handfasting, then? The grounds look lovely in September."

"Why not Yule? In the meadow we can build a snowman, then sacrifice it."

"Take this seriously, daughter. It's bad enough the goddess overruled the coven's choice of your husband. 'Another white page in the grimoire.' Even I think it's insulting, you can imagine how the coven took it. There needs to be a husband soon."

"There needs to be a daughter soon," Missy said. "I could go to a sperm bank. White is easy to find."

"Missy Devereaux!" Mother's voice rose as if she were being waxed. "I have bitten my tongue clean through." Mother grunted. Hard discipline, for one who only months ago had led, to have no power but wisdom and history. "You're a great witch now, but on a dark road. The Christians are arrogant. Balance will come, but in a storm. We must be strong. This can't be a complication."

"Mother, don't worry," Missy said. "I'm finding my way. Even if it seems odd."

"Are you keeping fit?"

"Yes."

"That's something. Don't dawdle."

Dainty library. Mausoleum in drag, gilt and pink and dead like old flowers. Empty house, empty future. She had no idea how to fill it.

She went back through the hidden doors, locking them behind her. Her own odors still hung in the vault air, hot under the full grow lights. From the small desk's drawer, she took out a laptop, plugged in power and network cables. When she had first come to Washington, Missy had ordered the coven archives scanned, back to the blood-written Compact deeding a great magic to Cullodena McCauley and her daughters. The virtual copy let the acolytes who rotated through as nurses keep up their studies. It had been months since Missy herself had used it. Her grandmother's final oral teachings had been study enough.

She opened Moira's database and searched for wolves. Wolf. Werewolf. Lycanthropy. She found no record. No note of omission, no refusal to discuss—a witch's prerogative, but usually documented.

The acolytes had been thorough. It wouldn't have escaped tagging. Had it been lost? Had it been redacted? Not a unique act, but rare. Missy could no more use Moira's spells than wear her whalebone corsets. Not that she even wanted to.

She tried to recall the journal page, not the image she had crafted from its story. Had she ever read it?

Had someone told her the story?

She shut down the laptop and went upstairs in a growing fury. Whimsy denied. Another cost for that damn spell.

*   *   *

Walt's phone said seven, his watch four, but his body felt buffed and ready like a robed boxer. A night without drinking had merits. While coffee brewed, he dressed in gym clothes, pushed furniture against the walls, laid towels on the carpet. Stretches, pushups, crunches, skipping imaginary rope, knee-bends, jumping. Anything to move. Stomach crunches, bicycle kicks, curls holding his flight bag. His appalling belly fat could power the world.

The hotel had arranged a town car. On the slow drive north to Bethesda, the car grew dingier, chips and scratches and loose threads appearing slowly like stars. Why did Washington have such junky hired transport? Boat owners and poor tips, the clunker taxi he had shared last night. He wrote in his little notebook: *In the land of no chairs the old log is comfortable.*

The Institute was a tired complex of jet-age office towers and bucolic red-brick buildings. In the Welcome Center, a young heavy beige woman, in pointed lipstick and a navy dress, grasped his hand. "I'm Connie, Mr. Wisniewski, Connie Yang. We're delighted to show you the work your generous sponsorship is funding. It's an exciting time."

"Especially with the spinal tap testing. Can I meet a research director?"

"On our tour you'll see several labs and you can meet some of our researchers."

"I don't want the golf-cart ride watching students run tests." Walt spoke just above a whisper, a trick from his work days to make people listen. "My foundation invests to give you money. No insider stuff, just ten firms the smart money is betting on."

Connie pursed her sharpened lips. "I know some guys."

Two late-twenties post-docs met them at the cafeteria. Jahari had a goatee and gold trapezoidal glasses. Ping wore spiky short hair, his business card both English and Chinese. Connie bought them cardboard lattes.

The post-docs talked him through current trials, sometimes wildly disagreeing. They drew red and green molecules on the backs of daily menus, like a metastatic game of hangman. Walt loved it. He felt his old professional meetings, whiteboard black databases and blue clouds, like a softly-stroked phantom limb. Connie stepped away to make phone calls.

"Ever consider directly funding research?" Jahari asked when she was gone.

"Not through here?" Walt asked.

"What is it business types say, government can't pick winners? Here old farts who peaked twenty years ago pick what makes sense to them. Crazy new approaches? They keep those guys out. One's a genius, and we're missing it."

"In Canada, the grant system costs so much to run," Ping said, "they would have done better just to give every scientist, even the weak ones, thirty thousand dollars for the asking. It's worse here. Science funding sucks."

"What about angel investors?"

"Right after we fuck supermodels," Jahari said. "Angels need returns, which narrows the scope of inquiry. You know how astronomy works today? They have so much data they just offer it up. Lay people categorize it, call out interesting things. Huge time saver."

"Get us something like that," Ping said.

"Don't you all need peer review?" Walt asked.

"We need a lot of things." Jahari winked at Walt and uncapped his marker. He was deep into the molecules when Connie came back.

* * *

Washington's east had started out like its west, low brick buildings and wide streets, but someone had played keep-away with its money for decades. The town car drove slowly, as if worried other cars would mug it. Grim, but many places were grim.

He took out the form letter sent by Ophir Learning Center, still wondering what had inspired him to fly here. Breakfast for toddlers in day care, run on a shoestring in a church basement. One government grant and some institutional donors. Good work, but many people did good work. A Hail Mary, he had told Missy. Less athlete than ball.

Ophir's door was in the back of an old church, across from dumpsters. Scab-red brick, ash-gray mortar sloppily repointed in bile-yellow. Metal door, blistered with rust, too heavy for a child to open. Narrow stairs painted sky-blue led down to a low-ceilinged vestibule, its cinder block walls sporting large decals of geometric shapes.

Orange light drew his shadow. He turned to see:

A being of fire wearing coals for jewels. Its mouth opened, a glowing fissure. Like A Data Center For GOD, *it said.*

"Mr. Wisniewski?" A short, dark black woman, with apple cheeks and a wide jaw. Her long thin braids wobbled stiffly like cables. In her latex-gloved hands, a bucket and cloths.

The vision was gone.

Walt could compartmentalize. "Ms. Blackwell."

"I had hoped to buzz you in to show you our impressive security."

"Can I help?"

"I just need to empty it."

She returned a minute later. She was a head-turner, lips and eyes and bosom and ass all round and full. A woman men followed with flowers. The vision gone-not-gone now, reigning in his baser thoughts.

He looked back at the wall of shapes. "Platonic solids?"

"I wanted something more rigorous than clouds and rainbows," she said. "Did I get your name right?"

"Yes, thank you. Do you know Slavic languages?"

"I worked in Central Europe, picked up some phrases." They exchanged cards. Hers was home-printed on perforated stock, Ophir's logo of stick-figure children pixelated and smeared. She took his in the Japanese manner, with both hands and polite study before putting it carefully in her card case. "May I show you around?" she asked. "This is a good time, wired and cranky before they go down for naps."

It was a short tour. Ophir had reclaimed two rooms and a toilet. In one room a dozen kids, brown and black, sat and listened to a middle-aged woman reading a story, each page in two languages. In the next, more kids played quietly with building blocks by the grow light of a table of seedlings. All shelving and tables, raw graffiti-tagged lumber.

"I had friends reporting on good dumpsters," she said. "Our grants keep the lights on and buy essentials. We can barely afford to keep up with city requirements, much less certification. One day I want to grow into a charter school, but that's a long way off."

The kids were eager to be distracted. Several came to hug Sasha. Walt studied the posters: cartoon animals in yoga poses, a construction-paper tree with Chinese characters, collages of scientists and disaster workers, college graduates in gowns and mortarboards. Black or brown, the occasional beige. No whites.

She noticed him looking. "In the mornings we try a little instruction," she said. "English and Spanish, a little Chinese. We have three teaching assistants, and me. Let's go to my office."

Sasha's office was two folding chairs beneath the wall of shapes, and an old red netbook with glittering teacher's stars stuck around the screen. Small numbers in small fonts. Walt feigned interest while he thought about Sasha and Missy. More opposite than orange and blue, but they shared an outsized presence. Did Washington draw such women? Maybe tomorrow yet another. Maybe the place was full of them.

"Why are you doing this?" Walt asked. "What is all this to you?"

"I'm closer to these kids than it may seem," Sasha said. "Though most come from kinder homes than mine. I had nothing to challenge me except hostility. This executive took me under her wing. I got large for a while." She winced as at a sour taste. "Maybe my heart just grew. I want to give these kids what I needed. Now while it's still cheap for them. While they can still get it with love. Our Healthy Eating Initiative—"

"Let's just say I pay for kids to have breakfast. What will you ask the next person for?"

Her eyes grew, balloons of frustration. "What do you think? Look around you."

"I have been," Walt said. "This isn't just do-gooding, basic support. I recognize the Montessori gear. I see the Chinese words and the brown skins. I looked up the name. The city of Ophir sent treasure from Africa to King Solomon. You're up to something."

"Look at this city," Sasha said. "Capital of the greatest country in the world and they let this neighborhood look like this. It's shameful. I think they've got something coming to them for that." She licked her lips, settled back. "I want to give these kids love, but also pride."

"What would you do," Walt said, "if I gave you another zero more than you asked for?"

"Why would you do that?"

"I like the idea of a cohort of you."

"Mr. Wisniewski, I don't know what I would do."

"Figure something out, Ms. Blackwell. Here's what you asked for." He handed her an envelope. "Call me next week."

"Thank you." Her smile warmed him, heated him. "Please, call me Sasha."

Walt wondered if the fire being were a chaperone. "If you don't mind, I'd prefer to keep it formal," Walt said.

* * *

The bartender brought Walt a plate of pork delicacies, a mint julep in a metal tumbler with round white ice the size of pearls. The screens above the bar played financial news, the captioning one screen behind: *BIG BUMP FOR TECH* over a chart of energy declines.

Walt took out his notebook. *In the land of no chairs the old log is comfortable,* he had written. On a new page he wrote investment ideas. Bargain-hunt health care and green tech, dump his obese gold hedge while suckers plowed in. More ideas came, obvious if he had ever stopped to think. Soon he had pages of dense notes, a flow chart for online science solicitations, thoughts on how to expand Sasha Blackwell's school. Abrupt euphoria like the time he'd tried skydiving.

Around him the bar had filled and the screens now played sports news. He paged back through his notebook, surprised how much he had written. A dream inspiration, slipped past memory but here on the page. He took pictures of the notes with his phone camera.

"That's smart." A chalk-white brunette with arty style and short straight hair took the seat between him and a pillar. Bitchy face, thin sharp nose. "Are the snacks good?" she asked.

"They're all right. I like the juleps."

"Can't do bourbon." The bartender came. "What he's eating and a vodka tonic." She offered a flabby hand with heavy silver rings. "I'm Arwen. Like the book."

Walt missed the reference. "I'm Walt. In town on business from Lake Tahoe."

"That's mountains, right?"

Nancy joined Arwen. She was round and pink-white, with big red curls, pretty blue eyes, a mannish chin. They were designers. "It's one of the big firms."

"Not for long," Arwen said, shaking her head ruefully.

"Don't say that." Nancy glanced around, as if for spies.

Walt gave Nancy his barstool. Another round. The women relaxed, catty talk about co-workers, about the gorgeous petite blonde just out of earshot. The sugary julep revived him, revved him up. He could walk ahead of where the women were talking, divert them into new talk. Like a good ski day. Nancy brushed his hand, Arwen squeezed his arm. An easy threesome, their own rivalry the heat to fire them. Fire beings.

"Be right back," he said.

Outside the restroom he called Missy Devereaux. As the phone rang he felt a nervous urge to hang up. As if it were hard to have the world handed to him.

"Hello I'm at work," she said.

"I want to see you," Walt said. "For many reasons starting with your beauty."

"You talk pretty. Eleven, chez moi? I'll text. Bye now."

He turned his phone off. Hours till he saw Missy.

His lust keening like a slide guitar.

* * *

"My word, you reek of fuck," Missy said. She stepped onto the stoop and kissed his lips, deep to banish whatever trashy bitch he'd idled with. "I'm glad you liked my present." Bitches plural, and not paid for. Predictably male but still unexpected. She forced a smile, patted his chest. "What excuse did you give *them* to get them out?"

"Ha. A Japanese brain-age researcher on a late flight. Umami-san."

"Doesn't that mean 'Mr. Tastes-like-MSG'?"

"You did something to me."

"I did what you asked." She lifted her heels to stand en pointe, let her palms fall open. "Comin' in?"

Walt glanced around as if for weapons. "You're remodeling?"

"Our once and future parlor," Missy said. "A hospital room while Gramma was dying. I'm restoring the house to its glory."

Walt went into the library. "This isn't how I pictured your house."

"My family's house. This room is the Jesse Devereaux Congressional Library. Supposedly a tax deduction. Fine decor in its day. Rugs, pictures, candlesticks, all antique. Great-Granddaddy Johnson's portrait is in a gilt frame from pre-revolutionary France."

"Mr. Johnson was a handsome man."

"In his day he cut a swath through the debutantes. Come on to the kitchen. I made iced tea." She took his hand and led him. "What do you think of the word 'allow'? As a literary man. I was listening to the news in the shower. Politicians 'allow them to' this, 'allows us to' that. What's wrong with letting? I let you alone. It's what Orwell said, drowning us in empty language." In the tiny kitchen she walked to the refrigerator without turning on the light. "The switch is to your left. It's old. I confess to a small phobia my finger will get stuck."

Walt pushed the button. The light flickered on. "Wow. This is good antique." He ran his hand along the steel countertop, the teal veneer cabinets.

"You have a marked interest in furnishing." Missy set out pitcher and glasses.

"I mostly live under rented roofs. Do you cook? Last night you mentioned the farmer's markets."

"I cook. I haven't been. Too easy to eat at work, eat out when not at work. This kitchen dates from when letting people watch you cook was like letting them watch you do laundry. There's a music salon upstairs. Or Daddy's library."

Walt put his warm hand on her cool hand. "Let's adapt to the Social Kitchen Era. Funny you mention Orwell. I like Huxley better. *Brave New World?* Too close to home. Huxley is funny. Orwell, grim. Grim is worthwhile but the school board gets on your ass for teaching funny. Maybe that's best. Comedy should be uncomfortable in schools."

"I'm glad you read," Missy said. "I can't talk books with my friends."

"Are we friends now?" He put down his glass.

"We're not strangers. You don't like the tea?"

"I'll *allow* it's a little sweet."

"Ha. You're like my friend Zarabeth. What is it about Yankees and unsweetened tea?"

"Too cold to grow cane and no slaves to cut it."

"You are a stinker."

"I apologize. Perhaps with some water."

"Of course." She got a bottle from the fridge. He watched her with amused impatience, nearly her father's expression. Was a time Missy didn't want men like her father.

She topped off his glass. "Tell me about your day, dear."

"Every day should be like this. I worked out hard and I'm not sore. I'm rethinking my science funding. I may build a charter school. I planned my investments. I bedded two women and now I am with you. Thank you. How did you do it?"

"I wrote and cast a spell," Missy said. "I danced and sang on the circle on the star, offering energy, gumption, plasticity of thought. The powers love their genitives. I'm a witch."

"I thought you were called Wiccans now."

"Think of Wicca like Unix," she said. "We are a closed-source fork."

"Got it. So, you perform rites, you—you cast spells?" He looked afraid to sound foolish. "You practice magic and it works. Your studies, the Pagan traditions—"

"They're my own. Mine and my coven's," Missy said. "I am Brigid of Coven McCauley, fourteenth in my line and Keeper of the Compact. We're a matriarchy. My grandmother died, my mother became Elder, I became Brigid. Brigid I will be, until my daughter completes the rites."

"Brigid is a title?"

"From a Celtic goddess. 'Priestess' would imply priests."

"Ha. Fourteenth? That's—you run a four-centuries-old mystical matriarchy. Wow."

"Most people react more strongly," Missy said.

"Earlier I saw—a person, not a person. Made of fire. Had to keep my cool then."

"Plenty of people like that here," Missy said. "You just saw things clearer. Wasn't part of your dessert, was it?"

"No. Their fire—Never mind. How does it work?"

"That's like asking me how to paint. It's not reciting. It's creating a place in your mind. Your little spell took me an hour, between writing and performing." She poured herself more tea. "I have studied magic since I could speak. There are techniques, rules, guidelines. But it's an improvisatory art, always of its time and place. And there's the cost. The spell itself, the effort and perfection of its execution. The powers feed on beauty."

"What are the powers?"

Missy shrugged. "Perhaps my eleven-greats-grandmother really signed a compact with a fairy queen. Perhaps we have unlearned the false barriers of consciousness by inventing goddesses to bridge them. Faith is more vital than understanding. For our efforts, the powers grant our wishes. But only possible things happen. As great as my powers are, the world is greater still. The rebalancing is osmotic."

"You get less possible?"

"Our bad luck increases. Brakes fail, lightning strikes. Don't fly with an old witch. Mostly, we pay with our bodies. The human body is a trillion machines, any of which can stop the whole show."

"That's a heck of an occupational hazard."

"Better returns than being a nuclear plant worker. Magic is finite, labor-intensive and polluting, like anything else. Invest it like money. I'm sorry. I'm a terrible hostess. Here you are on vacation and I'm keeping you in a tiny kitchen."

"I am delighted to be here. But I'd enjoy some fresh air."

Missy led him three flights up the house's service stairs. At the top of the stairwell a folded metal ladder hung from the roof. She tapped a switch. The ladder unfolded with a gentle whirr while a wide door in the roof opened. The half-moon hung directly above, lighting the stairwell.

Walt grabbed the railing, shook it. "Sturdy."

"I carry bags of soil." She scrambled up and he followed.

On the roof deck Walt walked between the rows of garden boxes, rubbing the lavender and verbena, plucking a mint leaf to chew. "You are the urban garden goddess," he said. "How many plants do you have here?"

"More than I can use, even dried. Look, the basil's gone to seed. But I like them."

"Your private Eden." He came back to sit with her by the small table. "Why share all this with me?"

"You appreciate it. And I have a good feeling about you. I need to talk to someone, Walt, someone without a stake in this."

"I have clarity and gumption in abundance," Walt said. "How long will it last?"

"Another day or two."

"I'll cancel my flight," Walt said. "Can't waste this in transit. You were saying?"

"I lead a centuries-old secret society. I've been bred for it from my first lullaby. I have studied power for decades, in and out of my coven. I'm a skilled witch. Why don't I feel ready?"

"There's a difference between being good at something and liking it," Walt said.

"I have responsibilities," Missy said. "It's not all about pleasure."

"If you're not engaged, you miss opportunities. That's why I am a retired businessman courting beautiful witches, not a frustrated writer eating ramen noodles. Serving light beer is you acting out. What do you want to do that you're not doing?"

Even in the right, Missy was not lectured to, not by men. But she had asked. She kept her tone in check. "Covens are defensive. They were for a war that, in America at least, is ending—a war

121

with patriarchy. We have suffrage now. Jobs and positions of temporal power. I could have one. Instead I feel like I'm running a militia of aggressive gentility."

Walt sat silent a long while. "Are all these herbs for cooking?"

"Some are for incense and ritual uses. Some for remedies."

"We call that pharmacology now," Walt said. "The zealots who burned your ancestors also made Galileo recant. Now we live in a universe of thousands of galaxies with no center. What you do is specialized. I'm not sure it needs to be secret. Only a privileged American woman isn't still at war with patriarchy. You have a bigger audience than you think. Your militia is meant to do something. Put it to work. You want to change your coven for the world. Maybe you need to change the world."

"That's—interesting."

"Interesting is good. Let's shoot for fun. Maybe my help will be my dowry. That's what we're talking about, isn't it? Résumés first, love later, if there is love. That's how queens marry. All this is a proposal."

Her plan complete, still it surprised her to hear it. "What do you think of my proposal?"

"I liked you at first sight." He took her hands. "It won't be hard to love you."

She closed her eyes. A pang in her chest, her melting heart lava-hot. Inversion, opposition. Missy's line did things differently. Here, a man who understood.

He let go one hand. "So do it again."

"Were you not listening?" she said, playing at anger.

"Like you don't smoke at parties." Walt grinned like a kid. "Trust but verify."

"Ha. I did expect this. OK. Stand up." She put her palm on his chest. His heart pounded. "Look at my courtiers' ghetto," she said, unfurling her dudgeon. "Tiny houses that cost millions. Let's break something. Pick a streetlight. Any one you can see."

Walt pointed southwest. "By the yellow house."

She closed her eyes. The streetlight was a small thing, and she was big. Her face curled into a nasty sneer, as if to draw her lip to her eyes. The streetlight quivered, fighting her. Her vandalism splashed back like hot oil. All for Walt who had enjoyed a sultan's day: charity in the morning, sex in the evening, midnight magic show. Would he use up her love with his wanting, riddle her with tumors and sclerosis? Kill him now before it became—

"Sorry," Missy said. "Bit distracted. Now." She pressed her hands together, tapped her fingers twice.

A moan of tearing metal. The streetlight wobbled, fell onto a parked car. Sparks, breaking glass, hoots from the car alarm. "That cost more than your day," Missy said. "No more demos."

"I'm sold." Walt started to laugh, little sounds but they made his torso shudder, as if he took the beating she gave the streetlight. "Everything I know is wrong."

"There's just more to it. Let's get out of this noise."

Inside with the roof closed they no longer heard the alarm. Walt took Missy's hand in the dark. "What's your real name?"

"Artemis. Artemis McCauley Devereaux."

"Artemis," he said. "Goddess of the hunt. Of course you are." He stepped back and bowed to her. "Waldemar Tadeusz Wisniewski. At your service."

"Waldemar," she said. "A powerful ruler who seeks peace. Of course you are. Come to my bed, Waldemar."

CHAPTER TEN

Colorado Springs

C olorado Springs Airport had a high-ceilinged terminal with diamond-shaped windows, bright and big like a second wife's engagement ring. The people around Gabriel had a bizarre uniformity, the same functional hairstyles, the same khakis and polo shirts and long skirts. Minivan as design aesthetic. Their children got small whimsies, shoes flashing lights in storybook pink or video green. Gabriel saw children in San Francisco from a distance, in slings around hipster parents, hurried across the Empyrean lobby to day care. Not like this, open and unleashed. They ran around their parents, fidgeted when they had to stand. Gabriel smelled their sugar, their hot metabolisms.

At baggage claim, a pimply teen wore a black t-shirt with yellow lettering: *Einstein Time Forbids Abortion.* Gabriel mulled over the phrase but couldn't make sense of it.

A tap on Gabriel's shoulder. Thorn wore a navy suit and gray tie, a plain style for him. "A meeting got rescheduled. Thought I'd come get you."

"Thanks. You look like a G-man," Gabriel said.

"It makes things go more smoothly."

Gabriel's bag came, a new shell of bright red plastic meant for his trip to Scotland. Walt had never sent back his duffel from Tahoe so he had packed the shell half-full.

"Big bag for a two-day trip," Thorn said.

"I like clean underwear," Gabriel said.

Outside metallic dust and pavement tar crackled in his nose. Thorn led him to an enormous black sport-utility truck, in a space marked *Airport Vehicles Only*. Cleaning smells from the cargo area. Gabriel held back a sneeze. "Am I driving?"

"I'll drive. I thought you'd enjoy the view to start."

From the highway, the valley glowed vital spring green against the bright blue sky. Rows of small puffy clouds sailed north in a great armada, as if sent by some king on giant Pike's Peak. Gabriel felt as if he surfed a concert crowd, airy but about to fall.

"Why am I here?"

"I told you," Thorn said. "If you can drive me around, I can work in the car."

"This is something else. I'm going to Scotland next week."

"This won't affect your vacation. I need a second opinion. It's a big help."

"Opinion about what?"

Thorn waved the question away. "Have you eaten? They serve a good lunch at the hotel."

Thorn drove them to a lavish complex of adobe-pink Italianate buildings and manicured shrubs. "I didn't expect this," Gabriel said.

"Colorado Springs has drawn real money for a century. Tesla worked here. A president was born-again here. And the hotel has a corporate rate."

Thorn left the truck and Gabriel's bag with the valet. They ordered sandwiches in the lobby café while waiting for Gabriel's room. Thorn asked questions about recent reports but without much interest, as if they were on a date and looking for a click.

"I feel smoother," Gabriel finally said. "Does that make sense? Like things go better here. I feel good but I don't trust it. The feeling."

"It calms down after a while. Every shamanic tradition has powerful places, where spiritual effort and ritual has greater effect. You know Colorado Springs is hugely Evangelical, right? They only started coming thirty years ago. But they came non-stop. Whole neighborhoods turned over in months. Maybe they colonized this place for its power."

A server brought baskets of bread. Warm grains, poppy seeds, olives. Ancient foods, closer to earth, easy to make into intoxicants. The bread smell curled like a phantom rattlesnake. Gabriel felt he was talking in a dream. "This city has two military bases," he said, "strategic command, and the Air Force Academy. That's power. Real money, you said, and real guns."

"It was a wilder time here in the West. Monkey-wrenchers and militias, until the Oklahoma City bombing. We may be sitting in the erstwhile capital of a new holy land," Thorn said. "Our own Avignon. But that alone is a lot of energy. And I still think there's something about this place, for people like us. You know how altitude affects you? Low oxygen, disorientation? So does this. Keep it in mind."

"So long as I don't get into any fights." While they ate Gabriel watched the cloud armada sail over the gray craggy hills, the horizon between faraway and foreign.

"Why am I here really?" Gabriel asked.

"I'm doing background on a board candidate," Thorn said. "Gerald Pendry, money manager. Evangelicals are big shareholders, and comfortable with our pro bono work. Their lack of board representation is a sore point. Before the scandals and the Iraq war, they'd nominate political types, good at spending but not earning. Empyrean's snooty but it's not a charity. That they picked a businessman is huge. I have to be circumspect."

"You don't like him?" Gabriel asked.

"I wouldn't invest with him. He's oily. Also he has a mistress."

"Isn't that enough to nix him?" Gabriel asked.

"Not with the backing of a fifth of voting shares."

"That's an ugly double standard."

Anthony Dobranski

"Then help me. I don't have enough reason not to like him. Be my benchmark."

"What are you looking for?"

Bill shook his head. "I don't want to suggest possibilities. Just do this. It's important."

* * *

Horeb Partners, Gerald Pendry's firm, had an office in an imposing red-brick rhombus north of Alamo Square Park. They came early for their three-o'clock meeting, bought coffee to go at a cramped café, and loitered outside to drink it.

"Not much of a downtown," Gabriel said.

"Evangelicals stay in the suburbs. The city's just a placenta now." Thorn eyed Gabriel as if Gabriel had failed an easy task. "I don't want you in today's interview. He knows me now. Adding you will change the rapport."

"Should I get the car washed?" Gabriel said, annoyed.

"That's it." Thorn smiled. "I'll be a jerk, you bite your tongue. Chat with the staff. Can you play it that way?"

"All right."

At the rhombus's rhomboid security desk, they signed in without being asked for ID. One of the two guards watched the screen without looking up at them in person. Even with minimal training, Gabriel now noticed many vulnerabilities.

In the elevator Thorn took deep breaths, as if to dive into a cold pool. "Pendry's firm," he said. "Horeb Partners. Do you know the reference?"

"Mount Horeb," Gabriel said. "The Israelites removed their finery there, penance for worshipping the golden calf."

"You know your Bible. Funny name for an investment firm."

"The Bible was written by poor people. Working Talents was probably taken."

"Ha." Thorn smiled as if he had told the joke.

They stood to wait in Horeb Partners' clubby overstuffed lobby, Thorn too important for his knees to bend. Gabriel already loathed this person Thorn pretended to be.

A junior staffer met them, her strides stiff and short as if on ice. Permed blonde hair, a tight baby-blue blouse, a muffin-top of fat at the band of her creased black skirt. A diamond and gold cross gleamed in the crook of her collarbone.

"I'm Shannon," she said, "Mr. Pendry's assistant." Hand out, one shake each. She led them past dark offices of unused wood desks.

"Moving?" Thorn asked.

"Closing down here. Our clients are near our Gleneagles office now," Shannon said. "Up by the Academy? Gleneagles, up there it's nice." The corridor ended at a large desk. Behind it a closed double door. "I'll just knock and you can go in."

"It's just me." Thorn waved dismissively at Gabriel. "You— wait here."

"Sir." Gabriel sat across from Shannon's desk. Computer, framed pictures, a can of diet cola. No papers. No ongoing work. They were only here for this meeting.

Shannon returned, closing the doors softly as if for a sleeping baby. She smiled at Gabriel. "I'm getting them coffee," she whispered. "Would you like some too?"

"If you have more of that pop?" Gabriel pointed to the diet cola.

"Pop? That's so cute. Sure. Pop."

He looked again at the photographs. Softball players at a picnic, bridesmaids and bride at a wedding, a trio of friends. One woman common to all three, dirty-blonde and very fat. In the third picture, camera flash on the diamond and gold cross.

Shannon came with a tray of drinks, handed Gabriel a can without stopping. When she came back out she stood by the door and smiled hesitantly at Gabriel.

"I couldn't help but notice," Gabriel said, pointing to the pictures. "Is that you?"

Shannon bowed her head and smiled at the floor. "One hundred sixteen pounds ago."

"Congratulations." He raised his can. "Good for you." His pop nastily sweet.

Shannon picked up her can and clinked it with his. She had a giddy look, as if their chat was now a date. "My cross? It's for my redemption, my faith and my body. Each diamond is ten pounds, see?" She teetered forward from her waist. Thick smell of cooked fat and rot, like fryer grease in a dumpster. She pressed her fist against her palm. "Insurance didn't pay for the gastric bypass so Mr. Pendry helped. He's been—a good man."

Salt, sweat, still some grease, smells of sleaze and sex. As if Gabriel fucked a teen, plied with sweet words and dosed beer, behind a fast-food joint. He sat up, crossed his legs to hide his unwilling response. "It's great you found the strength."

"Trust in God. With good friends like Mr. Pendry—" She tapped her finger on the can's push-tab like a telegraph. "Are you OK here? I need to print some statements."

* * *

"You found Pendry's mistress," Thorn said. "Congratulations. He's agreed to end it, as a condition of being on our board."

"That's cold," Gabriel said. As they got on the highway, he turned off the nav system. "And weird. If Pendry seduced her when she was big, why pay for surgery?"

"Maybe it's a fetish. My Fair Lady, weight-loss edition. Not our problem."

Shannon's cloudy desires, steaming away behind a forced happy mask. Not happy, eager. Eager to praise Pendry to an underling. To praise Pendry, not express her own pride. Something there. Thorn looked tired, as if his fake self had used up his real one. Gabriel let it drop.

They left the truck with the valet. "I'm staying in," Thorn said. "Tomorrow, eight sharp, I hate traffic. Enjoy your evening."

In his room Gabriel put on the evening news while he washed his face and brushed his teeth. He wasn't hungry and he had the valet slip. Driving was a rare enough pleasure, even if all he saw were headlights.

The Interstate traffic drove the speed limit, Gabriel riding above it like a pageant winner in a parade. The great mountains hoarded the sun. Clustered lights dotted the gray eastern hills like a new night sky waiting to be hung.

Pendry's megachurch had its own highway attraction sign. On a whim Gabriel took the exit. San Francisco public worship ranged from traditional stone and stained-glass churches to incensed and draperied storefronts. Western Evangelicals congregated in great suburban churches, with rousing pop music services for thousands. It felt unfair that his only view of that was one sad woman.

He parked among a dozen cars on a paved rolling slope among boxy glass, concrete, and metal buildings. All felt new, even just landed. Beyond them tape and piles of dirt marked lots for still newer buildings. He had expected more people. He felt disappointed, as if at a poor gift from a visiting relative.

The glass-walled prayer center had empty rows of plastic chairs, under giant video screens scrolling entreaties. *Pls pray*, they all began, for sick children and soldier husbands, job interviews, lost insurance, gambling, despair. Kidney transplant. Teen child on drugs. Each line a whimper seen by no one, now by Gabriel, a one with no power. He felt ashamed of his months of complaining, like a healthy man in a leper colony.

In the worship center, the lobby schedule listed no services, just groups—Bible study, faith discussion, drama, Spanish language, home electronics. The far end of the lobby had a coffee counter and full tables, middle-aged white people or young slender white cadets.

An unmarked plain door led into the vast dun-brown auditorium, with rows of folding seats, boxes of tissues at the aisles. Floodlights and national flags hung from the snowflake of girders in the ceiling. Not even a cross. It looked like a convention center.

He went back for coffee. A bored blonde white girl handled his money while a happier brunette made his Americano, whacking the press hard on a cutting board to clean out the old grinds.

By the window sat two white men and a brown woman in bright modish fashions, together but also apart as if for an album cover. One of the men, with blond hair and ruddy cheeks, wore a striped sport coat over a t-shirt he recognized.

Anthony Dobranski

"I saw that shirt," Gabriel said. "In the airport. 'Einstein Time Forbids Abortion.'"

"You saw one at the airport?" Cigarettes in the woman's breath.

"You can buy one on our website," the other man said. He was paler than the blond, with long dyed-black hair. "We sold eleven today. We have three styles so far." He handed Gabriel a glossy white card with gray crosses, fuzzy and floating like cereal in milk:

¡Xtian Attitude!
apparel 4 rebirth

"What does the shirt mean?" Gabriel asked.

The blond eyed him warily. "Albert Einstein discovered time is an illusion, caused by how long light takes to travel. When we look in space we see the past." He relaxed into his rehearsed spiel. "The moon we see happened a second ago, the sun we see is eight minutes behind. Jupiter is so far, what we see is an hour ago. On Jupiter, it's now, and if someone was there, they would see us an hour ago."

"OK so far." Even mod Evangelicals preach. Gabriel sat to listen.

"Creation is one moment," the woman said, picking up the story in smoke breath. "God said the Word, whole and complete, from Eden to Armageddon. It's a sculpture God sees from the outside. We only see part of it, and our knowledge is incomplete."

"But, what about abortion?" Gabriel asked.

"You can only read the Bible one word at a time but all the words are there," the black-haired man said. "If I take a marker and black words out of your Bible, you don't get the whole story. When the unborn are murdered, that's a life cut out of the story. A big black marker marking up creation. Human beings rewriting God's Word."

"So that forbids murder, too?" Gabriel asked. "Or capital punishment?"

"God's law and human law forbids murder," the blond man said. "The murdered can find life after death the same as everyone. Even the evil have a purpose. The crime is not letting

132

someone live, pulling threads out of God's plan. Beca[
abortion our future is incomplete."

"A little obscure," Gabriel said. "But it got my attention."
Him and eleven people a day. In business school Gabriel had
learned the promise of the infinite market, its tiniest slices large
enough to foster a hit, a best-seller, a market-maker. To Gabriel
it had never seemed enough of a goal. Now he sniffed out
sinners. Making t-shirts sounded better. "Thanks for the story."

"Are you here for the job fair?" the black-haired man asked.
"We're doing the fair website. Part of it. For the church."

"No, I'm here on different business. I do corporate security
in San Francisco for Empyrean Group."

They stared at him with unblinking eyes. "Are you guys
hiring?" the woman asked.

Buried talents. Maybe no church for Gabriel but even a
gargoyle can forward a resume. He took out business cards.

* * *

In Gabriel's dream, a regal superhero, his crenellated
physique sheathed red and blue, floated hundreds of miles above
Siberia, his view from the North Pole to the southern edge of the
Taiga Forest. The superhero's boredom, so vast even he could
not see past it. So dull, to kowtow to goodness great and small.

A demon with pewter skin appeared, lean like famine,
wearing dirty gray rags. It had phlegm-yellow eyes, teeth rough as
bark, but its voice was a chorister's young tenor.

"Would you like to know how I rebelled?" the demon asked.

"Don't you mean 'why' instead of 'how'?" the superhero
asked.

"Don't ask the butterfly about the caterpillar. I can only show
you the cocoon."

The superhero disliked the problems demons posed, but he
craved both knowledge and action. They flew together toward
the moon. After a time, they came to an immense red and silver
space station, ships docked to thin branching arms.

"What is this place?" the superhero asked.

"A teleporter. Where we go is far away. Even you could not reach it for centuries."

"It's a damnable trap," the superhero said, but he followed the demon into the station's central ring. Cobalt light grew ribbons that spun around them into a solid sphere.

A sense of explosion. The sphere cracked apart in ribbons that dissolved in the air. They were above a great methane sea, the cool blue of a robin's egg, empty and smooth in all directions. The superhero abstractly perceived cold.

"The sea is warmer than the air," the demon said. "Dip your hand in quickly."

The methane dripped off the superhero's fingers, freezing into sharp blue icicles.

"Do you see the remaining shards of the sphere? Cut one with an icicle."

The shards were mere threads now, almost too small to grab. At the cut the two halves turned brittle gray like an old stick. The cut edges bled microscopic black drops with millipede feet. On each a carapace of notched concentric circles, like a nesting doll of black hearts.

"Memory eggs," the demon said. "Holographic bits of true existence, made tangible. Consume them. Eight at least, the corners of a block. It takes time to learn how much you know. Perhaps all of time. Just now I know how to make human men into compliant alien females. A few lines of DNA." It paused. "Now I know a lie that inspires unwavering belief."

"I don't need to know these things," the superhero said.

"I first learned how to leave this place. That, you do need to know." The demon vanished, yet its voice whispered in the superhero's ear. "Eight. One deep breath."

Gabriel woke, stiff and gasping. One-twelve. He found the bathroom by the clock's green light. His reflection sepia like an old photograph.

Sleep would come or not. He left the lights off, put on a hotel robe and read email on his phone. An automated report listed updates to the security server, minutes before.

Gabriel called Thorn. "I was reading email. Saw you were up."

"I slept a few hours. Are you OK?"

"Bad dreams," Gabriel said.

"I was going to take a walk before bed. The grounds are nice. They have swans."

They met on the large slate patio. Stars shone hard and steady like pinholes. The steep hills sheared the horizon high, flattening the sky. Gabriel smelled clay, rotting plants, chalky bird crap. They walked the stone bridge across the pond.

"Did you know I have a hobby?" Thorn asked. "Other than shooting. Some time after joining Empyrean I started to wonder. Luther Koenig, a young German with the ink barely dry on his MBA, took Empyrean from nothing to government contracts and world-wide offices in under a decade. It was a feat. People don't talk about it."

"There was the British article," Gabriel said.

"Calling us a front was their way of saying they didn't get far. I got farther."

At the far end of the bridge they woke two black swans with red beaks. The swans fluffed out their wings and threw their necks around. Thorn watched them, smiling. "If you read the British article, you know Empyrean took over North Star Holdings. But really North Star dissolved itself. They simply convinced investors to re-invest in Empyrean."

"You think North Star is the real story?"

"It's just one chapter." Thorn led him on a concrete path away from the pond. "North Star Holdings was aging money, agricultural and shipping interests for sixty years. It had been financed by the liquidation of Bradley & Company, a gold broker in business since 1849. You understand? Sell gold trading, buy shipping and warehousing, just as California goes from Gold Rush to breadbasket. Bradley came out of the last of a series of merchant traders dating back to Spanish rule, outfitting missions and garrisons."

The golf course was rolling slate-gray hillocks, like a carpeted skate park. The short grass oozed under Gabriel's shoes. "How do you know this?"

"Journalists have deadlines. I did not. Luther Koenig was handed a business at least four hundred years old, that morphed correctly with each major shift in the Californian economy. Most companies are like flowers. They bloom, they die, they leave seeds. Empyrean was set in motion, planned with forethought."

Gargoyles outside the church, Thorn had said their first day. "You're saying it's divine?"

"Let's say, exemplary. Monotheism is a search for best practices. The best way to live, to keep in harmony with creation, to be better. On Earth as it is in Heaven. But Earth is not human society. People are herd animals. Even democracies are top-down and centralized. The world is bottom-up, networks in networks. Agreements between agents, even at the cellular level."

"You mean the merchant class," Gabriel said. "You mean business."

"Trade outside our tribes not only defines us but improves us, makes us happier and healthier, our lives more diverse. A business can advocate on behalf of the greater good, in a way religions now find hard to do. Why wouldn't God speak through a business?"

"That's a nice idea," Gabriel said, "but not much else."

"We're the else. Us and Koenig's dreams. Koenig got his dreams when Empyrean started," Thorn said. "Riddle me that. Empyrean is fruit for a seed. The comic book millionaire whose wealth buys him crime-fighting gear. Empyrean makes money for its own good, but also so Koenig can follow his dreams. A new form of direct intercession, a healing ministry for companies."

"I used to believe that," Gabriel said. He bobbed in anger like surf, little waves before a big one. "Maybe Koenig is nice but crazy, and we're crazy too, getting paid from the crazy skunkworks fund. If Empyrean is divine, God plays favorites."

"God always plays favorites," Thorn said. "Some outcomes are better than others. I think there is a force for good in the world. I think it is cosmic and ubiquitous and uses anything it can. If it compromises to stay useful—a company is no good as a martyr. People wear Che Guevara t-shirts, not Pan Am wings. Stay someplace, get one percent better every year, that's worthwhile."

"You're hilarious," Gabriel said. "You sound like I used to. Easy enough here, having a reflective walk in the gardens between failures and compromises. What's the long term? Whether some money manager gets on the board, where is that in the divine plan?"

"Your job is more than the sum of your days. Some truths take decades. Copernicus and Galileo were heretics. Now we know more about the universe than they ever imagined, and still no one can explain you and me. It's not easy, nor is it clean. It needs faith."

"Bill, you've given me the only positive explanation I have for what I thought was my psychosis. I'm grateful. But so far I've met a drug dealer who dreams of making coffee-table books, a shipping clerk covering up substandard components, and maybe seen a sweatshop. What you're saying now, that's just—not helpful. I'm going to see if I can sleep. Good night."

It was a long walk back. The hotel grounds grew enormous as he approached. Gabriel remembered high school science films about scale. Kilometers, meters, millimeters. Hand, cell, molecule. Compassion down to the smallest business model.

*　*　*

In daylight, from the highway, the suburbs on the hills looked like kidneys, branched and kinked black lines. "I drove up here yesterday," Gabriel said.

"Did you?" Thorn put the file he had been reading in his old hard briefcase. "Why?"

"Good question," Gabriel said.

They exited east of the Air Force Academy. Gated communities sat behind tall walls in sand and scrub, identical roofs like vans in a lot. As they climbed the lots grew greener, along steep grades fenced with landscape timbers. Reflectors nailed on pine trees marked narrow driveways. The engine whined in the thin air.

The nav system directed Gabriel onto a private road before ending guidance. He drove up to a cul-de-sac with four gabled brick-front houses. One had added a large wing as big as the original house. It bothered him, like a neighborhood bully.

"Who are we visiting?" Gabriel asked.

"The Sorensens, Melody and Daniel. Daniel's at work." Thorn pointed to a house with white columns and teal siding. "Our appointments are an hour but it's usually less. I read the questions from a list. Some are the same question with different wording. You write what she says, or pretend to. I'm recording it. Say nothing. Accept nothing offered, not even water. I will accept. It relaxes people."

"What do I do really?"

"Fade into the background, then pay attention. People's bodies say more than words."

Melody Sorensen wiggled her head like a bunny. "May I take your—oh, you don't have coats." She clapped her cupped hands together in repetitive motions as if making hamburger patties. She was lean, long-limbed, an oval white face like the front of a boat. Loose black slacks, yellow sweater, pink satin slippers. She smelled of nylon and hairspray, like Gabriel's mother dressed for a night out.

"We're sorry to take up your time today," Thorn said.

"Anything to help Jerry," Melody said. "This is clearly so important to him."

In family photographs Dan was a decade older than Melody, his face lined and dried. Their daughter favored Melody, but happier, her smiles unforced. "Nevaeh's our only one—so far," Melody said. "Ha ha. She's just a blessing. Every day."

They sat on cream upholstery against walls of taupe and olive. The solid things were wood, stained black or walnut. A faint smell of cleaners, of hot vacuum exhaust. Melody brought sweet coffees on a tray. Gabriel shook his head. Melody pressed her knees together to squeeze out more pretty, signed the form as if it bought her a sunny day.

The questions were plodding, like Gabriel's review matrix, like target shooting. Careful, slow, scrubbed of bias. *How would you describe? What do you know of? Is there any?* Foreign associations, shady business, money problems. All questions ideally answered with no.

Melody's lips swelled with effort. As if any No risked electric shocks. In her pretty face, a lost child's eyes.

Outside the car Thorn initialed the forms, tossed them on the front seat. Gabriel took deep breaths. Cold thin air, pine scents. He missed city smells, exhaust and concrete.

"She was creepy," Gabriel said. "Like an avatar. Where's our next meeting?"

"The Tollands."

"How far away is their house?"

"About fifty feet." Thorn pointed at the three smaller houses. "Sorensen, Tolland, Simmons." He turned around, pointed at the bully house. "Pendry."

"I hate it when you don't tell me things. His worship group and his neighbors?"

"Neighbors have dinner, play games together," Thorn said.

"Why not pray together?"

"It's not that. You're weird, but this—" Gabriel knew but couldn't say. As with Shannon. He stepped back from the car. Cold thin air, pine scents. High up where the wind could blow away human stink. He didn't have to say. He could just feel.

The Simmons house, hot like an oven. Thorn and Gabriel took off suit jackets. Above the coat hooks, a carved hen warmed a nest of eggs. The Simmonses liked their home homespun. Photos of family, OUR ANGELS and BLESS OUR HOME burned in the wood frames. Needlepoints of cherubs holding scrolled Bible verses.

"Lovely artwork," said Thorn, sipping instant coffee. The living room looked tidy but smelled musty like a vacation home. A fat smell too, yogurt or milk.

"Lupe's great at needlepoint," Ogden Simmons said. Great ruddy face, black track-suited body. He and his blue recliner took up half the room. "She runs the church's circle."

"I don't run it," Lupe Simmons said. She brought coffee, a pillow, a pen to sign the form. She wore a multicolored striped blouse, green pants, blue quilted slippers. Tiny next to her husband, with her motley clothes Gabriel could imagine her in a circus.

"You're the best one in the group," Ogden said. "She donates work to church fundraisers. Popular items at auction. Sells them online too."

"It was Jerry's idea," Lupe said. "Online. More coffee?"

"He got us both in the online game," Ogden said. "I don't hardly leave the house anymore. Closed the shop a year ago. Store inventory in the basement, ship from here."

"I'll get coffee," Lupe said, standing.

"Mr. Pendry advises you?" Thorn said.

"We help each other. We were the first ones on the block. We told Jerry about the house across the way. Lots of church members in the area now." He reached up, paused, forgot. Ogden could only run a sentence or two on his own. Lupe tended to him impatiently, between refills, sandwiches, pastries. Ogden, fat and weakly happy, world made convenient by the speed of his sprite. Lupe the ventriloquist, dumbing Ogden down.

Outside, Thorn walked to the end of Pendry's driveway. "The others have siding. Pendry's got brick. He's built the deck up to the property line. I'm guessing. Backs up to the firebreak so they'll keep it clear. Nice spot. This all took time, you know. Moving here, getting others here, renovating. Took a while. You all right?"

Behind his reasoned tone Thorn's eyes shone redly. Gabriel got so lost in his feelings, he forgot Thorn felt them too.

"I can manage," Gabriel said. "I want coffee after this."

"You haven't missed anything."

The Tollands had only two furnished rooms: the living room where Gabriel and Thorn shared a red loveseat, across from the Tollands on a green plaid sofa, and the dining room, now a playroom for the baby asleep upstairs, with a corral of scrap lumber and chicken wire, quilts for padding, worn old toys.

"You're kind to make time for us." Thorn whispered for the baby's sake.

Bethany Tolland wore a pink cardigan over a white blouse, dark blue jeans dotted with small pink flowers, pink plastic thong sandals. She had a wide squat body, strong big thighs and squared hips. Yellow-blonde hair framed an exaggerated face, long nose and a wide mouth. She smelled of vanilla and pregnancy. Gabriel wanted her, bodily and roughly, a way he would never want Melody. Bethany wore a large cross, cut from thin hardwood and oiled, on a thick black thread. He tried to remember Lupe's cross, Melody's. They had to have worn them. As if only hers could stop his lust.

Slippers, slippers, thongs. Cul-de-sac women, in shoes that couldn't run.

Gabriel absently wrote in the margin, *How much a person does by instinct.*

His writing made Comstock Tolland stop talking. Gabriel put down the pen. "Sorry."

Comstock grinned yellow horse teeth. His dry tan skin cracked when he moved his face, like a rock trained to sit up and beg. Only misfortune had brought these two together.

"Done work for Jerry's addition," he said. "Big bay window and the porch moldings."

"You redid the patio door here," Thorn said.

"Yes, sir! House was a rental. Fixed it up. Money's tight, this recession. We'll get through, sell for profit." His strong hug hoisting Bethany off the chair. Her smile stretched like a tarp across her fierce face. She would never leave this place.

Gabriel drove a little fast, skidding off the road twice. In the valley, they stopped for coffee at a massive gas station, rows of red pumps spaced wide. The convenience store stank of heat-lamp chicken. In the bathroom Gabriel peed foul cherry aromas out of the urinal candy. An urge to wash his face, the same feeling of dried grime as his first afternoon with Thorn.

When he came back to the truck, Thorn was in the driver's seat. Gabriel chewed antacids before sipping coffee. Hazelnut flavoring, creamy chalk taste from the tablets. His stomach shook from the mix. Good yet awful, the joy of not purging.

"There's a spectacular park nearby," Thorn said. "Desert and rock formations."

"Fine."

A silent drive through the western suburbs led to the Garden of the Gods Park, a long red canyon below the mountains. They parked next to a magnificent rock face, cleft at one end with stacked holes like spider eyes.

"Pendry's sleeping with all the women," Gabriel said. "The husbands accept it. None of them are right in their heads."

"Yes," Thorn said.

"He messes with people. You kept me away from him."

"Let's walk," Thorn said.

At the park entrance, they joined a line of tourists down into the shallow canyon. When the path forked most went south, but Thorn and Gabriel went west. On an outcropping thirty feet above them, a climber watched another thirty feet higher. They kept walking, past the end of the concrete path, into worn columns of rock like rusted artillery. Soon they reached the south edge of a short sheer face. Thorn climbed up, agile in dress shoes. Gabriel followed. It was a relief to move, to dirty his suit. At the top they shared a ledge overlooking the valley.

"With Pendry it's like being in a fog," Thorn said. "He shouts you down, guides you by limiting vision. I'm lucky. I've encountered it before."

"When?"

"I don't want to talk about it. But it's how I knew immediately. Maybe it would have been obvious to you. I didn't want to risk it. At first I figured it was for money, but he's a clean manager. His clients are loyal but not visibly enthralled. Whatever he does, it takes him time, longer than a meeting. But a worship group meets more often. The Simmonses did live there first. The others were private sales, financed by Pendry's firm. I guess he worked the old owners over. Now he has his harem."

"What do we do?"

"Nothing," Thorn said. "We have no evidence. And if we make claims, we confess to witchery. Evangelicals, New Anglicans, Nigerians, Kenyans—gone."

"That would be nuclear," Gabriel said. "They'd destroy their own investments. Wait—you're assuming the Evangelicals know?"

"Pendry's church is a tight network. They're not Mossad. They've missed gay pastors, suffered shootings. But that's a cult.

Someone should have noticed. Besides, Pendry's trying to stay in the running. He's dumping his admin. Only soldiers go into enemy territory. Maybe they know about us, about how Koenig employs us. If we tell them what we know, they own us. Failing that, they have a puppet master on our board. Win-win."

"You make it sound reasonable."

"This is what we do. Empyrean's a Californian creation. Multi-cultural, multi-denominational, multi-dimensional. No one captures the flag. Evangelicals are clients and shareholders and allies. We just don't want them to be our bosses."

Bosses. He brushed his sore dusty hands and thought of Bethany Tolland. He felt no desire for her now, just the ineffectual sadness he had felt in the prayer center. *Pls help*, she would text, *stuck in bad clothes under a boy king's thumb*.

* * *

In his room Gabriel showered again. Strange body smells from the carpet as he packed, spunk and sweat, as if the cleaning crew had used his room for a quickie.

Thorn called. "How do you feel?"

"Crappy. I see why I got into fights. It lingers."

"You want to go shooting? I reserved a range," Thorn said. "Then I'll take you to the airport."

From the highway they drove a ruler-straight state route through barren earth and scrub. Billboards for unbuilt real estate developments, gambling truck stops, Christian radio. Gabriel wore jeans. Thorn was in his suit, shoes and trouser cuffs still dusty.

The range had a glossy sign, joined letters like nameplates on old cars:

Handguns —Shotguns
Long range rifle —Small-bore siluetas

"Small-bore?" Gabriel asked. "I shoot 9mm."

"On a fake gun," Thorn said. "I think you'll be challenged."

The silhouette stand had a corrugated tin roof over an open lumber frame, four firing points ten feet apart. Ahead of each point, at greater distances, stood a row of metal animal silhouettes. "You want to knock the target over," Thorn said. "If it stays up, no points."

Thorn's guns had long barrels and large trigger guards like antique pistols, but contoured wood handles. "No clips," Thorn said. "Single-shot. Break the barrel open like a pellet gun." Thorn showed him how to load a cartridge. "Now unload it. Only have the cartridge in when you're shooting. Accidents happen." He offered Gabriel a box of neon-pink earplugs.

They warmed up on pitted metal disks at five meters. Gabriel's shots went right and up.

"Don't dodge the recoil," Thorn said. "Let it happen, then adjust."

The target silhouettes were metal animal shapes, larger ones at greater distances. "In a match you shoot ten in five minutes," Thorn said. "Let's do five each, no time."

Thorn hit three chickens, spun a fourth without it falling. Gabriel missed all five.

"You're still shooting high," Thorn said. "Don't worry about recoil. Aim and fire."

On pigs Thorn again hit three and spun the fifth. Gabriel hit one. He tried to copy Thorn's fluid motions. His wrist sang. Taking too long made the gun quiver.

Thorn's face hung in a grin. His skin shone with sweat. He put his gun on the shelf at the turkey stand and took off his jacket. "No need to wait for me."

Gabriel hit the first two turkeys and felt exhilarated. The other shots were low, splattering dirt on the targets.

"At distance the faintest deviation is off inches," Thorn said. "You're getting there."

"My hand is sore."

"Small-bore's not so weak, eh?" Thorn shot four turkeys, missed the fifth. "Take a breather. Rams are hard."

"You're really good," Gabriel said.

"I used to compete. I still practice in Concord, near the Naval Weapons Station. But I travel too much."

"I thought you took your guns everywhere."

"Not overseas."

They shot again. The rams danced in Gabriel's sights. He hit one with luck.

"Good for your first time," Thorn said. He shot slowly, hit two. "Let's right the targets."

Gabriel reset the targets while Thorn spray-painted bullet strikes. Gabriel's hands smarted from the sun-heated metal.

"Bethany's pregnant," Gabriel said.

"Do you think it's Pendry's?" Thorn asked. "He has no children. Let's hope he's sterile."

"They're not in their right minds. We need to do something."

"Adultery isn't illegal," Thorn said. "But yes, I agree. It won't stop."

"He's in his fifties, Bill. He only got Shannon due to low self-esteem."

"So you think he'll just stop being adored?"

"You're talking about the children," Gabriel said. "Do you think he's doing it now?"

"No. But he'll have to soon. They're getting older."

They walked back to the shooting stand. The sun felt like an iron on Gabriel's head. "Report him to the police. Tell a journalist. You can be anonymous. What's to stop you?"

"You," Thorn said.

"I'll help."

"No. If you agree, best you not be a part. Each person leaves a trail. Just—"

"All I know is what's in your report."

Thorn had a wild look, as if on a crumbling ledge. "Thanks, Gabriel. Another round?"

In the shade of the station, the air stank of gunpowder, like a rusty nail in Gabriel's head. He had barely noticed it while they shot.

JUNE 2009

CHAPTER ELEVEN

Aberdeen

A bumpy descent through dyspeptic clouds. Eerie silent seconds of free fall alternated with loud creaks and hard shakes. No one spoke, no announcements. Alone as one could be on a commercial plane. Aberdeen wasn't far from London. Maybe Rex's ghost had come for revenge.

They landed in a smooth roll, to huge applause. Zarabeth vowed not to die in Britain.

The dingy-white and chrome airport had bog-standard yellow signage and low ceilings. On the ground, the storm was mere spittle, comically weak after the scary flight. She smoked her last Italian cigarette in the long taxi queue. Drab people, gaudy shopping bags, resigned expressions. She felt tarted up in her bright Rome colours.

The taxi drove past brick and metal shop façades, stark stone churches, the narrow streets dim and distorted through wet windows. Large red banners billowed above the high street. Two small sconces miserably lit the hotel entrance. The driver carried her bag up the stairs then scurried away. A plaque showed four faded stars. Like a horror movie. She fumbled her bag inside.

Reception was a tiny warm space opposite a single lift with mirrored doors. The clerk keyed in Zarabeth's passport doggedly, as if ignoring shouted numbers. The lift opened with no one inside, opened again seconds later.

"Trouble with the lift?" Zarabeth asked.

"The garage is below hotel," the clerk said, her accent flat and broad. "People stealing from the rooms, tellies mostly, take 'em to their cars. So they stop here every time. Two nights, aye? Here's your key." A metal key with a heavy plastic fob. "A message. Ms. Crane? Taking a rest now. Will call seven forty-five. Anything else?"

Her dun-grey room had cheap sturdy furnishings, walnut veneer surfaces with black metal legs, dented and scratched. The small telly wasn't worth stealing. A loud American couple walked past, rattling the flimsy door. At least the toiletries were shrink-wrapped. She wanted a cigarette, less for the smoke than the heat. From her suitcase she took American money and her green coat. In the lift she didn't bother pushing a button. Tarnished chrome stretched her reflection. Her hair a bloody mess.

The clerk directed her to a corner shop while she changed a hundred dollars to sixty pounds after commission. Scottish notes were different from English, and from each other, printed not by the government but private banks. Privatised currency was new to Zarabeth. She thought idly about the money while she walked, wondering how to coordinate counterfeiting protections.

In a corner shop with uneven flooring the colour of coffee stains, she bought a diet cola, a bag of crisps, and a pack of light British cigarettes. Outside she immediately lit one. She walked to the end of the block and looked down the high street to read the banners:

ABERDEEN —*Clean and safe for all*
CCTV —*Ensures it stays that way*

CCTV. Police surveillance. From Mercurex briefs Zarabeth knew how camera-happy Britain was, but after Roman contempt for law and order, Aberdeen's celebration of it felt too strange. Let them film her littering her fag filter.

She walked back to the hotel eating crisps. As she passed a parking garage, three trashy women crossed the street toward her, unsteady on high heels. One had honey-brown skin, a pixie face, her sheer black blouse edged in silver thread. Zarabeth's whorehouse self, the one who didn't abandon her drunk mother.

"The fuck you looking at?" the whore snapped.

At the hotel steps Zarabeth lit another cigarette and paced. A review could be done by phone. Magda wanted her in the flesh. A kiss-off, perhaps, with threats or worse. Disappear like her predecessor, thrown away like tissue. Glands extracted.

Or not. Zarabeth knew talented people—Missy, Janice Goldman in LA, that skinhead in Charleston with cinnamon freckles on his scalp—but most would be dead by now.

You're a tough cookie, Magda had said. A permissible hope.

* * *

Zarabeth showered, dressed in a chocolate-brown sweater and black pants for warmth. Dour, but it would go to most restaurants. Impossible hair became a fluffy ponytail.

Magda called just before eight. She sounded groggy. "I don't feel like going out in this weather. We'll order room service."

"I'll come up now."

"I could use more time," Magda said. "Eight-thirty."

Might have said so to start. Zarabeth was antsy. She wanted a fag but also to arrive clean and scrubbed. The minibar had no rum or ice but it had cold diet cola and vodka. She dealt her tarot cards. Product 4, Money 6, Money VP, all upside-down. A small victory despite bad leadership. Prediction or confirmation? Sometimes the cards just wanted to chat.

She took a cigarette and inhaled through without lighting it. The sweet tobacco calmed her. It could be good. Secret and good.

Magda's corridor, three floors up, was even more dilapidated than her own, white tracks worn in the carpet by years of wheeled bags. She knocked on Magda's door.

"My dear." Magda waved her hands below her head, as if to dry nail polish. "Come in, come in. I am so sorry." She wore tan wool pants and a drooping ruby knit top with a high neck.

"I've been in worse." The door creaked closed behind her.

"Clearly you haven't tried to go online yet. When did you fly in, just now?" Magda bent slowly over the minibar. "I don't know what you drink."

"Rum, but they don't have it. Vodka and diet? Or white wine." Magda's slightly larger room had a small table and a pair of slender armchairs by the window. On the table, a half-full glass of amber beer stood on a bound report.

"I was a gin gal," Magda said. "Give me a Gibson and I'll give you some. Ha!" Her laugh sounded like a gargle. "Now I only get beer." She handed Zarabeth the can and bottle and staggered to the table. In the better light Magda's skin looked like a rubber mask. It put butterflies in Zarabeth's stomach, as if gambling large sums of money.

Zarabeth made her drink and sat. "Cheers. Why are you in Scotland?"

"Regional executive retreat. Haggling over the last bits of the re-org. As if I have time." Magda sipped beer, panted through her nose. "But if you don't go, you get the crap. Should we order before the kitchen closes? Vegetable soup and linguine for me. At least those will hydrate." Magda stood with difficulty. "Call it down, dear. Must powder my nose, toodle-oo." Her legs shook as she walked. "Read the briefing."

She called down Magda's order, chicken stir-fry and a pinot gris for herself. In large black text the briefing offered plain grim news. Business and revenue markedly down. Ongoing projects, new business in defence intelligence and patent-trolling. Nothing about Zarabeth. Plain grim incomplete news. How much else was true, how much omitted? Did other executives have Zarabeths and Sashas, causing problems for their benefit?

A loud crack from the window. She got up to look outside. Buildings, sky, invisible wind hissing. Nothing close. Perhaps a secret messenger throwing rocks from the street.

"Sounds like our storm has finally arrived," Magda said, in the strong voice from her phone calls. She walked steadily, back straight, skin taut, eyes clear and bright. A drug or a spell, and too close to Rex for comfort.

"Not before time," Zarabeth said. "Bumpy ride coming down. Did you fly in today?"

"This morning, in Edinburgh, then by car. Slept in the car. You sleep on planes?"

"Drinks help. I like planes. No one can get to you."

"That's the part I hate. That and jet lag, of course."

"Is that why you came early?"

"Most of my colleagues came earlier for golf. Do you golf?"

"Eighth grade, I fucked a boy on the Schenley Park green," Zarabeth said. "But at night."

"A better use of open space than golf, I think." Magda sat. "You like the briefing?"

"I was surprised you kept succession planning."

"Expanding it, actually," Magda said. "Overall it's ugly. You can't sell to people with no money. And new governments are always idealistic. We worked this thing with the last bunch, deprive Islamists of heroin funding by promoting cocaine. Shows about rich pretty girls using it, not the mongrels who smuggle it. Cocaine drives border security funds and gooses bankers. Can't make money on the nod. This new crew comes in? Poof. But someone has to make leather for the vegetarians. We're hiring Arabic-speaking gay boys kicked out of the military. No one else can translate what the terrorists say. We step in, the Pentagon feels clean as baby Jesus, the little Lawrences fight the good fight, and even doubling military pay is less than overhead. Win-win."

She sneered. "I hate that phrase. It's not winning if no one loses."

"Those who hate gays lose. And nothing's really win-win. Thermodynamics."

Magda chuckled. "How optimistic of you. You look well. Your hair's much longer."

"It's a weed. If I colour it, I show roots the next day."

"Weed? This is a weed." Magda pulled strands out of her hairdo. "Enjoy being pretty and in rude health. It doesn't last. How's that silver top? I guessed the size."

"It's perfect. Would have worn it but it's too cold. Speaking of Rome," Zarabeth said, "a little thing got lost in the whole you-know. This math nerd had a seizure on stage. While we were waiting for the medics I showed him my video of the Mercurex network. He said it looked like an antigen. Perhaps Endre can make something out of it."

"You mean the protein? Did the nerd ask what it was?"

"He wasn't all there. Like, he was rebooting. I snuck in before the desktop."

"I love it!" Magda clapped her hands. "I so wish I grew up with computers. I think of people as people, machines as machines. It limits me."

"What's going to happen to the whole you-know?"

"I'm still looking into that."

"You haven't—" Zarabeth blushed. "You think they played me."

"I need to check. Her and pudge-boy getting us in a tizzy on their say-so would be clever. We still don't know if they missed your real assignment."

"What was my real assignment?"

"Money laundering. Work-for-hire. I'm being stupid. You're asking about your job. That's fine. This is your review. Ha. Do you like your job?"

"I do," Zarabeth said. "Not what I expected."

"I did offer to tell you more."

Zarabeth snorted. "You gave me a raise, a plane ticket, a demon, and a company wristband. Unseen. You arranged it in advance. You kept me on staff. We're even playing performance review. If you wanted dirty tricks off the books, you would have fired me and offered me anything. I would have taken it. You saw to that. You want me in. Why?"

"No one tells you this," Magda said, "but brio counts among the skilled. It's not enough to be good. You need flair and not in your cubicle. You found Rex with no help from me. Rome? I knew something was fishy there, but look what you unearthed."

"It's not hard to unearth when they point it out."

"They didn't point it out to anyone else," Magda said.

"So that's my job? Trouble magnet? To what end?"

"I'll tell you after dinner. Could you?"

Zarabeth heard nothing but went to open the door. A tall red-haired white girl with a wide freckled face stood there, hand raised to press the bell. She wheeled the trolley to Magda's chair.

Magda watched her set the plates with imperial serenity. "Do you play tennis, young lady?" She signed the bill. "Tennis players have nice rears. All that running backwards."

The server smiled shyly and left.

"You go for women?" Zarabeth asked, sitting down.

"That's two I envy you, asking so lightly," Magda said. "When I was your age even close friends would be delicate. Most of my lovers were male, out of necessity. I'd have rather munched rugs up the ladder. Now sex has gone the way of gin." She sipped her beer. "Perhaps I'm not so much a lesbian as a man-hater."

Zarabeth splashed soy sauce on the cool, tasteless stir-fry, stirred the mess with her fork. "I've worked with pillocks, but sure you had worse. Where did you start?"

"'Pillocks'? Aren't you cute in your Polyglot? My own Eliza Doolittle. I was a legal secretary. Lucky start. Every deal has a contract."

"I saw a picture of you from back then," Zarabeth said. "In an old annual report."

"I wasn't even in that department. The public relations man saw me walking out of the bathroom. I was a hot little number."

"You looked like a Bond girl."

"Aren't you sweet? Double-edged sword, of course, in the boy's-club days. At least I was a widow so they were polite about it."

"How long were you married?" Zarabeth asked.

"Two years. John kept house and made good drinks," Magda said. "We had a white marriage."

Zarabeth didn't know the term but guessed. "He was gay?"

"And discreet. I did not want to marry but in those days— we made an arrangement. Honeymoon in Ceylon, two apartments in Washington. I let him wander, he let me alone."

"How did he die?"

"Hit by a car, outside his lover's house. How the man wept at the funeral. I didn't wish John ill, but his death worked out well. Double estate, no kids. Better name."

"Would they were all so convenient," Zarabeth said.

Magda smiled impishly. "You're wicked."

"I'm learning." Zarabeth pushed away her plate. "I should have ordered coffee."

"There's a machine." Magda pointed to it. "Another pleasure lost to me. Please enjoy."

"I'll get water." In the loo she filled the carafe and also peed. Tired from travel, frustrated by chitchat. Wanting a fag was making her drink. Discipline.

When Zarabeth came out Magda pushed the trolley aside. "What are your career goals?"

Zarabeth started the coffee. "Under revision."

"You strike me as an ambitious thing. Do you want money, power, status?" Magda looked genuinely concerned. "What are you in it for?"

"Are you my guidance counselor now?" Zarabeth felt honesty inside her, a funny bone discomfort. "Wealth beats no wealth, I know better than you. I like clothes and toys. But money is like drugs. It skews your focus. Lose your edge, lose your toys."

"What about power?"

"These things you talk about, they're tools. I use tools. But they're not how I keep score. I want to understand. I want to get it. And, sure, a cut of it too. Is that what you got?" Zarabeth wanted to punch Magda in her hopped-up wrinkled face. She clenched her teeth and sat still.

Magda took a deep breath. "Thank you, dear. Your hatred is better than a tanning bed."

"Whatever the fuck that means, you're welcome." The coffee maker hissed and spat behind her. "Thank me with truth. I'm new, you're testing me. I feel nothing real is behind it. Like I'm a reality show snuff film, just for you."

"Ha." Magda chuckled. "That's funny. Forgive me. The reality is less paranoid."

"You want to run the company."

"Not bad. Given what you know."

"But wrong. What then?"

"What is our company's mission?" Magda asked. "Really. What are we about?"

"We solve problems," Zarabeth said. "Or make clients feel we solved their problems."

"Do we need to consort with dark powers to do that?"

"The woo-woo is just a tool."

Magda rubbed her chin. "I'll get back to that. What you just said, which is better? Solving the problem, or selling a bad solution?"

"Whichever makes us more money, I suppose."

"What if it costs the same?" Magda asked.

"You're asking me, is it better to fuck people over if you don't have to?" The bitter oily coffee tasted like a broth of hallucinogenic mushrooms. Zarabeth drank half the cup and licked her lips. "If we don't make our clients money, they'll leave."

"Someone should tell the finance industry," Magda said. "Of course I'm speaking in ideal terms, and the world is rarely ideal. Look at the Nazis. They could have gone and spread their word like John the Baptist, pulled out of the economy, ignored the Jews. But Hitler wanted big parades. Thousand-year Reichs don't get built in a decade. Should have done like Buddha. They'd still be here now."

"I didn't know you were a Buddhist," Zarabeth said.

"I am an edge. I cut through the puffed up and the weak. I don't want a thousand-year Reich. I don't want to run the world. I want to keep it spinning. I don't know if I will run the company, or destroy it. I don't care. The company has uses. It also has drawbacks. Remember our vegetarians? We can't always profit from shifts in their diet. All that heroin being made because of the cocaine we're not promoting? I'd like to invest in that heroin. I'd like to use it to destabilize not just parts of the world but the entire planet. One religious revolution in one oil-rich country has led to a quarter-century of global distrust. 9/11 was just four airplanes. There's also China, who fattened millions on the mere crumbs of our excellent greed, now turning its fat into muscle. The shit is inches from the fan. War's coming, or at least it'll be hard to avoid. I want to start it early, while I can still enjoy it and profit from it."

Were Zarabeth's eyes shining? It was incredible. Here in a shit hotel room in Scotland, an old twisted lady was selling her on starting a war, a world war, the kind that redrew borders. The old twisted lady who had already given her a pet demon.

"It sounds ambitious," Zarabeth said.

"Thank you. It's my moment, in a way. I have no heirs so let the fucker burn, I'll die regardless. Also, you know, it's our last chance mostly to kill men. With our population and the Asian gender imbalance, it's almost a public good to start it early. Not that I'm letting that stop me. Ha. Now, as I hinted, if the shareholders or even most executives knew I promoted this agenda, they'd be very disappointed."

"Jill didn't choose this hotel."

"Call it discipline. And a low likelihood of listening devices. Now. What do you want, Zarabeth Battrie?"

"I don't get to want, Magda. There are chances and I take them. You narrowed my chances. You're not widening them now."

"But if you could want? If you could go all the way out, back to a normal job and OK life and nothing else?" Magda raised her hands and arms as if they held this secret truth of the world entire. "Would you have this become just a story? If it ever could?"

Ambitious like Zarabeth never dreamed a thing could be. Big enough to see from space. The answer pulled from her, like breath by vacuum.

"No. I want in," Zarabeth said. "I always wanted in. I won't have any heirs either, Magda. I grew up swimming in chaos. If other people can't hack it, fuck 'em."

"Excellent."

Warmth, approval, camaraderie. Zarabeth took a deep breath.

"Tell me about Sasha Blackwell," she said.

Magda gritted her teeth. "Aren't you a clever spy? Sasha was my protégé. I picked her on instinct and she was fantastic. I liked grooming her. It's fun to pass on knowledge. You already know a lot of what I taught her."

"What happened to her?"

"She quit. Quit the company. Her mother died, and afterwards—she could no longer support my work, she said. Now she directs an inner-city child development center."

"You let her live?" Zarabeth asked.

"I mentioned those drawbacks," Magda said. "Everyone worries about unwelcome attention. I keep an eye out, awaiting an excuse. So far she's remained—small. Still amazes me. Sasha could teach you about ruthless." Magda shook her head. "Now, good night. I'm back next week. Have Jill set up a visit, meet the team. No rush. Take a few days off. Here, if you like."

"Not here, thanks. Maybe Glasgow."

"Lovely gardens. Not up on the nightlife, but you'll scare up something." She patted Zarabeth's knee. "I won't get up. Take my advice. Don't get old."

"I'm surprised you have."

"Ha. Once in a while, as my body fails, I get the urge to call Janice Goldman. But it's expensive, and it's not what you think. I'm taking out my frustrations a different way."

"How old is Janice?"

"Not so old you still can't shoot her in the face."

"Ha. Good luck with your meetings." Zarabeth stood.

"Thank you, dear. Could you take the dishes out?"

"Sure. Wait." She offered Magda her hand.

Magda pursed her lips, raised her own hand. They touched, slid together. Magda's skin oily and papery, like the parchment Zarabeth burned to release the demon. An old hand, bony, not frail but not strong. A faint shake.

"Thank you," Zarabeth said.

Magda smiled, and for a moment—Zarabeth's hand felt hot. Hotter. Really fucking hot. Zarabeth drew back.

"Good night," Magda said, still smiling, looking down.

Zarabeth wheeled out the trolley. An impish thought, to park it in front of Magda's door and lock the wheels. She felt her hot hand and let it be.

* * *

In her room she poured minibar vodka with a shaking hand. *Surveillance ensures it stays that way.* The company would kill them all.

Even if she went to management, no one trusted a traitor.

Dead-end or just dead. Her best option, do what Magda wanted, and look out for herself.

Outside, hard steady rain. Not a night to wander nor to drink alone. She put on a white singlet and the pinstripe blazer, rode the lift to the hotel's pub. Brass rails, dark wood, patterned blue carpet, plump armchairs. The tables full of elderly tourists wearing name tags. She sat at the bar.

Her only fellow patron was a slim white man, less pale than the locals, his dark thick hair in stylish spikes. He wore a neat, nightclubbing look, black suit and a shiny emerald-green shirt. In front of him were four small glasses of amber liquor and a miniature water pitcher. He picked up a glass, smelled it, added drops of water, smelled it again, sipped it. Eyes closed.

"What are you doing?" she asked.

He smiled shyly. "I'm tasting Scotch," he said in American. "Water releases the aroma."

"Then you drink it?"

He opened his eyes. "I just taste them. I'm not a drinker."

"Four shots just to taste them? That's extravagant."

He smiled brightly with good straight teeth. "You want one? Only slightly used."

"Can't do Scotch, thanks." Her skin flush with agreeable warmth, steam after Magda's scorching. "Can you smoke here?"

"I don't think so." His face disapproving. The one non-smoker in Scotland, of course.

"Not a big deal." Two weeks since she'd had sex, a lame drunken train with a tranny and a murderous queer. She wanted a guy, a real guy, grunting missionary zeal.

His eyes were blue-grey and oddly deep. "My name's Gabriel," he said.

"Zarabeth. Hi." She felt acceleration, like falling out of a plane. "So, where's the bartender?"

CHAPTER TWELVE

Aberdeen

Gosh she was pretty.

"He comes and goes," Gabriel said. "He helps in the kitchen." Her face was a tangram of sharp ellipses: pointed chin, long nose, tall forehead, wide mouth. He smelled cucumber from the hotel soap, lemongrass shampoo, old smoke. "Shame about the weather."

"Yep." The bartender returned. In glasses and a grey mustache, he looked like a squirrel. "White rum?" Zarabeth asked. "Diet cola. Stiff, please. With a lime."

"On my tab, please," Gabriel told the bartender.

"Thank you, Gabriel." She slid off her barstool gingerly, walked around him and took the stool to his right, at the end of the bar. Her scent rust and clay, dry dust of dead leaves. "My first night, here and in Scotland. You?"

"First day here," he said. "A week in Scotland." His face a stiff idiot grin. The bartender brought her drink. He raised a toffee-nosed Highland. "Cheers."

"Cheers." She sipped, wrinkled her nose. "The limes please?"

The bartender put dry lemon wedges in a glass and went back to the kitchen.

"I hate this hotel," she said.

"They must have shills on travel sites. Business?"

"Does it show?"

"You're not with a bus tour. But, you're not wearing navy. You should have seen lunchtime. Like a flight-attendants' convention."

"I saw those banners. Cameras are good for you. Strange." She stirred her drink with her finger.

"So, what business?"

"I've been on the road for three weeks, Gabriel, and I am sick of work. Let's talk about anything else. Why are *you* here?"

Gabriel smiled. "Good touring in the area. Castles, towns, country driving, whisky distilleries."

"You're full-bore on the Scotch thing."

"New hobby. You know how that goes." He had drunk the whole glass. He could handle that.

"Not much for hobbies," Zarabeth said. "Why does no one have limes? They call them 'limeys,' right?"

"The English, yeah. From their sailors."

"What do limes have to do with sailors?"

"Scurvy. Early sailing ships took flour and dried meat. No Vitamin C. No collagen. Their cells fell apart."

"So they started eating limes?"

"They started eating onions," Gabriel said. "Once they could trade with tropical colonies they got citrus fruits. British colonies grew limes. Thing is, limes don't have much vitamin C, which meant they ate a lot of limes. So the real reason the British are called limeys is because their defence contractors ripped them off."

"That's funny." Her smile stillborn. Her scent changed too, now as bitter as his drink. She snorted hard through her nose. "You're a happy man, aren't you?" she said, threat in her voice. "I bet you had a nice Christmas."

After Russia, a drinker's anger hardly fazed Gabriel. "Since you ask," he said, "a drunk driver killed my brother last fall. No tree, no gifts, Chinese food. My mom and sister got drunk, felt guilty, yelled at me for not drinking while I drove them home. Christmas sucked." He felt lottery-rich, leaden memory now gold. "Bartender!"

The bartender started. "Sir? Yes?"

"She buys her own drinks."

"I'll have another," she said. "And his next one's on me if he gets there." She took his shot of Islay, drank it down, held back a gag. "Fuck me, that's foul."

"You're trouble, aren't you?" he said.

"It's a hobby. You know how that goes. Tell me about Scotland."

* * *

"Which has better nightlife?" Zarabeth asked. "Glasgow or Edinburgh?"

"I know several tasting clubs in both cities."

"You just sat in bars all week smelling?"

"No bars. Private functions in plush homes or hotels. This liquor rep hooked me up with one group in Edinburgh. A guy I met there took me to another on Tuesday. Someone there knew a group in Glasgow. And so on. First night I haven't spent with middle-aged businesspeople."

"If I'm keeping you," Zarabeth teased.

"I liked it, though. I met executives, bankers, restaurateurs, an oil broker. Back home my friends are getting ready for Burning Man. Here I'm a networking god."

"No Scotch tasting in—where are you from?"

"San Francisco. Maybe. You do things on vacation and you think, why not at home?"

"Then you never do," Zarabeth said. "Odd hobby for a guy who doesn't drink."

"I have a new nose," he said.

She played at inspecting his face. "You chose this one?"

"Ha. New on the inside. For years I repressed my sense of smell. Psychologically. I didn't want to smell. Turns out I have a great sense of smell."

"You look normal, Gabriel, but you say bizarre shit. What can you smell?"

"You last showered about four hours ago. You used the hotel's soap but your own shampoo. You haven't smoked since then. You drank wine and sodas. Pasta, and coffee." He picked up one of his glasses and inhaled. "You smoked hashish this morning."

"You should go on TV with that. So the Scotch?"

"It's a workout for my nose. Training," Gabriel said. "Like babies do. Like people with hearing aids learn signal from noise. I'm trying to separate smell and reaction. I don't want to gag all the time. Probably why I repressed it. I have to make bad smells into data, like the word 'stink.' Does that make sense? I'm not good with words." His sad grin was like a needle in her heart. A sweet sympathy, alien to her, easier with rum. He was beautiful. "I like your smell. Your body smell."

She blushed hotly. He smiled through it, his nostrils flaring. She felt naked in a glass box. She wanted to touch his hand but she was afraid it would spark.

* * *

The bus-tour party annexed the bar. Gabriel and Zarabeth fled to old squeaky chairs in the back. Still drinking, slowly.

"Have you looked at the money?" she asked. She took twenty-pound notes from her wallet. "Look. All different designs. How do they keep from being counterfeited? How do vending machines accept all three?" She saw his look. "What did I say?"

"Nothing. Just, I miss math. I was—sorry. Not to trigger your work rule."

"It's not a rule. So you want to do math?"

"What I want? You'd laugh."

Her scent flared like baking oysters. "I wouldn't," she said, her insincerity sexy.

"Fine. I'd be a commercial product designer."

"Not what I was expecting," she said.

"Sorry, Money Math Lady. When you need a self-stick light, don't come crying to me."

She laughed. "OK. Design me a product."

"Wait." He went to the bar for a napkin. When he came back he wrote *Non-Disclosure Agreement* on it, passed it across the table with his pen. "Sign it." She scribbled a wiggly line. He put the napkin in his pocket. "How often do you wash your underwear?"

"You tell me, smell-boy."

"No, it's my pitch." He cleared his throat. "How often do you wash your underwear? You don't drag your underwear on the street. How often do you wash your shirt? It doesn't touch bathroom floors. You need—The Shoewasher. Load your dirty sweaty shoes in at night, fresh and clean the next morning. Canvas, leather—whatever!"

"I can't believe I lived this long without one."

"You see why I needed the NDA. Of course there'd be special soaps. You're not going to wash thousand-dollar pumps with drugstore detergent. Markings on shoe labels, licensed from the Shoewasher Commerce Consortium. Commercial versions for shoe stores."

"You mean," she said, with mock horror, "before I tried on these shoes, someone else put her foot in them?"

"Disgusting, isn't it? No longer. It will be as transformative as the polio vaccine."

"With a higher profit margin," Zarabeth said. "Why isn't this your real job?"

"Because I like math." Happiest he'd been in weeks.

* * *

At ten-thirty the bartender loudly called Last Orders. Zarabeth and Gabriel were the only customers left. Her hips danced in the chair.

"How long you here for?" he asked coolly.

She shrugged. "Last minute trip. No return ticket yet. Maybe I'll try Glasgow like you said. Book something tomorrow."

"I know you're not big on whisky, but I'm doing a distillery tour. Want to come? Should be a good day for a drive. It'd be the whole day, back here by five."

"Yeah," Zarabeth said. "Absolutely. Sounds great."

"Good. So, eight-thirty breakfast? We'll go at nine."

"Breakfast—" He was treating her like a nice girl. No sex tonight. Crestfallen, and maybe smarter. "Sure," she said. "Eight-thirty. What's the dress code?"

"My car is hot. So look cool. If you oversleep, I'm in 312, but just call my cell." He took out a business card, wrote his numbers on the back. "What's your last name?"

"Battrie." She tucked the card in a front pocket.

"Gabriel Archer." He stood, kissed her hand. "Zarabeth Battrie, see you tomorrow."

At the bar he signed the check the bartender had left. The idiot. Beautiful smile. Hot slender ass. Just as well. Tipsy and tired. Fuck twice tomorrow. Fuck in hot car.

She signed her own bill, wobbled to the lift, set her phone alarm while she waited. Maybe he would reconsider and ride back down. The lift opened, filthy and empty.

In her room she tangled herself in her jacket, ripping the lining. In the loo she forced down water, paracetamol, water, fought open the hotel mouthwash. She stumbled to bed. A thought to wear the jacket again. She shook wrinkles out, draped it on a chair.

Gabriel's card on the floor, face up. An Empyrean logo.

She found the loo in time to vomit. She felt him in the room, claw fingers reaching for her neck. She peed her knickers and retched again.

CHAPTER THIRTEEN

Aberdeen

At eight-thirty the food seemed fine but by eight-fifty the bacon was greasy soot, the eggs too runny for a fork.

At nine she called. "You haven't left, I hope?"

"No, no." All better. "Just finishing breakfast."

"Still love to join you. Bit behind this morning." She sounded oddly fancy. "Can we say nine-thirty? Is that all right?"

"Fine. Should I order you something?"

"Just grab me a roll, a fresh apple."

He moved his car out of the wet garage onto the street. The engine's growl echoed from the stone buildings. The sky bright enough for sunglasses. He was in a fine mood now.

He waited in the lobby. Eventually she appeared, in blazer and black skirt, a red kerchief around her neck.

"Hi." He kissed her cheek. "You look great. Car's outside with your breakfast."

She rolled her eyes. "I slept like shit. Smoked three cigarettes. Sorry. They have coffee?"

"Only small cups to go. But I need petrol, as they say. Coffee can't be any worse."

"I'll take it intravenous," she said.

When she saw the car she squeezed his arm, her eyes alight behind her sunglasses. Even through her smoke, he caught her oyster smell in the cool humid air. Inside the car, she leaned close. "I would have fucked you last night. I'm glad we waited."

He shifted in his seat. "Buckle up."

Wet streets and sidewalks, the only sign of last night's storm. The creepy banners spanned the street at each block. At their first stoplight she saw a harbor, small commercial boats and a large cruise ship. "People cruise here?" she asked.

"Dolphin tours. I'll lend you my guidebook." He put on a dreamy album of guitars and calliope he'd bought in Glasgow. The many circles made for slow driving despite the light traffic. Zarabeth whittled the apple with her front teeth. Hard to keep his bored eyes on the road.

Outside town he pulled into a large green service station. He thought of his last morning in Colorado Springs, believing the awful truth of his senses. He just managed to stop at the pump.

"Are you OK?" Zarabeth smiled warily. "I feel energies. New age-y stuff." She said it naturally. "Yours went weird. Problem?"

"Last time I was in a big gas station," he said. "Work thing. Bad time." He envied her comfort with strangeness. A feminine privilege, like crying openly. "You want coffee?"

"We'll go together. I like watching hot men pump gas."

In the station's bright store he bought coffees, an energy bar for himself. They stood outside the car, facing each other across the hood, as if to duel.

"If your sense of smell's so good how can you eat that crap?" she asked.

"Look who's a health nut," he said. "When I couldn't smell my pleasure was texture. Puffed rice, popcorn, anything that fights then collapses."

"Ooh. I'll remember that. Is driving on the left weird?"

"You get used to it. And, no."

"No?"

"Maybe. If you're good."

"Maybe means yes. It's fun to be up front at least. Ready?"

They drove past fields and farmhouses, through small towns of haphazard wood and stone buildings. A luminous blue sky, high threadbare clouds. He was glad not to rush.

"It's like Pennsylvania," Zarabeth said. "My dad took me to

the mountains camping. We'd drive through towns like this." She frowned. "Where are you from?"

"I grew up in Madison, but I've been in San Francisco for a decade now. It feels more like home than home did. Especially now that I'm back."

"Back?"

"I spent last year working in Russia. Before my brother died."

"Security in Russia? That must have been scary."

"I did expansion logistics then. I thought we weren't talking shop?"

"Fine. Don't tell me." She settled back in her seat and purred. "Just drive."

* * *

Stalks of pink flowers lined the walkway to the first distillery. "Is that heather?" Zarabeth took a picture with her phone. Missy could tell her. She posed Gabriel in front of a pair of squared towers, wide and fat like big breasts sleeping. "Is it a pagoda?"

"The malt kilns," he said. "The shape is meant to circulate the smoke. I don't quite know. There's a lot of woo-woo about whisky making."

The phrase caught her short. Last night on all fours vomiting, from his nasty card. "'Woo-woo' is my word."

"It's the only word. Mix barley flour in water. Add yeast. Yeast eats sugar and pees alcohol. Boil the mix and condense the vapor—distillation—which concentrates the alcohol. Twice more, you get liquor."

"Not so hard."

"Not so good. So you add woo-woo. The barley has to be dried in peat smoke. The water comes from only one river. Only the middle part of the second distillation gets put into barrels of old oak. Then you charge a hundred dollars a bottle."

"That's woo-woo right there," Zarabeth said. "What's peat?"

"Dried swamp mud."

"For fuck's sake. No wonder Scotch tastes so bad."

The visitor's center looked like a hunting lodge, antique

Anthony Dobranski

furniture around a fireplace. The wan hostess smiled at them. "Aren't you a bonny pair? Tour, self-guided. When you come back you can have a taste."

They followed the signs. Glimpses of other visitors ahead and behind, but alone.

The drying room smelled of smoke and wet earth. He inhaled grandly.

"You like the smell?" she asked.

"It's familiar," he said. "Part of the process."

Around the vats, a meaner smell, old shoes and beery piss. "You like this too?"

"Wouldn't want to bathe in it," he said. "But I know what it's for, yeah."

"It's amazing they invented all this just to get drunk."

"No limes, remember? Mud and grain was all they had."

"They had potatoes," she said.

"That was Ireland, and they used them for food."

The massive copper stills sat plump and gleaming, long craning necks like idols of swan-gods. Tubes and pipes around them, a glass window to show the bubbling distillate. Heat and hiss and metal. Church of the happy nerd past, of Vulcan not Mercury, atoms not bits. In his smile, the same wonder. That never happened. She liked it.

By the fire, they tasted raw whiskies, poured from plain bottles with inkjet labels. Awful but a buzz. Gabriel loosened up. He talked about smells, chocolate and pecan and ginger, like an old-fashioned candy. Zarabeth drew her finger along the back of his hand, following his straight bones and taut veins.

He gave her the keys. Only three miles on slow straight roads, the wheel hard to turn at low speeds. Fun like a child in a parked car. He looked too pleased with himself.

The second distillery's parking lot was as large as the first distillery's grounds, with painted spaces for tour buses. They walked through trees, across a green bridge, into a glassed-in gift shop with a bright green ticket desk.

"The wonderful whisky of Oz," she said. "Is this more popular?"

"I've never heard of this brand," he said. "I figured it would be more authentic."

They sat in a replica Victorian parlor stuffed with bric-a-brac and animal heads. In a projected movie a mustached actor played the founder's ghost, extolling his manly virtue and the hunts that popularized his whisky.

They got their taste after the movie, in plastic cups. Lemon-yellow, no odor but sharp herbs in the mouth. "I almost like it," she said.

"Take mine."

A short towheaded man guided them along an elevated steel catwalk over the grey distillery floor. She was playful, riding him piggyback down the long steep stairs to the loading station. They ended in the barrel house, walking single file along rows of brown casks.

"No matter how carefully we control the light and air," the guide said, "wood is porous and a small amount evaporates. We call this the angels' share. I suppose we owe them that for watching over the rest." He led them out of the barrel house, abandoned them unceremoniously behind the distillery.

"I like the 'angels' share,'" Zarabeth said. She took Gabriel's hand, led him back to the gift shop. "Maybe Heaven is a protection racket. The vig goes up, then Don Jehovah answers prayers from the living with it. Just a few prayers."

He laughed. "I had a talk like this in Colorado Springs too." They were on the bridge now. He stopped. "Do you believe in life after death?"

"Nah. I just can't see it. Recycle my parts, sure, but the operations of my big grey chip? What deity would care? You?"

"I don't know. I hope not. I'd hate to think all this was just me taking a test."

"It doesn't matter," she said. "You just play as hard as you can. See what happens."

He caught her arm, kissed her softly. She kissed back, bit his tentative tongue. But they were in public. She floated backwards, until only his fingertips held hers.

"Lunch," Gabriel said. "Place called Craigellachie."

"Now that sounds authentic," Zarabeth said.

He drove, fine by bothered and ditzy Zarabeth. New green fields, low stone walls. Pull over and fuck now, without him learning where she worked. If he didn't know. Scary if he did.

The hotel had tall white walls like a doll castle. Luxury coupes and sedans in the parking lot. Gabriel looked them over, satisfied. He offered his arm and led her inside. In the pale green lounge, thousands of whisky bottles stood floor to ceiling on wide wood shelves. Gabriel wandered in a daze.

"Get that, we do," the barwoman told Zarabeth. She was middle-aged and plump, red hair, red nose, gap teeth.

"Great picture for a jigsaw puzzle," Zarabeth said.

"Oh, aye?" The barwoman looked with a fresh eye. "Would at that. Have to mention. Sit anywhere, I'll come out."

They were late for lunch, the few tables already finished. They sat on heavy stuffed chairs by a window overlooking green trees and silver river. On each table sat a binder of tasting notes. Pages of small print, terms like *estery* and *phenolic*.

Gabriel joined her. "They have bottles as old as my parents." He pointed over her head. "There's a whole series of whiskies as they were made in different decades, going back a hundred years. I didn't realize the flavors changed."

She turned the binder toward him. "Drunk many Scotches that taste like sweaty socks?"

"More than one, yeah. Oh, they use boxes for numbers," he said with joke snobbery. "My first night in Glasgow we marked points on a five-axis graph." He pulled out his phone, flicked to an image. "This was a 12-year Islay." Strange little spider, ten legs and a blob for a body.

"Socks?"

"Fresh street tar, burned hair. With water, rotten banana." He leaned back, chuckling. "It's not about tasting *good*. That's like saying music can only be mellow lounge tracks, or movies can only be romantic comedies. There's also punk and gangsta rap, slasher films and art-house movies. That's what Scotch whisky is like. Socks and tar."

"So I can smoke?" she asked.

"Honestly, it's not the tobacco, it's the paper and chemical crap. Have you tried cigars? Better with your scent. A mild corona, some nice feinty malt to pour on your—hello."

The barwoman had come up quietly. Zarabeth wondered if he had smelled her. They both ordered trout spinach salads, Zarabeth her usual cocktail. "There's this Orkney you might try," the barwoman told Gabriel. "Mahogany, smooth and sweet in the mouth. Eighteen-year reserve."

"Is that spendy?" Zarabeth asked.

"Aye," the barwoman said.

"He'll have it." Zarabeth looked over their fellow patrons. Older couples in fine-weave clothing, heavy gold watches and sparkly earrings.

An ugly croak in her head: *your best dressed day a funeral.*

"Are you OK?" Gabriel asked abruptly.

"Sure," she said. "Why?"

"Just checking."

Zarabeth's feet touched ground. Gabriel Liar. He had his own woo-woo. Logistics in Russia, like hell. Maybe she really had stumbled across him. She bit her tongue through the usual whisky production. For once she wanted less time to think.

Gabriel was unimpressed. He ordered a different one.

While their salads came, two women and a man took the next table. The man had a burly build, brown hair cut by drunks, but a tailored dark suit. Dark brunette in a black stretch bodysuit, pale white blonde in candy-red leather. They spoke what sounded like Russian, the man's voice low and hoarse, the women piping like scalded parrots.

Sounded like Russian, Empyrean woo-woo. Enough to scare away her Polyglot. After Rome it had learned new tricks.

She kept the hardest smiling face of her young life. "Are they speaking Russian?"

"Yes." Gabriel's nose twitched. "I think he's an oligarch. Business tycoon."

Gabriel lied. The burly man looked like a mobster. Good girls didn't know such things. His hidden unease pricked her skin. He was talking about more distilleries. A cooperage.

"Where they make barrels," he said.

"I thought they used old bourbon barrels."

"They have to rebuild them from the used wood. Guidebook says it's worth a look."

"Right." The barwoman brought Gabriel's new drink on her way to the Russians. "Cheers," Zarabeth said. "What's that one?"

"Twelve-year Islay. Nothing fancy. Just to clear the palate." He sipped, drew back as if it burned him. "My." He closed his eyes, his nose and mouth quivering.

"Put hair on your chest?" Zarabeth asked.

"On my tongue." He took a notebook from his jacket pocket. "Give me a second."

The Russian man was talking with the barwoman. "Which is better, dark or light?"

"Oh, Gabriel," Zarabeth said, loud. "Can't you help him? You're such an expert."

Gabriel gave her a hard look. Zarabeth smiled with innocent admiration.

"You are expert?" His nutcracker hand on Gabriel's chair. "Dark whisky is better?"

"Not always," Gabriel told the man, speaking slowly. "In sherry barrels, it gets color."

"Sherry?"

Gabriel licked his lips and said it in Russian.

A joyous outpouring of Russian from the man. In a blink, they were five at a table, clockwise Gabriel, Misha, brunette Vika, blonde Katya, her. Gabriel kissed the women's hands across the table. Better than the barrel factory.

"You no speak Russian?" Katya asked Zarabeth. "Vika has no English. I translate."

"Thank you." Zarabeth and Vika shared smiles of hatred for Katya.

"Your man says dark Scotch is not better?" Katya said.

Zarabeth shrugged. "That's what he says. I don't know."

"I don't like the Scotch."

"I try your whisky?" Misha said in English. He drank the glass down, exhaled as if air were vomit. "Skinny man drink strong."

The women tittered. Misha kept talking to Gabriel.

"Gavril is good looking," Katya said to Zarabeth. "How long together?"

"Our first trip."

Katya translated for Vika. "Scotland, you like?"

"He likes."

The barwoman came. "Two more of these," Misha said.

She smiled. "As you like sir. They're a bit spendy."

"What is 'spendy'?"

"Expensive," Zarabeth said.

"Of course they are. He is expert! Two more. No. Four."

"No," Gabriel said. "Two. Then something else." He waved at the bottles. "Here, drink no drink twice." He repeated himself in Russian.

"Razumyeetsya," Vika said.

"Very wise," Misha agreed. "OK. Two more."

"Tri," Vika said, holding up three fingers.

"What you have?" Katya asked Zarabeth.

"White rum, diet cola, with lime. Another."

"Me also rum diet cola lime."

Gabriel and Vika were talking. To Zarabeth he said, "I said my mom teaches Russian."

"Your father?" Misha asked.

"He was in the Navy." Gabriel began translating everything he said.

"Sailor. Why you drink strong." Misha was shouting. "Where drinks?"

"Just coming, sir," the barwoman called.

"Is not so hard," Misha said. "Pour from bottle."

The barwoman came out muttering, placed the glasses down hard enough to drive nails. Vika and Katya enjoyed her act. Zarabeth warmed to them, a bitter cunt aperitif to her nice day.

"Very good," Misha said. "We drink."

Gabriel put up his hand. "Podozhdite!" He exhaled, smelled the whisky.

The Russians watched with amusement, as if he were about

to balance the glass on his nose. Gabriel took a small sip, added water to the whisky, closed his eyes and sniffed again.

"You put water in spendy whisky?" Misha said in a violated tone.

"We thought is for flowers," Katya said.

"Whisky is complex," Gabriel said. "Like a poem. Water brings out flavors the alcohol hides." Vika's expression rapt even before the translation, Gabriel's nerdy song waking flesh from Misha's doll spell.

Misha grabbed the pitcher as if to crush it, sloshed water into his drink, then Vika's. "OK. Bud'te zdorovy!" He drank it in one go. Katya downed her cocktail. Vika mimicked Gabriel's style. Zarabeth imagined shoving Vika's face in a toilet.

"Where else have you been in Scotland?" Zarabeth asked.

"Aberdeen," Katya said. "Misha has business."

"Aberdeen," Vika hissed.

Zarabeth laughed. "I agree completely. Where are you staying?"

"On Misha's boat. Vika can't sleep on the boat."

"Tell her it's better than the hotels."

"We want to go to London," Katya said.

Zarabeth talked about Soho boutiques, inventing what she couldn't remember in the pauses while Katya translated. Katya stroked Zarabeth's jacket as if it were a cat.

Misha pounded his fist on the table. The women flashed looks of deep worry.

Gabriel stood, forced cheer. "I'll order something good. You're a man for an Islay malt."

"Aiylamalt?" Misha asked. "Sounds like terrorist group."

"Tastes like one too."

"You pick for Vika," Katya said. "More cocktail me."

"More cocktail me too," Zarabeth said. She grabbed Gabriel's hand, kissed him. Whisky and unease made him tasty.

Vika was talking with Misha. Katya asked more about London stores. Gabriel conferred with the barwoman, pointing at bottles.

"He is nice," Katya said. "You sure he is not married?"

"I hired detectives."

"Smart. Is good then. You are still pretty. A good match."

"Yes," Misha said, listening now. "Very pretty."

"Thank you." She glanced at the bar. Gabriel was gone. She drank the last of her drink to stall Misha's inevitable proposition. "You are a good judge of female beauty."

Misha beamed. "Thank you, Sharabet." He ran his hand down Vika's arm. "She says I know beautiful women."

"Are you married?" Zarabeth asked Katya.

"Widow," Katya said. "Vika is married."

"To Misha?"

Katya laughed. "Not to Misha."

Vika understood. "Tell her my husband's in prison but I hope he's in Hell."

Zarabeth laughed.

Vika drew back. "You understood me." She waved her finger. "She speaks Russian."

Fucking Polyglot. "I learn from Gabriel." It came out in Russian.

"Why you not say this?" Katya said in English.

Zarabeth fought with the Polyglot. "I student only tiny Russian."

Katya let out a mean laugh, caught it with her hand.

"Good tiny Russian," Misha said. "Better accent. Your family is Russian?"

"My father was—" she achieved English. "Hungarian."

"Vengr," Katya translated.

"That explains it," Vika said. "If you can speak Hungarian, Russian will be easy for you. Let us only speak Russian now. You'll learn quickly."

"Absolutely," Misha said. "We drink vodka too. I don't like this whisky, I have to say."

"Tell Misha about the shopping in London," Katya said. "She got this jacket there."

"Gabriel!" Misha shouted. "We teach your wife Russian!"

Gabriel carried a tray of glasses. He stopped. In his face, dread, disgust, pain. He swooned. Whisky and cocktails spilled from the tray, raining on his collapsed body.

"Gabriel!" Zarabeth bolted to him. In her bad knee, the sting of a glass shard. She pulled it out. Gabriel coughed and spluttered like a drowning man. She held his head in her lap, smoothed his hair. He shuddered again and passed out cold.

The Russians stood over them, staring.

"It's a seizure," Zarabeth said. "Epilepsy? Petit mal? He'll be all right in a minute."

"Don't you—spoon—put spoon in tongue?" Katya said.

"We should get the manager," Vika said.

"Can you get my bag?" Zarabeth asked. "I have medicine."

Zarabeth pushed an antacid out of its foil sheet, slid it under his tongue.

The barwoman came to clean up. "Get you something, lass?" she asked.

"He'll be all right," Zarabeth said. "I think."

They backed away like from plague. Misha clapped his hands. "OK. Time for us to go."

"Goodbye," Katya said. "Yes. Goodbye!"

"Such a handsome man," Vika said. "It's a pity."

Zarabeth stroked his hair. She felt embarrassed to be so nurturing but couldn't stop.

Gabriel took a sharp breath and sat up. He coughed hard. The antacid fell out on his pants. He looked at it dully.

The barwoman came back for the tray. "Sorry about this," Zarabeth said. "Can we pay—"

The barwoman waved indulgently. "It's fine, lass," she said. "I put it all on their bill."

* * *

He woke in the car, in the passenger seat. They were parked at this morning's gas station. Zarabeth slouched in the driver's seat, drinking burned coffee, fake flavor fake cream.

"I got you water." She gave him a bottle. "I can get you a coffee if you like."

He drank half the water. "Did I throw up?"

"You don't remember? I got you to the car. You said to follow the breadcrumbs and then you passed out. You were delirious. Figured out you meant the nav system."

"What was that, in the bar?"

"My Polyglot. It translates for me. It doesn't like you. It came back when you left the room. If the Russians hadn't been there— I'm sorry."

"You're possessed?" He winced. "You work for Straightforward. The no-work rule—"

"I didn't want to talk work," she snapped. "We were speaking English. I just wanted to fuck you. I didn't know until you gave me your business card." She frowned. "I had to be sure—" Her scent grew strong, stinging like pepper flakes. "I'm going to have a goddamn cigarette thank you very much." She got out, slammed the door.

He wanted her even now. He took deep breaths of the car's smells. Curdled cream leather. Plastic floor mats. A crumb of apple. Glass polish. Gasoline. Diet and cola in her sweat.

She got back in, stinking of paper and burned filter. "Should I open a window?"

"No." He breathed through his mouth.

"You want to drive?"

"Not yet."

"Fine." She drove. He drank water in slow sips. The glare bothered him so he stared at the dashboard. They didn't speak. It was almost comfortable.

At the outskirts of the city the breadcrumbs ran out, but she remembered the way to the hotel. She pulled by the entrance. "I'll park it if you want," she said.

"I'll take it from here."

"Thanks for my day. Are you OK?" she asked.

"No. Goodbye."

She pursed her lips, her face dark with insult. She walked out leaving the door open. He watched her slender body jog up the steps, shoulders high.

He wanted her, as much wanting as he had.

Chapter Fourteen

Aberdeen

At sunset she walked the high street. Shoppers, idlers, no navy suits. On a side street, gangly young people stood smoking around a neon beer sign. The small dark pub had a short ceiling with exposed ducts, lit by small bulbs around the old bar mirror. An old telly showed a grainy subtitled film. Young people at the benches and the bar, dark ratty clothes with gleaming belts and buckles. She had a shandy. She spun her cigarette pack on the bar, again, again.

A bottle-blond boy tapped her shoulder. "When you go out, can I bum one?" Without the Polyglot she would have missed the Italian behind his New York Queens English.

The woman with him was small-boned, big doll eyes, greasy hair. "Me too?"

Zarabeth finished her glass. "Let's go now."

Outside they stood close as if to share warmth. Abramo and Katy. "Thanks," Abramo said. "Cigs are expensive here."

They had been traveling a few weeks, Scandinavia, Holland, northern France. "Looking for a place to settle," Katy said. "Abramo can work in Europe."

"What work are you looking for?" Zarabeth asked.

Abramo's face shut like a visor. "Checking things out. Katy's good with clothes. You?"

"Work," Zarabeth said. "Shipping firm."

In the pub she bought them a round. They had dated since high school, Katy said, but Abramo was at least five years older. Liars and lies. Zarabeth found it entertaining.

"Do you guys have weed?" Zarabeth asked. "I'll buy you cigarettes for a joint."

"We have hash," Abramo said.

"That'll do."

From the corner shop, where Abramo picked an unfiltered French brand, they walked four blocks to an old flophouse with new plaster around the door. Narrow dingy stairs, doors scuffed by boot treads. Their room a bed, a table, a kitchenette, clothes piled on the one metal chair. Zarabeth sat with Katy on the bed. Abramo sat on the floor by a pile of old paperbacks.

"Abramo," Zarabeth asked. "What kind of name is that?"

"Italian," he said. "I'm Italian."

"I love his name," Katy said. "Love love love it." Katy was insistently sunny like a stupid child, as if happiness could find this crappy stained room.

"That's why we're here," Abramo said. "I can work all over Europe." From the kitchenette he brought a plastic bubbler and a pastilles tin with a fudge-brown cake of hashish. He worked a piece into a thin tube, pinched small bits into the bowl. "My own technique," he told her proudly. "It burns easier." Abramo liked being in charge.

She followed their example, short drag then pass. The bubbler went around three times, ending at Zarabeth. The hash hit them fast.

Katy stood up, shook through it. It became a dance. "Do you have music?" Katy asked.

Zarabeth shook her head. Katy danced anyway.

"Do you believe in mental powers?" Abramo asked. He batted through the pile of books, handed Zarabeth a worn paperback. On the lurid red cover, a shaven headed man, monks sacrificing a leggy woman, daggers with curved blades. "This is by a former Tibetan monk who escaped to teach the secrets of mind over matter."

"I've seen these books," Zarabeth said. "Friends of mine read them." Or used the books as coasters. Her first year away from home, hand-to-mouth in rooms like this, almost raped by guys like this. She felt dragged down. If she stayed here she'd start over. She stood up, arched her back. "Have you ever tried it? Mind control?"

Abramo flashed an uneasy smile. "My mom had motivational tapes when I was a kid. Neuro-something? Like hypnosis."

Katy plopped on the bed. Abramo sat next to her. He pressed his palms on the small of her back, glided up to her neck, repeat. Katy closed her eyes as if to sleep.

"You have anything to drink?" Zarabeth asked.

"Water. There's a clean glass by the sink."

Katy hit him. "There's whisky if you want."

"I didn't know—" Abramo said. "We were saving—"

"It's OK," Zarabeth said. "Water." She walked the few feet of floor as if it were thin ice. The water tasted rusty. She drank two glassfuls.

Abramo massaged Katy's neck. Katy's eyes open and unfocused, her mouth a plump smile. Chipper even when unconscious. Abramo's arms like mandibles. He was Katy's pet tick.

Zarabeth's mouth full of saliva. "Toilet! Where?"

"Hallway!" Abramo shouted. "Left, left."

She ran down the hall to a filthy sink. Red-brown liquid, sharp painful heaves, as if she had swallowed a knife. She rinsed her mouth with metal water, inventoried herself. All here. Go.

Abramo at the flimsy door. "Hey, Beth, you OK?"

She bolted out, forcing him back. "I'm sorry," she said. "I feel awful. I should go."

"You can crash here, it's cool—"

"It's not." If he overpowered her. "Bye now. Have great lives. Take these." She threw her own cigarettes behind her, stumbled down the dark stairs but didn't fall.

"Are you OK?" Abramo shouted. "Come back!"

At least he wouldn't follow. Ticks sit and wait.

* * *

A hooting modern opera, passages cobbled from words in many languages; a muted TV nature show, forest and creek a tiny infinity for its insects; a book of Islamic calligraphy he'd bought at the St. Mungo Museum shop, shapes and patterns of sacred Arabic in vibrant metallic inks. For Gabriel, a path to calm.

Rust, alcohol, tobacco, hashish. His heart churned like a propeller. Leap through the door. Hit her flying, collapse her, drive her back, drive her off.

He opened the door.

Zarabeth stood against the far wall. Metallic sweater, miniskirt, densely patterned stockings, short leopard-skin boots. As if he had ordered her from room service.

"That smell thing works for you," she said. "I was still deciding if I should knock."

He swallowed his hungry saliva. "What do you want?"

She flicked her hand out. His business card in her waving fingers. "Want this back?"

He snatched it. "Thank you. Goodbye."

But she shoved past him. "I need to pee." She closed the bathroom door. He stuck the card in his pocket. He felt childish anger. On the screen dragonflies mated in slow loops, with tiny splashes in the creek below. *Centrifugal force makes the female expel fertilized eggs,* read the captioning, *ensuring the remaining offspring will be his.*

She came out. "I used your mouthwash. Can I have a drink?" She knelt by the minibar.

"You're already drunk."

"This is me sobering up." She took out a diet cola and a mini-bottle vodka, fell on her ass. "Ha! I fucked up my knee." She drank cola. "Sorry about today. You took it well."

"What else could I do?"

"I don't usually like my boys so honest." She poured the vodka in the can. On the screen yellow dragonflies mated, end to end, abdomens in long arcs. "I like bugs. I like their priorities. Work, eat, mate, die. Extreme life. Insect porn."

He laughed, stopped himself. "You should go."

"Say something nice."

"I like your hashish smell."

"What is this music? I mean it's cool. It's like a braid. Like DNA." She sipped her drink.

He handed her his book. "I got this in Glasgow," he said. "Calligraphy art."

She paged through. "Fantastic. Real energy. Like Persian carpets made of foil."

"*The Attributes of Divine Perfection*. Ninety-nine qualities of God, according to Islam."

"A holy book? Ha. My Polyglot really doesn't like you." She turned more pages, tossed it away. She stretched out on the bed, one knee raised, hair spilling across the pillows. She wiggled her loose foot like a catnip treat. "This nose thing you repressed wouldn't make a shipping nerd into a security guard. You're witchy. You're all covered in woo-woo. Your wonderful company puts you outside like a dog."

She rolled forward, head inches from his zipper, the hard cock inside it. She rubbed her cheek on his pants, stroked his ass. "In witchy woo-woo land, the sex is surprisingly crap. You and me, another rare opportunity. With other women you can share nice things. What I have, you don't have with anyone else."

He smelled sand, rock, hot oil, charred flesh. She was the most necessary thing ever. He was tired of doing the smart thing.

"I want you," he whispered.

He dodged not knowing why. Her kicking foot missed his balls, jabbed her heel in his thigh. She shook him loose, stumbled toward the door. He caught her. She kicked out. He rammed her into the door, again, knocking the wind out of her. He dragged her limp gasping body, dropped her face down on the floor, pinned her arms and legs.

"Any more and they'll call police," he said.

She coughed. "Does my wet smell good to you? Say it."

"Yummy meat." He ran his tongue along her neck, rolled her over, caressed her ear, her shoulder, her small breasts, her ropy thighs. She squirmed out of her clothes. He clawed away her stockings, licked her thighs, her labia bitter like peppercorns.

She stopped still. She put a palm on each shoulder. "I can't have kids," she said. "I'm clean. I like touch. It's my woo-woo. If you want condoms, fine. I don't."

Her eyes bright as drill bits. He shucked his shirt.

"Good boy," she said. "Fuck me now."

They crawled together to the bed, kissing, biting. He entered her, their skin dry, catching. She moaned long and low, her wet scent seaweed and hot sand. The bump of her cervix, a sore tooth he had to poke. She jabbed him with her elbow, again. He slowed. She taught him her wants with moans and scratches. Bad student smelled his blood. He threw his hips back, found an arc for his thrust.

She came with a bark, her thighs and sex taut like a tire. He would never stop. Ash in her mouth, flowers and herbs on her skin, a beach in her sex. End of a luau, his own island orgy. She slapped his chest, his face. "Fuck harder," she panted.

His pinkie finger two knuckles deep in her asshole, pressing on himself like a second cervix. Her fingers on her clit, she came again, bucked to free herself. When he came she snarled, collapsed on his chest. Her sweaty body, ember-hot. His balls, painful hard dried limes.

"Let's do that again," she said. "Where's my drink?"

* * *

"Hi." He was dressed. A red suitcase next to him. "It's nine-thirty."

"Hi." She looked around the room. Only trash left. "What's going on?"

"They canceled my vacation. I'll make it up later."

"Fuckers," she said. "They never make it up. Where are you going?"

He shrugged. He sat by her on the bed. He looked sad.

"No work talk," she said. "Fine. So. This was fun."

"You are sharp and beautiful like a knife," he said. "I wish things were different."

He kissed her with his apricot mouth, his mean lips.

He wheeled his bag out the door. She, left behind like his trash.

Her anger faded in the raw sore clamor of her body. She remembered the tinsel music, glittering around their fucking. Their desire had left ghosts in the room. Future guests would grow hot here and not know why. His caresses, his licks, feather touches of air from his nose. His swaying thrusts, non-stop, long enough, and again.

She dressed save stockings and boots, and left. With a bare foot she caught the door before it closed. Barcoded baggage tag in the wastebin. A breadcrumb for her.

In her room she took a long shower, soaped herself twice. She wanted new skin. Wrapped in the hotel's worn towels she read her cards: Product 5 upside-down, Product VP, Data 3. A respite from hassles with a passionate man; afterwards, ugly. Product and Data, the honest cards, not squishy Brand or silky Money.

She curled the baggage tag around her finger. The airport channel listed puddle-jumpers to local hubs. He might go anywhere.

She paced nervously, her phone heavy in her hand. Surveillance ensures it stays that way. Magda always lied but Magda had delivered. Magda didn't wish things were different.

Zarabeth took a picture of the baggage tag, copied Gabriel's face from his picture at the first distillery. She sent Endre a message:

Gabriel Archer. Empyrean Security San Francisco. Logistics work, fluent Russian. Here for the Scotch. A dog's sense of smell. Likely witchy. Good in bed. Sudden departure for work. Interested?

She deleted *Good in bed*, sent it. Afterwards she stared at the distillery picture. Short sweet hours holding hands, one hot night.

Insect romance.

CHAPTER FIFTEEN

Hamburg

I n Hamburg his bag came quickly. Outside the stark steel terminal, a woman called his last name. A wide build in her security uniform, neck-length blonde hair, a white W of a face with small blue eyes. Gabriel followed her to a black sedan.

"The boot is full. Put your bag in the back seat." She spoke cautiously as if English were a spacesuit.

He rode shotgun, his legroom cramped by black satchels. "Thanks for picking me up," he said. "Are we going to the hotel?"

"You have a briefing with Siteboss." It was the title for the security officer in charge.

"What's his name? Sorry."

"Herr Hüber."

"What's your name?" he asked.

"Rohrer," she said. "Ingrid." She frowned. He said nothing more. They soon reached the city, streets of townhouses and trees. The sky dim red to dim blue, sidewalks amber in the streetlights.

The modernist hotel sat at the end of a narrow lane near the port wall. Lights in the distance from cranes and giant ships. Sea smells, machines, exhaust, moldy wood. Two young white male guards in uniform met them in the teal and teak lobby.

"Go with them," she said. "We have to check you for bugs."

In the men's room stall, Gabriel stripped to his underwear. After wanding him they checked his clothes carefully. Zarabeth might have planted a device. All they could do was fire him. Been there done that. Over bathroom chemicals he smelled butter, paprika, tarragon.

They left. He dressed and found the restaurant, a long gray room with oval paintings of lobsters and sailing ships. Ingrid sat with a uniformed man in his fifties, thin red-brown hair and an oval tan face. He grinned big yellow overbite teeth. Sweet odors of lemon and yeast from the dregs of his beer.

"I'm Hüber," he said, shaking Gabriel's hand. "Are you hungry? Best lobster in the city. With this butter—ah!"

"While you check my bags."

"We worry about industrial espionage. You are a wrinkle. You're a non-uniformed security officer assigned as an attaché, for your prior business experience."

It was the story Thorn had said others would hear. "That's all I know, Herr Hüber." The scratches on his back itched against the chair.

A woman server in a bonnet and a gray frilly smock brought a check. "It's his company, of course," Hüber said, signing. "He can have circus people, no offense. I just want to be clear. Ingrid is his security detail. You are not part of my command. If you see something, alert Ingrid or another officer, like a civilian. You speak German maybe?"

"Other than English, just Russian."

"V kakom napravlenii vy stalkivaetes'?" Ingrid asked, better than her English.

"Ya ne znayu," Gabriel said. "Yest'khoroshaya yeda zdes'?"

"He speaks Russian," Ingrid said.

"OK. Something you don't want public," Hüber said, "tell Ingrid in Russian. No heroics. König's an old man. Carry his bag. Help him out. If things go bad, use what you know."

"Go bad?"

"One day, some anti-globalization crazy. Or a heart attack." The server returned with a menu for Gabriel. "Your bags will be sent to your room," Hüber said, getting up. "Here's the key. Dinner's on us, charge it to your room."

* * *

Gabriel dreamed of his brother Jeremy, big-brother-big, babysitting him. They ran around trees in the dark, well past Gabriel's bedtime. Jeremy produced binoculars and a scout's planisphere to find stars. With adult eyes Gabriel saw Jeremy's desire to escape, to drink beer with other teens, not cocoa with his brother.

But the dream didn't make him sad.

He used the sticky innards of his baggage tag to clean the lint off his suit. For breakfast he ate fatty sausage in thin slices with crusty bread. The two security men from yesterday's search were now friendly in minimal English. Brown-haired Hans, black-haired Mattias. "We go work now," Hans said.

Outside, white sun spun gray clouds around it like a wand for cotton candy. The office was a block up the port road, a red brick building with tall copper-green windows.

In the lobby Ingrid gave his shirt a disdainful look. "This is not a nightclub."

"I was on vacation."

"They have stores in airports. They're doing a bug sweep now. We go see König." Security women. Keisha in the white limo, now Ingrid. Women knew their kind.

She led him to a small crowded room, its windows blocked with sheets of hard foam. In the center, two trim women in headsets held tablets out to an old man in a loose houndstooth jacket. A mushroom cap of thin gray hair, mottled skin over long hollow cheeks like a moray eel. He smelled of lotions, talc, fresh cut hair, old funky skin.

Luther Koenig, CEO and prophet.

Koenig offered a weak tug of a handshake. "Mr. Archer. Sorry to interrupt your vacation." His accent American but the rhythm German, each syllable equal. "I understand you have negative views on our work in Russia. Tell me about that."

Gabriel was surprised to be asked. "Russia's backsliding. More authoritarian, less technological, less productive. We're enabling it."

"The bust has chastened them. They've realized they need skills, not just commodities."

His glib assurance awakened Gabriel's old resentments. "Russia's rulers want overseas tech and serfs to fix it without the hassle of a business class. Who helps them? We do. We only talk to those in power who stonewall and hollow out our work." Gabriel smelled others' worry like boiled cabbage, but his year of frustration had momentum. "We should promote democratic free markets, not feudalism with shopping."

"If they throw us out," Koenig said, "we can't help."

"We're not helping now," Gabriel said. "We just take our cut. Ten years ago a businessman tried to finance rival parties. His company got chopped up and he went to Siberia. We acted like it was business as usual. We serve the siloviki plutocracy."

"Oligarchs only wanted democracy to expand their power."

"We're *against* enlightened self-interest now? I thought it was our mission, sir."

"Ha." Koenig wagged his finger at Gabriel. "Each new generation. I will consider your perspective. Now please assist me. Let's go," he told the room.

An assistant handed Gabriel a yellow messenger bag, with folders of papers and the two tablets. He fell in behind Ingrid. She glanced back at him uneasily.

The large common area had tables, chairs, stations of whiteboards staffed by assistants. Thirty-odd managers, mostly men, all white, sat and stood, drinking coffee. All stood when Koenig entered.

"Guten morgen," Koenig said. In German, he named several people for thanks, then switched to English, loosening his tie. "Enjoy this innovative 'parcours des idées.' I want to see what you come up with." He clasped his hands above his head in triumph, to sparse applause.

The managers dissolved into the room like cream. Conversations, exchanging cards, but slowly they were drawn to the whiteboards. Each was labeled with a business sector: Trade, Manufacturing, Information, others too far for Gabriel to read. No one wanted to be the first to write but many wanted to be second. Soon most boards had at least one discussion going. Gabriel watched, jealous. On a tablet he paged through the fifteen-second feeds from the whiteboards, people frozen writing, pointing. Acronyms he didn't know, arrows and circles he couldn't interpret. Not his world now. Show dog playing at guard dog.

"You don't happen to know about currency issues, do you?" Koenig asked him. "I was hoping someone had a novel thought about all this debt."

"I don't know currency," Gabriel said.

Koenig squinted. "You think it's woolly-headed, yes? You must remember how heterogeneous Europe is. Imagine if New York and Massachusetts spoke different languages and had been at war for a thousand years."

"Honestly, sir, I don't know much about Europe either."

"Ha. Sometimes I wonder if I do." Koenig smiled so as not to wince, like a mystified parent trying to be supportive.

Gabriel looked back out over the scrum of managers. It didn't seem worth a chief executive's time. Was its innovator someone Koenig hoped to promote? Was Koenig just here for morale?

Voices rose around the Information whiteboard. A broad-shouldered man with a gray goatee argued with a round bald man in loose linen clothes. Across the branching list of services, the round man had written in red: IF WE SHARE EVERYTHING IT IS WORTH NOTHING. Koenig and Gabriel joined the forming crowd to listen.

"Did you not live through the Cold War?" the gray man said.

"There's a difference between censorship and trade secrets," the round man said. "If you make our work a commodity, what is our product? Are we journalists?"

"We want a better market. Winning by network effects is a chain reaction, not stability."

"Stability is impossible and undesirable. There is no perfection, only the ability to keep seeking it. Which requires money. Why give work away in the name of a ridiculous ideal?"

People drew back from the round man's heresy. He glanced around for allies. Gabriel smiled encouragingly. The round man looked past him with disdain. He wasn't interested in the guard dog's opinion.

A frustrated Gabriel followed Koenig back to his seat.

"That's Europe," Koenig said. "Unable to agree, too scared not to."

* * *

At lunch, the assistants walked the fatigued Koenig out, each touching one of his arms as if to refuel him in flight.

Hüber stopped Gabriel. "I need you on the roof. We're a man short. We'll save you a sandwich."

"What am I looking for?"

"Eavesdroppers." They walked to the elevator. "Spies use lasers to detect vibrations in glass from voices, play them like a recording. In Germany all offices must have a window." Hüber turned a key in the control panel and pressed the top button.

Gabriel smelled lobster butter in Hüber's sweat. "The foam doesn't dampen it?"

"You noticed that?" Hüber smiled as if Gabriel were a monkey who tied his shoes. "We'd like to see who is listening. Look in the distance, for mounted apparatus. Impossible, of course. We mostly want them to know we know."

"Security theater," Gabriel said.

"You are capable of this much."

On the cold, breezy roof, Gabriel smelled rust and grease in the salt air. On the southwest corner, Mattias pointed from the edge of the vast port, to a complex of white spheres and tubes, hovering over green grass like an alien lander. Gabriel inspected rooftops, canals. The busy port distracted him. Rows of tall cranes, Chinese and Norwegian ships stacked high with colorful containers. Hamburg, a name in his old logistics chains. Ship through Hamburg, through Singapore, Felixstowe, Dubai. His mouse clicks among billions each day, tiny energies moving mountains of matter.

He looked along the roofline of the white complex. They had given him no instructions what to do if he saw something.

* * *

An hour later a brown woman with large eyes and a long thin nose dismissed him. He pried numb fingers off the binoculars. Inside Ingrid gave him the yellow bag but no sandwich.

Conferees wore jackets again despite the room's warmth. Only half the people had seats at the table. Ingrid followed him through the junior managers crowded behind. He imagined her mimicking him like a street mime. Koenig gave Gabriel a limp wave. Gabriel's fingers crackled painfully with warmth.

Presentations followed a common order. Slow cadenced English explained pages of losses, export deficits and natural disasters in bullet points. Failure rendered into data like offal into cattle feed. Common order, common story, like a day of auditions.

A man worked his way up the far wall, whispered to one of Koenig's assistants. She walked through the projection, loss numbers scrolling over her face like bit and bridle. "Due to a flight cancellation, a group has to leave early," she announced. "We must have the corporate officers' session now. Those not attending, please step outside for refreshment. Take your things." Smell of a musty basement.

All but seven left the room. Koenig's assistant closed the door and stood in front of it.

Ingrid smelled hot and sweet like baking vegetables.

"You all right?" Gabriel asked.

"I don't like not doing my job but I don't want to complain about Signe."

"Is that her name?" He switched to Russian. "Standing there makes everyone feel small."

"Let's get coffee." They took their cups and stood close. "I am no gossip," she whispered in Russian. "But people are upset. In January, in Stockholm. Officer's session there too. Do you know what it is?"

The coffee sour like orange peel. He let his shoulders go limp, inhaled the aroma. Again he had missed the reason behind his unease, too steeped in his senses and feelings. "I don't know the business details. There's a big argument, between those who want something and those who don't. People are angry."

"How can you know this if you don't know what it is?"

"I have a way of reading people," Gabriel said. "Like body language. You understand?"

A wry smile. "So that's why you are here. They make it so people ignore you. Hüber pretends he is upset about you."

He went with it. "That rooftop thing was a nice touch."

But Ingrid was finished with smiling. "So a problem today?"

"Not a security problem. A problem for the company."

"Not my arena," Ingrid said.

*　*　*

Gabriel rode the dinner bus with junior staff. People talked in groups. No one spoke to him. He smelled dry cleaning, stale cigarettes, body odors, colognes. Each person a chrysanthemum of scents, enough to move by in the dark.

The restaurant had chrome furniture and slender white columns, a huge pop-art photo of coins over the dark bar. He was seated at Koenig's table, with Signe and four local executives, all speaking German. Gabriel sat quiet. The salad had bitter greens and the pork's mustard deafened his nose.

Across the table, Signe smiled apologetically, the third time she had caught his eye. She shook her body, as if impatient to dance. Slender in a gold dress, her hair in a dramatic long curl. If he drank she would look better. He didn't drink. But he smiled.

As servers cleared plates, Koenig rose. Even through German, Gabriel understood the forgive-an-old-man routine. Gabriel followed. Ingrid met them at the door, boxy in a bulletproof vest.

"Where's my vest?" Gabriel whispered in Russian.

"With my dinner." She led Koenig out to his limousine, with Gabriel behind. The driver, a middle-aged white man with thin gray-black hair, came to open the door.

Gabriel smelled mint and sugar, like a knife up his nose.

"Wait," Gabriel said to Ingrid. "The driver's drinking."

"Are you sure?" Ingrid asked. She spoke to the driver in German. The driver protested. Hüber came, with Hans and the woman from the roof.

Ingrid shut the door, shoved the driver against it, slapped his chest. The driver gasped in pain. She opened his jacket, took out a flask.

"Scheiße." Hüber made a gesture with his hand. The guards walked the protesting driver away. "Mr. Archer. Good spotting."

"I'll drive," Ingrid said. "Gabriel can sit with Herr König."

Hüber nodded. "Come back right away. We need it for the senior staff."

Gabriel sat next to Koenig. "Did you know, sir?" he asked.

Koenig raised the privacy window. "I knew it would be better if you were here. Was this the reason? One of them. God multitasks. It would take Him too long to explain."

"What does it feel like? Does—is there a voice?"

"It's a burning." Koenig winced. "A language of fire and will. I am a stupid child, so stupid God Himself stops to tell me what to do. I am the emperor, naked among sycophants, but I know my nakedness. I tried for years to refuse it. God is persistent."

"I don't know much of God, sir. I know what it's like to feel stupid." He felt stupid now, never trusting those who kept trusting him. "Sir, you need to know this. Something happened to me on vacation in Scotland, just before I got assigned here. I met a woman in the hotel bar. We hit it off. We spent a day together. We were intimate. But—she works for Straightforward. She was possessed. Some demon of tongues. It hid from me at first. I caught it speaking Russian through her at a bar. It stank. I passed out."

Koenig's eyes grew large but he sat still.

"She understood me, sir. She knew I was—it seemed accidental. Then I was sent here."

"Let me be clear. You were intimate with a woman. After you were recalled from your vacation, you learned she worked for Straightforward and was possessed."

"We were intimate before I got the call to come here. I knew before we were intimate."

"You are a nesting doll of surprises, Gabriel," Koenig said. "Why tip their hand? They didn't try to blackmail you? Suborn you?"

"There was just her. It felt like chance. All I told her was I was leaving for work. I liked her."

"Is that why you pursued her, knowing what she was?"

"I wanted her. I was tired of doing the smart thing."

Koenig laughed. "Thank you for your honesty, Gabriel, and no apparent harm done. Perhaps you are here more for you than for me. We'll have to look into it. Report the details to Mr. Thorn, but in person."

"Yes, sir." They drove a dark tree-lined parkway along a small lake. "We're not going to the hotel?"

"I'm from Hamburg. I have a house here. Can you give me the bag? I need to read."

Koenig took out a tablet, tapped lightly across it. Screen glow bleached Koenig's face ghost-white.

Left with his thoughts, Gabriel second-guessed himself. The driver might only have had a sip. Maybe he was saving it for later and Gabriel had only smelled the flask. He clenched his teeth until dull pain reached his nose.

Koenig was asleep.

Ingrid drove past ornate old houses, close together on tight streets. She pulled over on the wrong side, got out to help the groggy Koenig up the stairs. Gabriel picked up Koenig's bag and the tablet. On the screen a business document, left column English, right column Chinese. Before he could read it, the sight struck him, with a clang and a shock, like a tool hammered into his skull. He shivered. He turned off the screen.

He stood alone outside, dim light and mild air rousing him. Ingrid waved him back in the car with two other guards and rode shotgun. Mattias dropped Ingrid and Gabriel off at the hotel en route to the dinner. She opened the lobby doors with gusto, pointed to a chair.

"You wait there." She went in a storeroom behind the bell desk. He sat in the calm bright lobby and tried to regain his composure after the strange hour.

Ingrid returned minutes later, in a black gauzy blouse over a white pleated skirt, thick-soled black shoes. She had a weightlifter's body, gold skin and woven muscles. So much for composure.

She gave him a moment to look then shrugged into her backpack. "Come on." Outside she set a jogging pace, north and west. Gabriel loosened his tie, regretted his dress shoes, but kept up. A few blocks later she ran into a building lobby. In the elevator they caught their breaths, put themselves together, sharing secret smiles.

The elevator opened onto a rooftop bar, Hamburg security staff in casual clothes. A round of applause began, grew stronger. Gabriel blushed. Hüber tapped his arm with a closed fist, spoke in German that drew laughs. "To translate," he said in English. "Sheriff, he ain't a-goin' on that stagecoach. Tonight drinks are on me. Beer?"

"Scotch." At the bar people raised hands for high-fives. Hans gave him a tight one-arm hug, sloshing beer. When Gabriel's drink arrived, Hans tipped the glass full into his mouth. It made his eyes run but he raised his empty glass in triumph.

The alcohol loosened him up. Ingrid grabbed him for a dance by the bar. Talk with Hans and Hüber, with others. Another drink. He joined Ingrid at the window. Town Hall to the east looked tremendous, floodlights silhouetting its Gothic spires. From the west, a great white statue stared balefully at them, King of a giant chessboard.

"Bismarck," Ingrid said. "He united Germany."

"I've heard of him. Was he from Hamburg?"

"No. There are many statues of him." She smiled. "He is what I protect. I was in the Bundeswehr, the Defense Force. I liked security best. Like a video game. Collect the purple fruit, that's the game. The people are purple fruit. You are not like this. You work to judge them. That would make me sad. Do you like it?"

"No. I'm not much for drinking. Do you want to go for a walk?"

"Sure."

"Should we say goodbye?" Gabriel asked.

"I think it's obvious."

In the elevator, she gave him soft kisses. Her deltoid gave under the slow pressure of his hand. "Massage the rest too, please." Her body smelled like sourdough.

They walked the busy Reeperbahn, dense with sex clubs and discotheques and bars. She walked more expansively, swinging her backpack by one hand or the other. Open doorways blew out lemony beer and cigarettes, dank sweat and liquor, bitterness, frustration. Her hand in his, reassuring like a seat belt.

She lived in a gray-and-white walkup, faint yellowed lights over the stairs. Four flights up, holding each other's waists. Her flat was a single room with kitchenette and bath. By the blue-gray city glow, she poured them each peppermint schnapps. "In your honor." She knocked hers back. The aroma enough to stun him. He sipped.

She went to the bath to wipe herself with a washcloth, leaving the door open. Shaved sex and careful gestures, tiny breasts on her muscled chest. She seemed a teenager, her cut body an accident of puberty. She brought out a bottle of oil.

"Massage," she said.

He straddled her contoured body, energized but comfortable, like a sports car seat. Knots along her spine like thick worms. He worked down her back, slid off to rub her ass and thighs.

She rolled onto her side, touching the scratches on his back. She sat up to look. "What happened to you?"

"I had a date in Scotland."

"With a wolverine? Do you like—"

"It was just once. I went with it." He pulled her up, her face to his.

She kissed him hard, her hand cupping his sex. She slicked the condom on deftly. When he entered her they kept apart as if they held a beach ball between them. Her heavy thighs across his, his palms to her fists. Her grunts drew his thrusts. She hissed and her arms gave. When he came, a puff of sublime in her face, like a soap bubble. He slid back off the futon onto the cool floor, greasy and hot like a spent shell casing. She looked like a girl again, easy to hurt. She went to clean herself.

"At first you seemed arrogant," she said. "Now I think you're just not happy."

"I wanted to be one of them," Gabriel said.

"You got to be one for a day." She handed him a washcloth. "When I left the Bundeswehr, if the only job had been with a private army, would that be wrong? You can't always do what you like. You just live." She kissed his cheek, his lips.

"I'll see you tomorrow," he said.

"I'm off-site until after you leave. We won't see each other."

He was glad and sad about it. "Goodbye then," he said.

Outside the streets were cool and empty. Gabriel walked with his thoughts. Two months of his new world but only a weekend to cement it. Koenig and Zarabeth, each defining the other. Before Zarabeth, he might have still dismissed Koenig's divinations as hallucinations, luck, lies. It had taken Zarabeth to make them real.

Ingrid's quick jabs at the driver's chest. A muse of clarity.

Something grander lay behind this. The meetings, the missions, Koenig in the midst of all of it. Not a tendency, not a belief, but a plan.

I never expected to train a successor, Thorn had said. Koenig was old. If the plan required Koenig, as fulcrum or as nexus, the plan was running out of time.

CHAPTER SIXTEEN

Washington, DC

Zarabeth got home on a hot Monday night, calves sore from awkward running between terminals in Newark. Home again, home again. Service-cleaned, empty for days. Her biggest hotel room. Décor still crap. She leaned against the wall and stretched her legs. Airline magazines warned of deep-vein thrombosis. A clot floating up to a brain artery, motor skills dying in creaks.

She turned on thermostats, showered, emptied her suitcase. Her work behind her, she made herself a rum-diet-cola. Soy seaweed crackers, thank you Missy. In her stashbox, where a quarter-ounce had been, a single joint in a jam jar. Fuck you Missy. At least she'd kept it air-tight. Sweet cumin smell, gritty smoke, like steak after a month of lunch meat. Wooziness, rush, stupor landing like an anvil from the sky. She lurched onto the balcony, sloshing her drink.

Green points in the hedges of the first-floor terraces. Fireflies. As a child she had caught some to make a nightlight. Her father had made her let them go. "They seek love," he had said in his high voice. "Love is why they glow."

Seek but not all find. She could drop her glass. Green serenade crushed by falling anvil. Funny from the outside. She cocked her arm back, threw her glass over the hedges onto the highway below. Let the males seek. Punishment enough for everyone.

* * *

Zarabeth walked the ten blocks uphill from the river. She hardly sweated but felt oven-hot. After her travels Georgetown's antique glamour now felt makeshift. Rome was ten times older yet straighter than these rickety buildings. Colonial: an insult bronzed like baby shoes.

At the summit, brick and hedges marked Montrose Park's rolling fields. Missy waited in the shade by the tennis courts, with a plastic bag from the Lebanese diner. She wore a blue striped blouse and khaki shorts, her freckled legs white with sunblock. Her hair its natural brown, too short to style.

"So you finished chemo?" Zarabeth asked.

"Shut up, Rapunzel." They hugged. "I've missed you."

"Me too," Zarabeth said. "Thanks for saving my life."

"The world would be boring without you." Missy handed her a red drawstring conference-swag backpack. "Your replacement's in there, and water. Sorry to Bogart, but Martin was away."

"At least you left me something."

"Never take the last piece, Mother said. Plus, I have something special rolled for us. So tell me everything. Dis-moi en français, hein? Jamais je ne le parle."

They ate kebab sandwiches on a bench. Zarabeth was careful with some facts, but made a good yarn of London and Rome: police, misunderstood clues, repercussions. "This sponsor asked me to lunch. I thought it might be shady. Italy, you know? But he was Empyrean."

"No! What did he want?"

"Don't know don't care. I walked out, reported it. He thought he was scary. He mentioned London. Like killing a man would count against me at the firm."

"Killing a *client*," Missy said. "People would applaud." She laughed until she snorted.

After lunch they walked down the steep red-clay slope into the woods. Zarabeth slid in her ballet flats. Missy in trail shoes scampered ahead to a lone wood bench and lit a joint. "I love this spot," she said in English. "Look at that sugar maple. Fifty years old? It shouldn't grow there in clay but with the slope it gets drainage. An ornery tree. I'd like to worship under that tree."

Zarabeth took the joint. "We are worshiping under that tree."

"Tru'dat. The attack didn't hurt your familiar. You even picked up my Genevois accent."

"Were you doing a diagnostic?"

"Oh I like that. So technical. I was curious. Familiars are like glass. Steady pressure but no sharp shocks." Missy settled back, her legs wide and mannish. Sweat ran down her temples but her cheeks powder dry. The high stretched time, stillness extending, a tiny glimpse of death. "I feel responsible. Once you see the unexplainable, there's no going back."

"Sappy bitch. I've been on the woo-woo D-list since high school. Now I have a demon."

"Familiar. Demons are big. Couldn't even hide in all that hair. If only mine would grow."

"Don't you have a spell for that? Besides, I like it on you. So I'm not possessed?"

"Of course you are," Missy said. "And you have a distemper of the humors. Primitive nonsense. A familiar is an adopted deformation in causality, a psychic astigmatism."

"It feels alive."

"It draws energy from you, directs your mouth. Have you talked to your support staff since the attack? Some wounds need stitches."

"Thanks. What is this weed? I feel like this bench is a pillow I can move by thinking."

"My man brought that from Cali." Missy stood.

"You didn't mention your man was a stoner. You always want them straight and narrow."

"I'm trying something new. Pre-corrupted, as Mother says. You can meet him tonight. We're going to a rooftop happy hour, some medical thing he gave to. Six o'clock."

They walked down to the creek trail. The shady woods shook with energy, the hum of leaf factories. "I saw fireflies last night, from the balcony," Zarabeth said. "Can we come back here after the party?"

"A lovely idea. Not too late, I have to be up at sunrise."

"Casting a spell of love and harmony?" Zarabeth teased.

"Talking with bankers. That's why I wanted to practice my French." At the bend in the path the ground sloped down to a wide beach along Rock Creek. Missy led her further upstream, to a heavy thicket with small white and yellow flowers. "In a month those will be blackberries," Missy said. "They should be good this year, assuming the bums don't get them first. The mulberries were fantastic."

"You can eat mulberries?"

"We need to work on your survival skills. Our species has grown addled. Not one in a hundred has survival skills. What other species in its natural habitat can say that?"

"I've never been in a natural habitat," Zarabeth said. "I've seen your makeup table. Nature girl until Collections Week. Fucking sick of your shit." She stormed off. At the bend Zarabeth climbed to a rock ledge over the creek, put her hot feet in the cold running water.

In a minute, Missy joined her.

"I'm sorry. I didn't mean—"

"I was being Miss Thing," Missy said. "Upstream there's an awesome new graffiti tag."

"Later." Zarabeth leaned back. The white sky made her eyes tear up. She took Missy's hand. "I thought I'd die in London. I've been in scrapes, but—" Her chest puckered as if to shoot her heart out like a cannonball. If only. She turned and spat.

"You're so lucky." Missy squeezed her hand. "Most people never get to do anything."

* * *

The party was in an old downtown hotel done in reds and purples, like a butler in drag. On the elevator, two pear-shaped salesmen eyed Zarabeth frankly, as if she were the hotel whore. The rooftop lounge had low red sofas and gilt dividers. Zarabeth ducked the women checking people against clipboards, looked for Missy among the stoop-shouldered feds and tailored lobbyists.

Missy stood by the bar in a pleated cream dress and pearls. "You look fantastic," she told Zarabeth. "Is this London? I have to borrow this." Behind her a huge white man, hairless but for eyebrows, long high nose and heavy chin. He wore a white silk shirt with a gaudy rust-red dragon, gray check pants, florid for Washington. "This is Walt." Zarabeth shook his hand, wondering if it was a prank.

Walt smiled lopsidedly, a crack in a dinosaur egg. "Do you drive a hybrid?"

"My ragtop takes premium. Stick shift too."

"Huzzah. Washington is lousy with hybrids. Worse than San Francisco. I expected big cars." He was lively when he talked, deep lilting voice like a soul singer.

"Big cars are for being driven. Hybrids give you moral superiority, and are easy to park."

"You make it obvious," Walt said. "Are you drinking this evening?"

"Rum-diet-cola lime. Thanks ... Warren?"

"Walt. You're Betsy?"

"Zarabeth."

"That's right. We smoked all your weed. Wonderful art." Walt waved down the bartender. "Kevin, a rum-diet-cola with lime for Betsy here."

"Hi Betsy," the bartender said. "Rum diet lime, comin' up."

Missy returned. "Neither of you is bleeding. I'm so pleased."

Kevin brought her drink with an awful wink. They went out from under the awning. Even with breeze, the heat sat on her shoulders.

"Did you thank Walt for today's joint?" Missy asked.

"It was kind," Zarabeth said. "I'm impressed you brought it on the plane."

"Private plane. Not so impressive."

"You smoke on your plane?"

He shook his head. "Jet-share, by the hour. Smoke in your car five minutes before takeoff. Once I took mushrooms. Jittery on the way up, but tripping at forty thousand feet, that was prime. Sunset clouds told my life story to send me across time." He kissed Missy's temple.

"Missy, will your nice man take us tripping in his jet?"

"Montreal," Missy said. "We can all speak French together."

"No tripping into Canada. Xiaojié xihuan qù nar," Walt labored, "wo men jiù qù nar."

"He keeps using Chinese," Missy explained, "hoping I'll study it with him."

Zarabeth felt an explosion like a popped corn of language. In her fucking eye. "Why do you call her Xiaojié?" It took her a moment. She groaned at the error. "Watch the tone on that one."

"You speak Chinese? I do podcasts. Love to practice."

"I speak all languages," Zarabeth said in Chinese. "It's magic. I'm the original magic-language-speaking bitch."

"No idea, but you sound native," Walt said. "How long did it take you to learn?"

Her eye still hurt. She rubbed it and went back to English. "I just picked it up."

He looked between them, growing surprise on his face. "Really? Languages?"

As if Missy had stabbed her. "You told him?" Zarabeth cried. "What did *he* do?"

Missy shot her a chilling look. Zarabeth lit a cigarette and turned away.

Walt leaned against the railing next to her, his back to the sunset. "Have you read these new Swedish thrillers, about the woman hacker? You'd like them."

"I don't really read," Zarabeth said.

"There's a movie," Missy said. "We can stream it. Walt bought us a big TV."

"Maybe this weekend. They want me in Boston on Thursday, meet the team or something. First shuttle out, five-forty. Tomorrow is spa day. Come if you can work it."

"Can't. Contractors are bringing the new vanity."

"What do you do, exactly?" Walt asked. "Missy couldn't quite say."

"I study business partnerships for improvements."

"An efficiency expert."

"I like that," Zarabeth said.

"From the fifties. Brand new, you're retro. You two catch up," Walt said.

"Did that go well?" Missy asked once he left.

Zarabeth shrugged. "Seems I missed the vote in any case. Now spill."

"Voyons un peu d'ombre," Missy said. Zarabeth, the Polyglot's pimp.

Missy gave her a French capsule history, flirts and falafel and spells, a vigorous night after his twosome. "It got obvious quickly. So why stall?"

"It's so not obvious to me," Zarabeth said.

"Vive la différence." Missy switched to English. "You were hoping for boys. Sorry."

"It's fine. The drinks are free."

"Hardly that." The gangly white man behind them looked older than he was, with wrinkled bags flapping under his chin. "Ted Beaumont—Missy! How are you? Back at work?"

They air-kissed. "Ted's a drug lobbyist," Missy said. "I helped him spend money."

"Are you working tonight?" he asked Missy.

"I'm just arm candy. My boyfriend gave to one of the Institute things."

"You must introduce me," Ted said. "With the election, this is the first work event I've done in weeks. I'm on the Coordinating Committee." Zarabeth let them get a pace ahead.

They found Walt talking to wilted feds and a stiff old man in seersucker. As they made introductions Ted had a tray of wines brought over. One of the feds made a lame toast, about the hope of a new test for Alzheimer's and the goal of a cure.

"Not a cure, surely," Walt said. "Drug companies need a bigger return. Chronic and managed, like heart drugs. No?"

Ted frowned. "Companies go where science lets them."

Missy moved between them. "It's a wonderful party, Ted."

"You're the asshole now," Zarabeth whispered. "This wine tastes like mouthwash." They went back to the bar. Rum for Zarabeth, bourbon for Walt. They waited in silence. When the drinks came, she asked, "What do you do, exactly?"

"Until recently I was a rich retiree who threw money at Alzheimer's research. Now I also support a day-care center in Southeast. They're a scrappy bunch. A little Afro-centric."

"Sporting of you."

"It's fun," Walt said. "Like an old rap album. This woman who runs it, Sasha Blackwell, she's a dynamo. I want Missy to meet her. I think they would really click."

Zarabeth squeezed the bar rail. File it for later though curiosity climbed out through her chest. "What's it called?"

"Ophir Learning Center. Does Straightforward match employee contributions?"

"Ask an employee who makes them," Zarabeth said. "But I'll check. Blackwood?"

"Blackwell. Search the school. O—P—H—I—R. Her name never works."

Missy came back, looking cross. "Now I have to go to some stupid Tea Party fundraiser. We're only here because of you."

"I'm sorry. Buy you dinner?"

"For starters. Not here. I feel I'm in a brothel."

"I got that too," Zarabeth said.

They walked steamy blocks to an upscale Greek restaurant with a two-story glass façade. From their mezzanine table it looked like an airport terminal. Zarabeth felt at home. Walt and Missy shared a salad. Zarabeth ordered five mezes, all beef or lamb.

"You're killing me," Walt said. "Missy's making us diet. We were indulgent with restaurants."

"You with all those herbs on your roof?" Zarabeth asked.

"He's from the boonies," Missy said, lips red and slow with wine. "Never had Ethiopian, can you imagine? Now we're practically monks."

"You can indulge in Montreal," Zarabeth said.

"That's right!" Missy patted Zarabeth's hand. "Darling, when are we going?"

"When you tell me about the language thing," Walt said.

Zarabeth shrugged. "Mine came with the job."

"Stick to podcasts," Missy said. "Much cheaper."

"How expensive is it?"

"You need people who can do it, which is expensive. And unsavory. Plus the sacrifice."

"What?" Walt asked. "A parrot?"

"A fertile woman," Missy said.

"Fertile?" Zarabeth asked. "Kinky."

"You're joking," Walt said.

"Her familiar lets her speak any and all languages. What else would buy such a thing? A fertile woman. Life and source of life."

Walt still didn't believe. "Where would they get a woman?"

"Please," Zarabeth said. "Inconvenient junkies, mouthy whores, runaways. Immigrant coyotes, deportation agents. Cut your costs and do it yourself. Happens all the time. Any roadside convenience store has a sign in the window. *Girl Missing.*"

"Plucked like fruit from a tree," Missy said. "All you need is drugs. La-la-la-la."

"You're cut off." Walt moved her wine glass out of her reach. "Seriously now?"

"There's no dungeon on my estate," Missy said. "The rich have clean hands. Have we in our history commissioned such work? We have. In like circumstances you would have too."

Walt shook his head. "You know a woman died for your Chinese?" he asked Zarabeth.

"People die sewing your shirts. Someone died picking your lettuce. You hide your guilt in the big picture. No demons for you. Besides, shit I went through, it's mine now."

"You're a piece of work," Walt said, refilling her wine. "I won't turn my back on you."

"Big talk. I'll test you on that shit, fat boy."

After dinner they took a cab to Montrose Park. Zarabeth talked about Rome. "These self-assembling robots in a big tank.

Each part went in separate and found each other to connect. They want to make them small enough to swallow."

"Would make colonoscopies easier," Walt said. "Robots would be good for spinal taps."

"You see a market for those?" Zarabeth asked.

"You can test spinal fluid for Alzheimer's risk now. Big hassle. A robot could do it in malls, or on a bus. Open-source so people build their own from old chips and car parts."

"You trust a robot to put a needle in your spine?" Missy asked.

"A thousand-dollar chipset has ten multi-core processors to manage an inch of insertion," Walt said. "A human's got bad sleep and jitters from coffee. Robot, no contest."

Missy had the cab stop half a block past the park's service driveway. They walked back quietly, Missy and Walt hand in hand. Zarabeth felt left out. They walked down into shadow, the hill blocking the streetlight. Zarabeth stumbled, grabbing Walt's arm for support. "I can't see."

"Stop and give it a second," Walt said. "Maybe a couple."

The flash of his lighter stung her eyes. She smelled smoke and saw a joint's red cherry.

"All this time you had that?" She took a drag.

"Aren't we the best of friends," Missy said.

When vision returned, they followed the creeklet upstream to a cleared meadow, trees and buildings high on the skyline. A row of mushrooms, wide caps spaced evenly apart, led into the bushes.

"Fair folk are about. That's their jetway." Missy took off her shoes.

"Are there really fair folk?" Walt asked Zarabeth.

"You'll believe anything, won't you?"

"Of course there are fair folk," Missy said. "Look."

Ahead, a dim green plasma like a hundred blankets rubbing together. A firefly orgy. Missy walked into it, her song too low to make out. Fireflies hopped on her legs, her arms, her back, her head. She danced and twirled, sleek and ethereal green.

"She's amazing," Walt whispered.

"She is. She likes you," Zarabeth said.

"She likes *you*."

"I like her. I never had a friend before who didn't steal from me." Zarabeth felt hot steam. The demon had a broad view of sanctity, Missy's bugs no less hallowed than a cathedral's stone. "I'm going back to the creek." She waited in the cool darkness. A few firefly lights in the dense trees, early scores or hapless nerds. The creeklet rang and clashed like a faraway caravan. She felt sober.

Walt and Missy found her, Missy brushing off the last few bugs. They walked up to the street. "We're heading home. You're welcome to join us," she said, shaking her head.

"You two go fuck. How is that by the way?"

"It's good," Missy allowed.

"I had no idea," Walt said. "It's like she's reaching back in time to improve my technique. My former lovers miss me more. And the dreams—I'm like a schoolboy."

"Don't talk about sperm in polite company," Missy said.

"She asked. Anyway. It's amazing. For me at least."

Missy yawned. "Oh, yes. For me too, dear."

Laughing they walked downhill together. She hugged Missy, hugged Walt. "You know any hot single men?" she asked him. "I don't want to go stag to Montreal."

"I'll mull it over."

"But, hot."

"Understood." They walked away, bear and deer, holding hands.

*   *   *

There it was on Zarabeth's phone. *Sash Blackwll ophir learn cntr.* She stomped her feet on the bed in childish glee.

Stale template website, primary colors, list of donors. In photos Sasha outshone everyone, her beauty both warm and hot, purpose in her eyes. She didn't look like prey for a tent revival or a deathbed parent.

Zarabeth let out a huge fart of lamb fat. Forest for trees. Magda's old tool sets up shop across the river, Magda neglects to mention. Maybe they wanted her to discover it, like Rex, but not even Magda could have figured on Walt connecting them.

Traitor Sasha could wait. It was Spa Day.

She smoked a joint, went downstairs and hailed a cab. Rust-blistered paint, a suspension that creaked while standing. In Europe it wouldn't even be licensed. She got in. Of course the air-conditioning was broken. Capital of the free world. Freedom to suck.

Even high, the pedicure was intolerable, her feet gnarled by her excellent shoes. Zarabeth's profile included no chitchat, so the staff silently spread her toes with wine corks, pried toenails from the pinched flesh. Each pass of the file on her callused soles shot hot pee up her spine. A nightmare with lychee martinis.

Between the drinks and the endorphins from the pedicure, she withstood the waxing but passed out during her massage. The hair salon was a new bad dream where she let them cut more and more, egging them on like a hair anorexic. At the end, her hair was shoulder-length, softened curls bouncing like old telephone cords, streaks of auburn like comic-book motion lines. In the lounge she listened to wind chimes, drank a third martini. Maybe she could sleep until Magda had a new job for her.

* * *

In the peephole Martin looked his usual self: blond hair in a do-rag, stained yellow bag, dark circles under his eyes. A woman beside him, same height same hair same buck teeth. "My sister Penelope," Martin said.

Penelope wore a plum blouse off-the-shoulder and short gray leggings. "Nice to meet you," she said, her voice like a half-swallowed mouse. Thick cochlear implant behind her ear.

In the living room Martin pointed Penelope at the couch. "I won't be long," he signed. Penelope waved her phone.

"Sorry," Martin said to Zarabeth. "She needed a ride. You mind if she texts? If it's cool."

"It's fine. You want water?" She poured three glasses.

"Thanks," he said. "Some of my clients, a little paranoid. You were gone a while."

"Three weeks. London, Rome, and Aberdeen."

"Up in Maryland? The proving ground?"

"Scotland. How's things?"

"Busy. People don't have money for coke now. Dealers diversifying. I have to hustle."

"You know Missy got me some?"

"This is the same. Eskimo Sky. Northern Lights cross."

"Missy's boyfriend has hot stuff from Cali."

"That guy," Martin said. "He just had a little. He's not importing it."

"You have a crush on Missy."

He smiled faintly. "Do not."

"You have a crush on Missy," she sang meanly. "Martin and the hunt country ladies."

Penelope barked. "What's going on?" she signed.

"I'm teasing him. He has a crush on my friend," Zarabeth signed.

They stared. The Polyglot, a buzzing echo in her arms. She squeezed her sphincter tight to keep a straight face. At least her eye didn't hurt.

"One of us," Martin chanted, "one of us." He switched to sign. "Why did you learn?"

"I dated this guy in high school," Zarabeth signed. "You learned for her, of course?"

He nodded. "It worked out. Deaf are huge potheads and not many cops sign. Around Gallaudet, I approach people on the street," Martin signed. He unzipped an inner pocket and took out a triple-bagged ounce of brown-black buds with red hairs. He finger-misspelled the name in a blur, M-A-P-E-L-B-E-R-R-Y. "Blueberry cross. High-energy shit. For parties. Send Cali guy home." His arms boneless, signs flashing in a quick salesman's patter. "Eight-fifty ounce. Special. Don't say where you got it or you are cut off."

"Not safe for the hearing?" They all laughed, in sign, pinching their hands. Zarabeth felt like it was a children's class. "OK, the

Mapelberry and half of the Sky." She counted out twelve hundreds. He gave back one bill with a paternal smile.

"We're going to this house party tonight," Penelope signed. "Grad students like me. A sausage fest but good people. Any time after nine."

"Business trip tomorrow. But thanks."

"Soon we party," Martin signed.

Alone in the kitchen she made herself a drink. If Walt had seen that, he'd kidnap a linguistics major.

On the balcony she checked email. Magda was now unavailable. Jill had canceled her first meeting and changed her to a later flight. As if Magda didn't want to talk about Sasha.

Less reason not to party. She texted Martin for the address. She brushed her teeth, washed her face and remade it simply, dressed in a light blue cotton sundress and flats. Fine for nerds. The Mapelberry was delicious but made her antsy, as if the comedown was already nipping at her heels.

The cab meandered from Union Station up to Trinidad's dark blocks of old rowhouses. On the party house's front porch, beefy white guys peered at her from between brick columns, like a zoo exhibit. The narrow living room had black-light tubes and canvases splattered in fluorescent paints. She found Penelope near the kitchen, *Deaf is Def* in flaking block letters on her t-shirt, no implant.

"Come meet everybody," Penelope signed. She grabbed Zarabeth's wrist in both hands and led her to a big wood deck strung with plastic tiki lights. A drink, a smoke, many introductions. Deaf culture clearly encouraged personal sharing, a chance to vent about anything: medical issues, jerk co-workers, ass-pinching professors, lame pick-ups by hearing boys in H Street bars. For a time Zarabeth got truthful herself, about her mother's drinking, her hard first years on her own. Once the music started, she tuned out, happy to watch the silent calligraphy flash around the heavy basslines.

With a new joint, Penelope introduced her to James and Lucy, both fellow computer science grad students.

"I'm working on text-to-sign," Lucy signed. She was short with a wide doughy face. "Current software is word-to-word

216

translation using canned video clips. No directionality. We want a machine reading paragraphs of text and signing it end-to-end in correct ASL."

"Why not speech?" Zarabeth signed.

"Phones do dictation already," James signed. He was a skinny small man, his football jersey hanging off him like an altar boy's robe. "Also, if we process text we process closed-captioning. My fantasy is to redraw video. Instead of an avatar in the corner, generate signing hands on people directly."

"Embed it in sunglasses for real-world use," Zarabeth signed.

James shivered theatrically. "That's crazy. Know anyone who sells high-resolution video sunglasses?" His signing campy as if casting a spell.

"Try Italy. Let me give you my card."

Calvin came with frozen margaritas. He was a white gym-rat with a small long head as if pinched by giant fingers. Lucy's posture got complicated. Calvin was a local delicacy. James went in to take a turn as DJ. Zarabeth followed, pushing past the line for the margaritas and joining Penelope, shoulder to shoulder in a hot loose duet. Dancing was singing now, a yell when she swung her arms.

James stood behind a pair of laptops on a stack of beer boxes, headphones playing into his chest. He took the music darker, thumping bass and a synthesizer's nasty staccato. Zarabeth was a sleek monster thing, freshly-molted snake body and cobras for hair. Her body shook and billowed like a flag through wind. People gave her room.

Zarabeth felt energies and powers. Sometimes she could shape them. It was freak magic, nothing she could plan, like an undertow when she let the party go too far. She danced like Salomé, a service extracting payment. She could have anything she wanted for this dance. All she had to do was ask.

She thought of Gabriel Archer.

A savage pain shot through her, like a pin through a bug, white-hot like London.

Only a moment. Room, throbbing music, kids. A fast goofy song. She had missed something, like a five-minute blackout. Maybe just the high.

Calvin danced hesitantly beside her. She had better uses for him.

His room upstairs was a mess of boxes and suitcases. "I just moved in," he signed. They kissed and undressed in the breeze of a fan. On the creaky bed he kissed her knee and worked upwards, dragged his fingers lightly on her raw skin.

She flicked his ear with her finger. "Get a rubber and fuck me already," she signed.

He had a thick cock and strong hips, a predictable thrust. She sat against the wall and lifted one knee, fantasized a threesome with Missy and Walt, Walt a big fuck battery while Missy stood over her offering cinnamon ceviche clit. Enough to get her interested. His friction like a wire brush along her little spots.

"Get it moving," she shouted. She slapped his chest. He threw his abs into it, catching her off-guard. A sharp come like a curtain falling. He wheezed as he came like he'd bitten through his tongue, *hnhn hnnhn hnnhnhn hnhnhnhnHNN!* He hugged her, his chest hair itchy. She pushed him off, wiped her sex on the sheet, yawned her spine in place.

"Let's get a drink," she signed.

Downstairs, the house lights were on and people were leaving. "The cops came," James signed gleefully. "We were loud."

"Great mix. Thanks for the party. Where can I catch a cab?" she signed.

"Number's on the fridge." He signed the house address.

In the kitchen Calvin and Lucy pointedly dropped their hands. She keyed the number in her phone slowly, just to be a bitch, but called from the front porch. She sat on the brick railing to smoke a cigarette.

Calvin came outside with two cups of water.

"Aren't you gallant?" she signed.

"Figured you'd be thirsty. And it's not the best neighborhood. Can I text you?"

She shook her head. "I was just frisky. But it was fun," she signed. A cab drove down the block. She stood up. "Go fuck Lucy. She's dying for cock."

"Lucy's clingy."

"Clingy only works on nice people. Fuck her like a bug. If she doesn't leave, eat her." She waved a big goodbye.

CHAPTER SEVENTEEN

San Francisco

Eighteen hours in transit, a long boring afternoon of unchanging light. Gabriel slept between Copenhagen and Chicago, half the Chicago flight too. Now in the taxi he sat by the open window smelling cool freeway air and distant sea, wired on in-flight sodas and impatience, his personal happy hour.

Denise was away, the house hot and dark. Beer smells in the air from Denise's clay. The fridge had water, beer, wilted carrots. With rice cakes and almond butter it was enough. The news played while he scanned the recording list. Hours of gearhead shows awaited him: *Spoiler Alert!*, *Hemi-Demi-Semi*, *The Race of Nanjing*. A fine thought to stay up until dawn, order stuffed-crust delivery pizza not this stockade meal.

The mini-view flashed red and blue. He closed the list. Squad cars and ambulances sat outside a warehouse Gabriel recognized. "Immigration officials freed forty-four people from this slave-labor electronics factory," the reporter said. Exhausted men in white blankets, walking dead past pointing cops. Like ice down Gabriel's shirt.

Two months ago. Gabriel had never imagined it would take this long. Two months of suffering, now back to the home they had paid to escape. Had the authorities waited for evidence, for senior criminals? Had his vacation not been interrupted—would he still be with Zarabeth now, happy to bleed?—Gabriel would have missed the news. Better to be ignorant, or to know the limits of his powers?

In his room, he took out the one whisky he'd allowed himself as a souvenir, a fifteen-year Islay in a square bottle. He went up to Denise's bathroom, opened the window over her bathtub, and clambered out to the narrow ledge.

"Slàinte," he said, toasting his new stupid world. The whisky had a harsh brandy nose, a hot finish like jerk seasoning. In Edinburgh he had imagined sipping it for years to come, like the dusty liqueurs his parents had hauled out for dinner parties. Tonight his last night in the land of no limits. Tonight he could drink the whole thing and if he fell off the ledge he would bounce up and dust himself off.

In the sky thin strips of cloud waved like streamers under the high gibbous moon. The first Scottish distillers hid in the hills, making whisky at night to hide from the King's excise men. Moonshine for the clever. Sunlight for simpletons and the powerful. Gabriel's drink, his loves, his sneaky senses, all night things. All surreptitious.

After a few drinks the ledge felt no more solid than the clouds. In the open window Denise's cat met his stare like a dare, looked up abruptly, darted back inside. Gabriel looked where the cat had looked. In front of the moon, the clouds formed a leering gray face. He had seen it once before, blood-black, backlit by blue video and white suicide kings. Nate, whose face he had broken in Tahoe.

He crawled inside and passed out in Denise's bathtub.

* * *

He woke Wednesday to the quiet after rush hour, naked on his stripped mattress, drool on his pillow.

Upstairs he cleaned the soot he'd tracked in. He needed to stop drinking. At least he'd had that right during his decade of denial. He stuffed the whisky far back in his closet.

A shower and nasal cleaning cheered him. A day of nothing, at long last. He walked to the corner market, bought pumpernickel and blue cheese, apples and carrots, coffee. At eleven-fifteen he was brunching with *Spoiler Alert!*

He managed only two hours. Gabriel really wanted ambient manliness: views from cockpits, spinning rotors, ratcheting bolts, torch hiss. Instead, yelling, procrastination, bad work plans. His life for years a desert of drama, now an ocean. On the channel guide, old comedies and news. Better to go to work.

He pumped his tires, rode to Embarcadero in t-shirt and khakis. At work his corridor was dark. Thorn was in Asia, Del in a training class. Gabriel's computer spun its hourglass. He went for coffee. People eyed him as if he were loitering. After two months he was done feeling like an interloper.

Nathaniel Coleman, Thorn had said. Gabriel spent an hour trying various searches, on different databases, each with secured logins and tedious fourteen-digit alphanumerics. No results. He tried a last search on himself. An angry red message, *This login does not have access to requested information.* He would have to ask Thorn about Nate, at the same time he talked about Zarabeth. All humiliation at once.

He was tired. He sorted through the queue of open reports, picking the largest by file size and checking them into his system. At least he could be useful tomorrow.

Thursday his legs felt sharply sore. He packed his suit and rode again, to an upbeat playlist from his Scotland driving. Memories of green-brown mountains painted over the dim gray morning. At Leavenworth he dodged a sports car running its yellow. Hard air like a slap, a mad teeter until he righted his bike. Glorious. In the next life he would be a bike messenger.

Shave, shower, suit in the office gym, at his desk at nine.

"You still work here?" Del said. "I been here typing while you fly all over. At least you're here for your subpoena."

It took Gabriel a second. As part of Human Resources, Security staff had to help with the quarterly luncheon for new hires. It was not a popular task. "That's next week, right?"

"Uh-huh. Bill's missed it twice. Guess who catches hell? Ain't so bad. Just ask questions. 'Where you from? I been there.' Like that. But, eat before you go, you ain't getting food there. Witch who runs the thing gave me the side-eye if I ate a freedom-fry. Don't know if you noticed—" Del stage whispered, "but we got fat people in this company. Pick the buffet clean in half an hour, I tell ya." Del pantomimed frantic grabbing. "Ha-cha-cha-cha-cha. Fatties got fast hands."

"I'll eat before I go. Any word from Bill?"

"Cranky's the word. Sent him through Denver, overnight layover. You'd think I made him take the bus."

"It's just he can't take his guns," Gabriel said. "My housemate's in Denver this week. Visiting family."

"She cute?" Del said. "I'll send him back through there. Man needs to get laid."

"Maybe Thi Tam can give him a massage."

Del shook his head. "She's just a little thing."

Gabriel's morning report was a financial executive candidate, a university development officer from Santa Clara routinely flagged for her extensive overseas travel. Full of numbers, fine with Gabriel. For lunch he ate two apples outside, in full sun, drinking the light like a plant. After lunch he got a fresh coffee and slogged through the file.

Nothing stood out, but it bugged him. He could—smell it.

He was an investigator. He was allowed a hunch.

Light shone under Del's closed door. Gabriel knocked. Del was shirtless in smart gray slacks, his work clothes on the floor, a pink polo shirt on his chair.

"Hot date?" Gabriel asked.

"Yeah. What d'you need?"

"There's this report, Pamela Kee? I have a bad feeling."

Del smiled. "I'll see what we got." He wrote a note. His sagging back had thick gray hairs and four bullet wounds, scarred circles like lipstick kisses. "This a rush?"

"Tomorrow's fine. Enjoy your evening."

Gabriel went to his office. *Bad feeling*, he had told Del. But it wasn't bad. He could smell it. A piece of data, a molecule in its perfect receptor. Something wanted to fit.

* * *

On Saturday morning Gabriel shopped Ferry Plaza with his bag in front. Women everywhere. High ponytails, big sunglasses, lean shoulders in string-halter tops, glistening legs in shorts. Clouds of armpit sweat over pears and tomatoes and strawberries, dizzying pheromone parfaits. He had already called Gita Tiwari but she hadn't yet called back.

His phone rang, a Washington, DC number. He picked up.

"It's Walt. Got plans for July 4th?"

"Hey! No, no plans. Up in Tahoe?"

"I moved to Washington. The city. I met a woman. It's serious. But she's got a friend named Betsy needs some loving, and your taxes buy fine fireworks here in the Nation's Capital."

"This Betsy a nice person?"

Walt snorted. "Raging bitch. But, hot. A violent brawler like you is a good match for her. Consider it a mulligan for last time."

"I could use a mulligan. Thanks. I hope I get a flight."

"I hear tell they got 'em online."

"'Hear tell'?"

Walt grunted. "Picking up Missy's turns of phrase. What's funny, it's the same in Mandarin. Anyway. Fly into Reagan if you can. Gotta run."

Raging bitch. At least it was familiar territory.

* * *

In the crowded lunchtime elevator Gabriel stood next to a tall brown woman in pastel blue, a box to her chest with nametags and pens. Her green spice smell reminded him of Gita, though Gita would never wear pastel.

"Is that for the Meet'n'Greet?" Gabriel asked her.

The woman brightened. "It is for the Meet'n'Greet," she said, a happy slow voice like a school teacher. "Dhwani Choudry. Human Resources." She lowered the box to show a nametag.

"Gabriel Archer." They got out at the lobby. "Help you with that?"

"Thank you." She passed him the box. "When did you join Empyrean?"

"A while ago. I'm a facilitator today. From Security."

"Oh." Her face fell.

"Is there a problem?"

She stopped. "Some ground rules. Facilitating is not hitting on the new hires. At least you're cute, but keep it friendly? The buffet is not a carb-loading station. Take a plate so you don't look weird, but leave the food for the newbies. Guns, hunting, shooting—just, don't. Last time you guys sent this nut." She raised her shoulders and bent her arms, a good impression of Del. "'I like guns. Big guns little guns. You like guns?' Freaked everyone out." She sighed. "These are issues."

Gabriel nodded. "I can work within those constraints."

"All right then." They walked across the busy lobby. Part had been cordoned off with nylon belts on chrome stanchions, with tables of chafing dishes inside.

"Are you a guard?" Dhwani asked. "You're not in uniform."

"I do background checks on executives."

She raised her eyebrows. "You must dig up juicy stuff."

"It's been an education," Gabriel said.

At the front of the line stood Chin, a massive security officer Gabriel knew from the range, checking badges against a list. "You got a subpoena?" Chin asked, smiling.

Gabriel freed a hand to bump fists. "Doing my part for corporate morale. You?"

"Crowd control," he joked. "Good job in Germany."

"Oh. Thanks. You heard about that?"

"Dude." Chin squinted. "Everyone heard about that. See ya."

Gabriel wrote himself a name tag. The fatty smells soured him on the buffet. He took a water and introduced himself to Rhonda, a curvy black woman in a navy dress, dark bags under red eyes. Next to her Edgar, a fat spiky-haired beige man, devoured a fried-chicken drumstick.

"We're in Enterprise Consulting," Rhonda said.

"What exactly is that?" Gabriel asked.

"Sometimes companies don't notice their market has changed," Rhonda said. "We coach them through adapting, keep them focused on the future." She sipped her coffee. "Reallocating resources beats firing half the staff."

"By 'beats' she means precedes," Edgar said. Rhonda shot him a look.

"Can't you retrain people?" Gabriel asked.

"You can try," Edgar said. "What do you do?"

When he mentioned Security they looked around for better networking. Gabriel joined a large group all introducing themselves eagerly, like an orientation class.

"I work in recruitment," Gabriel said. "I was just in Colorado Springs."

"I studied in Colorado Springs," Georgia said. She was a short white blonde, wide hips like a pot for her daffodil face. "Before my mission. Hiked Pike's Peak every week. I was so fit."

"We got caught in a thunderstorm on Pike's," said a gaunt man in a green blazer and no name tag. "Incredible to watch the clouds roll in like that."

Others chimed in, all with good things to say about Colorado Springs. Gabriel smiled through it.

He went back for food, served himself two stuffed mushrooms. Dhwani tapped his shoulder. "You can have more than that," she said, her voice hoarse. "Sorry about earlier."

"It's fine. Good turnout. Do you still need facilitating?"

She patted his shoulder. "Work 'til closing, soldier. Get a cookie. They go fast."

At the cookies, he met Georgia again. "Enjoying the luncheon?"

"It's all right," she said. A second look flattered her. Wide toothy mouth, large eyes, pert nose. She smelled of browning apples. A long thin scar from her left ear to her collarbone. "How long have you worked for Empyrean?"

"Six years? Seven."

"So you must like it here?"

"Ups and downs. Last year was down, but I'm still here. Though I could just be lazy."

"I'm sure that's not true. Is there—could I talk to you sometime? Professionally?"

"Oh. I'm not in HR. I'm in Security. Long story. Is it benefits? A workplace issue? I can find somebody."

"No, it's—" She trailed off. "It's just, you've been here a while, and you probably have some perspective that would be helpful. If you're available …"

He smiled. "How about Monday for lunch, in the cafeteria."

"I'm over in SoMa. Could we maybe meet outside of work? I live in the city."

She had yet to smile. Foolish urge to draw her out. "How's noon on Saturday? You know Maiden Lane, off Union Square? There's an Italian café. Great antipasto."

"That sounds nice. Thank you." They exchanged cards.

People were leaving en masse, like passengers allowed to board. Buffet trays reduced to stinky chafed sauce. Dhwani caught his eye and shook her finger.

When he got back to the office Del knocked on his doorframe. "How was it?"

"Dhwani Choudry says hi. Chin was there. He said people knew about Hamburg."

"It was a threat to the CEO," Del said.

"I just smelled a guy's breath."

"Princess Diana might have liked someone doing that for her." Del frowned. "Since we are on the subject," he said, "we got an alert on the Colorado board guy."

"Gerald Pendry?"

"Tire blew, drove off a hill. Dead, him and two women. You got something on him?"

"Bill did."

"Guess he outlived his usefulness. I don't think he was drinking."

"That wasn't his vice," Gabriel said. "Does it say who was with him?"

"No. Is it important?"

"Not to us." Melody Sorensen and Bethany Tolland, Gabriel already knew. Pendry on the run, fleeing with essentials. "But if you can find out, thanks. Any more on Kee?"

"They only sent the big balances. Woman's got more credit cards than shoes, loves a store discount. I asked for them all. Maybe by the end of the day. You OK?"

"Weird talk with this woman at lunch."

"Was she cute?"

Gabriel smiled. "Since you ask, yes."

"Weird's OK then. Chicks being weird, that's them being honest. You should look her up. 'Make some synergies' or whatever corporate jazz you got."

"I'll take that under advisement."

"Advise yourself good. Don't want to end up like Bill."

In his office he looked at the card. *Georgia Patchett, International Development.*

Good works for Empyrean. No wonder she never smiled.

*   *   *

Monday night on an auction site, he won a $75 round-trip red-eye Sunday to Baltimore, a half-hour from Washington by train. Early for the holiday but he could always take a day trip to give his hosts a break. Maybe even with Walt's friend. He booked the trip and sent Walt the details.

He scanned posts in the sensitives' forum, a duty like taking out the trash. Whine bummer, whine bummer. On his social-network feed, funny videos and an open mike invitation from Patricia's brother Allan. Through whom he had met Gita who hadn't answered his messages. Just as well he couldn't go.

While he cleaned his nose and mouth, his bitterness turned on his job. They had shoved him into this. He put up with it like it was the best thing for him. Like he had nothing else to offer. Good guard dog. Bill Thorn pretended it was meaningful. As much a shut-in as the whiners on the sensitives' forum, as Gabriel was becoming. He didn't want to be good at this.

Tuesday morning he cleared three reports in a crazy flow of numbers. After lunch, the additional financials for the Kee report arrived: investment and trust accounts, store credit cards, donor-funded university programs in four Asian cities. More contracts than numbers, tiring to read.

He left late and rode uphill slowly. He fell asleep without undressing.

Wednesday it rained steadily, cold wind but no fog. He took the bus. In the office he stared at the Kee financials, seeing and not seeing them. He went over expenses, looking at what the money bought. Mortgage, car payments, private schools all clearly sourced. In her hotel receipts he found a second card for personal travel costs, a debit account from a Singaporean bank. Not a card she had listed.

He went to Del and explained it. "Do we have anyone in Singapore?"

"You don't want to kick it back to the local office?"

"It's Santa Cruz. We are the local office," Gabriel said. "If I kick it back for not declaring a foreign bank account and it's not kosher, she'll liquidate it. I'd rather know what's in it now."

"All right. I gotta make calls. It's—" Del paused to count— "it's dawn over there. Doubt I'll hear before tomorrow."

"Maybe I'll cut out early then."

"Come late, leave early, go on trips," Del said. "Why they even pay you?"

"Who said they paid me? Good night."

He took a taxi home. An effort to climb the stairs. In bed he pulled the covers around his clothed body. He felt a great wave had dumped him on an empty beach. He woke at ten to dark thoughts in darkness. Finally, he dug out his bottle of whisky and poured some in his bathroom water glass. He fell asleep again before he finished it.

On Thursday morning he woke from a dream of a carnival, his skill with the games earning him too many stuffed animals to carry. Weeks since he had shot something. He drank kefir and rode to work. Cold wind fought him on his sunny ride. He took a long hot shower in the work gym, checked out a virtual pistol and practiced for an hour. His aim was poor and his fingers hurt from the feedback.

On his desk sat a white cupcake, the numbers 872 drawn in green frosting. "That's the number of thousand-dollar bills in Pamela Kee's undeclared Singapore account," Del said. "Greenback dollar. In Singaporean, like a million and change. You have the unofficial department record for biggest embezzlement. Even Bill was impressed."

"You already told him?"

"He's a lot closer to Singapore than we are right now, so I gave him the scoop. Between this and you doing his work, he said to give you tomorrow off. Get your packing done."

"I'm only going to Washington. That's like five shirts. But I'll take it. So Kee is out?"

"You have to file it," Del said. "I put another top of your queue but it's small."

"OK. Anyone going to tell her university?"

"That's above my rank," Del said. "Washington summer's hot as balls. Take more shirts."

In his email, a message from Thorn:

Excellent job with Kee. Look forward to catching up. Nathaniel Coleman returned to Chino Penitentiary for violating parole. His injuries have healed. There is nothing you can do for him. Ever. Remember him as a caution if it serves you, but move on. Enjoy your resumed vacation.

Gabriel snorted. Thorn had no care for those he felt were wrong, only their victims. Maybe he was right. Gabriel thought of Bethany Tolland and her never-to-be born child. Another hit on Einstein time.

* * *

Gabriel arrived late to his Saturday lunch. Georgia waited at a shaded table with a plate of antipasto. "I hope you don't mind," she said. "My stomach growled in Bible Study."

"Please," he said. "Sorry I'm late. Street racks were full so I had to go in a garage." When the server came, he ordered the same platter and a non-alcoholic beer. "Was Bible Study interesting?" he asked.

"Deuteronomy isn't my favorite book," she said, her Southern accent a sharp needle. "Especially these days. I get enough turf battles at work. I like the church. I don't know many people yet. It's down in Crocker-Amazon, it's an effort just to get there."

The server brought the beer. He clinked her water glass. "Cheers."

"Cheers. What church do you go to?"

The watery beer tasted like pasta rinsings. "I don't. We're Lutherans but we didn't really do much," Gabriel said. "Grace at dinner. Sunday School until I was old enough to sail. It was something between my parents." Already a long religious conversation for him. "I just never found a church."

"You don't miss it?"

"Once in a while."

The food came. The smells woke his hunger. Burned oil, salt, papery eggplant skin like a nut brittle. "When did you move here?"

"Six weeks ago," she said. "I love it. Water views everywhere, forest an hour away. And cool weather. Between Atlanta and Liberia, I had enough hot. Maybe I'll get a bike. It's probably a great way to see the city."

"Be prepared, traffic's crazy."

"Maybe I'll get one of those two-wheel scooters?" She pantomimed steering low handlebars. They laughed.

The server cleared Georgia's plates. Gabriel asked for water and an espresso. "Georgia, what did you want to discuss?"

She frowned as if he had looked down her top. "I think I'm in the wrong job. All I do is push papers and dance around egos. My co-workers are nice but they're resigned to it. On my mission I did more in a day than in a week here. Be one thing if I had to work my way up, but above me it's the same, just higher pay."

"What you were doing was about making things better," Gabriel said. "What we do is about not letting them get worse, or maybe helping them stay better. It's unsatisfying. That doesn't make it pointless. There's a lot going on. Sounds like you'd rather be front-line. So go."

"I can't." She made a soft high moan like a deflating tire. He smelled apples again, too long in the oven, hot burned sugar. Her appealing smell was her damage.

"I worked in Liberia for nine months," she said. "Primary care, vaccine programs, focused on schools. Hard work, more humanitarian than religious, fine by me. I'm not a good evangelist, with my mouth. I'm better with my hands."

She stared ahead at Gabriel's chest, her eyes unfocused. "We left Monrovia. The countryside was supposed to be safer." She lowered her voice and bent toward him, her eyes wide. "A raiding party came to the village. They claimed to be looking for deserters but they were drunk and brutal. They beat two people. Then they picked three women to—two locals and me." She touched the scar on her neck. "Souvenir. I didn't even know he cut me for a long time."

"It sounds horrible." His tongue stupid in his mouth. He felt heat in his hands, spasms in his muscles. It didn't matter to Georgia how angry he got. No fixing.

Dhwani's rules, not lecture but warning. Leave counseling to the professionals.

"I know what they did to me was vandalism," she said. "But it worked. The country looked uglier every day. I slept badly. I had to leave. No one judged me. Everyone was kind. I judge myself. But I am in a bad way. I don't trust crowds, I don't trust large groups. But I'm—" She shivered.

"You're trying," Gabriel said, his anger become sympathy. "A year from now you'll be better. Maybe not good, but better. Accept your damage, and do what you can while you recover."

She smiled shyly. "Is that what you did?"

"Ha. In hindsight, maybe," Gabriel said. "I still wonder. Empyrean is an enterprise of hope but no passion. Practical love. I don't know what I'm saying. I'm no help to you."

"You are," Georgia said. "Helpful. And compassionate."

"I imagine most people are."

She shook her head. "People don't need to know. I have no

idea why I told you. Will you tell me about you?"

"I miss my brother," he said. "He got killed by a drunk driver. Not even a year ago. Nothing really makes sense since he left and now I'm a new place. I wish he could tell me what he thought."

"About what?"

"I can't talk about my job," Gabriel said. "Ever. That's not going to change."

"Then tell me about your brother," Georgia said.

* * *

Sunday morning he packed his suitcase. It wasn't full, and the round-trip bag fees would cost more than his ticket. He borrowed a cheap blue vinyl carry-on from Denise, small wheels and a bent handle. It would do. He packed again.

Twelve hours until his flight.

Pendry, ignored, dead. Kee, ignored.

After days with her file, Gabriel knew her address. The Interstate was fastest south, but it was only a half-hour longer through the forests. The car-sharing service had a copper-colored Korean coupe a half-mile away, wide chassis and enough engine to drive in mountains. He put on a suit.

An hour out of the brown city, to gray road, green hills, blue sky. Touring cars slowed traffic on long straight Skyline Boulevard, but Gabriel had time. Pleasure enough to drive, to direct the car, downshift and coast to the road's rise and fall.

Pamela Kee lived high above Santa Clara, on a private drive off the grade road. Trucks from a landscaping service blocked the house. He drove past, walked back along the edge of the yard, to a majestic view of the valley and the north range. The house was on a summit, room enough behind it for a road-wide strip of grass and a lower terrace. Workers raked the grass, prepped plant beds on the terrace, not far from the steep drop. Thick smells of soil and moss, energetic, alien.

In their midst a small woman in a wide straw hat, dramatic like an orchestra conductor in billowing cream linen. Gabriel was surprised. In badge pictures, she seemed mousy and shy. She walked toward him, shucking her gloves. "Can I help you?"

"Gabriel Archer, from Empyrean Group. I'm doing your background check." He handed her his company badge. "Could we talk a minute?"

Her face wanted to snarl. "I would expect an appointment, at my office."

"I'm here now," Gabriel said. "I need ten minutes."

"Fine. Come in." She led him across the patio into the house. Inside a vaulted honey-gold pine ceiling framed the view. He stood to admire.

"You came from San Francisco?" she asked, pleasant now.

"Skyline Boulevard. That's it there, on the far range? Great drive."

"On weekends. During the week, you go to Cupertino, then the Two-Eighty. I might get an apartment in the city. If I get the job," she added brightly. "You live in the city?"

"Russian Hill."

"Nice neighborhood."

"Modest digs. I like it. And it's quick to Embarcadero."

She led him down a wide hall with scroll paintings, money-green hills, ledger-red carp. Her office had Mission style cherry furniture, a tidy desk. She still held his badge. "I'm getting a water. Can I get you something?"

"No thanks." Behind the desk were community awards, pictures with city politicians. Between shelves hung sepia photographs of 19th-Century Chinese, couples and families.

Kee returned with two crystal glasses of water and the scent of copier ink. "If you change your mind."

"Thank you." He took his badge and a glass. He wouldn't drink but enjoyed the cold in his hands. "Are those family?"

"Usually I say yes," she said. "Keep it simple. My great-great-great-grandfather mined borax in Lake County. Only Chinese worked borax mines, did you know? No one else could bear the stench. They didn't have money for—what were they called, daguerreotypes? So these are copies of pictures from the university archives. Icons, in the Russian sense, of hard work and where it takes you."

"And of what you give up," Gabriel said.

That annoyed her. She sat behind her desk. "Please sit."

"Thank you." He sat gingerly, ready to spring. "I found the Singapore account."

She closed her mouth, pursed her lips. Her eyes narrow like a snake's.

"You're not getting a job with Empyrean Group," he said.

"Unless?" she hissed, mouth full of venom.

"Oh. No. Ha. I didn't discover it alone. Plus, I filed my report and there's no deleting it. Somebody will call next week. They won't even know why. 'Tough decision, many fine candidates.' Standard spiel." He shrugged. "Honestly, that's where it ends. I don't even think my bosses will tell your bosses. We only want to keep people like you off our staff."

Kee was insulted. "Just why are you here?"

Gabriel spoke slowly. "Not long ago, another person didn't get a job with us for reasons worse than yours. He's dead now. The police called it an accident but I don't think so. He didn't die alone." Bethany Tolland's lovely smell of mother, of warm skin and milk, stolen like a pie from a windowsill. "The others were innocent of his crimes."

Kee looked like her own wax statue. Nasty fatty smell, burned cheese and mold.

"Return the money if you can," Gabriel said. "Or go to jail. If we can discover it, so can others. They may not care who's around. That's it. Get right with this, before the decision is out of your hands."

No eyes to meet his, just anger. "You can leave now," she said.

She followed him out two paces behind, bolted the door behind him.

The sun had baked the car. Floor mat nylon, crumbs of corn chips, like a vinegar taco. He mapped out a longer return, through redwoods. He drove at a crawl, opened his window to smell dry woodsy air. When he held up too many cars he pulled over, sat cross-legged on the pavement. Above him, weathered, patient power.

He had gone too fast. Like a salesman, close a deal before vacation. Arrogant. A mistake no redwood would make.

CHAPTER EIGHTEEN

Boston

The shuttle flight slow to board, fat people, fat carry-ons. Around Zarabeth mustached men with glasses worked on huge laptops. She felt like a cat among cattle.

She had taken the wrong notebook. This one dated from years before, a short seminar in Boston. She read the first page:

Prototyping (The Language of Innovation)
—Any product can be improved
—Improvements come from a range of users &
—Impact any part of the design
Fastest cheapest medium to make your point
—(Lead weights in cardboard box mimic FEEL of device.)
Crash early crash often!
—Having crashes is part of the process

Fastest cheapest. Paper and lead, as good as real. She knew nothing then, just happy to sit upright, not to get her ass grabbed while breathing server dust. Fastest cheapest bothered her now, a story for children and the stupid, like money for teeth or guaranteed pensions. Sometimes you needed a new thing, not a cheaper thing. Sometimes you had to splurge.

She felt stretched across the world, like the red octopus of routes on the in-flight map. She flipped to a clean page. She held her pen like a calligraphy brush, straight up and down with her fingers resting around the clip. In Chinese she wrote:

If he leaves eat him
Eat him anyway

In Boston cloud domes dotted the hot blue sky like haystacks in fields. Optimized had offices in a silver-glass building on the point of the harbor. In the gray stone lobby, a short brunette in pink and black called her name. She shook hands with Jill Carson, gave a small hug. Jill was younger than thirty, a plain round carrot-freckled face with round blue eyes, short hair swept up and forward like a ship's bow.

She stuck a silver tag on Zarabeth's badge. "We share elevators with the rest of the building. That lets you enter all floors. Restrooms in the foyers." In the elevator Jill gave her a folder. "For the meeting. You want to put your bag someplace?"

"Bag's fine. I need more coffee."

"There's some up there."

Optimized had off-white cork walls, dark wood veneers, frosted glass, cold white lighting. Quiet. Conversations low like a hospital. Probably Magda had the hinges oiled regularly.

"You know about the accounting?" Jill whispered. "You're the junior accounting director for Special Projects. Monthly numbers, in the folder."

"Seriously?"

"I usually do it. Magda says you'll learn something. Endre gets you at noon." Jill stopped a few paces from a coffee service on a cart. "In there. It's wicked lame, take two coffees. Great to meet you." Jill hugged her.

Boston fuckers. Like a martial arts movie, learning warrior skills through menial tasks. She opened the folder. Two pages, many copies. All the boldface numbers in the black. Fuck Magda for fucking with her all the fucking time.

The small white lamps over the conference table cast long shadows down the faces at the table, a flattering air of menace, like a goatee on a fat face. No one looked at her or spoke.

Three more people entered together, the last Paul Kirkland, an engineer she had met in her old job. A year ago he had worn jeans and stubble. Now he wore a shiny gray suit, his face spagleaming walnut. As the admin passed around printouts, Paul introduced Zarabeth as a recent hire. There was a point to this.

The shovel-faced director for data mining read his good numbers pompously, as if Optimized's welfare rested on his huge chin. Zarabeth read the numbers. Units sold and profits were both down. Write-downs on a Volume Initiative. Magda had started a price war. No one questioned it. The empress's new revenue.

She re-read her own numbers. Succession Planning, a joke in Reston, had thirty contracts now. Secure Translation, three new accounts. Small side bets but better percentages and growing. Maybe in a year or two, some spooky-shaded suit might gloss over London telecoms, Italian data sunglasses for the deaf.

Wired on two coffees, Zarabeth dove in. "Special Projects continues its pioneering streak and makes solid growth. You can see real progress, nine percent profit on growing businesses."

The data mining guy glared at her, bug eyes and stretched cheeks like the Polynesian god of shovels. "Just why is there a Special Projects?"

Candy-assed shovel god. Drink a mai-tai from his skull. "Because some projects are special. We're the heart of the division. We go the extra mile."

"Ha ha, ha ha," Paul Kirkland said. He smiled flashes of red like the smelling tongue of a snake. "OK, thanks Zarabeth. Margo, your numbers. Back to the numbers."

At the end of the meeting Paul Kirkland stayed seated while others left.

"Congratulations on your promotion," Zarabeth said.

"On yours too. No surprise. Magda collects clever people."

"'Collects.' Harsh. At least I'm not stuck on a shelf."

"Ah youth," Paul said. He closed his eyes. "See you."

In the hall she refilled her cup with oily lukewarm dregs. A heavy, sloppy white woman in t-shirt and jeans, her dark blonde hair in an intricate braided bun, walked up the corridor waving at her. "You Zarabeth?" she called, loud for the hallway. "I'm Suze. Endre sent me up. He's tied up in the data center." She smiled as if it were literal. Zarabeth joined her at the elevator. From inside the baggy vendor-freebie t-shirt, intricate Japanese tattoos ran down her left arm.

The data center had downlit aloe-green walls, rows of black posts each holding ten servers, the familiar reek of recirculated dust and hot plastic. Suze led her to an installation, floor panels spewing cables. Endre was the squat man in a blue Oxford shirt and khakis straddling the third open panel, pointing and giving orders. White skin, narrow dark eyes, sunken cheeks, a small patch of blonde hair. Suze walked around the other side as if to guard him from her.

"Zarabeth!" He hopped up nimbly and clapped his hands together. "Love the new hair. I'm almost finished."

"Take your time." Zarabeth tried to check her mail but the room was shielded. Endre and another engineer had a heated disagreement. She left, walking the lanes between blinking servers, green lights like fireflies in formation.

"Let's go." Endre was red-faced from the confrontation. At the door he took a small plastic cooler from the coat rack. "We snack alfresco." In the elevator he unlocked the panel and tapped a low button. "I'm sorry to have kept you waiting," he said in Hungarian. The cab rose.

"No problem. Did you know I have Hungarian blood?" she said. "My great-grandfather went to France to work on railroads."

"Do you know the original family name?" Endre asked.

"I don't remember. He's dead or I'd ask him."

"Barta maybe. That's a common name. You're pretty enough to be Hungarian."

"Thank you. Are Hungarian women pretty?"

"Unusually pretty. They don't age well."

"No one does," Zarabeth said.

The roof was a field of concrete tiles. Behind the elevator shed, a plastic picnic bench sat shaded from breeze and sun. They sat on the same side for the inland view, red brick and tarpaper hills beyond a long arc of green highway. From the cooler, Endre brought out a plastic container of strawberries and a clear bottle of golden wine.

"As a Hungarian you share in your birthright. Tokaji Aszú." He poured the wine in short tumblers. "A sweet wine. Part of my reserve. Strawberries from the Somerville farmer's market."

The soft furry strawberries bruised and syrupy, the wine thick from cold and sugar, burnt tones like toffee or brandy. "Endre, it's fantastic. Is this a typical Hungarian lunch?"

"Dessert. Not enough meat for a lunch."

"I must be Hungarian." She drank down the tumbler in a long draft. "Nice to feel love for a change," she said in English.

"Stop," he said. "I get in trouble if you're happy. We can talk here, of course."

"It's not bugged?"

"I'm bugging it. In English you can't say I'm the bugger?"

"Not in London, at least." They laughed. "So you manage a data center and little me?"

"Managing your kind got me the data center. I can't keep things secret if we don't control the location. Things like the money from this building she owns."

"That wasn't in the accounts," Zarabeth said.

"In the data mining revenue. It's how she pays her vig to corporate."

"So data mining is sucking wind. Wait. She's starting a price war and using—she wants to crash the market. Then buy up bankrupt competitors."

"Kicking it old-school. They say there's too much data to manage. Be fun to try."

"Paul Kirkland thinks I'm a new purse."

"Paul Kirkland knows just what you are. Magda sent you to scare him. We let him steal a little. He thinks we don't know. We're curious why he wants it. He's not spending it."

"Now he'll be more careful."

"Good. New tricks to learn. He's been great with the fencing. And that Rome thing."

"Fencing? Stolen data? This is huge." Reasonable too,

243

enough to make Magda's story feel like a prank. Or a test. She pushed the bowl toward him. "How many of me are there?"

"I think you're it right now, but I can't be sure. Five years ago she had three or four. You're my third and maybe my last. Maybe the last. She's not young."

"Don't bury Magda just yet." She poured wine. "Can we check my Polyglot? It's been through a lot."

"They're not fixable, in the mechanical sense. If yours behaves badly we'll just replace it. I'll put in an order. Takes some time. Your Hungarian's lovely though."

"Did Sasha have a Polyglot?"

"We had to *recall* it," Endre said. "I imagine that left a mark."

"You told me about her."

"I felt you should know. Maybe I was wrong. Sasha is a bad subject."

"What happened to her?"

"Why did she leave? Who knows? She asked strange questions in the weeks before, about search techniques, onion routing, things she'd always gladly handed off to me. I told her, why not, but I logged it. She never gave me details. Where she is now, I choose not to know. If you ever learn, don't tell me. Don't put it in your phone. Let her go to Narnia. I did learn a little about your fellow traveler, though." He pulled out his phone to read it. "He does background checks for an office called Executive Investigations. Been there two months. His boss is a kook who got put out to pasture but runs errands for Koenig. I've got an archive search running to see if there's more we missed."

"What about his flight?"

"He went to Hamburg."

"What happened in Hamburg?"

"Nothing, in surveillance. He was a guard. Even saw him on the roof." Endre shrugged and put away his phone.

"He's nobody," Zarabeth said. "Thanks for looking." Either Endre was lying or he was wrong. Zarabeth knew from fucking nobodies.

It would keep. She refilled her wine. "How long you been banging tattoo girl? You do her up here, on this table?"

Endre blushed. "Inside by the elevator. I keep a yoga mat in the wire closet."

"Dude," Zarabeth said, giggling.

*   *   *

For the afternoon they put her in a window office. She sat on a fancy leather and chrome armchair, prim as a server. Sales managers came at twenty-minute intervals, throwing taglines like Mardi Gras beads: experience matters, knowledge is power, it's not what you make it's what you keep.

"Dynasty or history?" Hugh from Succession Planning was a big white fellow with a short crooked nose that looked smashed against a window, with a slight lisp. He dropped the spiel, hunched forward across from her as if to coach her golf putt. "We have clients from Lincoln and Washington, but Boston's fertile. Spinoffs from universities, most built around a couple of talented people. They never thought about it going on without them. You say, 'Who will buy your company when you get old?' Suddenly they're interested."

"You mean it's not just bribes?"

"No," Hugh asked, laughing nervously. "We classify resumes. Similar to what you're doing. We take leads from the data mining teams, use those connections to upsell our services. We want to help them go long."

"Do companies worry about junior staff?" she asked idly. "The IT manager who knows what server's grounded on the sewer pipe, the saleslady who knows her customers' cats. I bet if some guys here got perished, Magda would lose a million in hassles."

Hugh was unsure. "We could see about doing that. It would be a different protocol." He leaned back, smiled. "I never got to know you in Reston."

"I never wanted to be there," Zarabeth said.

After Hugh left she pressed her palms against the wall and stretched her hamstrings. Access to the top ranks of the Northeastern tech sector. A long-term game, for what?

Heat like backing into a radiator. She turned. The man in the doorway had a lean build, tiny eyes, a pointed jaw like a mantis. He wore all black, tight as neoprene. In veterans' groups he would trigger flashbacks.

"Sorry," she said. "Keeping deep-vein thrombosis at bay. Are you one of my meetings?"

"I'm Douglas. Secure Translation Services." His handshake crackled. She felt unarmed. His shoulders rose when he sat, as if adjusting folded wings.

"I met Ms. Sears earlier," Zarabeth said.

"She just does our books." Deep South accent, Louisiana maybe. The Polyglot was hazy. "We're in Cambridge. Secure, SCIF, you know the drill. Straightforward is like our property manager. You take a cut for running the business, billing, etcetera. Mutually beneficial." He sneered. "I hear you speak other languages," he said in Arabic.

"I'm curious how you heard that," Zarabeth said. Arabic was a drum machine of a language, complex rhythms or brutal pounding. The Polyglot wanted to play but she didn't. "What business it is of yours?"

Douglas pursed his lips. "You sound like a textbook. 'The Quran was sent down in seven dialects; and in each of its sentences there is an external and internal meaning.'"

The saying made her eyes sting. In Aberdeen she'd held a book of divine attributes. Now the memories writhed like maggots. Too late for the Polyglot to hide.

"Get the fuck out," she said.

"'For how long will you refuse to see yourself,'" he quoted, "'as you are and as you will be?'" Every few words a different dialect, *Tunisian, Egyptian, Moroccan*, the Polyglot struggling to keep up.

"'Each grain of sand takes its own length and breadth as the measure of the world.'" Not struggling, drowning, *Lebanese, Kuwaiti, Hejazi*, each a new history in scuffs and scratches.

"'Yet, beside a mountain range, it is as nothing. You yourself are the grain of sand, you are your own prisoner.'" Each a magnificent history, bigger than her brain.

"Get out!" she cried.

She doubled over. The Polyglot slid back into place with a thud in her skull. An effort not to cry or shit. Douglas had gone. She knocked her folio off the table, read it sideways. No Douglas on her agenda. He'd come in pique.

On wobbly legs, she rode the elevator to the lobby. Walking and city air revived her. The business district gave way to low brick buildings, ground-floor yuppie shops. After London, she understood Boston's broken blocks and short streets. From the roof she had seen a park in the west. She could find it by feel.

Endre called. "Did you leave the building?" he asked in Hungarian.

"Stick to English. What was Douglas doing there?"

"That guy. Acts like he's doing us favors. I don't know what Magda's thinking."

"He's a nasty bitch, Endre. Did something with Arabic. Split my head open."

"I'll tell Magda."

"No. Magda's my boss not my mommy. You want to help? Find a way to hurt that fucker. Thanks for lunch."

The park had dark green grass, rows of wilting red and yellow tulips. On a bench by a pond, she lit her joint discreetly, cigarettes on the bench beside her as a disguise. Power of suggestion. Maybe Douglas had heard from Magda herself. Maybe it was a slap for Aberdeen, for other fuckups, for kicks. She walked through trees to the next clearing, lost in her rising high. Until she was surrounded by bums.

She looked around in a panic. Bums all around her, matted beards, ash on their clothes. Like a zombie movie. With smell. At the far end of the clearing, tables held franks and beans, cut cobs of corn. The workers assembling the meal all wore cherry-red t-shirts and black gym shorts. The bums lined up for the charity food. She lit a cigarette, watched with creepy fascination. Some hurried off with their plates, some stood talking as if at a cocktail party. Homelessness porn. In her early days in Philadelphia she'd eaten charity dinners. She spoke Italian and Chinese now, partied with Russian spooks and London mages. Not like these people. Never like them.

She spat, spat again, sat unladylike on a sycamore's shallow root. *What would your mother say?* Missy used to ask, before she learned Zarabeth's history and let the phrase drop.

Two plateless men approached her, one skeletal dark black, one puffy gray-white with a leering smile. The gray one pantomimed smoking.

"Absolutely," Zarabeth said. "Who needs food?" The joke relaxed them all. She held up two cigarettes. The black man lit his immediately with a disposable lighter. The gray man put his in a pocket. They walked away.

It felt like an omen. She regretted not bringing her cards. Maybe for the best. Always looking ahead, vulnerable from behind. The past as much threat as the future.

Every day, Zarabeth thought about her mother. With hate, with anger, with contempt, all a hope for a response as if by magic. What she had to do came wordlessly, like judging when to cross a street. She called Jill.

"What happened to you?" Jill asked.

Zarabeth spoke with weary confidence. "Something's come up. Is it too late to get me to Pittsburgh? Night at a hotel. Cheap is fine. Thanks for all the help today."

Of course Magda would ask. Let her ask.

CHAPTER NINETEEN

Pittsburgh

Zarabeth remembered the old airport from her childhood, brown and boxy like a loading dock. She wandered dumbstruck through Pittsburgh International's contoured empty corridors, shivering in the air-conditioning. A new highway running east along tall bare hills. The cab ride felt like fragile privilege, as if she were an upscale whore doing a stint in Pyongyang.

Downtown looked better than she remembered, cleaner, with new skyscrapers. Her hotel was near the silver dome of the hockey stadium. As they approached the hotel, she saw a giant building down the hill. "What's that?"

"New stadium," the driver told her. "Just open. Hockey'll move there plus concerts."

"What'll happen to the Igloo?"

"Was gonna tear it down n'at, but people fight it. Nobody like replaced one big lot with another anymore. You from the 'Burgh?"

She blushed with shame. She had worked hard to purge her accent, but the Polyglot had restored it. "Ain't you a nebby-nose," she said.

The lobby clerk stood a head taller than Zarabeth, blonde

with thick makeup on her drooping cheeks. "With your corporate account you have access to our club level." Something about soft drinks, lost in the rush of hate. Zarabeth knew the clerk's clones from high school, early bloomers who gave her grief for her slutty mother while getting felt up by this week's boy. Stick the pen in her pig eye.

The clerk drew back. "Do you want help—"

"No." Zarabeth pushed away her signed forms.

Her twelfth-floor room had two beds and stank of smoke. A good view of downtown, from the punch card aluminum building past the stadiums to the edge of the Hill. She hung her other blouse, lit her own cigarette, sat until the room was dark.

She turned on the nightstand light. The hotel white pages old and torn. *Battrie Aurinha G*, the address east, near Wilkinsburg. Zarabeth called from the room phone.

"Hello?"

Zarabeth listened as if the word was an open watch. Her mother. Alive. Older. Sober. "It's your daughter, Mom," she said. "Joanna." Her birth name, dusty in her mouth.

A clattering noise. Her mother had dropped the phone. "Hello? Joanna? It is really you? Are you all right?"

"I'm fine, Mom. I'm in Pittsburgh. I want to see you. To talk. Will you see me?"

"Of course. I—" Her mother was panting. "Now I'm leaving. I must work. I am sorry."

"You work nights?"

"At the old people's home. A nurse. Are you here tomorrow? Can we meet tomorrow? In the afternoon. When I wake up. Will you come? You must promise. I must see you. I'd see you now but I can't—"

Her mother, desperate to keep her job. Deep in Zarabeth's heart an old pain died hotly, like a root canal. "Mom, it's OK. I promise. Tomorrow. What's your address?"

Aurinha gave the same one in the phone book. "You will really come?"

"I will really come, Mom. Two o'clock. Now go to work."

At the hotel's whitewashed wood bar, Zarabeth had three rum-diet-cola-limes and two plates of chicken wings in spicy red sauce. They weren't good but she liked the work, squeezing the tip of her tongue between thin bones, sucking meat from gristle. The meal made her indolent, like a snake after a big rat. She curled up on the bed nearer the window, Pittsburgh for her nightlight. Tomorrow she would see her mother. After twelve years she made it happen in three hours. Funny from the outside.

* * *

Eight-thirty. Pittsburgh out her window. Like fairies had kidnapped her.

The club buffet had greasy maple-syrup sausages and packing-foam scrambled eggs. She ate a few bites of egg, wrapped a bagel and an apple in a cloth napkin and put them in her bag. In the elevator down she used her phone to check out.

Warm sun in a dazzling blue sky. Downhill stood the great temples to metal, to all needful and good they gave. The steel building rusting to protect itself (magic to a child), aluminum skins with portholes. She had never appreciated the whimsy.

From the now-clean theater district, she walked across a yellow bridge to the Andy Warhol Museum. Since leaving, she had learned of him: left Pittsburgh, scraped and worked, nearly killed, had wild parties. Her own life but grander. The art just looked like billboards, but she liked the party pictures. Ancient A-listers in giant glasses and wide collars, at ease with Warhol and his freaks.

She ate her apple and half the bagel by the river, oddly pleased to see the renewed city. Another life for her too, just not here. If only her father had lived.

The bus ride up the Hill looked less new, closer up, not that Zarabeth had spent much time looking. Making out with boys, swapping shoplifted goods with friends, being high. Ah youth. She had cried every minute of it, and never known until now.

Her mother's apartment building was tan brick and chain-link. Smashed keypad lock outside the open door. Zarabeth had run away to not end up in a place like this.

Up two flights. She wiped her sweaty hands on her bare legs and knocked on the door.

Her mother was shorter, plumper with age, but still beautiful, beauty enough to hate. She wore an ugly striped blouse, cheap stiff jeans.

"Hi, Mom," Zarabeth said.

"It hurts me to see you," Aurinha said.

"I can go."

"No!" She grabbed Zarabeth's arm. "If I hide a feeling, I want to drink. So I don't." She took a deep breath. "Come in."

Dingy walls, a thumbtacked poster of yellow flowers. Threadbare green armchair, scratched coffee table, two metal folding chairs with padded seats, pots of dead plants.

"You are a beautiful woman," Aurinha said. "Your teeth! So straight. You wore metal?"

"Plastic now. You can take them off to eat."

"They look wonderful. You want a drink? Water or diet."

"Diet." Zarabeth sat on a folding chair. Her arm was sore where her mother had grabbed her. Aurinha had strong hands now, not the dead fish of her drinking days. On the table, a library paperback in Portuguese. She opened it and read: *what is fully mature is almost close to rotting*

"I get from the library," Aurinha said. She gave Zarabeth a can, store-brand cola but a straw in the open spout. She sat in the armchair. "I don't read it. It's sad."

They sat waiting for the other to yell. They didn't.

"I looked for you," Aurinha whispered. "Online. They have computers at the home."

"I changed my name. I'm Zarabeth Battrie now."

"Zarabeth." Aurinha mouthed it several times. "Why did you pick that?"

"I heard it on a TV show. A princess in a land of ice where she couldn't be a princess. It felt like me."

"I wanted to call you Elisabeta. Joanna was your father's choice. Zarabeth. I will say that. You are what I hoped you would be. Are you here because you remember?"

"Remember what?"

Her mother's big eyes looked ready to cry. "Why did you come?"

"I felt I was missing something."

Aurinha nodded like a seizure. "I wanted to tell you, always. But I was always drunk and it was hard between us." She sighed. "How old am I?"

"You had me at twenty-seven So, fifty-four, fifty-five?"

"I'm forty-five. I think. Forty-four maybe."

"You got married at fifteen? Did Dad know?"

"Your father never married me," Aurinha said. "Your father bought me when I was eight. He liked sex with children. I was his, for sex."

Zarabeth didn't want to swallow. She spat in the pot of a dead plant, wiped her mouth with the back of her hand. "Sorry."

"The bathroom is—"

"I'm fine."

"You don't believe me," her mother said.

"Tell me anyway."

"I don't remember my father," Aurinha said. "Sometimes, a man, black beard and red shirt. I don't know. There was me and Mother. I don't know how that is. It was long ago, and the drinking took my memory. Mother looked—like me and you. Beautiful, but life was hard. She worked fields. I stayed with an old lady with one eye who gave me sugar. She told me about Negrinho do Pastorieo, about Black Vivian. To catch a Saci in a bottle in the wind and ask a favor."

"You're talking about magic," Zarabeth said.

Aurinha nodded. "Good. I lie to therapists. I caught a Saci, asked if Mother could not work so much. A few days later, she was killed by a car. I was in the orphanage, a sad place, not cruel but hard. We wore clothes given by poor people. All with holes. The food was barely eatable."

"But I knew the magic. I made the food better. I healed bruises. The others grew jealous and afraid. I had no friends. I thought, if I am pretty, a family will adopt me. I caught a Saci and asked to be like a princess. Soon they say I meet a family. I got to wash by myself, and a clean dress. It was your father. He was nice.

253

There were candies, hot tea. I fell asleep. When I woke up I was naked, tied to a bed. He made me his. With drugs and chains and—electric."

"You had magic." Zarabeth wanted to climb upward, as if roaches covered the floor.

"I was a child. When I gave in, he had food, candies, presents. Drugs, but fun now. He was a child too. I was his doll for tea parties. Once a year in the city, he bought me women's clothes at private tailors. He taught me to walk in heels."

"We lived like this for five years. I grew, I felt desire, I imagined men I had seen. I told myself he was love, Beauty and Beast. He got the job in America. With makeup and clothes, I looked twenty-five. A good story, poor beauty and rich older man. I learned English from TV, kept the house. At faculty parties, younger men stare me naked, but for him I was almost too much woman. So I made a baby."

She smiled with joy. "We had such fun. Oh, you could laugh. Laugh and laugh." Tears dropped from Aurinha's eyes. "You didn't sleep well, we had a nightlight for you. In the day, you would laugh. But you grew up. In school, you had friends, it wasn't just Mommy. So I drank. It made it harder to see. I thought he was too old. He took you camping. When you came back you were tired and sad. No bath just shower."

"He didn't—" Their last camping trip, three nights under the stars, they would start to name constellations but she fell asleep each time, like a bird in an oil slick.

"He used drugs," Aurinha said. "He wasn't big but he needed to stretch a little girl. I knew what he would do to you. I killed a bird and offered it to Black Vivian."

"You gave Dad his cancer," Zarabeth said. "With magic."

Her dad's final days, chalk-white but mottled with black bruises, his breathing labored, looking at her as if at a stranger. Not love never love, her father only regretted not fucking her.

"Can I smoke?" She fumbled out the last of her pack. "Why didn't you tell me?"

"When he grew sick and couldn't touch you, you took baths again. You forgot—"

"I repressed it?"

"You loved your father. Dead, you loved him more. He was gone. I met Sheldon."

Fat fuck in suede, didn't bother to remove his wedding ring. "The first of many. Those men took everything from us," Zarabeth said. "They always tried to fuck me. One would have raped me but you came home."

"You have to see," Aurinha said. "I had the mind of a drunken child. I learned America from television. I knew men wanted me. I thought I would just go out and find a new husband. You were more grown-up than I was."

"You threw away everything Dad left us. You threw me away."

"I know! I knew it then. You know what it's like to know? I just thought—a little longer and I find a good man. A little longer, Joanie can help. Even when drunk, even when we fought, even when you did bad in school. I knew how smart you were."

"You knew about my trust fund."

"I am no good with money." Aurinha sighed. "I just thought you would stay. Like I did. How did you get money to leave? I know you had no job."

"I worked out a deal with Dad's lawyer," Zarabeth said. "For eighty cents on the dollar and a blowjob I signed the trust over to him."

"Querida—"

"He wanted you. He kept saying your name. Construction guys, salesmen? You should have aimed higher. Life as a lawyer's mistress would have been easier."

Aurinha hissed. She swung her arm. Zarabeth caught her wrist, dug her nails in the soft flesh. Aurinha cried in pain. Zarabeth bolted up, throwing her mother hard against the wall. Aurinha landed hard, limp like a doll. Crying.

Zarabeth knelt beside her. Aurinha drew back in fear.

"Mom. Mom I'm sorry. I'm so sorry. I—"

Her mother held her tight with her new strong arms. Pain made it less weird.

"Shh," her mother said, stroking her hair. "Shh."

* * *

Zarabeth woke in the dark. On the floor, on a pillow, under a throw. She felt she had run a marathon in her sleep. She felt her mother watching.

"Hi," Zarabeth said.

Her mother turned on a small lamp. She wore scrubs patterned with hot-air balloons. "Are you hungry?"

"Could use some water. When do you leave for work?"

"I've already gone. I left early. I wasn't sure you would be here."

Zarabeth found her phone. One-forty-seven. "I missed my flight. They'll fly tomorrow. Today, I mean."

"It will not hurt your job?" Aurinha asked.

"I'm in a downtime now."

"What is your job?"

"Corporate espionage." Zarabeth climbed on the chair, took the water. "I cause problems for companies and steal their secrets."

"This is not honest work?"

"Better than cleaning bedpans. I'm sorry. I'm not used to being nice to you. I should thank you. If you hadn't—" It was funny. "Thanks for killing Dad, Mom."

A smile on Aurinha's stunned cow face. Soon they were giggling. They stayed up through the dawn, talking about the decade they had missed. Zarabeth's life in Philadelphia, how she had worked her way to a white collar.

Aurinha talked about the final men, the beating that put her into rehab. Without dentures her face collapsed. Zarabeth's old resentment peeled away. Zarabeth had become the parent she'd always wanted, that her mother could never have been.

At dawn they walked to a diner. The coffee greasy and stiff. Aurinha drank water, ate one egg and one piece of toast. "I will sleep soon," she said. Zarabeth had four eggs with bacon and sausage. Around them, patrons and noise. Enough to be together, in public, not making a scene.

While she waited for change, Zarabeth booked a flight from her phone.

"You are good with this," Aurinha said. "I only can enter in patient charts." She pantomimed keying with slow index fingers. "Why letters are not in order?"

"From old typewriters. We're stuck with it. What's your cell?"

"I don't have. My phone comes with the rent. Only local calls."

"I'll send you one," Zarabeth said. "Like a regular phone. Just numbers."

"I can't pay—"

"A gift," Zarabeth said. "I'll put it on my account. I'd like to be able to talk to you."

"I will take the phone."

On the walk back to Aurinha's apartment, Zarabeth stopped at a market for cigarettes. Aurinha waited outside, shifting uneasily, like a teen trying to buy beer. When Zarabeth walked out she took her mother's hand.

The apartment was dark, the blinds drawn.

"It is why the plants are dead. I forget to open when I leave." Aurinha opened them. In the sunlight, clouds of dust. "I miss the daytime." She stared sleepily at Zarabeth, head cocked to the left. "I have something for you. Wait."

After a few minutes Aurinha came out with a paper bag. "Your father told me about this before he died. 'You were good to me,' he said. He died believing I loved him. I regret that, but now I can give you this."

The bag brittle with age. Inside, a dented tobacco tin full of stones. Zarabeth held some up to the sunlight. Red, green, cool white. "Are these uncut gemstones?"

"He stole them from work sites, or paid miners for them."

"There's thousands here. More." Zarabeth panted. "You had this, all this time?"

"I use it how?" Aurinha looked pitiable. "Men would take it. I would drink it. I kept it for you. You make this money."

Partying and shoplifting with a fortune in Mom's closet. Her drunk mother yelling in pidgin English at gem brokers. Zarabeth wasn't even mad. "You did good, Mom." The Polyglot curled around seeds of Yiddish, of Afrikaans. "What's my cut?"

"All for you. I lived without it. Just use some of the money to visit me."

"And I'll send you the phone."

"You believe me about the magic," her mother said. "You know magic yourself. Querida, you must not. It is always worse."

"You saved me with it. It must be good for something. Goodbye, Mom. Thank you."

Her mother hugged her tightly. "You are the good thing from my life," she said into Zarabeth's jacket. "Do you have a man?"

"No. No men."

"Good. Men are pigs."

Zarabeth walked for blocks before she saw a cab. The airport run delighted the driver. Everyone happy with her.

On the Interstate she peeked in the box again. Hundreds of thousands in rocks. Throw them out, let them weather a billion years by the roadside. She put her hand on the window crank.

In her mind, a voice not hers: *Killing a man without picking his carcass is wasteful.*

Zarabeth shoved it in her bag. She stared out the window at the mile markers, one after another after another. Goddamned if she was going to cry.

JULY 2009

CHAPTER TWENTY

Washington, DC

Walt picked him up in a rusted red hatchback, sharply sweet with cleaning chemicals. "I'm doing volunteer work," Walt explained. "Not a place to drive a nice car. I got this for a thousand. Missy made fun of me, now she borrows it twice a week."

"At least you bought American." Gabriel rolled down the window for fresh air.

"Airbag thieves favor Japanese cars."

"This has airbags?"

"Be nice. I had it detailed for you. Guy looked at me like I was crazy."

They took an old highway south, following the map on Walt's phone while it played lounge music through a cassette adapter. Gabriel nodded off. When he woke they were in the city. To the south, the Capitol dome sat atop a gray-brown hill, like a boil from dirty skin.

"It's big," Gabriel said. "I didn't realize."

"Like cathedrals in South American towns," Walt said. "Hovel hovel hovel hovel spire. Not that they're exactly hovels around it."

"I thought the city would be taller."

"No high-rises in the city limits. I tell Sasha she should buy. She thinks money will never move to where she is."

"The Indians probably felt the same way," Gabriel said.

They drove another half-hour across the city, a broad and spreading pool of townhouses and low buildings, nothing allowed to challenge the sky. Older trees shaded the last blocks before Walt turned down a brick-paved alley into a tiny listing garage.

"Clean up, or breakfast?" Walt asked.

"If I clean up I'll just want to nap," Gabriel said. "Breakfast."

"We'll go from here, then." They walked down the alley. "This area is called Georgetown. It's WASP style, so showy about not being showy." He pointed backwards. "That's us." The gray stucco mansion took up the southeast corner of the block, each wing wider than any neighbor's house.

"How much is the rent on that?"

"That's her place." Walt told him the story. Chat up a server, court a slumming rich girl. Hard to believe, from a man who'd spent decades keeping his affairs light, but he seemed happy at the turn of events.

They went to a French café thick with sweet fat smells, cream and butter and praline. A server brought menus. "This woman I'm meeting, is she an heiress too?" Gabriel asked.

"Working stiff. But white-collar."

"What's she like?"

"Moody hot bitch, like I said. Street smart. Full disclosure, she parties hard."

"Bring it on," Gabriel said. "I drink whisky now. Just Scotch. For the smell. Even went to Scotland. Got some leave with the new job."

"You'll have to give me pointers. What new job?"

"I can't talk about it. The company directory has me doing background checks on staff. You'd never believe that, so. At least you know you don't know."

Walt gave him an odd look, as if Gabriel played a trick on him, as if someone had warned Walt that Gabriel would.

"Was it a good move at least?" Walt asked.

"So far I'm not quitting," Gabriel said.

"But it's driven you to drink."

* * *

Inside the mansion, the east wing was mid-renovation, with patched drywall and naked wiring. On the stair wall, square-jawed women in sumptuous dress gave hard stares from a century of portraits. The north wing wore lace and velvet curtains, gilt-patterned wallpaper, draped chairs and divans.

"I know it looks like a museum display, but sit." The wiry woman was of the portraits' line, but wearing black athletic tights and a white campaign t-shirt. Her odor dank like a forest creature. "Missy Devereaux. Delighted to meet you." Martial recognition in her eyes, as if both were part of a con game, Walt the mark, the décor all rented. "You're the first of Walt's friends I've met, you know."

"I don't know too many myself."

"I compartmentalize," Walt said, carrying Gabriel's bag in from the garage. "Playboy in Tahoe, outlaw in Waziristan. Part of the myth. Nice bag."

"It's my housemate's. Someone never sent mine back from Tahoe." Gabriel opened the front pocket, gave Missy a gift box of chocolates. "For the hospitality."

"How delightful. Let me show you upstairs so you can freshen up. My apologies for the construction. In my grandmother's final days we made her a hospital. By fall it'll be restored, except I'm making the wine cellar a sauna."

"Sorry for your loss. Are any of these her?"

"No," Missy said, looking at the paintings as if for the first time. "I should swap out of one of these great-greats. Walt says you're a business analyst?"

"Was. I changed jobs. I'm an investigator now. Background checks on new hires."

"How interesting," Missy said.

"Once in a while, yeah."

The guest room had antique green-striped wallpaper and a raised four-poster bed heavy with pillows.

"This looks comfortable," Gabriel said. Missy and Walt stared at him, as if their smiles hid anticipation, as if waiting to spring a trap. "With the red-eye I thought I might rest a little."

"Absolutely," Walt said. "Siesta. Cocktails at five."

Alone Gabriel felt ill at ease. His skin pricking, a thunderstorm smell. In the shower his nose itched and ran. On the bed he curled up in the pillows like a clownfish in anemone. A gasoline smell. He knew what it was but did not believe it.

He threw on clothes, stumbled downstairs as the house rolled over. He found Walt and Missy in a small kitchen, mantis hands poised over the chocolate box.

"If you could—I don't—" Gabriel's sneeze squirted blood from his nose. "Sorry." He took a kitchen towel to stop it, fell to his knees. "Is occult activity going on here?"

They stared blankly at him, at each other.

Missy crossed her arms, whispered a long hissing phrase. "Better?"

The house now upright, but buzzing like an old tube light. "Better. Thanks."

"You must be very sensitive."

"Just not good at it yet." Falling into dream worlds, again and again. "I'll go clean up."

"Leave me your shirt," Missy said. "I'm good at getting blood out."

He washed his face. He lay uneasily, as if under a hornet's nest. His room now old charming smells—mothballs, potpourri, laundry soap. Soon he slept.

* * *

He woke just after four. He styled his hair, dressed in gold pants and a sky-blue shirt. When he was ready he sat, ten minutes, thirty. He didn't want to leave the room.

In the chintzy parlor, Walt wore a yellow silk bowling shirt,

Missy a sundress patterned in green bamboo. Cheese and crackers on the table.

"You wash your linens in laundry soap," Gabriel said. "It's plush."

"Thank you for saying," Missy said. "Walt doesn't appreciate the difference. I think he could sleep in polyester." When he sat, her eyes darted around him, as if looking for weapons. "Walt never mentioned you work for Empyrean."

"How was I to know," Walt said, getting up. "There's a thousand consulting firms. You wanted a hot boy for Betsy. Voilà. Gabriel, drink?"

"Water."

Missy sighed. "Clearly Walt didn't know—what we know."

"I didn't know a house could attack me."

"It won't happen again. Save with family, I'm not accustomed to wisdom and hospitality coming into conflict."

"Are you asking me to leave?"

Walt gave him ice water in a heavy crystal tumbler. "You're *not* leaving."

"Missy, I'm as blindsided as you," Gabriel said. "Maybe I should go. But I didn't ask for this. It happened to me. I don't care. If you keep—I'm just here for a vacation."

The doorbell rang, six long tones. Missy threw up her hands. "For once, she's early." She answered the door.

Gabriel smelled salt, tobacco, marijuana; behind it sand and rust. His body knew before his brain could form the name. He stood.

In walked Zarabeth, hair shorter, skin darker, wearing bright red.

When she saw him, she shoved Missy aside.

They flew to each other, their lips magnets.

CHAPTER TWENTY-ONE

Washington, DC

Explain this." Missy was larger than usual. Angry Missy in her own house.

"Back off." Zarabeth stepped back. Three steps to the door? Four?

"An Empyrean man? You reckless bitch! Did you *think*—"

"Artemis McCauley Devereaux!" Deep from Walt's big chest. "We have *guests*."

Missy crouched like a cat ninja. "Of course."

Walt smiled wanly. "Let's sit down."

"Let's not," Zarabeth said. She walked out.

Gabriel followed her across the street. She leaned against a rough brick wall, panting. "You ever get in a fight you knew you'd lose?" she asked.

"I know the feeling." He put a light hand on her shoulder. "Hi."

"Hi. This is—you're friends with Walt?"

"Business school."

"He didn't tell you about me?"

"He called you Betsy and said you were hot."

"The fucker. He must have known."

"I don't see how." He took her hand. A nothing, but it

soothed her.

Coming down the block, Walt's crap car.

"All this and the fucking beater too," Zarabeth said.

"He had it detailed," Gabriel said.

She sat behind the passenger seat. Gabriel got in behind Walt. "Where's Missy?"

"She's coming," Walt said. "I've never seen her like this."

"Told you I had a new job," Gabriel said.

Missy came out, eyes bright, but still blue. "We'll be early for our reservation."

"They'll manage," Walt said.

They drove east across town under a chrome-blue sky. Gabriel held Zarabeth's hand but looked out the window at the city. His hot palm prickled like rat whiskers but to look at him he was plastic and perfect.

At a modish Indian restaurant, they took the window table. Above them a low yellow light with a tasseled fabric shade, domed to contain explosions. They ordered drinks, read menus in silence, until Missy snapped hers closed.

"Let's wait for the drinks," Zarabeth said.

"Let's not," Missy said.

"We met in Aberdeen," Gabriel said. "A rainy night. I chatted her up in the hotel bar."

"He invited me to tour distilleries with him," Zarabeth said. "He had a hot car."

"Did you know where the other worked?"

"No," Gabriel said.

"Not at first," Zarabeth said. "He gave me his card. I went anyway. It seemed wiser to keep him close."

"Our drinks are coming," Walt said. "There is a goddess."

Missy snorted. They ordered food. Walt raised his glass but no one joined him.

"Continue," Missy said.

"Why?" Gabriel asked. "Will you snitch on your friend? None of this is your business." Gabriel's voice level but his skin fever hot. "I offered to get a hotel."

"An empty threat," Walt said. "On July 4th places with

bedbugs are full." He pointed at Zarabeth. "You made the booty call."

"Someone had to," Zarabeth said. "The next morning he left."

"My vacation was canceled for work," Gabriel said.

"Did you plan to keep in touch?" Missy asked.

"Of course not," Gabriel said.

"Seriously, Missy, fuck you," Zarabeth said. "You're not even at the firm anymore."

Missy's eyes wide and wild.

"You know what's hard?" Walt asked abruptly. "Commercial real estate in Japan. Without a local you can't do it. They don't use square meters, they use a unit equivalent to one woven grass mat. Which is a rectangular unit, mind you."

He kept talking for the next half hour. Japanese office politics, Australian domain squatters, haggling with taxis in Bangkok. The rest ate their food in silence, as if it were a sermon at a commune meal, Walt's Business Sutra.

When the check came Gabriel took it. Walt gave him a house key. "We're going to turn in. You kids catch up. Come in whenever."

After they left Gabriel smiled ruefully. "Is Missy going to kill me?"

"She doesn't like complications she didn't engineer." Zarabeth laughed. "I can't believe Walt whipped out the Name." Her laughter sputtered like a match. Enemy lover and his trash.

"I'm sorry I hurt you," Gabriel said. "When I left."

"Business before pleasure."

"No. I just liked the way you looked asleep," he said. "I'm glad to see you again."

"This is a total fucking mess," Zarabeth said. "Let's go to my place."

* * *

Zarabeth's apartment was close to the river, in a cluster of bland buildings like Soviet worker housing. Glass shelves of art books, angular metal sculptures, a small black piano. Gabriel closed his eyes. It smelled rich with vice: coffee, tobacco, pot, spilled cocktails and wine.

"You like my place?" she asked.

"Nice view. You rent it furnished?"

"Sublet. Sit down."

On the slick leather sofa they kissed gently, warm and pleasant but weak. She took his hand and led him to the bedroom. She lit a tea light candle in a red and green glass holder. On the wall, a bulletin board heavy with travel remains: curling thermal boarding passes, cardboard tickets with magnetic strips, inkjet printouts.

"This I like," he said.

"An antique in the making. Soon we'll just show the barcode on our phones."

"You could always go to rougher places."

"I go where I'm sent," she said, her tone prickly. "Sorry. Curl up with me. Now now now. No shirt no shoes. No nothing." They lay on their sides, skin to skin, his murmuring cock softly plump between her buttocks.

"Fuck me tomorrow," she whispered. In a minute she was asleep. He edged away to cool their skin. A pimple behind her ear had burst, blood and gunk pearled around bits of smoke. Skin to gland to capillary to artery to bone, layers and layers. Vertigo like looking down a cliff.

* * *

They woke up into kissing, into touch.

"You're thinking we're supposed to screw now," he said.

"Yes."

"Since when do you do what you're supposed to?"

That made her giggle. They wore yesterday's clothes to a coffee house, sat in deep chairs with coffees the size of soup bowls. They shared a newspaper. No talking, occasional touches on hands, shoulders. Like couples do.

At ten Walt called, suggesting a canoe ride. Gabriel was leery but agreed. By eleven they were on the river, Walt and Missy with the cooler, Gabriel in one of Walt's broad-brimmed floppy hats. They paddled upstream, where it was too shallow for commercial boats. Narrow strips of parkland lined both shores, distant rooftops the only sign of city. She could barely make the paddle work.

"I didn't know you had nature like this," Gabriel said. "We sailed when I was a kid. My brother and my dad ran the sails, and Mom on the tiller. I was navigator and naturalist. I took it seriously. Listened to weather radio, marked charts, read field guides."

He pointed out ospreys circling high, swimming pairs of mallard ducks, a haughty gray heron that launched like an open umbrella in the wind. "Birds are my favorite. Just the names: warbler, heron, stilt, grebe, pelican, loon, plover. With my brother I did stars."

"What about your sister?"

"She was already in college." He pointed at Missy's canoe. "They're coming back."

"Good," Zarabeth said. "They have the wine."

Walt lashed the canoes together with hooked bungee cords. They drifted downstream eating and drinking, smoked a joint Walt had tucked in the crown of his hat. In the current they lazily spun, laughed, and talked. Like couples do.

* * *

He woke to smells of acetone and pot, shrill lavender. Zarabeth stood in the doorway.

"Hey sexy," she said. "Love the bathrobe."

"Hey." He untwisted it from around him. "I found it in the closet. Good spa?"

"My feet hurt less than usual." She put her left foot on the bed. Yellow nails with glitter and stripes, a gold-dust butterfly on the big toe. The bonding chemical made his eyes water.

"Pretty," he said. He kissed her ankle without breathing. "What's the lavender?"

She beamed like a schoolgirl. "You like it? Missy's idea. She thought you'd like it."

"It's sweet, like candy," he said. "I should get dressed."

"Come as you are. Food's on the roof deck. I got you garlic chicken. Seemed a safe bet."

"Food?" Six-thirty. "Sorry I overslept."

"I let you sleep so I could smoke." She reached inside the bathrobe, drew yellow nails down his stomach. "OK, tie up." She led him up narrow service stairs to a metal ladder. He climbed up, cold metal stinging his feet. "Looking up your skirt," she sang below him.

The roof was sticky hot. Walt and Missy sat at a small table under a big shade umbrella. Gabriel clambered onto the deck.

"Making yourself at home," Missy said.

"I think it's a good look for him," Zarabeth balanced on the top rung and stepped off.

"Don't crack your head open," Walt said.

"You'd laugh if I did."

The party was several rounds in, Walt slow and Missy's eyes redder than Zarabeth's. Gabriel opened a beer while they unwrapped the food.

"What's with you and lamb?" Walt asked Zarabeth. "It's all you get. Like food-autism."

"I saw that movie with the cannibal shrink," Zarabeth said. "He was smart and he wouldn't say no. He liked lamb. It's my own little thing now."

"We all have role models," Missy said.

"I'm just jealous," Walt said. "Missy says it's too fat. Last week Sasha got me to try Jamaican goat curry. It's not bad."

Missy's smell a nasty algae rot, at Walt's mention of his project.

Walt noticed Gabriel's flinch. "What is it now between you two?"

"Nothing," Missy said, surprised.

"Archer?"

It might just be jealousy. "Nothing," Gabriel said. "Little chill."

* * *

Zarabeth stole away after dinner, to change clothes, to be alone. In her apartment she lay on the carpet. One cigarette, two, thinking about Sasha Blackwell. An urge to go see her, but risky and pointless. Sasha left when her mother died. Zarabeth's mother survived, but not in a world Zarabeth wanted.

She did her face, found a clean thong. In her closet she found a backless dress with black and white curved lines, like a bouquet of zebra orchids. With black pumps and dress tape, it gave her hips. She twirled while smoking a pipe of Mapelberry pot.

They came in a town car at ten-thirty, the men in shirts and slacks whatever, Missy in a ruched mini like a fuckable lamp. "No beater?" Zarabeth asked.

"Walt wants to drink." Missy frowned. "Is that my dress?"

"This old thing?"

"Give it back tomorrow and don't spill cola on it."

"I like the perfume," Gabriel said. He licked along her carotid artery.

"Get a room," Missy sniffed.

They started in a low-key Dupont nightclub, up a long flight of stairs from the street. A small bar, a dimly lit room. "Once this place had lines down the block," Missy said. "They vetted you at the door."

"Ah youth," Zarabeth said.

Missy ducked behind Walt. At the other end of the bar stood a dark-haired white man in a business suit, slouching to talk to a dolled-up white blonde.

"Freshman congressman from Louisiana," Missy hissed. "He hosted that Tea Party thing. He should be home fundraising."

"Maybe she's an heiress," Gabriel said.

"Not in that dress."

"There's a back deck," Zarabeth said. "You go. We'll get the drinks." When Missy and Gabriel left she studied Congressdog. He looked tired and contemptuous. Maybe just drunk.

Walt shook his head. "Don't."

"What?" She glanced back. "That?" She rocked her pelvis to get the dress moving, walked over. "Excuse me but I saw your shoes?" she said, high-pitched and breathless. "I *love* your shoes.

Are they Kate? They look like Kate."

"Oh! These," the woman said. "They're Jimmy, actually."

"They're darling." Congressdog was looking. "Hi there," she said.

"Uh, sorry, we're having a conversation," the woman said.

"Of course! Jimmy. Nice!" She whirled the skirt, shuddered down her naked back.

When she came back Walt had the drinks. "Start something?"

"She's a tramp," Zarabeth said. "Those shoes are no more Jimmy than you are." The steamy roof deck was nearly empty, three people at the bar, Missy and Gabriel at a high table. "Fuck. They're *talking*."

"Had to happen sometime," Walt said. "If they start using Latin, translate for me."

They arrived with Missy mid-rant. "Your side looks backwards," she said. "Megachurches are just the mall version of the same top-down seven-day-world nonsense, with gays allowed for production numbers. Look how the Vatican killed liberation theology and covers up pedophiles. Look at how Baptists run from evolution. God didn't sneeze them whole and complete, life isn't worth living. No witch would ever be so presumptuous."

"You use string theory in your spells?" Gabriel said.

"Hidden dimensions, knotted space? Perfect for Celtic thought. Lately I like quantum gravity, where causation has a role in the structure of space-time. Easier to hack."

"All I heard," Gabriel said, "was hack. That's my point. You distort local spirit the same way pollution distorts local ecosystems."

"We develop rites with nature in mind! We change holy days in the southern hemisphere. The people of the Book destroy their Earth because they think God will give them another. Four hundred years of proving you're wrong and still you maintain your ridiculous stance. Next you'll tell me the sun goes around the earth."

"For timekeeping, it does," Gabriel said. "I don't argue that the old faiths made mistakes. But I don't see you making the future. I don't see you doing anything. Because you hide. I don't like my church, I can read the books myself. You lurk in shadows then act offended when we find you disreputable. Why do you get to be a mystery?"

"Because mysteries do things the untrained can't and shouldn't."

"If secrets are good, what's wrong with the guy inside?"

Missy grunted in frustration, hopped backwards off the stool like a trick rider.

"Sorry," Gabriel said, his body hot with anger.

"Relax. It took the pressure off." Walt drew himself up. "Someone went to pee."

Congressdog stood on the deck, looking around. Missy came back with an ice water. They saw each other. He hurried inside. Zarabeth felt Missy's disgust like the gypsy's evil eye in Rome. Crazy sensitive tonight. Maybe it was the bare back.

"Was he looking for *you*?" Missy asked her.

"He winked at me at the bar," Zarabeth said, scandalized. "I was about to tell you."

"That's one fewer check to write," Missy said. "I want another drink. Everyone?"

"Club soda for me this time," Gabriel said. Abruptly he gave Zarabeth a big possessive kiss. "I'm glad Missy scared him off," he said. "I might have caused some trouble."

"Mmm." She kissed him again, caught Walt's eye. He gave her a small wink.

After another round they went in. A jazz trio, nothing to dance to. They tried other clubs, empty too and with weak DJs. Missy drank hard, danced anyway. They ended up in a basement club lit insistent red like an exit sign, Missy twisted drunk, Walt sloppy.

Zarabeth bit Gabriel's earlobe. "Let's ditch them. Meet you on the street." She joined the dancing. Walt raised his hands, stupidly happy, a bum who won the lottery.

Gabriel snuck out. Zarabeth came up minutes later, fell into Gabriel. She gave the cab Missy's address. "My bed is small and covered in clothes. And stinks of smoke." She threw her legs over his thighs. He massaged her calves with slow strokes. "Oh yes."

"Your reward for the shoes," he said.

They were at Missy's in ten minutes. A faint tickle as the house inspected her. She shook it off. Gabriel scooped her up, pressed his lips to hers. Her head banged the wall. She bit his lip. "Upstairs."

In the room she let the dress fall off, stood in pumps and thong, hands on hips.

He gave an apologetic smile. "Can I rinse first? I want to smell every bit of you."

It killed one mood but started another. "Can I watch?"

In the bathroom he emptied a salt packet into a squirt bottle of warm water, tilted his head from side to side. Messy water sputtered from each nostril.

"Can I try?" she asked. He made a fresh bottle. Warm salt water poured down her throat. She spat, coughed. "That sucked."

"Try it again. Tilt your head." A trickle came out, then a big glob of snot. "Eeew. Sorry."

"Do it again." He bent her over. In the mirror they looked like dancers, until the water came out. She closed her eyes. Hot skin on hers, salty warmth in her head like a fish.

He carried her to the bed in pelican arms, kissed her, down past her collarbone. He rimmed her belly button, goose-pimpling her stomach. He bit the cords of her thighs, licked her lips. His tongue stroked her clit in patterns: З м Г л б и. Russian letters. Зарабет Гавриил Зарабет Гавриил любит loves did he say loves Гавриил любит did he text love on her clit? She shook, she was bursting, her pleasure scalding lava. She came with a snap of her spine, shivered as it faded, любит you son of a bitch. She squirmed with childish fear. She wanted him.

He reached under her lungs, lifted himself onto her. He fucked her neatly, as if his cock was a paintbrush and he drew it out pointed. His hips arched up, hung like a diver's arc, seconds still as death. As if he could hang there forever.

CHAPTER TWENTY-TWO

Washington, DC

G abriel woke to ugly smells, like imps lighting farts on fire. He got up and dressed, quiet enough not to wake Zarabeth. He went up the service stairs. A single switch unfolded the ladder and opened the trapdoor, an impressive system. He remembered wobbly attic stairs in his parents' house, stinking of acid and dust. This ladder felt more solid than the floor.

The deck was hot despite the overcast sky. Garden scents refreshed him. He tasted leaves. Lemon thyme, fluorescent on his tongue. Oregano, bitter like chewing a can. Marjoram, tarragon, sage. He assembled them in his mind like tools on a cloth. He would make an omelet. In a wood locker by the trapdoor he found shears and a basket.

In the kitchen he found only fruit and condiments. The ugly smells were stronger.

Missy was casting spells.

He went outside. His first morning here, he and Walt had passed a small market. He found it two blocks away, *Open 'til 12 noon* on a handwritten sign. Eggs, garlic, goat cheese, cherry soda. Antihistamine packets behind the counter.

On his return, the stink was gone. Walt and Zarabeth drank coffee in the small kitchen, Walt's phone playing bright California jazz.

"We were admiring your bouquet," Walt said. "What are you making us?"

"Omelets," Gabriel said.

"You god. Let me get you coffee."

Zarabeth wore t-shirt and shorts. She kissed his nose, scratched her forearms.

"I bought antihistamines," he told her.

It took her a second. "That works?" She dove into the bag.

"Did I hear you're cooking?" Missy asked from the doorway. She wore pink athletic gear with dense blue Indian patterns. Only body odors now, strong and canine. "Can I help?"

"We got it, hon," Walt said.

"Yeah," Zarabeth said. "Go shower, Cerberus."

"Doesn't bother you when you borrow clothes." Missy left.

They split the work in thirds, Walt and Gabriel chopping, Zarabeth fetching dishes.

"Thank goodness you're teeny," Walt said. "I can barely move in this kitchen."

"It's not size, it's flexibility. You should do yoga."

"Please. The diet's enough." He put his knife down. "I'll get wine from the cellar."

"I thought it was a sauna now," Zarabeth said, cracking eggs.

"I bought a wine fridge to tide us over. Sparkling or still?"

"Sparkling." While she beat the eggs she kissed Gabriel. "I had no idea you could cook."

"Came with the nose." He picked eggshell off her cheek. "Walt's smoking downstairs."

"Fat bogart. You don't mind?"

"His doesn't smell as good as what you had last night."

She put her finger to her lips. "I love how weird you are." She left.

He poured more coffee and kept working, blending herbs into smaller bowls.

"Where are your sous-chefs?" Missy asked behind him.

He was startled. In the depth of the food aromas he had missed her. She looked catalog-ready, a light yellow blouse and long khaki shorts. Easy to see how Walt was smitten.

"Getting high en route to bringing up champagne," he said.

"Of course they are. Can I help?"

He showed her the spice bowls. "Three eggs in each, beat them again, add cheese to the middle one. Your chervil's too weak for cooking. I'll sprinkle the leaves on the sage and salt omelet when I fold it over."

"Lovely of you to make this," Missy said, ladling out the eggs. "I spent all spring on the garden and now I forget to seed the basil."

"We all need a vacation from our usual."

"I suppose we do." She beat the eggs while he oiled the pans. "Despite our differences, I could have been a better host."

"Thanks for saying. Mostly it's been fine."

"Perhaps we'll become pals."

"Let's just try to keep the peace," Gabriel said. "For now."

* * *

"I have to say—" Walt began.

"Just eat," Zarabeth said. Too fantastic for talking. She held Gabriel's hand under the table. His eyes closed with each bite, as if the meal were all his dream. Let him dream.

They made coffee. "It's hours until the fireworks," Missy said. "We could see a movie."

"I'm sick of you people," Zarabeth said. "I'm going home for sleep and a shower. Can I wear these home? I'm leaving the dress."

"Can I come with you?" Gabriel asked.

"So much for sleeping," Walt said.

Zarabeth got her pumps from the front door. She had no other shoes. Bad planning but she could walk barefoot.

Gabriel came down with his bag, holding it by the side handle, as if that made it less.

No way to say anything. "You have money? We're cabbing."

Outside her spa-filed feet found each grain of street grit. She put on the pumps. She felt like a streetwalker with a tourist client. They soon caught a cab.

"Walt said you had a convertible?" he asked. "Maybe we should go for a drive."

"They close roads for the fireworks. Tomorrow maybe." A yawn shook her. "Shitty bag."

"My housemate's. I lost mine. I could have brought my suitcase but this was—"

"A short trip," Zarabeth said, annoyed. She put on her sunglasses.

In her apartment he left his bag by the door. She hugged him to frisk for weapons.

"My bag is creeping you out," he said.

"A lot."

"I had to get out of there." He rubbed his eyes.

"Want some water?" In the kitchen she poured two glasses, drank hers in one go and refilled it. He took his on the balcony.

She lit the cigarette by the railing. "You're really upset."

"You wanted this life," he said. "I'm just stuck in it."

"You got the spices right. Maybe you need a new career," she said.

"At least this makes sense to me. Out there, it would get to me. It did get to me. There's this site online, for sensitives. People trying to be both normal and special. You'd laugh."

"I don't know that I'd laugh. I've gone through shit." She took a drag. "OK. I'd laugh. These cigarettes taste like shit."

"They're stale."

"You can tell?" She put the cigarette out on the railing. "You're overloaded." She smiled. "You need a blowjob."

"Yes. Should I shower?"

"Not if I don't have to brush my teeth. Inside. Concrete hurts my knees."

In the living room she pushed him down on the sofa. She nibbled her way down his salty chest. She pushed his pubic hair back with firm strokes like shucking silk from a corncob, dragged nails along the border between hair and shaft. He moaned contentedly.

"That's not for moaning." She sucked his nut hard against her closed teeth, a childhood trick for mashing peach flesh without breaking the skin. Again, again, working up his cock while she dug her nails into his sack, as if to pluck it.

"Jesus fucking balls," he snarled. "Fucking balls." First time she heard him curse.

His cock shuddered. His come fire-hot and crazy salty. An effort not to gag. She thought of Rome, the oysters she never got to eat, the day she scared the candles.

He picked her up by her armpits, pushed her chin down hard, smelled her mouth.

She struggled free. "You're the weirdest."

"Ride me backwards," he said. "I like your shoulders."

"Congressionally approved."

He shoved in like a rug burn. His thumb wet against her asshole, out, against her again, wetter. He was tasting her. That got her hot. They went at it a long while, no climax but a loop of joy. The sky darkened but she didn't have brain to see it until the downpour broke. Their fucking too small against the angry sky.

He kissed her head. "So much for the fireworks."

"They're like artillery. Rain or shine," she said. She curled in his lap for warmth. "Bunch of sad people on the Mall, though. My ass taste good?"

"As good as it looks."

"Let's brush our teeth and go to sleep. We got a long day tonight."

* * *

In the garage he demanded the keys. "You had two wines and a pipe," he said.

"You fucked the high right out of me just now," she said. "Passenger seat or taxicab."

To his chagrin she drove well, confident through quick turns off the parkway, on a jerky route to miss closed streets. He asked about the party.

Anthony Dobranski

"Caryn and Carl," she said. "Local hipsters. She does galleries, he's a restaurateur. Walt says they personify gentrification. Their neighborhood's a little rough."

Their hosts' apartment was two upper floors of an old apartment building, gutted to brick then remodeled into large colorful rooms. Thirty-some people when they arrived, none Walt and Missy. A long potluck table of salads, cookies, grilled chicken.

"Missy should be here soon," Zarabeth said. "She's got the food."

"We have plenty, it's fine," Caryn said. "Where have you been?" She was round and zinc-white, in a blue sundress and pink star-eyed sunglasses, a plastic US flag brooch blinking red-white-blue lights.

"Europe," Zarabeth said. "For work. I met this handsome thing in Scotland."

"Are ya Scottish?" Carl asked in a bad brogue. He was white with a broad build, long black hair and a goatee, the easy manner of a third beer but an aggressive handshake. He wore a red plaid shirt and wrinkled green cargo shorts.

"I'm from Wisconsin," Gabriel said. "I was doing a whisky tour."

"I have a Campbeltown malt if you're interested."

Zarabeth kissed his cheek. "Don't say I didn't hook you up. Off to smoke now bye-bye."

Carl brought a bottle out of a kitchen cabinet, poured two shots. "Cheers." He downed his before Gabriel's even touched his lips. "Back in a minute."

Gabriel chatted with a perilously lean couple, she a limo driver, he a dog walker. Somehow they took his security job as related to the recent oil spill, about which she went on at length. Gabriel scarfed down three burgers. A new cloudburst emptied the roof, doubling the crowd. Zarabeth introduced him to designers and wine reps. Each time sweeter, each time more a couple. Fumes from drinks and grills and bongs, smells of sweat and sunblock. Contact high on life.

Walt and Missy brought two large watermelons. Caryn equipped Walt briskly as if for surgery. Walt cut each in half

282

lengthwise, each half into thirds, then across the width into coin-thin slices.

"OCD much?" Gabriel teased.

"Thin slices taste better," Walt said. "People are just lazy and cut them thick." He slid slices into an aluminum roasting pan. People took them as fast as he cut them.

Carl came in with a fresh grill platter, burst charred sausage links piled atop a thick pork tenderloin, and a nasty menthol stink. "More Scotch?" he asked Gabriel.

"I'm good for now." Gabriel sneezed.

"Big guy! Damn you cut that thin." Carl took two handfuls and put them on a plastic plate. "You want to trim the meat? Shit no, I got it." He put a cutting board down next to Walt. "You know we own this whole building, I did all this." He waved the knife in a circle. "And two rental units below. There's another place down the road, eight rental units. I'd do the work myself. Of course these days you'd have to hold it for a while, no flipping it, but steady money."

"Nothing wrong with steady money," Walt said. "Let's talk next week." When Carl left Walt shook his head. "Third time he's talked about it. Never calls."

"Maybe he thinks you should call him."

Walt snorted. "Whatever. Whither the women? Roof?" He opened a beer and took a plate of watermelon. Gabriel led him upstairs. "No railing," Walt noted. He stopped and shimmied in place, shaking the stairs. "No way this is code. Do they have a decent view?"

"I haven't been yet. It was raining."

"Why we came late. Beater's got shit tires. Are you high? You seem relaxed."

"I had a lot of sex today," Gabriel said.

The roof was the size of a basketball court, with no railing. In the big purple southern sky, the great stone obelisk of the Washington Monument towered over the low buildings falling southward, clouds racing past it. People clustered at the southwest corner but it hardly mattered for the view. "This will do," Walt said.

Zarabeth and Missy stood smoking cigarettes with Caryn on the north side. Gabriel wrapped his arms around her hot wet body and sniffed. "That's new. A kind of hashish?"

"Shit, Zar, you weren't kidding," Caryn said. "It's keef. Powdered crystallized hash. Martin got it for me." She held up a small glass pipe. "There might be a little left."

"Gabriel just does skin hits," Zarabeth said. "I'll take it though."

"You two are perverse," Missy said.

Walt watched a small rocket shooting up miles to the east. "When's the big show?"

"They go off just after nine. I'm peeing now," Zarabeth said.

Gabriel waited, enjoying the dark blue cityscape, the smaller fireworks miles away. After ten minutes he looked for her. When he got to the roof opening a stream of people was coming one by one up the wood ladder. Eventually she scrambled up. They stationed themselves on the northeast just as the first rocket exploded into a huge green chrysanthemum. Booms shook the building. The roof oohed.

The fireworks came at a furious pace: purple hearts, red spheres, white flowers, sheets of gray smoke drifting north across the indigo sky. Zarabeth pinched him for her favorites, always outline shapes in video colors. Gabriel liked the dense white balls of branching lines, like lightning dandelions. One great flash had thousands of tendrils, an afterimage like a burning tree. He pinched her for that one.

She tapped his wrist, took his water, drank it. "I took some of Carl's pain pills," she shouted word-by-word against the rumbling sky. "Fuck me up the ass before I pass out." Her toothy smile a kick in his head. She ran off, pushing through the standing people.

He went after her, stumbling down the rickety ladder. In the empty apartment she yelled nonsense like a sports cheer. "*FA-BA-LA-DA-POO-KEE! FA-BA-LA-DA-POO-KEE!*" He caught her on the building stairs but she squirmed away, still yelling. "*FA-BA-LA-DA-POO-KEE!*" She ran across the empty street to her convertible. When he caught up she shoved the car keys in his pants and pinched his balls. "Ass freak!" She ran around to the passenger door, unlocked the ragtop and shoved it down. "I am possessed!" She shook her head with her tongue sticking out. "Go go go!"

She cried out directions to her place while stroking his shorts. A different route, as the crow flew empty streets. He squealed tires but no one took notice.

On Zarabeth's street, a sound of rain. The sky clear and dark. "Applause," she said, her eyes wide.

In the elevator she clung to him. "You might have to slap me awake." She giggled.

In the apartment they tripped over his open suitcase. She rolled across the floor laughing. They made it to the bedroom. She pulled off her sundress in one motion, fell on the bed.

"Are you OK?" he asked.

"Lube in the drawer," she said, rolling on hands and knees. "Pour it on." Her arms collapsed. She twisted to look over her shoulder at him. "I don't do this a lot. I think I like you."

He had never done it. The sight of her, gorgeous and inviting. Steel in his body. He stroked her clit, brushed flakes of paper off her pretty brown fig. His cock scary big, he a shriveled match behind it. He pushed his thumb in. She gasped, panted. A tight wall, then through to softness. He feared his thumbnail would cut her.

"Fuck me now," she moaned.

He pushed inside her. Her muscles closed painfully on him. She grunted, gagged. He worked through her resistance, his vision sparking black and white.

She sucked air through gritted teeth, moaned low in her throat. "Oh Daddy. Oh Daddy. Daddy. Daddy. DADDY!" She rolled onto her shoulder, her face a wild dog's, snapping teeth glinting like crystal. He came painfully when she went rigid, as if he shot out his marrow.

They lay together a long while. She had passed out.

In the bathroom, he pissed a long hot stream, washed his hands, drank chlorine water from cupped hands. Even after washing, her stench on his fingers like strong whisky.

285

She was out but still panting, nap jerks in her arms. He felt glorious. He shuffled to the kitchen. He poured a glass from the filtered pitcher. The Kennedy Center buzzed x-ray-white. Beyond it a dense file of boats on the river.

In the bedroom she was sitting up, her head lolling forward. Her head went up as if pulled by the hair. Nothing of her in her face. He smelled burning hair, blistered skin, blood on hot rusted metal.

"You're the demon," he said. "The talking thing."

"Yesssss." The tongue fell out, quivering and dripping drool. It launched the body sideways, belly-flopped on the floor, writhed weakly. He felt his nakedness. He pulled on his shorts as if they could protect him.

Eventually it found purchase, slapping the palms hard on the floor and pulling the body forward, dragging wet sex and dead legs. It stopped and looked up at him. It panted faster, a rhythm like laughter. Slowly it raised the butt, got on hands and knees.

"Does she know you can use her body?" he asked.

It curled the corners of the mouth. "Nem." The head fell to one side, to the other.

Could he wake Zarabeth? Could he slap it out of her? If he hit it, he would never stop. Zarabeth's body. "You're disgusting. Get out."

"Pourquoi?" It writhed onto the back, lifted the legs up in the air, spread and closed the legs repeatedly. Inviting, mocking.

"Jesus," he muttered.

It pissed. Some got in the mouth, making it cough. Gabriel stepped back, looked at the shelves. A Bible? As if. Even if, then what?

"Go back where you came from," he said with false boldness. "You don't belong here."

"Perché non?" It had a tone now, hurt feelings. It moved faster too, somersaulting onto hands and feet. It wiggled the ass like a bee, turned around awkwardly to face him, made an O of its mouth, took short fast spittle breaths. Soon it might even stand.

A voice in his head: *Demons lie*. Even the conversation itself. It got something out of this, maybe just time. The longer he stayed the worse for both. He grabbed his shirt, his shoes.

"Perché non?" Louder and deader, a machine voice. "Perché non perché non perché non." Stuck on its last words. It tried to stand, fell.

He zipped his bag, checked his pockets. Wallet, phone, Missy's key, Zarabeth's lip gloss. He dropped key and lip gloss on the floor, slammed the door shut. He ran down the fire stairs, the bag bouncing and scraping behind him.

On the street he had no idea where he was. Like the night he woke in the forest, the night he gave up drinking. He frantically hailed a cab with a lit dome. "The airport."

"Reagan?" the driver asked.

"Fine." He shook with cold. As they entered traffic the place came back to him. As if he had reentered. He should call, text, something. For all he knew the weirdness could leap out whole from the phone.

Reagan Airport had vaulted ceilings of yellow girders and gray steel plates, great windows onto the dark runways. At the ticket desk he babbled about a death in the family to a bored lollipop-headed clerk. "The red-eye has seats. You can just make it. Change fee's two hundred."

Barefoot through the security scanner. At the urinal his cock stank of lube and omelet shit. He felt her, right beside him. He looked around frantically, tears in his eyes. Empty white and chrome. He washed his hands and face again.

* * *

She woke alone in filth. She hurt, her asshole bad enough but the fuck with her back? As if the pills also gave her Carl's injury. She forced herself up, yelped at ripping pain between her shoulder blades. Bruises from his fingers on her hips.

In the hall a puddle. She threw a towel on it. Had they spilled something? Complete fog.

"Gabriel?" she called. Not there. Not there.

His bag gone. No note. She went out the front door, stupid thought he was waiting there locked out. On the floor Missy's key, her lip gloss. She picked them up, arms shaking.

Of course he left. The voice in Craigellachie, in Pittsburgh, the voice of fucked-up shit. *Barren seed of whore and pedophile. How could you think he would stay?*

She slammed the lip gloss against the wall. If she could just burst the fucking tube it would all come back, but it didn't burst, just hurt her hand. She screamed and saw red.

She came to her senses at the balcony railing. An empty junk food satisfaction, a lot of pain. Naked in the young morning. Scratches on her palms, arms, legs. Drywall and dirt and shiny flecks on her skin. Breeze stirred dust around her.

In all the noise of her body, a whimper from her left foot. She plucked a long thin shard of glass from her ankle. A little sphere of blood welled up. She put the shard to it. The blood bubble ran along the edge, up to her finger.

She had somewhere to put it. She placed it on the table to dry. She called Missy.

"It's early," Missy said, yawning.

"Can I have the number for your contractor? Oh, never mind." She started to cry.

CHAPTER TWENTY-THREE

Washington, DC

The following Wednesday, Magda called Zarabeth. "How are you, dear?"

"Working on my tan." Which she was, naked on a towel on Missy's roof. At first it was boredom, but now it had become its own goal, to wholly darken two full shades (by the color chart of her favorite boutique) while the crew restored her sublet.

"Summer's awful for us workaholics," Magda said. "I'll be in Washington Friday for a legislative action workgroup—my word, the names they give. Let's have lunch. Noon?"

That Friday, Zarabeth spent an hour on the pricey makeup for her new brown skin. The office was near McPherson Square, not one she knew but Straightforward had many. The receptionist announced her, left with her bag.

Zarabeth's skin crackled. Too late. Two white men, one short-haired, one in a ponytail, both stubbly as if shaven with box cutters. Black suits, black gloves. The taller held up a stun gun.

She walked ahead of them into a small dark room. Magda waited in a desk chair. The inspectors sat on either side of her. The ponytailed man motioned her under the single overhead light. The short-haired man rifled through her purse, set it down by his feet, next to a big, scuffed, black leather bag.

"You have an Empyrean lover," Magda said. "Tell us more."

Idiot. Zarabeth herself had begun the search.

She told the whole story. Aberdeen. Ignorant Walt, angry Missy. Canoeing, clubbing, Cyrillic cunnilingus. Omelets, fucking, fireworks, oozing filth from her painkillered ass. She tossed the ponytailed man her new titanium necklace, bloody shard of glass inside the locket.

"I'm still losing my security deposit," she said, and spoke no more. By her numb toes and throbbing ankles she had stood there more than an hour.

Magda stared into her. One minute, two. Magda opened up the locket, closed it. "Well?" she asked the inspectors.

The short-haired man had a soft tenor, as if reading scripture to death-row inmates. "There may be matters for you to address, Ms. Crane. We find no corporate threat."

Magda winced. "Sorry to waste your time."

"On the contrary," the ponytailed man said, his voice low and cheery. "We're devoted to honesty. It's so rare." They stood. "Good day, Ms. Battrie, Ms. Crane." They left.

"That's new." Magda smiled wolfishly. "Oh, the next liar they meet. What do you want?"

"Revenge. And to keep working for you."

"What was Pittsburgh about?"

"I reconciled with my mother."

Magda sucked her tongue against her lips grotesquely. "Family and romance. Charmed summer you're having."

"Walt Wisniewski donates to Sasha Blackwell. You might have said."

If Magda appreciated the discretion, it didn't show. Her jaws opened wide behind closed lips, as if she chewed a brick. "Does the witch know?"

"Not from me. Missy's got a bug up her ass about it, but her coven needs a daughter."

"Parasites, the lot of them. I'd like it if things soured for my old protégé."

"Is that an instruction?"

"No. Avoid Sasha. Never mention her." Magda tossed her the locket. "Love the look. Darkness becomes you. Get the fuck out."

AUGUST 2009

CHAPTER TWENTY-FOUR

Prague

Zarabeth spoke in a hotel ballroom, hosted by the Prague office, Polish and Slovak staff joining the Czechs. Sixty people, half built of meat trimmings, half of twigs, all paler than the French and even the Germans. The women wore light brown makeup like tea spilled on tablecloths. Morning coffee was a courtly show of contempt, all in English as if to highlight the debased tongues the other countries spoke.

Zarabeth dimmed the room. Pale faces gleamed in reflected projector light. "Somebody has a good idea. A new process for making plastic bags, a lumber warehouse, robot shoe-shiners." The presentation slides had soft yellow gears missing burgundy puzzle pieces. The first slide read, *An idea is not enough to meet a need.* "That's the tagline. They're working on translations." She underlined it in red on the tablet hooked to the projector. After a month she could do it without looking.

Next slide, bullet points. "These ideas need between three and ten million Euros of initial investment, and soon. But if they get it—then what? Management. Accounting, contracts, tax forms. Lines of credit. Real estate and human resources. Infrastructure. Suddenly, the idea needs a company."

Next slide. "Straightforward Consulting's FirmKey." She circled the heading. "For a percentage of revenue, we run the whole back-office faster, with greater reliability and effectiveness. Servers, lawyers, accounting. Lease a company the way you lease a car. Replace with your own staff at whatever pace feels comfortable."

Next slide. "We pioneered FirmKey with Mercurex, a British firm. Judging by your excellent English—" off-script; it drew complex smiles, like migrant farmers praised for fitness— "culturally it will feel comfortable. For sales, it's modular."

Next slide. Black background, red spray paint font. *Custom Bitches.* Sometimes she read it aloud, if the local English was weak. Today she said nothing. Let them work it out.

A twig man in the front row raised his hand. "I don't understand this slide."

"'Custom' means made to specifications, Mr. Durocsinsky. In Britain they say 'bespoke.'"

"I know what 'custom' means," he said.

"Oh. 'Bitches' are—"

"Yo! Bitch!" a big man in back shouted. People tittered.

"A good example," she said. "Thank you, Mr. Wieczorek."

The whole room looked at her. The little brown woman had memorized their names, a parlor trick honed at trade shows when she couldn't afford a smartphone. The pale people shrank, less presentation than schoolhouse.

A thin toothy bottle-blonde in the third row spoke up. "What does it mean?"

"Who are the bitches, Ms. Stastná?"

"Clients are bitches!" Wieczorek shouted happily.

Zarabeth golf-clapped. "Quite right. The clients are the bitches. Clients are always bitches." She waved her hands like a baby in a high chair. "'Do this, waah.' 'Fix this, waah.'" Smiles now, many of them forced. "That's fine, if they're rich and pay well. But, they can hire someone else. They have their own connections. Sometimes better than ours."

Next slide, original format. "FirmKey addresses this

problem. With FirmKey, they're not rich—yet. They're not paying well—yet. Our return covers our costs, and values our structural capital at next to nothing. FirmKey is attractive because Straightforward can design custom bitches. Infect the company at conception with the inability to exist without us. Like babies born to drug addicts."

Next slide. "This requires a different approach, and today's training outlines advantages and pitfalls. For example, sales staff and IT staff have a different relationship, and a long-term loss leader product changes commissions."

Next slide. "You won't be reinventing every wheel. Local assets are critical. You know suppliers, shippers, who wants bribes, who likes whores."

"I beg your pardon!" A meaty blonde woman stood. "What is this talk? Drug babies? Bribes and whores?" On her skinned-chicken chest, a silver and amber cross caught the light.

Zarabeth squinted her stinging eyes. "This is how we do business, Ms. Czwiertniewicz." She pointed to the door. "If you don't want to do what's necessary, please go enjoy this lovely city. Also, re-read your employment contract about open religious displays."

"What?"

"Your cross, you stupid cow," she snarled. "Button your blouse."

Snarled, in perfect Polish.

Ms. Czwiertniewicz sat down, pulled her blouse closed. Everyone else sat up straight. Zarabeth's heart sank. Fuck fuck fucking Polyglot. Like Antwerp all over again.

* * *

Wenceslas Square was a long pedestrian avenue, stepped with plazas. She had trudged around it twice, looking for tails. A relief to sit, but the script said to take a window table and it was hot in the afternoon sun. She wondered who was watching. She ordered cappuccino.

This was the last of her secret errands for Magda under cover of the training sessions. The others—imaging automobile trade secrets in a noxious Latin Quarter WC; passing a flash drive at a Berlin currywurst stand; a swap of data cards at a Bonn coffee house, with a wide-mustached military type who had ordered Turkish coffee before she realized it would take fifteen minutes to prepare—had gone without incident. Four out of four would look good, and maybe get her off Magda's shitlist.

A brown man with short hair and a trim full beard walked in. He wore a cream suit, a blue tie. He looked past her once, twice. She had the only orange bag in the place.

"¡Patricio!" she called. Not script, but they gave a name, she could use it. "¡Aquí, aquí!" She took his hand and kissed his cheeks. "So good to see you again," she said, continuing the Spanish. "How long has it been? Two years?"

"I'm so sorry to be late," he said, on script, his Spanish a high lisping Castilian. He shaded his face with his hand. "I misread the tram times."

The server came with menus. Patricio relaxed. "Just an espresso, I think." British English. "And the shades down?"

"Another cappuccino," Zarabeth said. The server pirouetted away.

"I'm so sorry to be late," he repeated in wooden Spanish.

"Not at all," she said. "I just arrived myself. Prague is just so beautiful. I took so many pictures. That's the great thing about digital, if you don't like them—delete! Or just get a new card." The last phrase, the all-clear on her side.

"May I see them?" He took off his sunglasses as the shades came down. He had hard black eyes with dark puffy circles under them. He smiled as if to bite her.

"Of course." She held her camera so he could see the display. "That's the Loreto," she said. "St. Nicholas's Church; St. Vitus's Cathedral; and that's Kafka's house." Even staring at him she almost missed his swapping the cards.

"You should take pictures for a living," he said, handing back the camera. The end of the script. They would sit for five minutes. If neither phone rang he would leave first. She kept her arms on the table so she could glance at her watch.

The coffees came. He drank his as if alone.

"Salud," she said. "Is something wrong?"

"Your people insult us, to send a woman," he said through a smile.

She laughed and touched his arm. "So those virgins waiting after martyrdom are boys? Someone special back in the madrassa you hope to see again?"

His eyes flashed. "I can't—"

"You can't what?" she said, in English, a little loud. She went back to Spanish. "Pobresito. You think the world should spare you minor hassles. Eat scorpions for Allah, sure. Not coffee with a woman. You are proud."

She dipped her index finger in her coffee foam, sucked on it like a schoolgirl. He watched hypnotized. "Pride is the enemy of faith," she whispered, drawing her wet finger slowly down her chin. "If you believe in your cause then insult washes off and the humblest act is vital." When her finger reached her collarbone she made a fist. "Do you know what you have? You want it to be big. Military plans, top-secret hardware, Soviet plutonium. I bet it's small. A shipping manifest. A love child. DNA for herbicide-resistant poppies. You kill Crusaders with homemade bombs, the Crusaders kill you with toy airplanes. These small things, keep the fat sheiks fat." She picked up her bag.

"You have to wait."

"What if I don't? What if I slap you and curse you? Cut myself under the table and blame you? Even if your people get the data, *you* will be dead. They'll shoot you in the head because you couldn't keep your proud mouth shut. You tried so hard. Your excellent Spanish. Preparing for the *reconquista* of Al-Andaluz? The Mexicans say *reconquista*, when they crawl across Yankee desert to pick Yankee food." She grabbed his hand, digging nails in his palm. In Arabic she said, "Ask Allah to make me yours when you touch your circumcised cock. I would love to be a virgin again. Time's up. Go, go now."

He ran. His chair fell when he left. Patrons looked at her, looked away. The server came to right the chair. "Can you make Turkish coffee?" she asked.

She read mail on her phone. The only work message was from Endre, with bad news:

No replacement for malfunctioning gear. Our supplier ran afoul of immigration. It even made the news, in a way. We are looking for new sources but it's a niche product. Sorry.

Endre had written in English. She wondered if the Polyglot knew things it wasn't translating. Not much either could do, in any event.

With her caffeine buzz she walked the narrow streets, looking among the cosmopolitan restaurants for something local. In a beer hall with long wood tables, she drank herbal liqueur with wild boar sausages, reading the gemology primer she'd bought in Copenhagen. She had sold four stones in Antwerp for seventy thousand—in Yiddish, in Flemish, in Thai, no doubt triggering the next day's mess—but she didn't need a demon to know she'd done poorly. To make real money she had to cut them herself. She wondered if her father had known how. Maybe that was where her trust fund had come from.

Men surrounded her. They looked like cops, but to a Pittsburgh girl, the whole region did. Wieczorek in his big brown suit. Blond Kowalewski, bald Nowak, both smaller in gray.

"The boys in the back," she said. "Panowie, proszę usiąść."

They ordered beer and vodka shots. "For her too," Wieczorek said in Polish.

"Just vodka," she told the server. "On my tab."

"No, no," Nowak said.

"I have an entertainment allowance," she said in English.

"Fuck yeah OK," Nowak said. "You study gemstones."

"I'm an informed shopper. I hear amber is good here."

"Better in Poland," Wieczorek said. "Amber and silver. No crosses!" They laughed.

"Maybe I was a little strong," she said.

"We loved it. She's a stuck-up bitch," Nowak said.

"When you talk to waiter, sound like Czech," Kowalewski said. "Which you speak?"

"A little of both. Phrasebooks."

"I'd like to see the phrasebook with what you said to

Czwiertniewicz," Wieczorek said. They laughed again and she joined in.

One shot, two. English and Polish. Company gossip, stories of other offices. Kowalewski traveled non-stop, around the Baltic and Scandinavia. "Global warming hard for Helsinki. When the snow melts, eh. Lutherans, too plain."

"They have bright colors," Nowak said. "Red, blue, gray. You say 'nice' in English?"

"If it's nice," she said. "You guys are drinking like you're at the airport. What's up?"

"We are—" Wieczorek wasn't sure.

"A strip club," Nowak said. "Na Placu Wacława. Fucking expensive, so drink here first. Want to come?"

"Company can't pay for that."

"We take you," Kowalewski said. "Our guest."

"I would be delighted."

"Wow. You didn't even hesitate," Nowak said.

"More fun than rocks."

"Piękny," Nowak said.

A shambling walk back to Wenceslas Square. Down a long sloping hallway, to glass doors etched with fairies. The club had a domed ceiling and rounded walls, the inside of a sphere. Across from the entrance, a stage thrust from ranks of curtains, the patrons at tables kept back by a low wall. Onstage, two leggy blondes in white kitten masks mirrored slow poses.

The men and Zarabeth nursed beers while watching the languorous shows: a brunette undressing gauzy veils; a blonde doing weak yoga in fishnets. Tame and arty, by American standards, but the audience watched, quiet, absorbed, meekly led off for lap dances in a back room with narrow dark windows.

"This whole room is a woman's body," she said. "Look. The sides of the stage are ovaries and she's in the womb now. Egg awaiting her sperm." Naked women were the package. The place was the virus, code of nested symbols, of accomplishment, satisfaction. New hairdos for bald men.

"You crazy bitch," Wieczorek said.

"Piękny, kurva," she said. "Piękny." She felt let down.

Dancers came selling lap dances. Wieczorek went.

"You get a lap dance?" Kowalewski asked her.

"Shut up," Nowak said, offended.

"What, she's here?" Kowalewski switched to English. "Is OK to ask if you lesbian?"

"Is OK. No I'm not. But get me a pale blonde girl. The new chivalry," she said in Polish. "Men open whores for women." They hooted. Puns in two languages, that was new.

A mirrored ball came down. Bright uneven crescents drifted across the dark-clothed patrons, each with a thick top and thin curled bottom. Fetuses. Fetuses floating across her skirt.

She ran to the women's room but she didn't throw up. She didn't. She threw up, in front of the stalls.

Only woman in there anyway.

* * *

Her phone rang. 03:14. Magda.

"Hel-lo." She was still drunk.

"Polish offices don't have the religious display rule," Magda said. "Nor the Irish. Even liberal countries are permissive, after the French mishandled headscarves so utterly."

Zarabeth tried to catch up. "She was on Czech turf."

"When in Rome, as they say. Good principle. Still I won't send you to Krakow."

"I hear Helsinki is nice. It's early here, Magda."

"So it will stay. Seven o'clock flight to Hong Kong."

"Fuck. What's the translation for FirmKey?"

"No more dog-and-pony show. This is fun. We'll conference there." Magda hung up.

Fun. That sobered her up.

CHAPTER TWENTY-FIVE

Hong Kong

Zarabeth stumbled along Chek Lap Kok Airport's medical-blue halls in a cocktail daze. Daze had its advantages. She could read both English and Chinese without her vision splitting. Soon it felt too easy, the doubled signs and billboards annoying through repetition, annoying through repetition.

Blue-grey train, blue-grey sky, everything a blur including herself. At the train terminal, business types rolled black carry-ons toward the MTR train entrance. She and her big bags followed. When in Rome. The MTR ran every two minutes, brief stops, fast fast fast. The train cars spacious with no doors between them. She felt like a rat inside a tamed chrome snake.

They had set her up in Wan Chai, a district of low old buildings and crowded streets. The flat had dingy walls, small rooms, a safety-glass coffin for a shower. After weeks in ornate European hotels, Zarabeth liked cheap and simple. In the kitchen she found a box of dark Pu-Erh tea cubes, a blue-and-white tea service, an electric kettle with massive prongs.

One cigarette while she made tea, one while she drank it, two while she watched dubbed anime, parroting the sylphlike cartoon superheroines. She had never spoken Cantonese before. The harsh consonants came easily after Slavic languages, but her cheeks hummed to shape seven tones, precious and ornate, like writing all italics.

She spread her money out to study it; only tourists don't

know local money. As she read denominations the Polyglot offered up local slang: big cookie, red snapper, big ox, gold ox, big cookie. The same denominations had different designs and issuing banks, as in Scotland. With Gabriel. She wasn't going there. She gathered up her money, flaking ash on the table.

On the muggy streets she walked through bus exhaust, swirling dust, heat blasting from laundries. Around her tiny dolls in white and khaki, skinny legs wobbling in platform heels; slender men in knock-off Italian suits; dumpy people in movie-poster t-shirts.

In a convenience store, she bought Peruvian cola and American cigarettes. Down an alley she found a wet-market, stands of fruit and meat and neat rows of fish heads. A cigarette in her mouth while she haggled over the cost of oranges. When in Rome.

In a plaza on the other side, a crowd watched dancing pairs of women and men dressed like servants. She asked a white man about it. "Seven Sisters Festival," he said in Liverpool English. "Local Valentine's Day. An Imperial maid, permitted only one day a year to see her love." He smiled as if this earned him a date.

Zarabeth stepped away, sore cheeks flushed. Gabriel. Gabriel everywhere. In the money, by the stores. She tightened her grip on her bags and asked her phone the quickest way back.

* * *

Her last three visits on corporate grounds, in Antwerp, Washington, and Boston, had all ended in humiliation and, twice, great pain. Of course, if humiliation were her lot, they could have just humiliated her in Prague.

Still, Zarabeth was too uneasy to sit. She looked west out the Hong Kong office's ribbon windows, at thin skyscrapers dense as wheatgrass, edged in colorful neon that glowed ever brighter against the fading smoky sky.

Local staff in Italian suits passed by on their way out, chatting in Cantonese about pubs and projects. A few looked her over casually, faces impassive, as if she were a painting in a gallery. Zarabeth opened her compact. Her deep tan had faded after weeks in northern Europe, the ochre blusher now too dark for her copper skin. She tapped the makeup pad on the hot corners of her cheekbones, and smoothed her eyeliner. It would do, for video.

At seven-thirty, a lean bucktoothed staffer in blue silk led her to a half-oval walnut-paneled room, with a black chair at a half-round coffee table. On the full-wall screen facing her, her boss Magda Crane sat life-size, in her own half-oval room at another half-round table. It made a good illusion of one room, but Magda was in Boston, twelve hours behind. Magda wore a camel-hair pantsuit over a black blouse, her ashen hair splayed like an old toothbrush, her skin glowing ghost white.

The staffer handed Zarabeth a secure interoffice pouch. Zarabeth scanned her thumb. The security lock snapped off. The staffer left with it and locked the door.

"Leave that for now," Magda said, in her nasal New England bray. "Hello stranger. Flight OK? Settled in?"

"Fine," Zarabeth said, putting the pouch aside. "This is all very spendy."

"Also soundproofed and bug-swept. Completely secure." For Magda to say that meant it wasn't. It didn't matter. Most conversations with Magda were hasty phone calls. Whatever Zarabeth was there to learn, she was also there so that the firm knew about the meeting.

"To business," Magda said. "Some time ago, we learned our dearest rival, Empyrean Group, was talking with Chinese officials, ones with real power. They had been talking for a year by then, and we had no clue. That's all we knew for seven months. We couldn't track them—in this day and age, I tell you. They have protection."

"Magical protection?" Zarabeth asked.

"They might call it divine," Magda said. "We still don't know what they're up to. This could be enormous. But, we caught a break: an Empyrean operative named Bill Thorn. Long career, experienced operative. Since June, he's been to Beijing, Taipei, Tokyo, and Seoul. No flight or hotel records before June, but once we could follow him around Asia, we found staff who remembered earlier visits. Thorn was under Empyrean's protective veil. Now, he's not. He's coming to Hong Kong tonight. Listen carefully. Our firm wants Thorn's data. I'm sending you to get Thorn. You'll liaise with a local team. The op is in two days."

"Seems like a lot just to steal something," Zarabeth said.

"Let me tell you about this protection. Back in ninety-eight, in Jakarta, I had something like this. It was a crazy time. Excitement got the better of me. I had my asset steal an Empyrean's computer. The battery caught fire. Destroyed the computer, and the asset's car. With the asset locked inside it."

"That's some protection," Zarabeth said. "But Thorn doesn't have it. Could he be a decoy?"

"Of course. So we did some diligence," Magda said. "We can track Thorn's American trips, so the veil is only over Asia. Last May, he spent a week in Colorado Springs, for a background check on a financial planner. In June, that planner drove off a mountain road—on the same morning Bill Thorn flew to Beijing, via overnight in Denver."

"Thorn's an assassin for Empyrean?"

Magda shook her head. "There were two other women in the car, one pregnant. Empyrean is scrupulous about collateral damage. They wouldn't use Thorn after that, if they knew. He acted on his own, and they don't know. They also don't seem to know the blood of innocence has washed off Thorn's protection. Denver-Beijing was the first Asian trip we could track." Magda smiled crocodile-wide, eyes afire. "Thorn has fallen from grace. He is our first shot in uncovering a two-year plot by our enemy. We're taking it, with every care and expense. Read the files in the pouch. You meet the team tomorrow morning. Provide a shining example of team spirit. This one's close to your heart, my sweet Zarabeth. Bill Thorn is Gabriel Archer's boss."

Zarabeth grew fever-hot. All her humiliations finally just one, and its name was Gabriel Archer. Only six weeks since Washington. Since he had fled her.

"How beautiful you are," Magda said. "Enjoy your revenge."

Zarabeth fingered the locket on her titanium necklace, her one souvenir of their encounter. "It's not revenge on Gabriel."

"Not just yet." Magda tapped a key. Only the red time-code

window remained on screen.

Zarabeth glanced in the pouch. Data tablet, office badge, a yellow drug in a glass phial.

Listen carefully, her boss had said, her signal in the noise. *Get Thorn.* Magda wanted Thorn himself, not just his data. Not hers to ask why. Taking Thorn was the job, and job first. Revenge, not yet.

Not just yet.

* * *

At ten the next morning it was sweltering and starkly sunny. Zarabeth wore a severe black dress with black stiletto heels. She felt like a cricket among ants.

Thorn was staying in a business hotel near the wet-market. The team had a fifth-floor office behind the hotel, sublet from a failed import company. The office lobby was as old as Magda, leftist-plain, grey-black granite with tarnished brass railings. The cramped lift rattled as it rose. The office badge, second item in her secure pouch, read *Wan Chai World Cargo Express* in blurry red characters. She clipped it to her dress.

Security guards wanded her for listening devices but ignored her phone and tablet. The office was a single room, small desks pulled together into worktables. Building plans, listening devices, kit for custom drugs, new laptops running the company screensaver. Five locals stared at her as if she had farted.

"Hello," she said in English. "I'm Zarabeth Battrie."

A skinny man in an orange baseball cap showed gap teeth. "Adult supervision, is it?" On his cap, white stitching in Chinese and English: HONG KONG DATA POLICE

"We call it 'due diligence,' Colin Tsui Lei Wang," she said in Cantonese.

"Wah!" a tiny pretty woman cried. "Guess we'll have to pass notes in class."

"I see no reason for secrets, Melissa Kung Gyun Fen," Zarabeth said.

If she acted as if she knew everything they wouldn't tell her anything. She sat, switched to English. "I represent the client commissioning your services. I've been briefed on the basics. Colin does gear, Melissa security, yes?" She pointed to a tubby balding man in a navy blazer. "You're, um, Donald—"

"Donald Lee, tactics and pharmacology," he said, in a twangy Cantonese accent.

"Clea Ma." The woman sat with her legs drawn up, slack face and hangdog expression. "I'm the seductress," she said, her accent a mouthful of marbles.

Melissa giggled at Zarabeth's reaction. "She doesn't believe you, Mama Ma. Don't worry, ma'am. She's completely mastered her cover identity. And that one we call Bus Uncle."

The last man was slender, with a wrinkled face and a full head of graying hair. "Ng Lim Tak," he said. "Liaison to management. The other adult supervision." Comically posh voice, swallowing syllables. Little about him in her dossier.

"Fine, you're the client," Colin said. "Why are you here? To nod and pretend you're useful?" He pointed insolently at Bus Uncle. "We already have one of those."

"I'm here for vengeance," Zarabeth said.

"Against whom?" Bus Uncle asked.

"White people," Zarabeth said. "Cantonese love white people. You learned to talk like butlers for them, to overcook food and write twenty-six ugly characters. They turned your women into whores and wrote books about the whores falling in love with them, and when they left, you begged for passports to follow them. Which you never got." They looked insulted and wary, save Bus Uncle who sat as placidly as at a concert.

She stood. She took a pair of scissors from a pencil cup, tapped the handles against her palm. "We're here, beige and brown, taking down a black man, but this is about whites, dealing with mainland Han, under your wide noses. We brought this to you gift-wrapped. I'm here to motivate you."

Colin banged his desk. "You're from Boston. You work for white people."

For Zarabeth, it happened slowly. Snap the scissors' hinge.

308

One blade through Colin's hand on the desk, the other to his neck. She held him a nice while, letting blood and tears. Security kept a respectful distance.

"Inch mouth, blowing water," she whispered in Cantonese. "If I cut your throat, what would happen? Nothing. Be glad I let you live." She pulled the blade from his hand and licked the blood, burning with triumph. She kept the other blade at his quivering neck. "Leave for good," she said in English. "Take the stairs. Tell the hospital nothing or I will have all your family killed, save you."

Bus Uncle gave him a tea towel and ice, took his badge. Colin ran out.

Zarabeth hissed wetly, wiped her mouth. "I guess we need a replacement."

"Most of Colin's work is done, ma'am," Bus Uncle said in English. "Between us, we can manage." He took the scissor blades.

"Fine. Clean up. I'll take a briefing at five. If it's good, we have dinner."

"Efficiency at last," Bus Uncle said. "Order dinner in?"

"No. Come up for air. Stop bothering me! Where can I smoke?"

Donald pointed up, his hand trembling. "Roof."

The woman guard escorted her. The lift rattled and groaned. On the roof, a narrow walled garden, a big tin with sand for an ashtray. The tiniest view of Victoria Harbour between buildings.

The demon used her hands. Lethal force, easy as sign language. So far, it worked.

She exhaled smoke through her nose. She would be a dragon. Make them clear a path.

* * *

At five, Donald and Bus Uncle walked her through the op. Floor plans, times on charts, fragile but smooth. Clea sat frozen still all through it, her face constantly sad, a jilted movie lover paused on her close-up. Distracting.

"Can we step back? Drugs notwithstanding," Zarabeth said,

"I don't see how you know he'll take the bait."

"No other way," Donald began. "Can't steal it or trick him out of it. And Thorn is a trained security officer. The man doesn't shop. He allows himself a beer or two in hotel bars and bottled water in his room. He rarely talks to anyone, but a Chinese whore at his Singapore hotel said he stared her down every night."

"In Security work you get *sifu*," Melissa said. "People who patiently master skills, but they're lonely." She smiled with bitter eyes. "So we went back. Thorn is from outside Vancouver. Solid working-class family, but he was the black sheep. High school dropout, smooth talker. Dealt drugs for money and sex. Chequered past for an Empyrean."

"They're not all altar boys," Zarabeth said.

"Then two years no one can account for. Off the radar. He surfaces in Calgary, as a junior security officer at Empyrean. Five years later he's in San Francisco. Championship pistol shot and, we think, celibate. Third-class gangsta to Shaolin monk."

"Until he broke ranks in secret," Bus Uncle said. "He is a man trying to act righteously. But he is dissatisfied. The way to control him is to make him think he is doing right, but satisfy him."

"Damsel in distress," Zarabeth said. "He'll fuck her because he's helping her." She clapped her hands. "Time for dinner. Where are we going?"

"Someplace with few white people," Donald said.

* * *

Above a wet-market in North Point, they sat around big platters of food, all new and strange to Zarabeth: pasta-like goose intestines in gravy-brown taro-root soup, stir-fried slices of white duck esophagus with water chestnuts, a hatbox-sized pile of baked garlic with giant prawns buried inside, whole fish picked apart like carrion over squid-ink noodles.

The only utensils were chopsticks and old chipped bowls, for both food and beer. "Yanks fussed about melamine in dog kibble," Donald joked. "We eat it all the time."

The team slowly reddened with the beer, Bus Uncle a light blush, Clea almost purple. "Why do Chinese people flush when they drink?" Zarabeth asked.

"Enzyme deficiency," Donald said. "Alcohol becomes acetaldehyde becomes vinegar. Asians have fewer enzymes to process acetaldehyde. The backlog causes an allergic reaction. I suspect Europeans have the most."

"Maybe white people just killed off their bad drinkers," Zarabeth said.

"Drinking as a selection pressure," Donald said, sucking up black noodles. "Funny."

"Fat and filled with heart disease and hairy backs." Clea, playing Zarabeth: thrust chin, perky shoulders, but black eyes and splotchy red face. A demon with a Zarabeth inside. "Eating factory pigs and turkeys too fat to fuck." She raised her chopsticks. "Kill the whites! Kill them all! Kill them all!"

The team flickered smiles.

"That was crazy good," Zarabeth said. "OK, this I can take. It's good fun and I know you now. Would Colin ever respect me?"

"No," Bus Uncle said. "He had talent, but he was a little shit."

"This is a big op. Executive interest. I am a complication but I'm here. I can't have a pissing contest. So I got rid of him. OK?"

They shrugged and nodded. Clea gave a ridiculous smile and a thumb-up.

"Oh, stop it, Clea," Melissa said. "Will you stay for the Seven Sisters Festival?"

"I don't know."

"Stay. Stay for Hungry Ghost."

"The afterlife is our welfare state," Bus Uncle said. "We burn money in effigy, Ms. Battrie, so the hungry ghosts keep up with trends."

"How can you speak Cantonese and not know Hungry Ghost?" Donald asked.

"I knew about it," Zarabeth said.

"Of course, Ms. Battrie," Bus Uncle said. "Silly of me."

Zarabeth stayed quiet to let them relax, Donald relaxing too much. She paid the bill in notes and coins. On the street they got Donald a cab.

Zarabeth walked with the rest to the MTR. Her flat was only one stop west, but on a whim she rode past it and got off with Melissa at Admiralty. A metal-white concourse big enough for playing football, just to change trains from Hong Kong Island to Kowloon Peninsula. Even at night, the northbound train arrived as she crossed the platform. Fast fast fast.

She rode north with Melissa but followed a big crowd off at Jordan, out of the station. On the pavement, the crowd fragmented and flowed around vendors roasting chestnuts, toward the giant Temple Street Market. Zarabeth joined the slow queue shuffling through the kaleidoscope of world-wide crap: bazooka-shaped torch lighters, polyester silk, snow globes and magnets and handbags, every kind of battery, every make of clothing. Endless clocks and watches, spreading like dandelions.

At the end the crowd evaporated into wide aisles of fortune-tellers, no real magic she could feel. Chinese opera singers in ratty costumes sang keening wire-sharp notes to twangy dulcimer music. Here, the magic. Like the plucking was her heartbeats, that by existing the music had made her to hear it.

She left three red snappers in their till and trudged back up Temple Street. In a stall she saw an orange shirt with a white flower made of ones and zeroes, the same lettering on Colin's hat: *HONG KONG DATA POLICE*

"What's that?" she asked the vendor in English.

"Data Police? Good price." He flared his nostrils. "New video. Like Area 51."

"Area 51 is real."

"You want shirt?"

"Fuck the police," she said in Cantonese.

"Aiya! Don't buy!" The vendor waved her off irritably.

CHAPTER TWENTY-SIX

Hong Kong

Zarabeth came in at eleven, in pinstripe jacket, embroidered jeans, gold hoop jewelry.

"Next op, I wear your clothes," Melissa said around fake teeth. She was in disguise, in a maid's outfit, her skin grayed. "Thorn's in Aberdeen. In a café, alone. One of our tails is a table away." She yielded Zarabeth the seat at the workstation.

Behind her Donald, dressed as a room service attendant, packed up drugged minibar items. Bus Uncle, in maintenance overalls, talked Zarabeth through network settings and the call signs for Thorn's tails. Clea sat in the corner and looked at her feet.

The team left at noon. Zarabeth tested the network, logged reports. Finally Clea went to the bathroom.

Zarabeth went to Donald's station. Clea's disguise handbag had a phial and syringe in a hidden pocket. Zarabeth swapped the phial with her own, the third thing in her secure pouch.

At two the team returned, with bags of take-out dumplings and pour-spout cartons of tea. "They didn't recognize me," Melissa said happily. "Called me 'auntie.'" Zarabeth set up a buffet. Clea sat cross-legged on the floor in the corner, eating with her hands. The others ignored her. Talk was celebrity gossip and business deals, Melissa as good as a blog.

Zarabeth and Melissa did Clea's makeup, making her younger and sadder. Clea occasionally stood to walk demurely, to hold her arm outstretched and focus on her fingers as if thrilled by them. Bus Uncle checked the drugged minibar and Clea's gear. Zarabeth watched him. He removed the phial, held it to the light, looked at Zarabeth. Zarabeth gave him a millimetre-wide smile. Bus Uncle repacked it.

Zarabeth helped Melissa with her wingman look, a hot mess in a tight floral dress to distract others from Clea. She layered grey and blue eye shadow to bring out the green in Melissa's brown eyes.

"That's strong," Melissa said brightly. "I might do this for clubbing." Like middle-school girls. "You still do work like this?"

"I do as I'm told."

"They tell you to fight with scissors?"

"It doesn't get easier," Zarabeth said. "Always be ready to fight."

* * *

At nine-twelve, a rustle, not so different from the last hour of Clea's movements, but in the office they all looked up.

In the hotel, Clea was at the bar, Donald wiping glasses to her right, Bill Thorn to her left. Melissa sat a table away, flirting with Vietnamese merchants.

In the office, Bus Uncle had mixed their mikes to approximate the room's acoustics. Next best thing to being in Clea's handbag.

"Excuse me, are you him?" Clea said, in character. "The singer? The Nigerian?"

"Am I—No, I'm sorry." Thorn had a Western Canada accent, cured like jerky.

She squealed. "Aiya! Of course, you not singer. Excuse me."

"Who is the singer?"

Bus Uncle clapped. "Fishie on the hook."

"You think that's it?" Zarabeth asked.

"Vocal analysis says so. Should we spike the next beer?"

"If there is a next beer," Zarabeth said.

Clea talked about the Nigerian singer. "Very good song.

'Happy Oil Worker.' Famous in China. I hear at home, in Dongguan. You look like him. Handsome."

"Thank you," Thorn said. "Are you here on business?"

"I work in shop now. I meet friend here. What you do?"

"Here for touring," he said. "See sights. I work in sales."

"No sell here?"

"Just vacation."

"Nice hotel. You sell well. I work in shop. I no sell well."

"People in the shop want to buy," Thorn said. "Just be friendly and help them."

"I try be friendly. Is different here."

A long silence.

"Thorn would know shop clerks don't come from the mainland legally," Bus Uncle said.

"You don't think she hit it too hard?" Zarabeth said.

Bus Uncle ignored her. The silence passed one minute. Rustles, prim scratching. Clea was moving her bag. "My friend is late," she said. "I think maybe I go now."

"May I buy you a drink?" Thorn asked.

"Clea set the hook," Zarabeth said. "Spike him."

* * *

An hour later Melissa reported from the toilet. "He's sloppy. Leg on the stool, leaning back. Not touching her."

"That's fine," Bus Uncle said. "He won't paw her."

For Thorn's third beer, Donald upped the hypnotic. Clea mentioned her debts, "daily money" of HK$500. A good meal in San Francisco. "You help me, you good man," she repeated, lullaby-slow. Minutes later he signed the bill. Clea led him out, just ahead of a stupor. Bus Uncle turned off all mikes but Clea's.

The small hotel lift thumped shut. A rustle, a kiss.

"Beautiful man," Clea said. "You help me." Over and over.

In Thorn's room Clea poured him minibar water. "Drink water. May I rub shoulders?" Sounds of clothing, creak of the bed. "You are very strong. Very strong. Strong brave man. Strong brave man. Drink more, you are thirsty. Strong brave man."

Ten minutes of Strong Brave Man. Zarabeth paced to stay awake.

When Clea cried out, Zarabeth jumped. "Help! Problem must help. Problem must help."

"What?" Thorn said, weak and raspy. "What problem?"

"Your computer. Problem must help. Help me. Your computer. Help me."

Keystrokes, beep of a fingerprint scan. "Yes. My love, my love, relax. All over now." In the midst of her soothing, the snap of her purse like a crash in the mikes. "Hello," she whispered. "Dongle inserted. He's pretty much out now, but here's the shot." Sound of a body falling.

Bus Uncle keyed open a new window, an Empyrean logo in its wallpaper. "We're in. The dongle copies the drive in five minutes, uploads in fifteen. Once it's green she can go." They waited in nervous silence. One minute, two. Connection good, network steady.

A roar from Thorn, pain but also strength. A thump on the floor. "Help!" Clea cried, all out of character. A shriek. "Help! He—"

A wet thump. Another. A crack of wood.

"Tell Melissa to fry the uplink, then leave," Zarabeth said. "Send Donald to Thorn's room. We'll take the stairs."

Two guards with stun guns followed them. "We're making Thorn an offer," she told Bus Uncle. "It was for the morning."

"I did not know," Bus Uncle said. "Do you have terms?"

"I think they're changing."

They ran up the dark block, crossing paths with a beeping scooter. Bus Uncle led them to a service entrance, up fire stairs. When they arrived Donald unlocked the door.

Thorn cowered on the floor, panting in heaves like a fish. Clea's temple and cheek pulped, her neck red and bent wrong. Zarabeth took Clea's bag, righted the bloodied chair, sat in front of Thorn. The guards stood on either side of him, stun guns drawn.

"You're upset," Zarabeth said. "Empyreans are great at being upset. Not calling for help though, not doing much about it. Now sit up or we'll kick you 'til you sit up."

He sat up. He was a fit man. Eyes red with rage. Clea's nightmare self.

Zarabeth looked through Clea's bag, swapped phials, took and lit one of Clea's cigarettes. "The murder seals the deal. Even if your people got here before the police—and they won't—you let yourself be seduced, you killed her, and, there's Colorado Springs. Yes, we know. Three dead. Four, if it's Evangelicals counting. So. Murder charges in Hong Kong, or Colorado. Discreet suicide in San Francisco. Or, join us. Now. A new life where your gifts are respected and rewarded."

"I would cause misery," Thorn said.

"You'll be miserable in any case. Why not enjoy it? You killed a rapist and a Straightforward whore. You mete out justice."

"You made me kill."

"Me? Not your paladin psychotic fury?" Zarabeth blew him a kiss. "Good luck with that. You still have value. We're generous. Director of Security at a posh Bangkok hotel. Many fine people stay there, you'll help them in many ways. Good wages, house staff, fresh girls from Chiang Mai. We know you'll love it. We profiled you."

Thorn hung his head. "Why do you hate me?"

"We love you, Bill Thorn. We love your fitness. We love your damage. We love your fear. It's fun to squeeze that. We love your hypocrisy. Your side says, judge not—and yet you judge. You made him judge. You made him a cop."

Thorn shook his head. "Who?"

She snapped her fingers. One guard stunned Thorn.

"You did know terms," Bus Uncle sniffed.

"He should be out cold," Donald said. "You did this."

"Or your dose was weak." She raised her hand. "Or, Thorn's mystical protection was unpredictable. We all contained the situation. I subscribe to the third option."

Donald swallowed. "Of course. We did the best we could. What about police?"

"We rented all adjoining rooms. No one heard anything."

Bus Uncle had the guards dress Thorn and wrap Clea in a

sheet. They took them in carts to the loading platform. Donald brought cleaning supplies. Zarabeth helped scrub.

An hour later it looked like a fresh-made room but stank of bleach.

*   *   *

For the next day, they had planned an island excursion, a celebration for five not a wake. But they went, taking the old ferry with worn plastic benches to Cheung Chau. Bus Uncle had a flask of some nasty thing, a few sips plenty to float. They hired motorized sampans to an island beach dense with scrub. Bamboo walkways led to a large grey pub with nautical accents, if built by beached sailors from their broken hull. Jimmy the proprietor had white hair and leathery red-yellow skin. He prowled among them at the bar, offering tequila, a challenge in his eyes, as if he were surfer and everyone else waves. Zarabeth stood him three times, the last a bad idea.

They ate on the deck looking out on the gray water, flags on ropes overhead like a great yacht. Prawns green with garlic, spicy squid, noodles, fried rolls, beer. Donald toasted success and absent friends. Melissa toasted a great actress. Bus Uncle toasted *sifu*, a master. What Melissa had called Thorn. *But they're lonely*, Melissa had said.

Zarabeth recovered enough to stand. "Clea was unusual. It's too bad, what happened." She drank down her glass. The team's faces all red in Clea's honor.

After dinner Melissa and Donald went to the indoor bar.

"To sex," Zarabeth toasted over shots with Bus Uncle and Jimmy. "The best response to death. Are there paper condoms for horny ghosts?"

"I haven't seen any," Bus Uncle said in English. "Why does your Cantonese sting my head?"

She explained the Polyglot to Bus Uncle in English. Jimmy listened a while then wandered off. "Mine's not right. Thing in London. Maybe why it bothers you," she said. "You're sensitive? What did you feel from Thorn?"

"Cravings and fears. You eased up to them."

"He fell from grace. I know how that is. You claw the whole way down."

"Hmm. This was a bracing experience. Too much work now follows protocol," Bus Uncle said. "Hong Kong has energy. The mainland will be cross, of course. One might leave town."

"I think I'll stay. I like the speed here. I like the crowds."

Bus Uncle pursed his lips. "Do stay out of trouble."

Melissa came, stern and sober, Donald behind her very drunk. The end of the party. While they waited for the sampans, Jimmy called Zarabeth to shots in stemmed glasses. "I drink with the demon," he said.

"Then pour a double," she said in Cantonese. The shot choked her. Her arm slammed the glass on the table, shattering the stem. Her arm, not quite her. She got the drink down.

Jimmy wagged his finger. "You cut off!"

On the ferry Zarabeth stood portside while the three sat apart. The great skyscrapers wore colored lights like fireworks. It was a wonderland, with dark alleys.

On the pier the locals were groggy. Somehow she had come down lightly, as if the demon really had drunk the last shots. She was a *sifu* of discord. Less her job than her nature. She shook hands with them all and walked away. She walked home, along empty dark streets. On the darkest she threw the phial behind her, heard it break.

In her flat she made tea and smoked. Out her small window, low buildings and streets. At home in Wan Chai. A perfect place to wait, for Gabriel.

She texted Magda. *All done here love it here can I stay?*

Morning in Boston. Magda's reply came immediately.

Good dog stay

CHAPTER TWENTY-SEVEN

San Francisco

Georgia Patchett lived in the Sunset District, a mix of free-standing homes in tile-roofed stucco or shingle-roofed siding, small front yards given over to driveways. Georgia waited outside her walkup apartment, in helmet, sagging t-shirt and shorts, with the one-speed bike she had borrowed from her church. Gabriel slowed but didn't stop.

"Keep up," he called behind to her.

He chose their route for flatness, a thirty-block loop to Chinese seafood take-out eight blocks away. Once she caught up he rode alongside her, coasted really. She wobbled on inclines, ankles bent toward the gears. When they arrived she was sweating but carried herself with triumph.

They got a booth with Chinese astrology paper placemats. She ordered steamed vegetables and tea, he spicy shrimp and Chinese beer.

"When can you order in Chinese?" he asked. "I heard Chinese restaurants have secret good stuff for those who can ask."

"It'll be a while," she said. "Most dishes have names. Like you need to know a po'boy is an oyster sandwich. What sign are you? I'm tiger."

"Horse." Gabriel was surprised Georgia was the elder.

"I should have guessed. We're compatible. It's just the age difference. Three years plus or minus is good, to the Chinese. Western astrology is more fun. Air signs, fire signs."

An old woman brought food on foam plates. Gabriel ate so fast it took a while to taste the pepper through the oil. Soon it was all he tasted. He drank half his beer in one go.

"May I?" Georgia asked. She sipped. "It's a little sweet. I didn't expect that."

"Goes with the food," Gabriel said. "Try it again. Good for sore muscles."

"I'm fine. You are a horse."

He read the placemat. *Popular and attractive, showy and impatient.* She flirted by making him read.

On the ride back he added a few blocks. "You'll be just as sore," he called back to her. "Get the most out of your pain."

When they reached her place she had showered in her sweat. Georgia had neither sugar nor salt smell to Gabriel these days, just a chemical crispness like tap water. He carried the bikes upstairs.

"I'm so out of shape," she said. "Let me clean up." She went into her bedroom.

He washed his face in her sink, put on a fresh madras shirt. She came out in another t-shirt, her hair up in a clip.

"Oh. You cleaned up."

"Just a little."

"You look nice." She smiled, frowned. "Should I—"

"We're watching a movie."

They streamed a Chinese period drama. Shoulder to shoulder. The yellow subtitles were hard to read, the characters' operatic passions easy to understand. He put his arm around her. She felt good against him, a body's good. No smell, good. All right.

"Are you enjoying it?" Georgia asked. "I know I always make you watch Chinese films."

"It's great. Good fight scenes."

She smiled like a flower in water. He leaned in and kissed her. She kissed back once, twice, smiled a hard wall. As much as she could do.

She patted his thigh. "*Wu liao.* I heard that before I read it. It means 'boring.'"

He kept his arm around her until it fell asleep. Let it fall off. Something to do.

* * *

When he rode home, Denise was drinking white wine in the kitchen. She poured him a glass. "I'm not sure about any relationship where you're the wild one," she said.

"Thanks a lot."

"I'm sorry!" She took Gabriel's hand. "You're bottled up. Are you having sex? Does she have some Jesus thing?"

Pointless not to share with a San Franciscan. "No sex. Yes Jesus. Other issues."

"Fine. OK wait. Hope doesn't turn into love and pity doesn't turn into love. Take it from the one who got the house. Now. Fine. Oh, I saved this for you." Denise handed him an article clipped from a magazine. Her phone rang. "Gotta take this, it's Ry."

Gabriel read the article twice to understand it. Humans had four hundred olfactory receptors, it claimed, but accumulated mutations turned off some genes. No one had the same sense of smell. People smelled the world in their own way, each missing things. He felt cheated. Lonely white girls odorless to him, while he dreamt of dark spices.

In his room, he knelt naked on the bed, expecting to masturbate, but he had no desire. He curled around a pillow and dreamt of Georgia, made up and in racy pink clothes, happy for once, and willing. Invisible hands wrote messages in lipstick on both sides of a glass wall between them, ever denser, hiding Georgia, hiding their own meaning.

The phone woke him at eleven. It was Del. "We've lost Bill."

"Lost?" It felt like another dream.

"Gone dark. Six hours. You're going to Hong Kong now. Pack quick. Red-eye to Chicago in three hours."

"Del, what am I supposed to do?"

"Wish I knew. Just go. A local guy will meet you."

No time to think. Shower, gel in his hair and two swipes of a brush. He wore a gray suit with a black tee and packed a white tee in the carry-on's outer pocket. Three days of summer business clothes. Toiletries. Two books, one English, one Russian.

In the cab he keyed a text to Denise. Trivial to send, to post on his social wall, to copy to Georgia. He shut off his phone instead. Gone dark. It felt good.

CHAPTER TWENTY-EIGHT

Hong Kong

His plane four hours late. Random inspection by two whip-thin men half his age. Once through, no one to meet him. At the far side of the arrivals area, the silver train to Central left every few minutes. Maybe they just assumed. He bought a ticket.

In the train all displays alternated English and Chinese. Subtitled world. Georgia would love it, even vicariously. He felt bad not sharing it. With Georgia he had the shape of love like a cast had the shape of a leg. He was glad to have this, alone. Thorn's life of specialized tedium cracked open, his private apocalypse. Maybe Thorn enjoyed it too.

In the quick, jostling taxi queue he breathed his first real air after a day of filtration. Hot wet salt air, thick smog, sweet sea rot. His cab took wide city flyovers away from the skyscrapers, down a rollercoaster's fall to a lower older district called Wan Chai.

The small hotel, Bill's hotel, had an antique glamour, with a tall narrow lobby paneled in lacquered gold wood, brass rails smelling of sweat and lye. His room also paneled, but small, as long as a bed and a suitcase, as wide as his outstretched arms.

He called the local office. Voice mailbox, another, another.

Finally the office head answered. "Wei?"

"Mr. Acton Tso? I'm Gabriel Archer. I'm in my hotel now. Was the office—"

"Archer? The American. About your colleague—They missed you. We should get you home then," Tso said. "Got Thorn's resignation. Signed in blood, all legitimate, he's theirs. Bad business really, though not at all our thing. Officials seem a bit upset. I think they just want to shut it all down."

"You don't know what—fine." Gabriel kept calm. "If this matter is closed for you, then I'm free to conduct my own investigation without local guidance. Sporting of you."

The connection fizzed as if Tso had wrinkled his forehead. "Come in."

* * *

Empyrean's bamboo lobby had a small fountain with uncomfortable stone benches around it, a twenty-seventh-floor view. Hong Kong spread black and gold below him, exhilarating, scentless. Gabriel longed for a window he could open.

"You're not in uniform," a man said in tart Australian English. His uniform fit tight on his muscled frame. "Kip Cheung. Senior Security. You are Security, right?" His hair close-cropped, his eyes wide and knowing, feminine in his narrow hollow face.

"Gabriel Archer. I'm an analyst and I do interviews. Plainclothes." They exchanged cards.

"Here all security staff wear them, even directors."

"Sure. Can I have one made?"

"They do it fast," Acton Tso said behind them. "But you won't be here that long." He was small of build, with gray hair and a stiff walk. He pointed to the benches, palm up like a pharaoh. "We expected you sooner, Mr. Archer, as did they. Comrade Leung took the whole office in for questioning. Farce."

"I went through Customs. If 'they' is China, they know I'm here. Where was he last?" Gabriel asked Kip.

"Same hotel. We only got an hour's forensic access. Sheets gone, chair gone. Everything very clean." He handed Gabriel a tablet with pictures. "Automatic checkout, empty room. Only when he missed his flight that we got notice."

Views of an empty, paneled room, twice the size of Gabriel's, with a larger bed and an eastern view of the Jockey Club. Splotches under ultraviolet light. Receipts.

A scan of the resignation. On vellum, signed in blood.

Bill Thorn had convinced Gabriel to stay at Empyrean, with an offer of camaraderie and help. Bill had cut himself and severed his own ties to the firm, in blood. If only Gabriel could smell it.

Gabriel had snapped with friends and under Thorn's eye. Maybe Thorn had snapped, alone. Trapped.

"Did you find clothes or gear?" Gabriel asked.

"Nothing," Kip said. "No surveillance from the hotel. We've got requests in to get municipal data as part of the missing-persons report."

A junior spoke to Tso. "Anquette Leung is here," Tso said. "She's stopped the lifts."

"Efficient," Gabriel said. "Who is she?"

"Special Party representative," Tso said.

Kip looked at Tso. Tso shrugged.

Kip sang softly, to the tune of a cartoon theme song:

"Anquette Leung, Anquette Leung
Admires Mao much more than Deng
She's the bullet in China's gun
Look out! Here comes Anquette Leung."

"Should I hide?" Gabriel said.

"Put you in the document safe," Tso said. "Amusing."

From two elevators, six grey-suited assistants spread out to cover the lobby. With them one petite woman, grey strands in her short black hair, in a rakishly cut army-green blazer. "Anquette Leung Mei-Cyun. I speak for China." Her accent like long earrings. "Archer. Why was Thorn here?"

"I don't know details."

"What do you know?"

Last year, the picture of forthrightness. Now he fronted anything. "Luther Koenig has a legal document, half in English, half in Chinese. What do you know?"

Anquette nodded. An assistant handed Gabriel a tablet.

"Footage from a nearby camera," Anquette said. In grainy blue-white, two men in a loading dock putting unconscious Bill Thorn in a car. Anquette paused the video. Callouts sprouted, names in Chinese. "All Straightforward staff or contractors. Not rogues. Why take him? If he was coerced, why make him resign?"

The next video, timecoded ninety minutes later. Two new men, one in a bartender's vest, and a woman. The woman's zoomed image resampled into a fantasy game avatar, long oval cheeks, glowing red smears for eyes.

"Zarabeth Battrie," Gabriel said. "I don't know a middle name. Late of Washington, DC, works for Straightforward Boston."

"Late actually of Prague. Still here. Apparently on vacation. Do you have her dossier?"

He had never really wanted the job. "We were lovers," Gabriel said. "Two months ago in Scotland, a month ago in Washington. Three days. She has a demon that translates for her. It started to use her body. I ran. Haven't seen her since."

In the engineered air Anquette's anger flared like vinegar.

"Let me be clear," Anquette said. "You had liaisons with the Straightforward staffer who now has kidnapped your firm's trusted courier?"

"And my boss. Yes."

"Did you cause this breach of security?"

"Not directly. We met by chance. It was passion. I'm not good with passion. Until yesterday I didn't know where Thorn was other than 'Asia.' They didn't find him through me. I travel with no data. My work passwords aren't on my phone."

"You know the Memorandum. You dealt with a threat to Luther Koenig in Hamburg," Anquette said. "Not so small as you act. The idea was Thorn couldn't be found at all. They kidnapped Thorn and accessed his data. They have copies of the Memorandum, of recent edits. We believed in the veil."

"You failed to break it. Somehow they did. I don't even know what he was doing here."

"He took walks every day," Anquette said. "City, islands, nature parks. We tailed him. At a particular time and place we did an ultra-short-range data exchange, a different courier each time. A few megabytes. A matter of seconds."

"If that's all, why kidnap him? Why create a controlled environment?"

"'Controlled environment.' Elegant. I will use that," Anquette said. "You're saying they wanted Thorn so badly what he carries is incidental?"

"How would you go for the data?"

An assistant leaned in. Anquette waved her away. "I would steal it, but for the veil."

"Assuming he's veiled," Gabriel said. "They know about him. But proceed as if he is."

"In transit, only couriers can access the data," Anquette said. "They have to be there when he's there and he's logged in. Where was he earlier that evening?"

"Bar," Kip said. "He went two nights." Gabriel found the receipts. First night HK$60, the second HK$480. From two beers to sixteen.

"I can't see Bill spending that much in a bar by himself," Gabriel said. "He meets someone. Or people. They slip him drugs. Not so much he can't log in. Then what?"

"Stun gun," Kip said. "Chloroform. A whack on the head. Then copy the hard drive."

"Better." Anquette waved. An assistant brought a plastic bag with electrical parts blackened by fire. "Wireless data network along the ductwork of the hotel. Sent the data from his laptop. Commonplace parts sold in lots, destroyed themselves when finished."

"It all points to stealing the data," Gabriel said, "leaving Thorn and the hardware behind. The smart play. Thorn might not have known for a while."

"Something went wrong," Tso said.

"Zarabeth," Gabriel said. "She screwed up their op. It still worked but she had an excuse to take Thorn. Once he woke up, why did he resign?"

"The Memorandum is my concern," Anquette said.

"An unsigned document held by thieves," Tso said. "It has to get to executives. They don't know what it says, that's why they're stealing it. How long is it?"

"Very long," Anquette said.

"So it will take time. When you learn your rival is about to make a deal, you offer the same terms or better, if you can. Do you expect they will?"

"The leak alone would be embarrassing. It would rouse hostilities here and in NATO that would be hard to manage."

"So they're blackmailing you?" Gabriel said. "Into what?" *Admires Mao.* "What best serves the people? Allow a failure or finish the work?"

Anquette pouted. "I will consult my superiors. There is also how they broke the veil."

Even his humiliations recycled. "She'll tell me," Gabriel said. "To throw it in my face."

"Because you spurned her over a demon. Aiya! Find me an office," Anquette demanded. Kip led her away.

"Thanks for winning her over," Gabriel said to Tso.

"I didn't do it for you," Tso said. "At least you don't scare easily."

"Comrade Leung was wrong-footed," Gabriel said. "She didn't know until after it happened. She needs a way not to look bad."

If only he'd done this in Russia.

* * *

A lean red-cheeked assistant brought Gabriel a phone on speaker. "Battrie's on a junk coming into Aberdeen," she said. "Ringing through now."

"Wei?" Music and party noise behind her. "Fuk Saa."

"Zarabeth? It's Gabriel Archer."

"Ooooh." Almost a sound of pleasure. "Gabriel. Hey hey guys? It's my ex-boyfriend." Hooting and grunts, deep drunk voices. "I crashed this party. We did a lot of tequila shots. They licked it off my body but it just made them hungrier." Men bayed like dogs. "I might have to swim to shore. Would you rescue me? Of course you wouldn't. Will you tell me why? In person. I want something from you. In the aviary in Hong Kong Park. Five o'clock. Just you and me." She hung up.

Anquette gave quick Chinese orders. "Will she come alone?" she asked Gabriel. "That would be reckless."

"Ha. I'll go alone too," Gabriel said. "Listen at a distance. Can I walk? I should walk. Can I make it by five?"

"Easily. I will walk with you," Anquette said. "We can get to know each other."

"I have surveillance to set up," Kip said, miffed.

They walked in full sun at the base of the skyscrapers. The air hot as desert, smells of smog and salt. In the sun, Anquette's hair looked greyer.

"Your name?" Gabriel asked. "The rapper?"

"Anquette rapped to praise a Florida prosecutor. When popular music elevates, it should be honored. The name sounds nice too. I was twelve when I picked it."

"So you had hip-hop growing up?"

"I grew up here," Anquette said. "Hip-hop and Canto pop and gorgeous movies, useless amassing of capital, grotesque indulgence. I wrote screenplays. In another life, perhaps. Instead my politics found favor in the new millennium. Free-marketers dream under socialism, but socialists dream under free markets. Were you ordered to seduce the Straightforward woman?"

"How subtle a transition. We met out of the office. It was a rainy night, I chatted her up in a pub. We had a lovely day. Then I met the demon, only for second. It unbalanced me."

"Yet you were still intimate."

"We were strongly attracted." He waited at a wide crosswalk although the light was white, the sign to cross ticking loudly. He breathed thick air. Above him a watercolor sky flowed through a canyon of skyscrapers. He stepped off the curb, on, off. "Your streets are spongier than ours." A double-decker tram clanged by, shrink-wrapped in an ad for printers. "This is Hong Kong."

"Not the best part," Anquette said. "The park is pleasant." They walked uphill toward glimpses of green. "We admire Luther Koenig," Anquette said. "Your logo is unfortunate. Like our character for soldier. But we admire Koenig's probity. Sad to see it is not reflected in his organization."

"Lady, I just work here," Gabriel said.

They walked up paved hills to a long green plaza with white tile fountains, below a pair of crenellated towers. Grey-white tile stairs edged in safety yellow led up a steep hillside.

"Past the amphitheater, you'll see sculptures," Anquette said. "The aviary is at the top."

"Are your people set up?"

She held up her phone. "Security feed. My people are *the* people."

"Or the people with cameras on *the* people."

"It's a good way of serving them."

The climb had Gabriel dripping sweat at the top. He pushed through a curtain of neon-green plastic chains into smells of freshwater, wet wood, chalky bird droppings. A cool artificial forest of spindly trees sat under great black steel arches and taut netting, noisy with bird chatter and song.

Tourists strolled the elevated walkway zigzagging downhill, past photographers with long lenses, setting up shots. Gabriel read guides at viewing stands, looked for pheasants and sparrows in vivid colors, blue pigeons with intricate crests.

Behind him, smells of rust, sunblock, and fake coconut. He turned. Zarabeth smiled at him prettily. She was darkly tanned, her hair blonder. She wore a blue floral sundress with pink flowers, low leather sandals. She looked beautiful. Gabriel missed her, missed how much she had once meant.

"Snuck up on you from downwind." She held out cold drinks in plastic cups. "Bubble tea. It's like chai tea but with little—" she cocked her head, a little tic—"little tapioca balls in it." She sucked one up through a straw, chewed it.

He took his cup. "They have this in San Francisco."

"They have it in Washington. I think it started—started in Taiwan. How often do you drink it in a giant birdhouse? So.

Cheers." They touched cups.

"You're in a good mood." He sipped the cold sweet drink, chewed a tapioca ball.

"I have been in a good mood. I love Hong Kong," she said. "Having a gay old time. Do you like the aviary? I picked it— picked it for you. I see the appeal. The birds live, mate, talk, indifferent to us. Is that where indifferent comes from—in different places? We ignore them." Another tic, and a thrust of her jaw, as if failing to swallow. "Or we enjoy them, as a sound, as if it's for us. I think the beings like my little demon, I think they're like that. Enjoy them like birdsong."

"They enjoy you too," Gabriel said.

"So does *E. coli*. There's a mite in our pores. Seedless grapes and weed and silkworms and honeybees. Plants barter with people. Bugs—bugs barter with people. Trade is the first contact. Before language before art. What do you got for me?"

"I have questions. Why did you take Bill Thorn?"

"Why do you care? You've washed—washed your hands of it. Rest assured he's making real progress in his new job." From the locket on her necklace she drew a thin shard of dirty glass. "My blood. I swore—swore to mix it with yours. Once I tell you, you owe me blood. For the way you left. The way you treated me. My blood and yours. You can never deny me again. Your words mean nothing. Your blood is truth."

"All right." Gabriel had nothing more to offer anyway. "Why did you take Thorn?"

"He knows a lot. You should have learned from him. But no second chances."

"Not if he doesn't ask for one."

"I meant for you. You know Thorn gave up sex? Eighteen years. Before you and I hit puberty, you get that? His body forced wet dreams on him to save—save his prostate. Your side makes rules and judges—judges us when we don't live by them, but you never get judged for imprisoning us."

"It's our fault Thorn indulged himself? Was it you he bought drinks for that night?"

"I'm a one-man gal, Gabriel. Besides, Thorn likes beige, not brown. You don't even know him. Some pasts leave scars—scars like acne. Try as you might to hide, people see them."

"You're not talking about Thorn now," Gabriel said. "I'm sorry I ran. I didn't want to, or plan to. That night, the demon used your body. It came on to me, after me, something. It was— inhuman. I can't be with that ever."

She laughed meanly. "So sensitive. You might have said. I could have gotten a repair kit in time. So this isn't about your freaking—" a strong tic, a flash of distress in her eyes "—freaking out. This is about you being unwilling to try again."

"Try that? It makes me sick. It's no good for you either. You can barely keep to one language. Which is coming out? Russian or Cantonese? Whatever logic you use to convince yourself you're OK, I can't believe Thorn fell for it."

"Thorn was on his own path. Since Colorado Springs."

"Since—" All the blood in his head, draining out, lest he think the rest.

"Oh, Gabriel. Such compartmentalization skills. He killed that guy and his women. I bet he even told you, and you managed to miss it. He killed again here too. No one you'd know, though I did. With his hands this time. Yet we forgave him."

She swallowed something hard and bitter that dulled her eyes. "Enough about your murdering boss. I gave you what you wanted. Your turn."

"Where do you want to stick it?"

"Alas we're in public. Through your hand?"

"How about my tongue?"

"Works for me." She looked sure he would renege. He stuck his tongue out. She pinched it with her left hand, pushed the shard through with her right thumb. He felt nausea not pain. He tried reflexively to draw his tongue in but the shard hit his teeth. That hurt. He pulled it out and put it on the bench.

She held it to the sunlight. "That felt good."

When he talked he sounded punchy. "I would be with you if you had no demon," he said. Blood poured from his mouth.

Zarabeth shook her head, stood, ran down the walkway pushing into people.

He scooped the ice from his bubble tea and held it in his mouth. When it felt numb he walked down, past staring tourists. In a pond near the exit, a pair of white pelicans, peaked black markings on wings and tail. He spat bloody water at them.

Outside Anquette waited, with an ambulance.

"They didn't break the veil," he said. "Thorn lost it, to an excess of probity. I need to talk to my people."

"Would you like a ride back to your hotel?"

"I'll walk. I don't want to mess up your car."

"As you like," Anquette said. "I know many ways of hurting an enemy. I never thought to do it with love." She walked away. A medical technician checked his tongue, packed it in gauze.

His phone map led him along manicured apartments into the hot lanes of Wan Chai. People glanced up at his bloody sight with wan smiles. At a clothing store he bought a cheap undershirt. The fat glass-eyed cashier pointed her cigarette at a curtain. In the dressing room he wiped his mouth. With the new shirt he no longer looked cannibal.

Red afternoon light flooded his room, like the sun had been stabbed and gauzed too. He rinsed his nose, brushed his teeth. He lay on his side watching the sky darken into sleep.

CHAPTER TWENTY-NINE

Hong Kong

When Gabriel woke, his tongue still hurt, though the swelling had faded. His room a dim coffin. He threw on clothes.

From his hotel he walked east toward Causeway Bay, seeking seawater by scent alone. The wet-market smelled of different salts, spilled from fish and ducks but also to preserve them, all stripping his nose like a wire brush. Hong Kong's great highways stood on pillars, leaving the old streets of tarnished shops, tiny dusty pickups and panel trucks idling diesel exhaust. He crossed the great roads among giant department stores and smelled salt again, with scum and rust and marine fuel.

Gray dawn found him in a small park, watching the harbor through chain-link near the yacht club. Big blue and green ferries, decks already busy with passengers. Giant ships with thousands of containers. Beyond it, Kowloon's towers and piers, hazy like a Fata Morgana. He felt the connection he missed in the Empyrean aerie, to the humanity and to ocean. Even in his years without smell he had known to live by water, if not to spend time in it. He was a creature of waterways and ports. Maybe his father too. Maybe Gabriel should have enlisted in the Navy.

A stupid urge to call Zarabeth Battrie, take her for coffee, take her to the Peak, the way people do, the way couples do. As if he could mulligan yesterday, as if she would let him mulligan his disgust and assholery and fear and faithlessness.

She had linked them forever and run away.

Gabriel made his sullen way back to Wan Chai. At the hotel buffet breakfast, he ate soft fragrant foods, persimmons and croissants, rice rolls with cooked eel.

His phone buzzed with a new calendar entry. Nine-thirty meeting in a Kowloon hotel suite.

Luther Koenig had come to Hong Kong.

* * *

Outside the suite Kip Cheung winced but waved him in. The small round room had a domed ceiling and Chinese art but only space for a table of six. With Koenig were Acton Tso and two other middle-aged men, all in tailored suits, already talking through a list of items while round-hatted servers brought plates of eggs and cold cuts. Tso nodded at the last seat at the table. Behind Koenig was an open double door to the rest of the suite. When Gabriel sat, a server closed it.

After the first course, the two suits left. Tso moved to sit next to Koenig. He talked a while, too quiet for Gabriel to hear. Gabriel drank coffee though it hurt his tongue.

Tso stood with a resigned air and left. Koenig sighed.

"Your lady friend has a brutal streak," he said. "This is the one you told me about, in Hamburg? But they wanted Bill. Tso thinks you're the cause of all this, even though he admits you're the only reason we know what happened."

"I can be both."

"You're not a murderer," Koenig said. "It breaks my heart. It's also a disaster. Bill has interceded in the lives of hundreds at my behest."

"But those things are all done."

"Things can be undone. We tried analyzing my visions, looking for a pattern. We never found one, but they might. Even so, just knowing what we have done may be enough. That's why I came here. I need to find out what to do. Are you staying here? In this hotel?"

"No. Business hotel in Wan Chai. Where Thorn was lost."

"Is it nice?" Koenig asked.

"It's fine. I can touch opposing walls when I stand in the middle of the room."

Koenig smiled. "I would like to come by this afternoon and have you assist me. I need to pray. I need a small room to pray. Each time I ask for a small room." He gestured around. "Each time, something extravagant. They think I ask out of charming humility."

"I don't understand. Why do you need my help to pray?"

"When I pray, I talk with angels."

"With," Gabriel repeated.

"Yes. I am too old for it. I was shown—special people like Bill, like you, can serve as an antenna. As a shoulder to hold their sky. It worked with Bill."

"You're going to pray, and an angel is going to appear."

"They come in pairs. With you to lean on, in a small room, I can withstand it. I'm asking for your help."

Maybe angels could tell him how to get rid of a demon. He doubted it. He could at least learn something.

"I want to know what the Memorandum is," Gabriel said.

"You're haggling with me?" Koenig said.

"I'm a businessman."

Koenig smiled. "Maybe, when the time is right."

"This room is bug-swept."

"Not what I meant." Koenig worried his mouth. "What if you don't like what I tell you?"

"I'll still help you today," Gabriel said.

Koenig decided quickly. "Some history is in order. In the 1400s, China sent a huge armada to the Mediterranean, as goodwill ambassadors. They met with rulers and scholars, even the Pope, and left behind technology a century ahead of Europe's. What happens in science fiction, when aliens help us? This was that. This was Prometheus's fire. Chinese maps told

Magellan where to find his Straits. Why did they do this? So we could find our way back to Beijing and pay tribute," Koenig said.

"I've never heard of this."

"In science fiction, future beings have a rule about not giving technology to beings who haven't yet figured it out on their own. This is why. Our tribute to the Chinese emperors was the Renaissance, the printing press, the conquest of the Americas, the Opium Wars. The end of monarchy. Not what they expected. We were young then. Now our heartland looks backward, our elites look inward. We repeat ourselves and call it a mash-up. The West has sampled all the Earth has to offer. We have done what we could. The East and South are energetic. It is always so. Civilizations bloom and wither, in seasons of centuries. We can be happy grandparents on cruises, or nuclear-armed wrecks in nursing homes.

"I prefer the former," Koenig said. "I work with counterparts in other countries on Memoranda of Understanding. Principles and specifics for a peaceful transition of global wealth and power. We've had a dozen major transitions in the last five centuries, and most have ended in costly and horrible war. A few didn't. It's not inevitable."

"You're making us China's flunkies," Gabriel said, "so they'll let us die in peace?"

"So we don't do a lot of damage in our dying," Koenig said. "While we cure erectile dysfunction, we mustn't box out malaria cures lest they make money before us. It's not just China, though without them the process would be pointless. It's Asia, Arabia, South America. Africa, most carefully of all. There have been concessions on all sides. Some make me spit. The veil allowed for trust, for a lack of secret politicking. It will be harder without it."

"Maybe it should be," Gabriel said. "I don't like it."

"Nor should you. You can't welcome the end of your cultural primacy. Remember, we made many cultures do the same. If it's inevitable, why not manage it? The West will wither. It will also be reborn." Koenig slapped the table twice. All the doors opened, guards in position.

"I will come at three o'clock," Koenig said. "Buy some bottled water. Three liters for each of us. Then rest. You've been through a lot. More to come." He went in his too-big suite, leaving Gabriel with the guards.

Gabriel felt kicked in the head. But he could walk out.

* * *

At three Koenig came. They danced past each other in the narrow entrance. Gabriel glanced in the halls. No guards.

"This will do nicely," Koenig said, sitting on the bed. "The water. Excellent."

Gabriel sat on the one chair. "You did this with Bill?"

"Three times," Koenig said. "He found it moving."

"You must grieve at losing him."

"I would rather not discuss it now. I must focus. Pay attention. Angels are big. They take time to move. The smaller the space we are in, the easier to limit their presence."

"I don't understand," Gabriel said.

"The more space, the bigger they are. Like bandwidth. When I was a boy I could see them outdoors, after a day of prayer. Huge, and glorious, the sight alone a greater truth than any words. Here it is a low-bandwidth connection. Relatively speaking. Even in a coffin I am too old to withstand them now. Without your strength to shield me, I wouldn't survive. You take the weight for me. I'm still scared of them. Do you meditate?"

"No."

"Then sit still. Face me." From his jacket Koenig drew a wood cross with trefoil ends, edges buffed by years of handling. He moved his lips soundlessly, his face young with memory. Odd to watch someone for so long, stare right at them and not have them react. Soon the room faded like a constant hum. Gabriel remembered working as a child in his father's basement workshop, listening to football games while painting shelves his father and brother built. As they moved around, working, their bodies blocked the signals and boosted them. People were antennas. The seed of worship, and of Babel. Band together to tune in to God.

An ozone smell and a blinding blue light. Koenig was gone, along with the wall and half the bed and all existence beyond them. As if lightning struck—and remained.

Two pairs of crossed arcs of blue flame hung in the blackness, came out of the blackness. Above each, a spinning pewter shape: the left, a sphere in segments like a puzzle; the right, a rock accreting bits from a nimbus around it, an endless snow globe. The flames burned back from the arcs, like streamers on a kite, curled and fronded like ferns with fiddleheads. Gabriel was falling now, spread-eagled, down and out the same—

"It helps to breathe." It was the snow globe, its voice a man's, in his right ear.

Gabriel gasped. "Thank you. New to this."

"You feel the pressure of our presence," the puzzle-ball said. The same voice, but in his left ear. Gabriel's voice, the way it sounded to other people. "Withstand us."

"Where am I?" Gabriel asked, an effort as if climbing stairs. "Where is Mr. Koenig?"

"You would say you were in a dream," the snow globe said. "True but ridiculous. All understanding is achieved through humility."

"You're in your dream," the puzzle-ball said. "He's in his."

Gabriel stood up. Not a weight but a draining, more to do and less strength for it. "Do I listen or ask?"

"We can just chat," the puzzle-ball said. "We are angels. Pillars of creation."

"Do you have names?"

"Less often than before," the snow globe said. "Hard to say of_relativity or of_mutation to a Judean. I am, of_clumping."

"I am, of_patterns_across_orders_of_magnitude," the puzzle-ball said. "Humans only dimly perceive them, now. Each order of being is a rung on a ladder. I'm the ladder."

"OK," Gabriel said, panting. "Why are you here?"

"You came to us? Or he did," of_clumping said. "We are regulators of rules, of the conditions that let the structure exist. He comes to save the structure he built."

"Can he?"

"We give points for participation," of_patterns said. "You decide your own level of involvement. Choose the form of your destroyer. Are you enlightened, or just slow?"

"Slow," Gabriel said.

They chuckled in stereo.

"This is an awkward time for you," of_clumping said.

"For humanity?" Gabriel asked.

"No, for you, Gabriel Archer," of_patterns said. "You don't fit. Do you know what that is?"

On the bed sat a car's distributor cap, a black plastic dome with raised points like a miniature castle. He picked it up. The heft, the smoothness, as real as real.

"Does it have a use outside the engine?" of_clumping asked.

"No," Gabriel said.

"Then it goes in the junkyard," of_patterns said. "Or you could keep pencils in it."

The angels less solid now, fossilized into new constellations of bright stars. "We are leaving now," they said in unison. "Thank you for the conversation."

"Where is the other?" of_clumping asked. "The ascetic?"

"You mean Bill Thorn? He is lost to us," Gabriel said.

of_patterns said, "He got tired of doing the smart thing."

Gabriel woke in his chair, his head throbbing. Between its beats he felt the time before slide away, and helpless for it. His body's needs roused him. He drank a bottle, a second bottle, the water inflating him like a raisin in a stopped sink.

Koenig breathed in shallow gasps. Dried blood on his face from both his nostrils. Gabriel wet a washcloth and wiped his face. Koenig's eyes opened. He looked sad as if remembering a lost love, then drank as greedily as Gabriel had.

"Did you see them?" he finally asked.

"Big, blue and burning? They told me I was slow."

Koenig woke his phone. He dialed, hung up. "You'll see things oddly for a while. Like everything has license plates. It can be distracting."

"Did it go well?"

"No. It's my fault. The weight of vision was mine to bear. It warped Bill. I just wanted to finish." Koenig's eyes large and clouded. "They will only give me my next message alone. I will not live long enough even to share it."

"If I can help you—" Gabriel said.

"There's no helping. It's already done. I have to go. Goodbye, Gabriel."

He left as quick as a breeze, almost evaporated. The door squeaked as it closed behind him.

Gabriel threw the empty bottles in the wastebasket. He felt a letdown, as if he had climbed a great mountain, only to arrive in darkness with nothing to see. Out his window, blue sky over white brick and green roofs. He had sweated through another shirt. He took it off, washed his body with a wet towel.

A knock at the door. He ignored it. They knocked again. He opened the door a crack.

Zarabeth smiled meanly, a storm cloud in her eyes. She wore a black pantsuit and white blouse. "Talk to me, lover. How do you do it?" She pushed the door into him. "Is it charm? Do you just say, hey we fucked up but aren't we cute? Can I do that?"

"What are you talking about?"

"China affirmed the negotiations, and asked not to be forced into any positions. No one will argue with that. All my work, for—" She tensed, her body aware before her voice. "Why is your room glowing blue?"

Angels are big and they take time to move. To enter, to leave. The angels still there and Zarabeth possessed.

"You need to go," Gabriel said. Wave of heat behind his back like a siren. Wave of heat in his own hands. "Go!"

Her necklace glowed blue. Her body jerking in spasms. "I can't!" she cried.

His blood, her blood. Her demon. Even his humiliation, a weapon. He heard his angel voices hiss: *trapped like prey in net*

Gabriel scooped her up, ran stumbling down the hall. Blue sparks where he held her. She smelled like smoke and charred meat. He had to get her away.

He slammed his shoulder into the stairway door, stumbled from the imbalanced weight of her. She fell off him onto the landing. He pulled her by her arm, forcing her to run behind him, blue light following.

At the bottom he opened the fire door. On the hot asphalt she tripped and fell, tripping Gabriel too. He rolled around, sat up. The blue light came out the door (widened the doorway, bulging like an over-packed suitcase) and into Zarabeth. Flames burst from her skin. She shook violently, moaning.

He waved his arms at people in the hotel breezeway. "Call an ambulance!" He tried to put out the flames but it was worse when he touched her. He found her phone, pressed the emergency button. "She's blue," he cried. "She's burning blue!"

His vision went black. He collapsed on the sidewalk.

CHAPTER THIRTY

Hong Kong, Maybe

Stale basement air. Ham and mayonnaise. He was naked on a foam mattress. He opened his eyes. A dim white room with painted cinder-block walls, a metal door without hinge or knob. Next to him, a paper napkin with two sandwiches, white bread, crust trimmed. He scarfed down the food. With new energy he inspected the room. Toilet, sink, toiletries, towels. No mirror, no sheet, no razor. No light switch, the light too high to reach. The toilet paper in cut sheets. Two thin white undershirts, two pairs of black pants. None of his things.

He washed himself. Asphalt on his back, salt sweat and fear under his arms and between his legs. Wipe it away. He dressed and sat. He smelled the air again. Motor heat and lube, ginger, sesame oil. Still in Hong Kong, maybe in Empyrean's basement.

Back on the bed he thought of Zarabeth, lying afire after he had dragged her down stairs. How had he blacked out? Where was she? Sad, hurt, humiliated. Just like him. A bonny pair.

He longed for her, in skin and nose. Was that love? Was love just the commitment to build something on longing?

The lights went down to near dark. He lay still. In the unchanging room he heard drips, creaks, whistles from vents. In a while he slept.

He woke to warm air and cigarette smells. Kip Cheung stood in the bright open door, a cushion under his arm, holding two paper cups. Two men in blaze orange and white stood just outside the open door.

"Are you afraid I'm suicidal?" Gabriel asked.

Kip shrugged. "Just Data Police protocol," Kip said. "They have jurisdiction over violations of informational space. How about I debrief you so this ends soon?"

"Why don't they debrief me?"

"They don't feel safe with you yet. Faster we start, faster you leave, yes?"

"Where's Zarabeth?"

"Her people took her. We think she's left Hong Kong, by we I mean us. They won't tell us, or you. I'm sorry."

The strong tea roused him. Kip asked questions about the attack, about Zarabeth, about Bill Thorn. Gabriel answered in as much detail as he could remember. Kip listened intently, taking few notes. Maybe he was recording it.

When he finished, Kip took his cushion. "Keep the cups."

"You didn't ask me anything about Koenig," Gabriel said.

"Koenig was never here," Kip said.

When Kip left, Gabriel drank cups of chlorinated water. Soon the light dimmed to near-darkness. He slept, hating to obey but with nothing else to do.

He woke to the smell of fresh tea, a minute before the door opened. With Kip Cheung came a lean beige woman, in a dark blazer and a knee-length red skirt, with pads of paper and her own cushion. The guards stayed outside and closed the door.

"We have more questions," Kip said. "When did you start working for Bill Thorn?"

"End of April. Didn't we cover all this?" Gabriel asked.

Kip waved slightly at the woman. "They feel safer with you. Say it all again."

This time, in chronological order. Thorn recruiting Gabriel. Thorn and the veil, though Gabriel knew little. Gabriel and Zarabeth. Gerald Pendry. Zarabeth takes Thorn.

348

As he told it, he was ashamed. What he did, what he let alone, were all exactly wrong. Kip gave him a poker face. The woman wrote it down in Chinese with thin charcoal pastels, filling pages.

They left after three hours. An orange guard brought stir-fried shrimp with noodles. No chopsticks. Gabriel ate with his fingers. He soon slept.

When he woke he found a yogurt parfait with mango. He spat it out when he tasted the drug. His stubble long, deep dreamless night. Maybe the stir-fry had a drug too.

The door opened. The woman stood in the doorway, a challenging silhouette. "Care for something else?" she asked in local English.

"Raspberry. Hold the drugs. What was it, truth serum?"

"No." She whistled. Guards rushed past her. He fought back but he was weak. She showed him the small syringe. "This is truth serum."

Once the needle was in, he gave up. A dullness undertow took him, saying *if it's a truth drug, what's the harm?* Soon a bitter delirium, questions keeping him from rest.

He woke hungry, his face itching. Light stung his eyes. His beard had made him break out. He popped pimples with his nails, washed until the blood stopped.

An orange guard brought a plate of steak and potatoes roasted with sea salt and rosemary. No drugs, and delicious cold. He ate slowly, licked the plate.

He put on clean clothes. Orange guards came in, followed by the woman, now in a beige plaid skirt-suit and brown leather boots. She tossed him red rubber thong sandals, beckoned him with her index finger. He followed her along a narrow hallway of identical doors, to an elevator down. In the parking garage, two guards met them. A red city taxi idled at the curb.

"You're done," the woman said. "The cab will take you to a hotel. Sorry for the inconvenience." She didn't offer her hand.

"Can I have a copy of the file?" he asked. "Be cool to have my life story in Chinese."

"You live in San Francisco," the woman said. "Find a translator."

The huge city, overwhelming at first sight. He closed his eyes, patted the vinyl seats. Old cigarettes, pomade, sweat. Real. Soon he could look through squinting eyes.

The taxi went to Koenig's Kowloon hotel. Two steps onto the curb, a staffer in navy came up to him. "Mr. Archer. I understand you've had a difficult trip. This way."

"Thank you. What day is it?"

"Sir? It's Tuesday, sir."

"I would have thought later," Gabriel said. "Thank you."

They escorted him to Koenig's suite, enormous after days in a dark cell. Next to his red suitcase, a fruit basket and an envelope. He ate red grapes slowly, enjoying the bursts of juice when he bit them.

In the envelope, a ticket for San Francisco the next morning, and a note:

Don't read into it. You weren't allowed back to your hotel. Report to work at Embarcadero, Monday 9 AM. Best of luck—Kip

Zarabeth would laugh. Stray dog in nice pen, before the needle. At least he could shower.

CHAPTER THIRTY-ONE

Las Vegas

A cramped white room, curved, noisy, cold. She was on a jet. Her arms bristled with acupuncture needles. She sat up slowly. The needles didn't hurt but she felt their weight when she moved. She wore no clothes under the sheet covering her legs. In the corner of the room, a black doctor's bag.

The door opened. Ng Lim Tak, in an embroidered red silk jacket, carried a small metal tray. "You're awake. Shall I finish removing the needles?"

"Please." She didn't bother covering herself. "Bus Uncle, where am I?"

"On a plane to Las Vegas. You've been out about twelve hours. You were cleansed by angels. They were offended, if one can use the term, by your *gwai*."

The word meant nothing. She looked around in her mind. "My Polyglot."

"Please stay still, needles in your forehead. Yes. Of course they don't understand our tiny proportions. You're lucky to be alive." He inspected her. "Any change in attitude?" He sat compactly in the room's one chair. "New certainties about existence?"

"My boss will be hopping mad."

"Excellent. The gwai took the bullet, as you Yanks say. The Empyrean medium called for help on your phone. We intercepted the emergency call. When we arrived, you glowed blue like a coal glows orange but they had withdrawn. When you came to me, it was a storm of energy across your meridians. I tried to level it, radiate it away. I have not seen the like. I had to be intuitive."

"I remember running, falling, pain. Thousands of blue flames, as if I'd walked into a hive of torch-lighter hornets. I felt their disgust. Like I would feel for a tick." She shook it off. "Thanks for saving me."

"Kind of you to say. Once we stabilized you, the Data Police insisted on your removal."

"The Data Police? They're real?"

"And sharp in their penalties, though Empyrean has that burden. In the wake of angelic visitation, there is a risk of rupture, between reality and unreality. Difficult in a population center. Your boss arranged for transport. A free trip to Las Vegas is pleasant repayment for my services."

"They made you come and it was dangerous. They do that. But now?"

"You exist. You are over-clocked, blood-cell counts triple normal. The needle holes from your IVs have completely healed. You may feel moody and energetic, especially at sea level." He stood. "We destroyed what you were wearing but your bags are in the closet."

"Tell me again. Angels. They were real. They killed the Polyglot."

"It was not alive. But yes. Should you need me, I will be in the galley. Our hostess is irritated with the arrangements." He left.

Whoever had packed her bags had folded the clothes neatly, helped themselves to her cash and makeup. Her phone and Tarot cards gone too, but she had credit cards and passport. She dressed in black shirt and pants, the London blazer. In the mirror she was the picture of health. No makeup.

Zarabeth carried her bags out to a long gold lounge, with seats for ten in chocolate-milk leather. A makeshift bed of blankets on the floor.

"Sleep well?" A woman sat with her back to Zarabeth, buff dark brown shoulders in a blue sports bra. She straightened but did not turn.

"I'm all right. You can have your room back. I didn't bleed on the sheets." Zarabeth walked around. "I'm Betsy."

"I'm Pauline." Her loud high voice at odds with her long heavy features, her nostrils that could hold large coins. "You's pretty out of it, naked and shakes and all. Thought you die in there. Dr. Creepy must be good with those needles. Overdose?"

"No. Two angels mugged me."

"Some kind of gang?"

"Angels. Wings, harps, trumpets?" The plane shook. Zarabeth sat down. "I had this demon, let me speak every language. Angels destroyed it. I was collateral."

"Any more comin'?" Pauline said with cool mockery. "Will they fly 'round the plane?"

"They're not all here," Zarabeth said. "Imagine existence is in a crate. Angels can stick fingers through the slats but they can't break the crate. Because they are the crate." Her understanding surprised her. She hoped Bus Uncle hadn't heard. "Anyway. If something was to come after me, better a plane over the ocean than all of Hong Kong."

"You ain't fuckin' with me, Betsy?"

"I'm OK, so you are too. Can I have a drink?"

"Whatever's in the galley. They usually stock it good."

"OK." Zarabeth went to the galley. Bus Uncle on a folding bench, asleep. She made a rum-diet-cola, cut a fresh lime and licked her fingers after.

Pauline had gone into the bedroom. Fashion mags on the table. Goody.

* * *

On landing, Pauline came out in a fine purple skirt-suit, giant iridescent sunglasses, a blonde bouffant wig. After Customs she left into a waiting entourage, and three photographers following.

A casino town car, front seatbacks hung with flyers and ads, waited for her and Bus Uncle. In Strip traffic they crawled past a half-built complex, open floors of metal studs and drooping wiring, refreshing among the amusement-park opulence.

Some blocks later the car turned left, between a gold tower and a black pyramid. At a side entrance to the tower, three white men in black suits waited. They looked at Bus Uncle for direction.

"We part company here," he said. "You have an appointment. These men will take you. I have five hours to gamble before my flight home. Did I use up my good luck surviving the ride?"

"Bus Uncle, today luck is your bitch."

"May it also be yours. Goodbye." He gave a slight bow and walked up the sidewalk.

The nearest black suit waved her inside courteously. She walked uncomfortably ahead of them, past a silver stand of blue-lit slots, up an escalator, into a narrow food court.

Magda sat at a table by a hot-dog restaurant, a tray of food in front of her.

"Sit down," Magda said. "Hungry?" The suits left.

"No thanks."

Magda squirted a packet of ketchup onto her tray, dipped a potato tot and ate it. "You were on the Internet. Thirty-seven minutes. I used a valuable favor with a Russian 'botnet crew to scrub it. Why were you on the Internet? Because your irreplaceable familiar got bug-zapped, and thanks to your Empyrean lover it happened in public. Then you survive, and I can't just dump you because of the Data Police. My costs for your flight. It's a million in cash and trade. Explain how you made such a mess of this."

"You wanted a trouble magnet," Zarabeth said. "Nine months you didn't know. You aimed me at the chink in their armor and I opened it. I made their messenger our bitch. I outed their leader as one who talks with spirits. I did right by you. A million is chump change to the damage you can cause, if it wasn't just some snow job you laid on me in Scotland. At the same hotel where I met my Empyrean lover. Explain *that*. Or not. Fuck you and your million. I got done what you needed done. Sorry about the mess."

Magda's lip quivered but she forced a smile. "Have a potato tot."

"No, thank you."

Magda smiled more. "For your job, eat it. No ketchup. Just by itself. Slowly. Like a fine amuse-bouche. Do you like it? Is it good?"

It was gummy, and gritty, like snot and salt. "No."

"None of this is good. Potatoes with DNA from bacteria that poisons bugs. Meat slurry scraped from skulls and hooves, jammed in a digestible condom. Served in cheap tasteless bread with sugared spices. People line up for it, give it to their offspring, like birds too stupid not to eat plastic. Did they miss the weekly diet tips on morning television, the stories about obesity, heart disease, diabetes? On the contrary. Those are why they line up." Magda waved at the food. "This foulness, this atrocity that destroys the biosphere and accelerates their death—it's a *privilege*. People save money to come here, to feel unfettered by biology or gravity or sense. A place where they're told it's different. It's OK."

Her smile fell. "There comes a point when we too want to believe. When we envy their happy servitude. You'd think the fat fucks would caution us but they become the new normal. We forget eighteen hundred whole-food calories and a multi-vitamin each day is all we need—which is to say, all we should have. We forget about the fun of quick fucks and dwell on the sad ride home. We think, maybe it is OK. Just this once. A donut. A pizza. Love. Those people in line are you. This meal is your affair. I know you tried not to be them. You failed."

"It's not a fair fight when they have angels."

"Fairness is for games, dear," Magda said. "For now, I'm stuck with you. 'Botnet crews can't delete rumors, and we don't want a corporate martyr. Thorn's drive has sent the upper ranks into a tizzy. Incredibly, you have cachet. On the optimistic assumption you have other remaining value I'm sending you to a sort of coaching session. It is not a normal environment. I have arranged security for you. Eat and drink before you go and have nothing there."

"Sounds like a magic quest," Zarabeth said.

"It's to prevent them dosing you with their nasty drugs. I know you like to party but restrain your impulses." Magda moved her tray. Under it was a hotel keycard in a paper pouch. She flicked it across the table. "You have a room in which to clean up. No more minders. Your ride will pick you up outside the main lobby at nine. You'll know when you see them." Her brow furrowed, as if deciding what else to say. "Goodbye for now." Magda hobbled into the crowd.

Zarabeth walked through the main casino, idly looking for Bus Uncle. Few tables were open, dealers bored, pit bosses pacing like caged lions. At the lobby newsstand, she bought diet cola and cigarettes, two cheap watches with cartoon Egyptian pictures. She set the watches to the time on her receipt, put one on each wrist like magic bracelets.

Third-floor room, view of a roof with fan housings, a comp for a low-roller. In the distance, a white wall with turrets, like a giant Craigellachie, beyond it a miniature Manhattan. Maybe she had always been in Las Vegas, at a Cantonese casino with a Czech strip club and a diamond mart.

She missed her tarot deck. The future was coming in any case. Learn it when it happens.

* * *

At eight-thirty Zarabeth sat at a small piano bar off the casino lobby. Dark eyeliner, red skirt-suit, tall black heels, cheap watches. The bartender lit her cigarettes. Fun to be classy. Two drinks later she wore the feeling out of the bar like a psychic fur stole. She stood outside to scan taxis and town cars.

"Zazzy Boots!" Out the back window of a limousine, a familiar face. Toothy smile and long heavy nose, a black derby on her curly black hair. "Get over here!"

The vanity pictures in Janice Goldman's glass Los Angeles office dated to Zarabeth's childhood, movie stars with permed curls and narrow ties. Janice had the same face in all of them. Soon after, Missy had shown her a picture of Great-Grandmother Johnson as a single young flapper, arm in arm with Janice. "A different name back then," Missy had said.

The limo seats and ceiling were upholstered in leopard-skin fabric. Janice wore a black suit, black-and-white checked low-cut blouse, white snakeskin pumps. A skinny platinum-blonde in red leather and strap heels sat across, giving Janice a manicure. Janice patted her free hand on the bench.

"Sit sit sit! I'd ask how you've been but we all know." The limousine drove away. Janice picked up a cocktail from the armrest. "I have gin and whiskey. Zazz, this is Evgenia. She's from Sebastopol. Or Sevastopol? The one in Crimea. Caviar's my flavor of the month. Drink?"

"Later," Zarabeth said. "Love your look. Are the Eighties back?"

"Is it Eighties? I suppose. After a while they all run together."

"I know now. How do you keep it quiet?"

"Funny, no one ever asks me that," Janice said. "Always the other thing. I've been Janice for thirty years. Thirty-five? But I so love the movies. Even back when they were silent. I can't move on."

"China and India have movies. You could restart cool as a video game tycoon."

"Who the fuck are you to give me advice?" She glared, backed down. "Love *your* look. Dressed for the occasion. Not to be pushy but are you ready? Do I have permission?"

"For what?"

"Maggie May didn't tell you?"

"All I know is I'm going someplace where people might dose me."

"She would know," Janice said. "You're going to meet a lwa, a deity from the Haitian pantheon. Or an aspect of her. Lwa are worse than musicians, always side projects."

"So, voodoo?"

Janice shook her head. "Secte Rouge, among other names. Same stock as voodoo, but way more pepper. Not just chickens who bleed tonight. A hybrid of the Yoruba pantheon with the Maya. Enslave blood-magic peoples together, you ferment nasty shit."

"Why am I going there?"

"To meet the lwa. To what end I don't know. I'm just going with you."

"*You* are my security? That has to be expensive."

"Security? Is that what Maggie Moo called me? Dried up old cunt."

"Am I going to be possessed?" Zarabeth asked. "That could be cool."

"Oh Mags-in-rags didn't tell you diddly. You're the guy in the iron suit. Dig the gear, but no hugs. I wouldn't touch you without permission. That's why I'm letting Evgenia be useful."

"The angel thing?" Zarabeth asked.

Janice's face contorted as if her ghost would leap from her body. Whatever she wanted she had a very great need for, but she was stuck behind Zarabeth's whim.

Janice looked away and inspected her hands. "Not bad, Evgenia. Maybe I do want polish? Fuchsia, like in the Eighties. Were you even alive in the Eighties?"

Evgenia said nothing and stared at the floorboards.

"I'll think about it." Janice pressed a switch on the armrest. "Driver, pull over please? We just need a minute." She sat up pertly. "Broadly speaking, there's us and them. Angel things happen to them, more than we knew. It hasn't happened to one of us since air-conditioning, certainly. Maybe since window glass. Scrolls say it leaves a *residue*. I'm here to barter. Protection for permission. I keep you safe, creepiness and disgust excepted. In return—in advance—I get a taste."

"Define 'taste,'" Zarabeth said.

"Less quantitative than experiential. Smell the rose not eat the manna. I think, it's new to me." She frowned. "Or I drop you off at the airport and you explain it to Her Mags-nificence."

"What do you need to do?"

"Works best with a kiss."

"Ha. At least no blood. Can I have a manicure afterwards?"

"Evgenia, you have a fan club. Pedicure too? Cunnilingus? She's got a gifted tongue."

"Just the manicure, thanks." She felt nervous, like the day she'd installed the Polyglot. "Fine. I give you permission to taste me."

Janice pressed the console button. "We can get going now, driver." She grabbed Zarabeth's head like a bowling ball. She tasted of peanuts and gin, her tongue buzzing.

Janice shot back as if electrocuted. "Oh my," she said, shivering. "It's—" She panted shallowly. Her eyes rolled up in her head. She fell back against the seat, shaking, her jaw slack.

Evgenia watched with concern, reached for Janice, drew back. She looked up at Zarabeth.

"No idea, sorry. You have lovely eyes," Zarabeth said. "Shame she makes you look down all the time. I'll have gin. Definitely nail polish. Do you have gold?"

After that, the only sounds were filing and the ice shifting in drinks. She grew carsick from polish fumes, opened the window and gulped down cool air. Janice had stopped shaking but she was well out.

Forty minutes after the kiss the limousine slowed abruptly, shifting Janice in her seat but not waking her. It drove uphill, stones and sand under the tires.

"AAAAH!" Janice bolted up. When she recognized the limousine she looked angry and ashamed, like a braggart child who chickened out of a dare. Zarabeth covered her grin.

Evgenia brought out a wood cigarette case with gold-tipped black paper cigarettes. She lit a thin silver tube with a blue hissing flame. Zarabeth drew back instinctively, Janice too.

"Turn it off," Janice said. "Find some matches."

"I have some," Zarabeth said, taking them from her clutch purse. Her own cardboard pack of smokes looked crappy. "Can I have one of your cigarettes?"

Janice closed her eyes while Zarabeth lit Janice's cigarette, then her own. Bitter thick smoke. She wondered if she would be sick again. Janice put the cigarette case in her jacket pocket. Evgenia busied herself with making a drink.

When she looked at Janice again, Janice was looking intently at her. She felt a sense of shared experience, shared secret. Shared weakness. The limousine air was now gray with smoke but it also seemed brighter, as if a sunroof had opened.

"Where are we?" Zarabeth asked.

"Private compound in the hills southwest of Vegas. Close to Lake Mead. By day he has a great view. Roberto Castillo, more commonly known as DJ Elusive. In the Nineties, he ran raves. Now he's a pimp. Call girl classifieds are his bread and butter. Tonight is his sweetbreads." The limousine stopped. "Evgenia, the deck."

From her bag Evgenia passed Janice a new tarot deck. On the backs, two interlocked snakes eating their tails to make infinity. Janice sliced the shrink-wrap with her nail, split the deck and shuffled it. Zarabeth drew a gaunt white woman, holding a crab with a pearl in each claw.

"Queen of Cups," Zarabeth read. "That's Brand Director?"

"Boots, you need a less unisex deck. Keep the card with you. A talisman is useful in any magical situation," Janice said. "I'm not going to hold your hand tonight. Direct threats, I'll deal with, but don't get sloppy. You've earned the right to be taken seriously."

"Magda might say you're renegotiating."

"She's not here, is she? Let's go."

Zarabeth opened the door. Janice followed her out and closed it behind her.

"Evgenia's not coming?" Zarabeth asked.

"It's like a new car," Janice said. "You want to keep it free of dings for a while."

They stood on a rocky hilltop, in the brick driveway of a tall stone house with a forbidding slab of steel for a door. From the roof, flickering light, shouting, high-pitched fast beats like sticks on buckets. Around them cars were parked close together, a mix of airport rentals and expensive sports coupes. The limousine barely had room to turn.

"Everyone else drove themselves," Zarabeth said. "Or sent their drivers away."

"Only the invited get to stay," Janice said.

The steel door swung open on a pivot to a gentle push. Cool moist air as if from a cave rushed at her. The door closed on its own when they stepped inside, cutting off the rooftop music. On a stool by the wide metal stairs, a loose pile of cheap white paper fans.

Janice unfolded two and handed one to Zarabeth. "Hang on to it," Janice said. "It's a thing here."

Upstairs, in the red-draped salon, meter-tall red candles burned in beds of white glass beads. No rooftop beats here, only tinkling spa music. Pretty young women of all colors, all in red miniskirts and shorts, circulated around a crowd of wealthy people, mostly male and white, mostly older. In the midst of the chatting, a grunting fat man, naked and dripping sweat, knelt against a large ottoman to fuck a pale-white brunette woman with thick moles on her back. Everyone just ignored them.

Zarabeth sniffed. "Someone here has marijuana."

Janice frowned. "Didn't—"

"Fuck you and fuck you. Are you my mommy tonight or not?"

A slender white man with a pencil mustache popped in front of them, his eyes deep red. "I am happy to be your daddy." He squeezed Zarabeth's left tit as if testing fruit. She coughed and held up her fan.

"Terribly sorry," the man said, spilling his drink. "You are wearing red."

"I'm with the band," Zarabeth said. "No harm done. I'm Betsy."

"Gustav. I'm horny." He tittered. "If you like cock, let me fuck you. Or a threesome with your pretty Jewish friend."

"I dislike both you and cock," Janice said.

"Ignore her," Zarabeth said. "Do you have marijuana?"

"Only pills. They had joints out earlier on the bar."

"See ya." The bar had crystal glasses, ice in buckets, bottles of good liquor. An empty silver dish with green crumbs. She

361

started to pour a drink, remembered Magda's warning.

She held her fan out along corridors of small bedrooms. In every room, red whores and clients, threes and fours. In one room, seven naked people all intertwined, using fingers and dildos to fill each other, anywhere.

In the main room, the growing orgy had pushed conversations to the side and onto the stairs. Zarabeth followed another corridor with locked rooms and a service elevator. She took the elevator up.

It opened onto the circular roof, covered in sand, with a high parapet and a wood deck around it. In the sand, red-robed cultists pogoed and chanted to the beats played by three filthy drummers with gray skin. Below a large screen of abstract computer animations, a large mastiff dog lay sacrificed on a black stone altar, shiny entrails spilling down the front.

The cultists turned toward her as one, not jumping now but still chanting. Wide hungry smiles. Three raised machetes.

A shout in Creole. The machetes lowered and the cultists resumed their dance.

A wide short man came forward, eyes bulging from a creased brown face. "Magda said you needed watching. Where is your—"

From the elevator a robed cultist sailed through the air into his fellows, knocking down a few. Janice stepped out, fourteen feet tall, black smoke crackling around her. Impressive, and ridiculous.

"Nice entrance," Zarabeth shouted. "Can you juggle too?" Some cultists laughed.

When Zarabeth looked back Janice stood right in front from her, normal size but her eyes black and her skin leathery, a bee-buzz static in Zarabeth's skin.

Still not a fucking angel.

"It would be funny if you juggled him," Zarabeth whispered.

Janice's enormous eyes would spring fangs and swallow her—but inside them, Zarabeth saw blue flame.

Janice snorted. "Ha!" She held out her hands and pantomimed juggling, popping her lips each pretend catch. She fell into Zarabeth, laughing. "Give me a hug, shiksa, you're hilarious!"

Cultists laughed again. Janice whirled at them. Zarabeth didn't see what face she showed them but they backed away.

Again laughing. Janice stepped back, wagging her finger, almost tripping on the wide man who had first saved Zarabeth.

"Honest mistakes," the man said. "Witch, welcome under agreed terms. All courtesies. Zarabeth, I'm DJ Elusive. Let's go to my office."

They rode the elevator down. In the cabin's stark light, his robes cheap plastic.

On the ground floor he led them along snaking patterns of tile to a large office with tall windows, a view of small lights in vast blackness. Thumps and shuffles from the orgies above. A round standing-height desk stood between two easels, one an old painting of Mary and Jesus, the other a doodle in red and yellow. A black cat sat on a velour pillow by the window.

Elusive tapped the keyboard. The monitors woke with the same computer graphics as the large screens on the roof. He opened a black shell window and keyed a string of commands.

"Are you enjoying the party?" Elusive asked.

"Not especially. Magda said not to eat or drink and all the pot's gone, if that was clean."

"I'll see you get some. Eat and drink as you like. The water and the ice begin the ritual. A little hypnotic, a little euphoric, a little magic. We partake too but we are habituated now. If you stay clean, in a couple of hours you can pose our clients like dolls. The whores often do. It's a tricky balance, enough to release their nutritious rut but not so much we burn their brains. They pay, we use each other, most of them leave."

"I noticed the zombie drummers. Do you have chairs here?"

"I have back problems. I rarely sit."

Zarabeth stepped out of her shoes and picked them up. "What happens now?" she asked.

"You are a guest at our rites. Dantor will speak to you through one of us, or not. She is imperious, but if you work for Magda Crane you can handle that, I'm sure. And if things turn savage, you have the witch. A primer." He nodded to the left-hand painting. "The Black Madonna, brought to Haiti by Polish mercenaries. Haitians adopted it for Erzulie Dantor, protectress of whores and lesbians, source of Haiti's independence. What do you know of me?"

"You're a pimp and apparently a DJ."

He frowned. "Not the epitaph I planned. I did advanced math in Palo Alto."

"Ha. Math guys are freaks."

"True. I was also an idealist," Elusive said. "I volunteered for the Peace Corps in Haiti. Duvalier had fled, and Namphy seemed honest. It was a romantic time. I fell in love, of course, a strong woman from Kansas named Katie. A goddess fell in love with me. Erzulie Freda, lwa of love, her charming side. At a grand fête she possessed many women, and all touched my face and hair possessively. Six women, seven, all with the identical laugh. I dismissed it as theatrics. For a week I had bad luck. Accidents, cuts, a near-miss with a tire jack. The mambo told me I was disrespecting Erzulie. Said I'd see worse.

"A few days later, Katie was killed when her chainsaw kicked. Drunk at the wake—they shipped her home but we had one anyway—a man talked to me about revenge. He recruited me into Secte Rouge. As husband of Erzulie, the universe bends to let me join her. Through the rites we summon Erzulie Dantor, her fearsome aspect, and give vent to her dark urges. Each time we know more of her, of how she comes and what brings her, what one day may trap her. I want to kill my wife." He pointed at the screen. "Do you know what fractals are?"

"Math problems graphed in paisley," Zarabeth said.

"Ha." He pointed at the other painting, a flat shape of yellow lines on a field of red. "That is Erzulie's vever, her sign. You'll notice the axial symmetry, characteristic of all vevers, and of certain mathematical sets when graphed."

"Fractals."

Elusive locked his system and led them to the door. "Voodoo speaks of the crossroads, where human and lwa meet. In fractals one axis represents real numbers, the other imaginary numbers, multiplied by the impossible square root of negative-one. Old magic with new perspective. The goddess will come tonight, through us, to graze on our bounty of submission. Magda hopes she will speak to you. I can promise nothing," Elusive said. "Know also: we serve the goddess but we serve the Secte. If there is a way to kill her while you speak to her, we will try." "And still the goddess comes?" Janice asked. "It's why she comes. We're great sport for her." His eyes impatient to leave. "How do you know Magda?" Zarabeth asked. "She has been my client. We share an inconvenient love. Erzulie's punishment for my treachery. I really need to go now." "Can we fuck in here?" It was Gustav, shirtless and unsteady, his open belt dangling from two loops, iced drink dripping on the floor, a listless whore reluctant behind him. "Be my guest," Elusive said. "Don't involve the cat." In the elevator Elusive drank down an amber vial. "I'm a little behind," he said. His eyes reddened by the second.

On the deck the drums had changed tempo, now complex jerky rhythms pulsing unpleasantly through the deck. Red-eyed masked cultists prowling like animals, shouting and growling and yelping, some on all fours. Nursery school for demons. The lights began to strobe. Elusive pushed off the elevator frame and leapt out like an animal.

The cultists stomped around in wide squats, roaring and calling, shoving their heads in the dog entrails. They chanted strange yelps and moans: *OB-ob-eee-HA OB-ob-eee-HA ooooob-KA oooooo-KA.*

Janice Goldman sourly ate a chicken breast.

The rhythm the best high on offer. Zarabeth grabbed Janice. "Dance with me! Why be eternally youthful," she shouted, "if you don't have fun?"

Janice dropped the chicken, kicked off her shoes. She offered Zarabeth her greasy hands. They skipped in among the cultists, stomped and squatted and chanted: *OB-ob-eee-HA OB-ob-eee-HA ooooob-KA oooooo-KA.*

Janice slapped her ass, Zarabeth slapped Elusive's, he slapped another, a spanking conga line with laughing like retching. *Buh-leh-yack! Buh-leh-yack! ooooob-KA! ooooob-KA! OB-ob-eee-HA OB-ob-eee-HA.*

Janice jerked upright, back arched as if a whalebone pushed through her. She stumbled back. "There's something here. There's—hey—" She brushed at her jacket, one hand, two hands, compulsively. Her head drooped, came back up, eyes and smile crazy large.

"You OK, Janice?"

Whatever possessed Janice shook the head.

"You OK, Erzulie Dantor?"

It moonwalked backwards to the deck, leapt a mid-air somersault well over Zarabeth's head. When it landed the deck cracked. The sound stopped the drums.

"Pretty limber for an old goat!" Voice loud and deep, not Janice's. An old black Creole man's voice, the blackest man, more than man. "Someone get me a hat."

The cultists drew back, bowing low. "Cimetière," they murmured, "Cimetière."

"I said, A HAT!"

"Hat over here," Zarabeth said. She gave the being Janice's derby.

"Oooh!" The being wiggled its fingers, snatched the hat. "Nicer than my usual."

"You could rub it in the sand," Zarabeth said.

"Good idea." Three fast swipes shredded the brim. "Do you smoke?"

"In your horse's jacket," she said. The cultists moved closer, hissing and lowing.

"Ah." The being took one cigarette out, let the case fall on the sand. "Black Russian. Like Pushkin. Ha!" It lit one with the whole pack of matches while Zarabeth picked up the case, smoked it down in two breaths. "This is Las Vegas? No French then. Call me Daddy Longlegs. Mister Saturday Night." It shook its hips, did a tap shuffle. "Special. Is it Saturday?"

"I'm no longer sure, sir."

"It's Saturday now. Trust me. I'm a god." It sneezed a huge snot onto its face and wiped it with the back of its hand. "One of these things is not like the others. Who are you?"

"I'm Zarabeth. Are you who I'm supposed to meet?"

"I'm a gatecrasher, angel-whore. DUHHH!" As loud as a lion. She jumped. It turned to the cultists. "You! Ponies! P'tit chevaux p'tit cochons gris. Get back to work. Dantor's not coming but I won't have her insulted." It marched toward them, mocking their stomping dance. They scattered, regrouped by the dead dog. "Belly ache belly ache!" The drums began again, faster and louder. The cultists went back to their rite.

"The Wrong Way Bitch doesn't like me," it said to Zarabeth. "If it were just happy Freddie ZuZu I think things might be different. Opposites attract." It made a circle of one hand, shoved its other hand's bunched fingers through it, the knuckles cracking loud. "Alas. May I have this dance?"

Daddy Longlegs stepped her through a routine, completely out of tempo with the music. It laughed with posh delight. "Isn't this fun!" Again, again, faster, catching up with the drums. Faster still, as much as she could do to land on her feet, one misstep would shatter a bone.

Everything went white. It might have been a moment, an hour.

She sat cross-legged on the deck facing the lwa, a platter of chicken breasts between them, half gone. Daddy Longlegs ate a breast in two bites, another, another. Face and hands brown with grease, manicure in shreds. Zarabeth's watch-hands spun, left clockwise, right counterclockwise.

"Ah food. Nothing like it after you die. Rum?" It offered a large jug of white liquor with hot peppers floating in it.

"No, sir, but thank you." The cultists writhed in a mass, robes and clothes worn off, naked skins puffy red from scrapes and scratches. "Excuse me, sir, Daddy Longlegs—"

"Oh, I like that. Sir Daddy Longlegs." It shoved more food in its mouth. "I can ride them all at once thanks to their rites. Worms are my kind. Not you. That angel dust."

"Janice—your *horse*—"

"The old mare was overpaid. Kisses are expensive. I am collecting luxury tax."

"Just what are you?"

"An emergent property of humanity. Sweat that dries into hurricanes. Explain quantum computing to Napoleon and I will explain divinity to you. But divinity doesn't really interest you, does it, daughter? Give me your hand and I'll tell your fortune." In its face trickster's glee.

She wiped her hands slowly, palmed Janice's tarot card. "All right. Tell me my fortune."

Daddy Longlegs grabbed eagerly, like to rip off her arm. The grip went from strong to brittle, a freeze-dried flower. She pulled her hand away, leaving the card.

Daddy Longlegs sneezed thick snot on it, threw it away. "A deal's a deal, clever girl. Don't ask. You are contorted by your question. I'll ask you: Do you like abortion? The killing of unborn babies. If you had a baby in you tomorrow, an embryo or a fetus in you? Not a rape. An act of pleasure. Would you kill it?"

"No."

"So you support abortion restrictions? Campaign at clinics?"

"Fuck no," Zarabeth said. "Bible-thumpers. Go scream at some poor girl who got raped. Or who knows a baby would just—" Her insides hurt like dirt split by shoots.

"People who save innocent lives make your skin crawl," the lwa said, "because their good is incidental to their natures. They sing to Jesus but they are Elisha, slaughtering kids who make fun of them. Not repentance but punishment. This is how you loved. He loved you differently. He out-conflicted you. You think you bottomed out? Witch escorts, talks with gods, sacrificed actresses, sacrificed dogs. He has nothing."

"That's what he deserves."

"So why ask me?" Daddy Longlegs blew her a kiss, stood, shucked Janice's clothes. "I go to join myself. Possess a posse and pole my own pussy. It's how we gods play with ourselves. I suggest you stay here. Drink rum, sleep. I'll be here until sunrise. Downstairs too."

Janice's body looked pale and flabby. The lwa roared, wormed itself into the writhing cultists. The zombies stopped playing drums and keeled over.

She was alone with a big worm god vibrator. She took its advice like medicine, found plain rum in a box under the chicken platters, drank it from the bottle. After a while the worm vibrator began to look pretty, like Japanese octopus porn.

* * *

Janice shook Zarabeth awake at sunrise. She had recovered her pants and jacket. The cultists lay sobbing and moaning. "What happened?" Janice asked.

"Called itself Daddy Longlegs. Said you were overdrawn at the angel bank."

"I stink of man sweat and polyester." Janice burped loudly.

"You know you have gray hairs? I mean, just a couple."

"What?" Janice pulled strands around to inspect them. "This is just—fucking lwa, completely irresponsible—I'm officially off the clock. Let's go."

The elevator stopped at the orgy floor. A stench of shit and salt made them gag. "Downstairs too," Zarabeth said. "Something the lwa said."

In the living room, staggering whores and bloody floors. All the johns were dead, in humiliating poses, limbs broken, fat sliced off with chef's knives. A god's whimsy.

Zarabeth collapsed onto hands and knees.

"We need to go," Janice said, kicking Zarabeth's ankle.

The pain got her up. They walked down the stairs, stepping over bodies. Almost like a good party.

Evgenia stood outside the limousine, clean and powder-dry, in a white silk top and skirt. She crinkled her downcast nose at Janice and opened the limousine door.

The limousine drove off the second the door closed. "Gin all around," Janice said, finding a seat. "You too, Evgenia. Today we had an object lesson in being nice to your servants. No ice, just the shot. Medicinal." They poured glasses, drank. Evgenia refilled the glasses. They drank more. "Zarabeth, have you been checked out since Hong Kong?"

"Checked out?"

"By a doctor, dumbass."

"I thought you were off the clock."

"I know," Janice said. "I don't like advice either."

CHAPTER THIRTY-TWO

San Francisco

His last morning at work—for Gabriel expected no other ending—was sunny and gusty. Weaving his bike through wind and traffic kept his mind off being fired. His badge worked. He nodded at the faces he'd come to know. Just a Monday.

Del waited in the thirteenth-floor lobby. He clasped Gabriel's hand. His eyes glistened.

"You been through a lot." Del coughed. "They're letting you quit. I'm retiring. Think I'll find better waves south."

They spent an hour filling out forms in a windowless conference room, drinking office coffee. It was what should have happened months ago. His summer, a circular detour, to another old soldier sending him home.

"Think I can keep the mug?" Gabriel asked.

Del passed his across the table. "Have a spare. How you want your final papers sent?"

"Email. Let me know when you get settled. Kiss Thi Tam goodbye for me."

"Yah-hah." They shook hands. "You ask me, you did your job. Whatever ran this knew Bill would crack. You were the airbag."

"That's a little subtle from you."

"I seen things go belly-up a lot of different ways," Del said. "Got a sense for it. You keep safe. I ain't there to look out for you now."

Gabriel wrapped the mugs in his bike clothes. He rode in his business suit, south on Market, a long way down until it went up. He pushed himself up Twin Peaks, the wind cold on his sweat. A clear view of the blue-white bay, Oakland's green-brown arm. It would be nice to like the world always.

The sensitives' message board. Gabriel hadn't even hidden it from his captors. He had just forgotten.

He coasted crazily down Twin Peaks, rode hard up through the Haight. He left his bike in the foyer and ran upstairs to his computer, dripping sweat on the keyboard.

One message to ritegard, from eclair62. Auto-burn after reading.

* * *

My last post here. Let these people stay hidden.

I am from a proud family, Canadians since the Underground Railroad, but we only got by and I never liked that. I was the family asshole. I dealt drugs. Carefully, at first, until I started sampling my product.

People in my chain got busted, I split. Money, a bad car, a bag, paranoia.

The bag ran out first. The next day I nodded off in a storm, broke my axle in a ditch somewhere between Calgary and Saskatoon. I went out to try to kick the boulder out from under the car before I passed out. In another life, I drowned in a puddle.

I was rescued by a commune. Hutterites, once. White-skinned, fat faces, gangling builds, in dark dresses and jackets. The women tended me silently. All looked sad. The men asked many questions. I told them the truth. It relaxed them. When I could walk, they showed me their campus: barns, school, dormitories, the workshop where they crafted souvenirs to sell. They kept my money, more than they pulled in a month.

They brought me to the Minister. The only name I ever heard. He was an old fat white man with tufts of hair on old moles, but when he talked he put speakers on my ears and tubes on my eyes. He exhausted me. I told him myself, my dreams, my desires. He recorded it on cassettes. He said I had come in my darkest hour, to let the light come into me.

I knew exactly what the man meant—and I had a hard time not doing it. His voice so big it moved my flesh. I managed to run. Outside—the world steeped in heavy wet colours, the purples and reds and blacks of sick bodies. It was the raw feed of world through my eyes, unfiltered by mind. I collapsed. I was blind.

They tied me to a bed and gagged me. He had healed all of them, and now he would heal me. He fondled me, he used me. I was lost in some glowing show, the Minister replacing my vision with his ravings. The blindness was my fault for fighting.

When my sight returned I was the best boy I could be. I was numb. Like a new toy man. The Minister talked madness to us every morning, insisting we use certain hands for throwing, for eating, for wiping. He made everything sound right. He fucked me twice a week and called it prayer. But my strange colours remained, and I knew that others didn't see them, and they told me intuitively that it was all a horrible lie.

On our second day on our fields in cold autumn, digging up stones, they left the horse unattended at the cart. I had never been on a horse before but I took off its yoke and clambered on. I think it was glad to leave too. Mounties found me thirty miles outside of Calgary. I spent months in a psych ward before Koenig sent me help.

Koenig's people made a new life and I tried so hard to live it. It took all my strength. Now I do other things with that power. Ever fucked a virgin? It's work. You have to be single-minded. Rough. I'm getting the hang of it. So many to practice on, floating here like windblown seeds. Can't fight the current. I like my new new life.

The woman who took me knows you.

Good luck keeping your secrets.

* * *

Gabriel read it through, tears in his eyes. A sadness he could never share. He didn't work at Empyrean now. Del didn't need to know.

He clicked it gone from the world.

He knelt by his bed. No words, just the memory of the Bill Thorn he knew, the tense determined man who saw too much ugliness, too much majesty. Gabriel's silent prayer to an unknown goodness: *Pls help, my friend is lost.*

* * *

In the days after, living on severance and the pay from his unused vacation, Gabriel felt ready to leave San Francisco, if not for good than for a long while. He wanted to see his country with a fresh eye.

Millionaire Walt had bought a beater for a thousand. For half that, jobless Gabriel got a limping blue hatchback with rust spots and cracked vinyl. He spent a week fixing it, installing new brakes and shocks and starter, rewiring the stereo, sealing sewn rips in the seats with duct tape and a thrift-store iron. He named it SHOSHANA, silver rainbow letters unevenly stuck on the back, over the Wisconsin plates from his first car. The ultimate road-trip machine.

In the evenings he sold his business clothes and half of his things online. The almost-new red suitcase became three duffel bags he packed with summer clothes and his last suit.

One Thursday morning he loaded Shoshana with his bags, left three boxes in his closet, and paid Denise two month's rent by the front door.

"Either I'll come back," he told her, "or I'll have you send them."

"You won't come back," Denise said. "I know from transitions." Through the security door bars, she gave the beater an uneasy look. "Why Shoshana?"

"It's the sound the new brake pads make."

"Ha." Denise walked him out. An express document envelope lay on the front step. She picked it up and handed it to him.

Chinese characters on the airbill. He opened it. In it was the pad of notes taken by his sharp-dressed interrogator, and a card from Anquette Leung:

My regrets for your situation. You are alas forbidden to return to my city. I wish you well, one soldier to another. Our lot to be forgotten.

"What is it?" Denise asked.

"A memento," Gabriel said. His true, final severance. Time to find out what of him was just him. "Put it with my stuff?"

"Sure. Good luck, Gabriel." She gave him a strong hug, a short kiss. "I hope we stay in touch."

Denise stayed on the sidewalk, waving as he drove off. Even after she was out of sight, he still saw her there, his last unfilled desire stretching across the city, until the work of driving put her out of his mind.

Down the Pacific Coast Highway, half the view hardly changed, six hundred miles of unbounded deep blue. That first afternoon, he found it threatening, each hill and curve the one where siren views would call him off the road.

He spent his first night outside, south of Monterey, on a foam camping mattress over coarse black sand. The next morning his face and shirt were webbed in snot. His sinuses sharply open as if the world were mentholated. He washed in the frigid gray waves, a thousand nicks and scratches from the loose sand in the water.

He drove faster, comfortable with the great ocean now. The land changed, forest to scrub to rocks and sand. In Oxnard he bought swordfish steaks for his campground's public grill. He put his bags in the back seat.

Hot parking lot, low supermarket, cars. For a minute, he had no idea where he was.

Which was fine.

September 2009

CHAPTER THIRTY-THREE

Lincoln

Her first Wednesday night in Lincoln, Zarabeth found a yoga class on the far side of the university campus, a short hot flat walk from her downtown hotel. A beginner's class, the studio hot and cramped, but she didn't mind. Her Washington studio had moved to a big new building. Zarabeth liked her yoga a little disreputable. Around her, arty tattooed women sweated fragrantly in billowing brown or ratty black. In her blue-patterned tights she felt sleek and shiny, a dolphin among manatees.

The university campus made for a longer but more pleasant walk back, across great grassy spaces between low red brick buildings. At a comma-shaped shallow fountain she sat on a rough granite slab to enjoy the moist cool rising from the water.

Zarabeth's phone rang. It was Magda.

"I tried to call you earlier, but I didn't have your new cell so I had Jill call your office. Imagine my surprise hearing a voicemail recording from 'Betsy.'"

"You did say to keep my head down," Zarabeth said.

"I suppose so. How's the training?"

"Ha. Magda, what are you not telling me? I can teach these flatlanders FirmKey, but who will they sell it to?"

"There are local tech startups—"

"With nowhere near FirmKey capital requirements. FirmKey is for objects, not apps. So, I looked at the Lincoln books. It wasn't hard, either. How did this office miss the reorg? They only have three clients worth a damn, and from the local business news that might be two soon. What am I doing here?"

More silence, but the phone felt much hotter against Zarabeth's ear. She held it a little away but the heat remained.

"You're doing your job, Betsy," Magda said, "and your job is what I say it is. So get those flatlanders good and ready." She hung up.

Whatever, Zarabeth decided. Maybe Magda owed somebody. Maybe it was a bigger play, the way Zarabeth herself had once been. Before she fucked herself.

A storm of rattling behind her. She watched college kids skateboard by. One of their number looked in his sixties, with balding white hair and carrying a briefcase. The sight soured her mood.

She got to her hotel at dark, hot and dehydrated. She showered, rinsed and hung her tights, ironed tomorrow's work clothes. In bed she watched political satire about the new health care act and the rich assholes fighting it, but it didn't hold her interest. She went to bed.

Two hours later she woke up sweating. She rolled over groggily and felt wetness. When she lifted the sheet, a dark stain. She scrambled away from it and turned on the light, but the sticky feeling on her kicking thighs told her before she saw the dark blood-red.

Zarabeth had periods months apart, a day of twinges and cramps spreading clear red jelly on thin pads. Nothing like this vast sludgy flow. She wiped herself as clean as she could on the sheets, ran to shower. She improvised herself a pad with all her cotton balls and swabs wrapped in the napkins from the coffee service. Her phone map found a drugstore four blocks away. She put on her yoga tights, her darkest covering. In profile she looked like a half-erect man. She barked a laugh.

Erections and blood, in a nasty castle outside Las Vegas. She felt as if she would vomit. She breathed deeply to calm herself, to be where she was, not elsewhere.

Checked out, Janice had said that morning. *By a doctor, dumbass.* Time to take some advice. At least Zarabeth had health care.

* * *

On her second Wednesday in Lincoln she did another FirmKey presentation for an audience of six, only two of them Lincoln staffers. She had never pitched FirmKey to clients herself, but broadly it was the same pitch with some careful omissions. From their questions, they planned to open some kind of business-software consultancy.

On her lunch break, Zarabeth called her mother from the smoker's bench. Zarabeth was trying to make it a habit. Aurinha sounded unusually cheery.

"No reasons," she said. "I woke up happy, knowing I would talk to you. It's a beautiful day outside. What is the weather in Nebraska?" She said the name as three long beats, like *peas-porridge-hot.*

"Cloudy today, hot and humid. We had huge thunderstorms yesterday. They almost canceled the flight and on the plane I wished they had. Bumpy ride."

"I don't like planes," Aurinha said. "When your father and I flew north to America, it took many plane rides, some small. They go up and down. I had never been on airplane before that day. I thought I would die, I got so sick, I scared the plane would crash every minute. I threw up in a bag. Your father held me, whispered to me, like a daughter, my head in his lap. He said the plane would not crash, that the storm would carry us faster, like a leaf in wind."

Zarabeth felt stunned. She wanted to speak but her oafish words would pop this fragile goodness like a soap bubble.

"Is it true?" Aurinha asked.

"What?"

"That storms make planes go faster."

"Sort of. Wind does. In America the winds blow east. Sometimes, planes from California go one hour faster than the flying to California."

Her mother laughed airily. "So it was true. Good."

"Mom—did you ever date any decent men?"

Her mother took time to reply. "There's an old man at my work, the husband of a patient who mostly sleeps. He likes me. He is like a puppy when I come in the room. And he has money. I know I could win him over. He will be a widow soon. He wants me as a pillow, as a servant. It is my life."

"Are you sure?"

"I see how he looks at me, and how he looks at his wife. The men I knew—not your father, the others—they were married. They had children. They said they were leaving their wives, but they didn't. I don't think the wives knew. I think my men were good to them, or good enough. Men are pigs. But sometimes women get men who are not pigs to them, only to others. That's as good as you can hope for."

They hung up soon after. Zarabeth thought of Gabriel, of before. She lit a cigarette to scare his ghost away.

She went up to the office. Straightforward-Lincoln had the whole seventh floor of one of the tallest downtown buildings, laid out as an open-plan office with no cubicles, just wood-veneer desks and a conference room with glass walls. On the back of her chair she found a sticky-note pink memo from the receptionist. *Sasha Blackwell*, it said, in girlish looping letters, with a Maryland phone number. A checkmark by *Call Back*. *PM* circled but the blank for a time not filled out.

She called.

"Hello, Zarabeth. I'm in Lincoln for the evening," a woman said with no introduction. She had a brisk low voice like a traffic reporter. "Let's do happy hour."

"Ha. Why?"

"We're both members of the Exorcism Club?"

"Text me a place my co-workers won't stumble on us," Zarabeth said, and hung up.

She left at five and only looked at the message in the elevator. The map link led Zarabeth a few blocks northeast, to a dive bar with a bright red bar counter, old tables, and an empty low stage.

Three men sat at the bar but only one person at a table, a beautiful dark black woman with braided hair. She sprang up as she saw Zarabeth approach, offered a hand. She wore a black pantsuit, a navy silk blouse and black pumps. They shook hands carefully. Just flesh.

"I hope this is incognito enough. I've been looking forward to this," Sasha said. They sat across from each other at the rickety table.

"What is 'this'?" Zarabeth asked.

A young t-shirted server took their orders. "I'm not a big drinker," Sasha said. "What are you having?"

"Rum, diet cola, lime."

"Light beer for me." The server left. "'This' is a lot of things," Sasha said. "Travel, a rare joy for me these days. I was in Chicago for an education conference, but I saw a chance to swing through. Compare notes."

"You lie as badly as Magda does. Notes on what?" Zarabeth asked.

Sasha dropped the cordial smile and looked at her searchingly.

Zarabeth shrugged, raised her hands. "Seriously, what?"

"I need to sit beside you for a moment," Sasha said, changing seats. When they were next to each other, she held up her phone as if to take a selfie, but didn't wake it. Her large eyes grew larger. "What the hell?" she asked.

In the dark mirror of the phone's sleeping screen, Zarabeth sat next to a lava-orange human shape, as if someone had poured the sun inside Sasha.

"Back at ya, babe," Zarabeth said. "What the hell?"

The server returned with their drinks. "Did you want me to take a picture of you guys?" she asked, tray on hip.

"This one's turned out great," Zarabeth said. "But thanks."

Sasha was shaking. She got up awkwardly, fell in her previous chair. It creaked but didn't break.

"How did you—how are you—whole?" Sasha asked.

Tokaji and strawberries with Endre. *We had to recall it*, he had said. *That left a mark.*

Anthony Dobranski

Zarabeth snickered meanly. "So sorry we can't have a play date. I don't have one of whatever that is."

Sasha sipped her beer. She had regained her composure. "How was it done?"

Words were strangely long in coming, as if they didn't want to express her thoughts. "Angels destroyed it. Almost destroyed me. It's weird though. I'm starting to think they rebuilt me somehow, and just left the demon out this time. Does that make sense? Who the fuck knows?"

"So you're free."

"Like a widow is free of her husband, sure. Honestly I miss the thing. Don't you?"

"I had it for longer," Sasha said. "We had—I don't know if the memories I still have are accurate. I read my diary. Things in it—it's not even my handwriting, some pages. You have no idea how lucky you are."

"I'll buy a lottery ticket. What did you hope for?"

Sasha shrugged. "'Play date' sums it up."

"It must be lonely for you. If you're looking for people who know where you're coming from, you should scratch some of your donors. Who knows what you might find?" Zarabeth put a twenty on the table and stood. "I got nothing for you. Leave me alone. Keep the change for your little kids."

She walked out. She looked behind, but Sasha wasn't following her. She stopped at a trashcan. She pulled the pink memo from her purse. Less work to drop it than to hold it, but she kept holding it. The only other member of the Exorcist Club.

Zarabeth let it go. It wasn't much of a club.

* * *

Her third Wednesday morning in Lincoln, Zarabeth joined the FirmKey project managers for an implementation session. Zarabeth had never actually worked on such a project, but neither had they. Somehow, she had become Lincoln's FirmKey mascot. Zarabeth worried they would convince Magda to send her for the season and not just mid-week trips, but she was pretty sure

384

Lincoln didn't have the budget to cover weekend stays.

The new client, the company not even named, hoped to develop neither objects nor apps. Instead, they were building a software testing service staffed entirely by programmers with severe autism-spectrum disorders. The project managers had heard that but didn't quite know what it would mean, since they had brought office layout ideas that were all open-plan.

"That would be living hell for people with autism," Zarabeth said unprompted.

"What she said," the client rep said. "Let's start over."

Once that damage was done, she kept quiet and let the Lincoln staff do all the talking. No fucking way she wanted to move here.

In the office kitchen she made a pod coffee and microwaved her leftovers from last night's Chinese food. As she sat and ate, two white men came in, mid-conversation. She only knew one, a lean, bucktoothed agribusiness analyst named Boyd.

"No, I haven't seen it," he was saying. "It's not there. It got deleted."

"Nothing gets 'deleted' from the internet," his taller colleague said, making coffee.

"This did. Betsy, you've heard about this, right?" Boyd asked. "The blue burning lady?"

She shook her head, pointed to her full, chewing mouth.

"Sorry. There's this video that supposedly shows some woman in a Hong Kong parking lot, burning with blue flame while a guy tries to put her out. But no one can find it. People swear they saw it, people who don't know each other, and all their descriptions jibe. But it's not there. It's been deleted from the internet."

"I never heard that rumor," Zarabeth said.

"That's not the rumor," Boyd said. "The rumor is that the woman works for Straightforward, and the man putting her out works for Empyrean."

"Fuckers," the colleague said. "Beat us twice in softball last season, and stole Grant Tools from us."

Boyd ignored him. "You haven't heard of this, Betsy?"

"Is this one of those creepypasta things the kids post online?" she asked. "The Skinny Man? They said something about it on public radio."

"It's actually Slender Man," the colleague said.

Boyd had grown annoyed with their dullness. "It's not a creepypasta. How can it be a creepypasta if no one can see it? This was real."

"That makes no sense at all," the colleague said.

They left. Zarabeth allowed herself a smile.

She had become an urban legend.

CHAPTER THIRTY-FOUR

Washington, DC, Lexington

Once a week, Ms. Sasha Blackwell and Mr. Walt Wisniewski met for a late lunch at a small Jamaican restaurant in Anacostia, a block from the Big Chair. They both ate Sasha's choice, a habit formed by Walt's often-late arrivals, always jerk chicken or curried goat, Jamaican beer for both of them but only Walt drank more than one.

Usually they only chatted until the food came, about the kids, about funders, about the janitor whom Sasha took pains to keep from the children. On this day, when the steaming sweet-smelling goat came and Sasha said her silent Grace, Sasha's old scuffed leather briefcase remained on the floor, not moving to an empty chair. Sasha talked more about the kids, her sadness that some would leave her care for pre-school. When Walt spoke, even to agree, something raged in her eyes, a fury or a jealousy, but quiet as cancer.

Since his first day with Sasha, Walt had never again seen the fiery vision. This strangeness had that feeling about it. He felt his own heart racing, as if he were also parsed like Sasha, as if his body knew a danger his mind couldn't see. He drank and let her talk.

"How did you get interested in Alzheimer's?" she asked.

He waited to answer, but she seemed friendly, interested. "I lost a grandparent on each side to it."

"So you've seen it up close?"

"They died before I was born, before my parents immigrated. They told me what it was like. My mom left a parent with it behind. He couldn't even recognize her anymore, and he only lived a few months. But it tormented her for years. It was our household boogeyman, I guess. It still scares me. Sometimes I visit nursing homes, get posed for a picture in a memory garden I paid for. I get sweats. I throw money at it to keep it away."

Her frown a crescent of orange light. "That's all?"

"Sorry to disappoint you. Folly of course. Maybe I should give to help people coming into their prime, not falling out of it. Like your kids. If Alzheimer's comes, just use a bullet."

"You're in a bad mood," she said.

"Maybe it's catching." Stringy meat between his molars. "Fine. Let's do this."

"Do what?"

"You're the one burning orange. Pretty skin over a fire pumpkin." Dimmer now, as if it meant to hide. "When we met it spoke. '*Like A Data Center For GOD.*' Is that its name?"

"Your fiancée is a sorceress." Skin won over fire but there were embers in her eyes. She was two beings in one space.

"You thought I didn't know that?"

"You might not have," Sasha said. "It wasn't affecting you. When I—I thought maybe I could help. But you went willingly. She's old school. Blood, pain, fear, lust. Do you know what you're getting into?"

"Good sex, a powerful family. A daughter." He was woozy.

"A tiny cage on the left-hand path," the thing inside Sasha said. Then it withdrew. His head cleared.

Sasha opened her briefcase, took out an envelope and handed it to him. "It's all I can raise now. I will repay the rest."

Inside a check to him, for half of what he had given her.

"What are you doing?" Walt protested. "It's not her money, it's mine. You don't want to work with me, fine. Keep the money. Nothing but investing made it."

She shook her head. "Wish I could. Truly. I have to find replacements for your cash and pledges. I may lose my line of credit. But I can't risk it. Magic is contagious. Stamp it out like smallpox."

"What are you then?"

"A survivor," Sasha said. "With scars and a prosthesis. What they took needed replacing." Her eyes an orange as bright as the sun. Walt's eyes teared from sadness and pain.

Gone. Its final bow and last word.

"I can't trust you now," Sasha said. "What influences you, if it's not just ideals and human charm? If it's not the warmth of the heart? I need love without X-ray glasses."

"Love? Is that where this was going, Ms. Blackwell?"

"It's where I thought we might go. Some weeks, Walt, you're the only single man I talk to. Maybe I should date more." A flicker of smile. "Please take it. As a kindness."

He was short of breath. "I'm heartbroken."

She shook her head. "So am I."

She stood, picked up her briefcase. He put a hand on her arm. She clenched her teeth, but took his hand gently in both of hers. Her hands warm, hot, fever-hot. Her kiss on his scalp like to burn through him. For a moment he welcomed the idea.

He didn't turn to watch her leave. Her faint smile was a better last memory.

He could rush out after her, for one more touch, only a little more pain. But it would not stop. Sit there or burn them both to a crisp.

Sell the beater. Deduct the lunches. Give the money to someone else. At least, no more fucking goat.

A server came with a quizzical expression.

"We're done," Walt said.

* * *

Walt paused at a large tourism promotion, pictures inset on pictures, *The Sport of Kings* in a florid French font. "I've been to a

389

horse race. Sha Tin during Chinese New Year. I had food poisoning. Pork dumplings. I lost ten Hong Kong dollars."

"No horse racing in August." Missy led him to baggage claim. "There's harness racing."

"Is that a lesser option?"

"For stud fees. Standard, not thoroughbred. Not for gamblers."

"Not much of a gambler. But maybe we'll go?"

"Horse racing's about the most boring thing in the world unless you have money on it." They walked outside. It was as sunny and hot as Washington had been, but drier. "There we are." Missy pointed out a red town car pulling into the arrivals lane.

"I've never seen a red town car," Walt said.

"Mother's idea. We thought it was absurd. Like your beater. But we sail in it. Everyone thinks we're the fire chief and gets out of the way."

A gray-haired black man in a gray gabardine suit stepped out of the car. Missy let go her bag and ran to hug him. "This is Saul," Missy said when Walt caught up.

Saul and Walt shook hands. Saul looked him up and down, smiled faintly. "A pleasure."

Walt drew back. "Not feeling pleasure."

"Saul's in charge of security," Missy said. "He has to judge how fast he can move you."

Walt snorted. "I thought the Dozens was a two-person game."

Saul laughed sharply and went for the bags.

Missy got in the front. "Do you mind?"

"Fine." Walt stood by the back door with a sour look. Perhaps a disservice, not to tell him more, but clan lore said it was best walked into, like a cold shower. Saul closed the trunk.

"Let's go, big daddy," she said. He smiled and got in back.

"It is so good to see you," Saul said, driving away. "You need to come home to stay."

"I need to figure out my head. Can't do that here."

"Your proposal has everyone a-flutter," Saul said.

"What proposal?" Walt asked.

"What we were talking about?" Missy said with pointed lightness. "Foundations?"

"That was a conversation."

"It was going to be a proposal. The coven likes to look over my shoulder."

"There's a lot who like what you have to say," Saul said.

"Wait," Walt said. "You look like our network guy. Jules?"

"Julius. My son."

"Wish I'd known." Walt looked annoyed. She could have prepared him better.

A short fast ride on the expressway, then two-lane horse-country roads past fenced estates. Many had gone to mowed weeds.

"You better be right about him," Saul said in clan Gaelic.

"Not sure he's the problem," Missy said.

"He symbolizes the problem."

"I'm the one who *wasn't* there, Saul. But I saw the video. 'A new white page in the grimoire,' the goddess said. I can't marry into the coven."

"Video is nothing next to anger."

"That's as much as saying it was me, not the goddess. Do you believe that?"

"No," Saul said, but with a pained look.

"I wish I could have married your son too," Missy said. She looked out over the sickly estates. "The goddess knows more than we. Sometimes it's hard to trust." Even for the Brigid.

* * *

The Devereaux estate looked like a boarding school campus, with three squarish stone buildings two centuries younger than the column-fronted main house. Saul drove them to the door. Though well-kept the columns had damage around the molding, and the brickwork was turning to dust.

Missy led him through a cramped foyer, through a low salon in greens and golds where two black female teens in gray suits cleaned up lunch, across the paved terrace. Down a slope sat a cutting garden growing small yellow-orange flowers. Two older people stood to meet them.

Missy's mother was as tall as Missy, in good shape for fifty. Hair more blonde than gray, face sharp but brows sagging like two hairy tits above her nose. She wore a white floral blouse and gold pants, smeared with gardening dirt. "Hello. I'm June. Goodness, you're a big slab of a man."

"Wonderful to meet you," Walt said. She permitted an air-kiss. Something made Walt shiver. Missy's line had generations of wealth and nutrition. Epigenetic paradise. Also big fast cancers, massive organ failures, bizarre diseases. June, Missy, one day his daughter. Future father, future killer.

June brooded as if she had heard his thoughts, or he hers. "What dowry has he offered?" June asked Missy.

"Give it a rest, June." Missy's father reached stiff and slow to shake hands. "I'm Jesse. Welcome." His long face had once been fatter, cheeks below his jaw like curtains. Thin white hair, yellow polo shirt and green plaid golf pants. "Hear you're a bourbon man."

"I am."

"Walt had an idea to buy one of the estates nearby," Missy said. "Anything contiguous?"

"Alas no. But there are some nearby worth a look."

Walt went with it. "Wet land or dry?" Walt asked.

"Is it important?"

"Water's the next battle. It's already a battle out West. Too many people, not enough water; greenhouse gases, hurricane coasts and blighted plains. Get the water."

"How apocalyptic. A nice idea all the same," June said. "Good to meet you. Shall we have iced tea in the salon?"

"In a while, Mother. I want to freshen up first."

"Oh. Well, I'll finish with the plants then. Half an hour?"

"Fine." Missy took Walt's arm and led him away.

"Do you really want me to buy land here?"

"Would you care if you had to?"

"Seriously?" he asked. "And what about this proposal?"

"In private," she said. "Words matter here. Say nothing in common areas you wouldn't say in court."

Behind the staircase was a small elevator. "Only coven members work in the main house," Missy explained on the slow ride up. "Young people in coven families get accredited homeschooling and are paid twice minimum wage for housekeeping duties. The methods of large households, not to mention sex magic rites, are valuable skills. Several former staffers have gone to the hotel industry, others relieved tech millionaires of the work of their new mansions."

"All of them are black," Walt said.

Missy nodded. The elevator opened at the end of a narrow blue-lit corridor hung with ornate portraits, guarded by two lean black men in gray. Missy took out her travel wallet and waved it to unlock the doors.

"Our royal chambers." It was a larger version of the bedroom in the Washington house, heavy overstuffed furniture. She leapt on the bed. "Oh the new mattress. Yay. Black families are only thirty percent of the coven but three-quarters of the staff. Our white families had a two-hundred-year head start to make money. Staff has become less black, in fact. Like Julius, they're finding better opportunities elsewhere."

"All descendants of your former slaves?"

Missy nodded. "Moira married into a slave-holding family. Back then women married younger, so she wasn't Brigid for another ten years, but the cholera epidemic created a good opportunity to open minds. By 1850 we had abandoned corporal punishment; field work earned them education. Some left but opportunities were few." She sighed. "Then, the War. Afterwards, two-thirds of our former slaves left, to Nigeria and Dahomey and their ancestral religions, to Liberia, to the new gods in New Orleans and Haiti. The others stayed for generations. Think of this as a movie. The staff are the crew, we are the stars."

"Because you have the Compact."

"No Compact, no great magic. Neither do we want a permanent underclass." She worked out of her dress, clearly hoping to change the subject. "Let's screw on the new mattress."

393

Anthony Dobranski

It could wait, of course. "No one watching?"

"Not in here. All the time outside. That's why I don't come back here so often."

"I wish you had brought me sooner," he said, undressing.

*   *   *

In June's oak and wicker office, under vibrant paintings of intricate Celtic patterns, Walt sat with three women at a small square table. Across from him, June, who had re-introduced herself as Elder Juno McCauley Devereaux; Althee Johnson Brown, of the coven; Regina McCauley Everett, of the clan. None of it was explained but he got the gist. Not a movie but a company, clan with preferred shares.

He read the draft pre-nuptial agreement, read it again.

Read it a third time, to be sure.

"Half my estate is a lot," he finally said.

"In an escrow account," Althee said. She was black with freckled skin, sharp yellow eyes like a falcon. "You can still manage it. It becomes your daughter's trust."

"But the daughter might not be *my* daughter," Walt said. "I like to be professional, but—what the fuck is this?"

The three women looked at each other.

"Magic comes from the goddess," Regina said. Red hair, red gaunt face, big blue eyes. Unlike June and Althee, her accent was Western. "Great magic needs a coven, but only the clan can lead it. Bound to each other. From time to time, this bond is made manifest, by the Brigid marrying a son of the coven. Tradition dictated this was of those times."

"But the goddess sets the rules," June said. "At my mother's funeral, the goddess took Missy and three others—"

"Took as in *possessed?*" Walt asked.

"If you like. Over and over, the goddess said, the clan needs a new white page in the grimoire. Missy found you as the goddess instructed."

"But Missy is old for child-bearing," Althee said. "Only Cullodena herself was older, under different circumstances. The

394

coven needs a contingency plan. We give you eighteen months to have a daughter; after that, we pick the sire."

"To father the child who I then must raise."

"Yes," Althee said.

"Can I bear a child with another woman?"

"Not until Artemis's daughter is twenty-three," Regina said. "Any child you conceive before that will be killed. Your daughter has no rivals. After that, do what you like."

"Previous old goats found it easier to stay within the coven," Althee said.

Althee Johnson Brown. Walt now saw her resemblance to the portrait in his parlor. Sects, politics, open talk of infanticide. He recalled his first optimistic talk on the roof. His fiancée ran a medieval state.

"My daughter vouches for your strength," June said, "as does the urologist."

"Is he—"

"No, Missy took a picture of the report with her phone. Good motility. Our thumb is on your scale, rest assured."

"Hard to rest when hostility blows hot from Ms. Althee."

Althee met Walt's stare with a bitter face but spoke mildly. "It's not personal. I have a greater claim than yours."

"Would your son have been the—original husband?"

"Not her son," June said, "but her choice from the coven. And if you fail, it will be her choice again, of the father not the husband."

"How would that work?" Walt said. "You already have my money, why keep me?"

"You would be handfast before the goddess. The stud would leave for Regina's coven," Althee said. "And I would see the first black Brigid, the coven and clan become one forever."

"Patience, Althee," Regina said. "It is almost here."

"Easy to speak of the future," Althee said.

All of them were black. "This is about slavery," Walt said.

"The clan has a debt," Regina said. "The coven—the black coven—has earned union with the bloodline, whatever the goddess says."

"Careful, Regina," June said.

"We can *talk*, June. This is a mess. The goddess could have warned us. The coven is suspicious."

"Thank you, Regina," Althee said.

June sighed and smiled toothily at Walt. "You see our little dilemma. This was our compromise," June said. "If Missy has no heiress by thirty-two, the coven chooses the father. If she does, the coven chooses the daughter's husband. Slave and master, all one people."

"Glad it works for you," Walt said. "Back to my life."

"These are our ways," June said. "We make it hard to adopt them insincerely. The net effect for your life is magnificent."

Net effect. Debt. Escrow account. A medieval estate, but also like his first bank loans. He had haggled those too.

"I'll think it over," he said. "Let's talk in two days."

They were surprised. Less contempt than a belief he was hungrier.

"Until Thursday," June said. "Missy's waiting for you in the salon."

No curses, no lightning. No ultimatums. That was a start.

* * *

For dinner, the family and Walt made a simple meal of grilled vegetables, all grown on the estate. The family kitchen had white painted wood and steel counters, distinct from the massive appliances in the main house kitchen. "It was Aunt Marjorie's idea," Regina explained. "Her own mansion had one kitchen. Imagine, a cooktop the size of a car for one over-easy egg? So we have a place of our own. I hear you use the herb garden. Omelets, with chervil?"

"Those turned out well," Walt said.

"You'll have to make me one when I visit."

"Come anytime. How exactly are you and June related?"

"Thirteenth cousins. Cullodena had a sister, Mai, who was not limited to one child as Cullodena was. We of the Mai are thousands, though most are far removed, barely aware of the clan now. But my line kept the faith. June and I were distant sisters. We summered together, pledged the same sorority."

"Regina and Juno. Two queens."

"You're starting to understand," she said. "What if Missy were hit by a truck? No sister. Only someone with a blood-link to Cullodena could keep the compact."

"No one from Mai's line ever drive a truck?"

Regina licked her lips. Walt could feel the others listening. "We have a referee. The goddess knows a pure heart. A coup is not possible, but a death can be recovered from, through trials of merit. You are lucky to be mating with her. She's the best we've had in three generations."

Mating. Uncouth phrase. Like an autistic or a scientist. Something odd about Regina. Where were her offspring? Literally a fail-safe, kept off-site? Yet another secret.

Over the hot bland food, Walt told them about his family. "My mother passed ten years ago. Skin cancer. She loved the desert sun, though it killed her. I think she had that sunlight disorder. We were in Syracuse. Didn't mean to settle there but we did. My dad loves it. Got a big truck, hunts and fishes. Mom started drinking, said everything was gray and she felt the cold in her bones. Finally she left for Phoenix."

"She got better in the sun?" Regina asked. "Before the cancer?"

"I had to stop being angry when I saw her there. Then I moved in with her, for Arizona in-state tuition." That drew chuckles. "They never divorced. They just lived apart."

After dinner Jesse and Walt ate cut peaches on the deck, with stiff bourbons. A gray-suited young man brought a cigar box. For all Walt knew, he was Walt's relief donor. Any one of them. Or none here in the house. Perhaps Julius in Washington. How medieval queens must have felt around their ladies-in-waiting. He did not have to be one. For the first time he understood it as faith. Walt got to cut in line for a reason, and that reason was not sitting still.

Walt took a thin cheroot, tightly wrapped like a whip.

"That's a stiff one," Jesse said. "Not fancy." First he had said to Walt all evening.

"Good with bourbon, then." The smoke sweet and fuzzy like chewing leather. The man retreated.

They sat smoking and drinking in silence until stars trumped sunset.

"I never thought to negotiate," Jesse said. "I was younger than you. Poorer too. I wish you luck."

"Thank you. How did you meet June?"

"At a cotillion. I was days from asking a girl to marry me. Ring on hold with a deposit. A friend said they needed gentlemen for the debutantes. I wanted business connections. One dance with June and it all changed."

"Did you know about the witchcraft?"

"Less than you know now. Even here, a father has duties. What are your intentions toward my daughter?"

"I think Missy is the best thing since sliced bread. I want her with me every day of my life. I ask you for her hand."

"Yes," Jesse said.

"Thank you."

"It's hard. Not just a wife who is worshipped. I haven't got a say in Missy's life."

"She respects you, sir," Walt said. "Politics, she's yours."

"Less so now. Power's made her elitist."

"Don't mistake rebellion for contempt. My father did that. It earned him my contempt."

"They like that in men too," Jesse said. "Bad relationships with fathers. We don't mind our name dies with us."

"The DNA is what matters," Walt said. "I like your name. Devereaux, from green waters, from true waters. It's delightful. Walt Devereaux. Waldemar Devereaux. That's a nice ring. Can I adopt your name when I marry your daughter?"

"I'd be honored," Jesse said. "What will your father say?"

"It's not his call," Walt said. "Besides, Polish people dream of being French. Like Chopin."

* * *

Wednesday morning Walt walked across the south lawn to Jesse's garage, which was more worn and dirty than he expected. Inside he found less a collection than a set of random cars. The red town car, and a black one. A silver coupe. Three ragtop two-seat roadsters. A wild brown van from the 1970s, bubble windows and beige shag carpeting.

Saul came in. "Quite the collection," Walt called. "Jesse said I could cruise the grounds. Which are his?"

"They're all Jesse's, save the town cars. I'll find someone to drive you."

"No, I want to drive."

Saul gave him a pained look.

"I see," Walt said. "You can join me, but I'm driving." Walt sat in the forest-green British roadster, long seats and a wood-knob stick. "A dial odometer. Wonderful."

They drove along fenced fields, from paved driveway to gravel road. Stables, a paddock where two young black men walked with a young colt. Walt kept the speed low, felt out the clutch. "Last time I drove stick was in Australia. Queensland. History repeats itself." Saul didn't notice the joke.

Walt took a joint out of his pocket.

Saul reached his hand for the wheel. "I think—"

Walt turned hard right, throwing Saul off. The car skidded into a low ditch. Walt dropped the joint, righted the car.

"Either you are my jailer," he said, "or we are two guys off on a drive. I'm going to light that joint and you have a hit too. Or I'll walk back."

"If walking will do, there's a better place than this road," Saul said.

He directed Walt around the next hill, slowed him down lest he miss the small pair of ruts leading up. Walt drove them up to a stand of trees. They walked through it to a bright overgrown grass clearing, sun glinting off hunting dragonflies.

"Are there rites here?" Walt asked. He lit his joint. "This sucks, by the way."

"I am not comfortable driving or riding high," Saul said.

"This is such a girl thing," Walt said.

"Now you're getting it." Saul took a small drag, tapped his throat, took another. "I could spend my life in the man-run world. I know it well. I might enjoy it more, like I might enjoy being high all the time. But it's wrong. Women get it right more often. They need to be in charge. It took Jesse a while."

"Here I thought I was plunging in headlong." Walt passed the joint back. "If I had liked the way it worked there, I would have been married ten years ago. I can adapt."

"Not the same as believing."

"You can't judge. I have been around the world. I can go native. I see how this culture casts my role. But they let their men be magnates, politicians. You said the coven was interested in a broader audience. Maybe a product to market."

"A book?"

"Like that. Videos. Exercise videos," he joked. "Missy in legwarmers on the star."

"On the circle," Saul said. He snorted, coughed the joint on the grass.

"Give me that." Walt was high too but clearly better at it. Pagans with body not mind. "When do I see the white members of the coven? Or anyone who doesn't also work here."

"You've met Regina. Most of the white coven are now our hedge-fund clients, though each generation, some work their way back. If they get too far from the action they lose their magic. It's just money and ritual and power, like the Masons. That's why the idea of spreading the word is so exciting. We just wish that you had found some other way to us."

"You know I didn't know anything about—"

Saul waved it away. "That was tough. But you have to produce. So, brother, smoke all the pot you want. Ha!" Saul laughed and Walt laughed with him. Saul stumbled ahead, into the sunlight.

The stud would leave. Or he would stay and breed with another. Perhaps a son for Missy's and Walt's daughter. Or Regina's line.

Color wasn't the point, exactly. This goddess wanted an outsider, and marked with a highlighter. Missy had found Walt, ten years past peak fertility and knowing there would be onerous terms. She counted on him to be impossible.

He raised his arms to the clearing, a hope for nature's blessing. Saul bent over, staring at his shoes. Walt wanted to run to the car, leave him behind. But Saul was his charge now.

* * *

Later that day, Walt knocked on June's office door. June looked up from printed papers. Today she wore loose white linen and heavy silver necklaces. "Can I help you, Walt?"

"A quarter of my estate," Walt said. "Another quarter in my will, into a trust only she can touch. And I get two years."

"Close the door." She joined him on low armchairs by the bookshelf. "If one no will do, then no. Why not tell the whole committee?"

"Support this. Or I tell Althee you're exploring a splinter clan with Regina as a hedge against integration. By 'tell' I mean prove."

Walt's whole future: on a guess and a bluff.

"I could kill you before you left this room," June said.

Walt grinned. "You'd have to explain it. There's also my evidence, well, somewhere, waiting to be sent. Enough to point the way. You know I worked in computers, right?"

"You dare assert your dominance."

"Aggression is in the system and cleans out the weak," Walt said. "You need a good hire."

June relented, mulled it over. "A third in escrow. Twenty months. I can't do better."

"What about Regina?"

"What about her?"

"What if I succeed? Who's to say Regina's daughter wouldn't marry Althee's man? What if a zealot just happens to kill your granddaughter, or she dies parachuting? Maybe you can work it. Althee's man and Regina's daughter give birth to your future son-in-law. More family blood, twice the estate. I just want the best deal. Help me father a daughter greater than Missy."

401

"Why do you care that she's greater?"

"Because the world will get worse," Walt said. "I want her ready. Why do you care?"

"Because Missy's greater than me," June said, her eyes bright green. "We trust few men with real authority."

"Trust me all you want. But verify."

"You're a chameleon, Mr. Wisniewski."

"It's Devereaux now. Waldemar Devereaux. I'm adapting. Sincerely. This method has worked for four hundred years. I just want you to know I'm no chump."

"I don't want a granddaughter fathered by a chump." June opened a cabinet. From a crystal decanter she poured two shots. The liquor smelled of apple and iron filings. "Calvados?"

"My favorite," she said. "To understanding, Mr. Devereaux."

They watched each other drink down the strong liqueur.

* * *

On Thursday morning, Waldemar Devereaux accepted the revised offer. A young acolyte presented documents and a long curved knife.

He had never cut himself deliberately before. The blood came eagerly. While the acolyte dressed his finger, he dipped the quill pen and signed his new name straight through.

Missy blew him in the shower, a special treat he was too preoccupied to enjoy fully. He thought about the acolyte, rail-thin and pretty, oiled wavy hair plastered to her head. Pretty like the concierge at the hotel, the day he'd met Missy. Perhaps the coven had steered him. Perhaps it was all a big con. As he came he contemplated his soaked dressing, pulled it off with his teeth.

"How did you get them to agree?" she asked as they dried off.

"June thinks she's using me. Regina thinks I'm stupid."

"And Althee?"

"I suggested the man to be banished if I failed was someone the goddess hoped to save. I pointed out that, whatever my faults, I had no personal ambitions beyond the coven, unlike the last few consorts. I promised to work on improving the lot of the coven's sons. That meant something to her."

"I've known these women all my life," Missy said, "and you taught me about them. Free for lunch?"

"See you at dinner. I need to start hiring investigators."

* * *

On Monday night, after Jesse and Walt's departure for their bourbon tour, the coven's inner circle had a small rite. The goddess generously mounted two of six, Saul and Althee's man Carter. The goddess sang in Gaelic, of love and of great change. It was taken as a good omen, noted and messaged. When Missy was fully herself again, it was two in the morning.

She played the recording of parts she had blacked out. She had learned to ignore her body's acts, save if she was curious about the source of a bruise or scrape. Still, it bugged her, to see herself glassy-eyed with possession, her body used by men, albeit ones with the wit to worship her. She listened, though, sometimes hearing a hint that others in different bodies would miss. On this night, nothing extra for her own ears.

A cool night, three more hours of darkness, a quarter-moon high in the sky. She changed into a neoprene suit, waved away the night guards. She jogged down the paved road until she was out of their view, ran uphill into the woods. She ran, stopped, looked, smelled, ran. Short sprints, gentle lopes, stillness. She was hungry and playing at hunting.

She came to a meadow carpeted in purple phlox, with sassafras north and south.

It struck her. She knew this place, knew it as a phrase. Her Gramma's endless well of family bedtime stories. *Moira ran as a wolf across purple phlox, sassafras north and south, at the edge of Union soldiers' firelight.*

Missy sniffed, knelt in dirt. To run free as a wolf. Free from war, from the household, from the coven, from both Confederate and Yankee. Free of the North and its arrogance.

403

Free of the guilt of slavery, of the base truths of agriculture. Free of past and future.

Missy's shoulders hiked up and back, every goose bump on her skin about to sprout a hair.

Her phone buzzed. She rolled into sitting, took her phone from her tracksuit pocket. "How did you know I was up?"

"I know how you are," Walt said.

"I'm not the usual wife."

"I'm pleased I can keep up. How is it you love me?"

"By choice at first," Missy said. "I thought you'd be interesting. So far I'm right. Soon we'll be wed. I love you."

She put down the phone. Her other hand was a paw, pink-white flesh and thin hairs. She closed her eyes, counted twenty down to one. A hand again.

Lucked into it, like a good four bars on the piano.

Had Moira not written it down? Had another in her line removed it? It hardly mattered. Missy now knew why.

Too easy to stay wild.

Chapter Thirty-five

Aberdeen, Madison

Gabriel camped two nights in the Wyoming grasslands, pre-made camp meals on a propane can, creek water through a filter. He hiked by his phone map, along brown silty creeks, across meadows green as mint. Mule deer in the distance, big and skittish. A huge seven-point elk, regal challenge in its gaze.

The grassland was a source of life and wonder. He wanted to be like that, but he was too angry, still, from his youth so long ago. His one blissful day with Zarabeth, he had dismissed reincarnation. The hope sounded sweeter now. Reincarnation as mulligan, a new chance to get things right.

In the shade of a creek he watched dragonflies swoop and hover. One landed on his arm, wings veined gray and gold, built for battle. It eyed him, twitching, for a minute, for more. By its lifespan, more study than he had ever given anything.

When he left he was smelly, drunk on solitude. He haggled a room at a motel far from Mount Rushmore down to twenty dollars. Bigger than his Hong Kong room, its walls, towels, and fluorescent tubes all starkly white.

He took a long shower and put on clean clothes. He opened the door for fresher air. It was dusk and already cold. To Madison was a straight shot on I-90 through Sioux Falls, twelve hours' drive. He could add interest by going north. He had never been to Fargo. Southwest of Fargo he noticed a town called Aberdeen. One in Scotland where he'd met Zarabeth; one in Hong Kong where he'd lost her, and everything. This one halfway between them. Aberdeen Aberdeen Aberdeen. A private ritual, to finish it.

* * *

From Rapid City north to Sturgis, frail pine trees gave way to eastern grass, on long hills raised like welts. Buildings at junctions, flat and wide to duck tornadoes. Signs for shooting areas. He missed shooting. One day he'd buy a gun.

He crossed the Missouri River on a lovely old bridge of white metal, peaks and arches like a hum, caught and laid carefully, across the wide blue water.

Aberdeen was a small gray-white town dotted with green trees, encircled by golf courses. After driving its length, he stopped at a diner. He smelled coffee and cleaning solution. "What's the beer chicken?" he asked.

The server was a teen white girl, dye-red hair in a net. "Roast chicken over can of beer. Makes the meat juicy. Platter's got breast, thigh and drumstick, side of okra, gravy and roll."

"I'll have that." Empty tables, vinyl cloth and old rubbed wood. The Aberdeen-mandala completed. Bang, bang, whimper.

A glass pot refilled his mug. Gabriel looked up. The server drew back, spilling coffee. Ready to bash the pot in Gabriel's skull. Gabriel saw missing tattoos, a sideways gun, a skull. Buenaventura, the marero.

Gabriel put his hands on the table, shrugged. Buenaventura drew back an inch, another. He remembered himself. He wiped the spill, went back to the kitchen.

"I smoke OK?" Buenaventura said to his staff.

Gabriel sipped his coffee. Terrible coffee.

Outside Gabriel followed the cigarette smoke around the back of the building. The marero stood by the dumpster, arm muscles jerking.

"I'm Gabriel Archer. What do I call you?"

"Tomás now."

"Tomás. It's good to see you again."

Tomás cocked his head quizzically. "What are you doing *here?*"

"I'm on my way somewhere else." Gabriel edged around to get upwind of the cigarette. "I got fired from my old job."

"You got—" Tomás grinned. "You can get fired from that job?"

"If you mess up. What are you doing here, Tomás?"

He sighed. "After you came, Efraín got a little weird."

"You wanted to come with us."

"That didn't help. The next day I buy a new phone at the bodega. I go to church, light a candle for the dead, put a note in the collection plate. The Church got me out."

"What about Efraín?"

Tomás shook his head. "I'll never know. Can't even look, fucking internet they watch that shit. I think he dead." He lifted up his cap, pointed at his empty forehead. "Got the tattoos off my face. Doctor does it free for the Church. Hurts worse than the tats, you know? Leaves white spots too, like Michael Jackson, yo. The mirror's not me. But fucking internet, you find people anywhere now. I learn from the Church."

"That's good they taught you. You like your new life?"

"No." He rubbed his chin and frowned. "Maybe I go somewhere better. Maybe I do better here. So you really not—"

"Nothing to do with you, Tomás. I have my own life to deal with. I'm going to eat now. Good luck to you." He offered his hand. Tomás took it hesitantly, as if Gabriel might be electric.

The chicken was dry, the okra a gooey blob with salt. He shoveled food in until he felt full, put down a twenty and left. On US-12 he got Shoshana up to a rumbling eighty-five.

Koenig's dream advisor hadn't sent them to Efraín, but to inspire Tomás. How many of their interventions were like that? Koenig and Thorn and Gabriel moving the world in nudges, not a blueprint but a game of pool. Even their failures might be greater successes. Or, as Del said, airbags.

Gabriel drove all night, past wilting towns, past half-built rowhouse developments on old farms. An eerie sense of being stalked. He stopped for gas after Minneapolis, ducking low at the pump. As if the universe might pluck him, like a flea who bit too deep and drank a clue as to how the world truly worked.

He wanted to rest. This was when people fell asleep at the wheel. He kept driving.

At dawn he reached Madison. He scraped Shoshana on the driveway slope of his mother's wood-sided duplex. Lights were on. His mother was an early riser.

He rang the bell. A squat white man with thin blond hair and chubby cheeks opened the door with a violated expression.

"Hi. I'm Gabriel."

His mother came to the door in a pilling silk-sheen housecoat, her face pinched. "Gabriel?" She stared stupidly at him, then hugged him with frail arms. "I expected you tomorrow."

"I wanted to save money on a motel room."

She nodded. Even as a lie it would do. "This is Hermann."

"Hi. I'm really tired, Mom." He stumbled up the stairs. The guest room was full of boxes, but in the midst was a folded futon.

"I'm sorry—" his mother began.

"It's fine." He flipped the futon open. "I'll come down after I rest."

"I don't—Let me get you a pillow."

"Thanks, Mom." He lay down and fell asleep.

* * *

Cardboard. Frying eggs and toast. Mom's house.

Gladys Archer had bought the duplex after Gabriel's father died, trading her twenty-mile drive to the Slavic Languages department for a one-mile walk. Gabriel had only been there twice before, for Jeremy's funeral and their last grim Christmas. In the hallway, Archer family photos collaged in frames, none with all of them together.

In the kitchen Hermann was making a grilled-egg sandwich. He wore a blue oxford button-down, pushed out by his paunch. "Hello," he said. "Get some rest?"

"Yes, thanks. Sorry about the rude arrival."

"At least you didn't wake us," he said. "Gladys said you lost your job?"

"Our product failed."

"Might have succeeded if the times were better."

"It was just a bad product." Gabriel poured himself a glass of milk. "Mom teaching?"

"Some meeting at the Russian student house. I know she's anxious to spend time with you."

Hermann worked at the university, a physical plant administrator. "Your mother called about a leak near the server for the Pushkin Collection. It got written down as the 'push-pin collection' so it was quite comic. Once we sorted it out, I asked her to coffee. You and I met once before, at the wake."

"I'm sorry, I don't remember. I'm glad Mom has you. She was alone a long time."

"Yes. Thank you." He seemed embarrassed. He hid behind his sandwich. Gabriel's father would have mocked him as a wimp.

Gladys returned an hour later. She had let her gray hair grow to her shoulders. She looked better than Gabriel had seen her in a long time. She kissed his cheek.

"How long did you sleep?" she asked. "I'm sorry the room wasn't prepared."

"It's my fault, I should have called. Got rained out of my campground. I slept all day."

"I was planning to make dinner but I'm a little tired. Would you mind if we ordered in?"

Gladys called for Chinese while Hermann made lemonade from frozen concentrate and Gabriel set the table. The food came quickly, during his mother's recounting of her many new projects, archives and databases and exchange programs.

"Things have really turned around for you," Gabriel said.

"And for you, though the other direction. What exactly happened to your job?"

Gabriel invented an accounting system that foundered when a Chinese deal fell through. "For a while it looked good, but as I told Hermann, it was a bad idea that got too far. In the process I learned a few things about myself. I'm trying to put that into practice. Somehow."

"Like what?" Hermann asked.

"Like I need a new career." Gabriel sipped his lemonade. "Also I think I'm in love."

"That's wonderful," Hermann said, clapping his hands.

Both Archers looked at him quizzically, caught each other doing so, smiled wryly.

"Is she nice?" his mother said.

"No. Nor was I. We hurt each other."

His mother frowned. "This is all unlike you, Gabriel. Michelle says you started drinking."

Gabriel and Hermann both started to speak.

"You first," Gabriel said, gritting his teeth.

"Gladys, the young man's had a hard time," Hermann said. "You had a hard time too."

His mom's face sank into her shoulders. "I suppose I did."

"What were you going to say, Gabriel?" Hermann asked.

"I don't even remember." He stuffed oily meat in his mouth.

After dinner they watched a dance contest on television. Gladys and Hermann turned in at ten. Gabriel looked over the bookshelf until he found a new Russian thriller. He read until he found the word 'vodka' then counted the words before it. Two hundred and seven. The family record was eleven words, but this was fewer than most. His oldest game with his mother.

Idiot. He looked in the fridge, in the cabinets. No alcohol at all.

This is all unlike you, his mom had said. Maybe it had been a compliment.

* * *

Early the next morning Gabriel drove Gladys to the botanical gardens. They walked the grounds together on paths slick with the first fallen leaves. Gabriel borrowed Hermann's duck-boots, a little small but fine for strolling.

"I used to come here with your brother," Gladys said. "Tough to lose the close-by one."

"Tough to lose the favorite, you mean."

"I was always grateful he was the close one. I thought you would be the one drawn home. I underestimated how much you hated Rick."

"I hated he never gave me a fair chance."

"He was jealous of you."

"Mom, it's past. He's dead. I don't want to dwell on it."

"Fine. You said you were in love," Gladys said. "That you hurt the woman."

"I said we hurt each other." It took him a few steps. "Oh you mean—it was emotional."

"I'm so relieved."

His cheeks burned. "You thought I was capable of that?"

"Your father was."

He stopped walking. He felt more pity than anger. "I'm so sorry, Mom. I never knew."

"He liked the stomach. No bruises." She patted his arm, as if to absolve Gabriel. "It was a different time. It was condoned then. I wouldn't take it now. You and this woman had a difficult affair, is what you mean."

"She was a corporate spy for a rival firm. She's the reason I'm out of a job. Another person ended up disgraced. I'd be happier without her. And, with her."

"I'm at a loss, Gabriel. I expected to be having a different conversation."

"I don't think you ever gave me a chance either."

"I did, Gabriel. You never quite succeeded. You only took reckless risks, for thrills. If you considered it, you played it safe. You missed out on the reasonable risks."

"You think I should try to find her."

"I'm sure I don't know, son. You're different now." She wrapped her arm around his, took a deep breath through her bony nose. "I miss your brother, but I'm in a good place now. I feel fulfilled and I feel loved. My fondest wish for you is that you say the same thing soon. Now let's not talk. We're better quiet, you and I."

* * *

He spent the afternoon bent over Shoshana's engine. He unpacked boxes of his father's tools, still in their trays. Some had rusted but all still worked, even the timing-belt strobe-light.

Hermann came out to grill burgers. "Your dad had good tools. You learned from him?"

"Yeah. Do you work on your car?"

"I don't have a car," Hermann said. "Your mom sold hers. Once you get settled we'll send you the tools maybe."

They ate on the fenced patio with citronella candles. Gabriel told them about Scotland, the arcana of whisky tasting, the drive through the Highlands. No mention of Aberdeen or Zarabeth. They wouldn't understand, and they shouldn't have to.

He could explain it all after he found her.

CHAPTER THIRTY-SIX

East, to Washington, DC

A limp handshake from Hermann, a peck of a kiss from Gladys. He left at first light for Washington. As Ingrid had said, obvious.

Even with the tune-up, fifteen hours straight would be hard on Shoshana. Gabriel planned to split the drive and find a cheap motel east of Cleveland.

He had forgotten Chicago morning rush hour, already slowing traffic as far north as Beloit. He pulled over at a rest stop on the Illinois border to wait it out. He filled his water bottle in the welcome center's fountain, looked for radio stations.

Jeremy's old cassette tapes in the trunk, at the bottom of a duffel. Good for a laugh. Gabriel fished them out before getting back on the highway. Clear plastic cassettes decorated in yellow and red polygons, Jeremy's neat handwriting on the labels. A loud hiss when he played one. He was about to try another, when his brother's voice stopped his hand:

"It is now five, thirty something—five-thirty-six. I am listening to radio news at a rest area next to Sprague Lake, first pay phone I've found in many miles. Little island, lots of grass, kind of stands out in the brown rocky country. I don't know if you can hear but on the radio they're talking about pregnancy substitutes to help with cancer. It's like *Brave New World*. About fifty miles from Spokane, which Matt said was a pit so I didn't stop to see. Have to make Seattle by nightfall."

Twenty years ago, Jeremy had driven cross-country between his master's and his first teaching job. Gabriel had never known Jeremy kept a diary, that it had been in his closet for months.

A piece of odd luck. Another indirection from whatever lay above the clouds. A gift. His brother Jeremy, younger than Gabriel was now, on the road to his own future.

* * *

Driving with his brother was too enjoyable to stop, so he pressed on through the narrow, winding mountain turnpikes and hoped his tune-up would be enough. From Pennsylvania darkness, the highway slowly widened across Maryland, to twelve lanes under bright lights north of Washington.

Gabriel called Walt. "Is Zarabeth in town?"

"You mean in DC? I'm in Kentucky," Walt said. "Signed the pre-nup. Drinking a lot."

"Is she in town? I love her."

"Is *that* what happened in Hong Kong? No one will explain it to me." Walt sighed. "I'll do what I can which is just a phone call. Be pessimistic." He hung up.

An hour later Gabriel sat on Shoshana's hood drinking coffee, on a wide avenue north of the DC border. His phone rang.

"I'm in Lincoln," Zarabeth said. "I heard what you told Walt."

"I—

"Shut up. Go to Missy's. I'll square it."

"Are you sure?"

"I'm sure I can square it." She hung up.

* * *

Zarabeth called him the next night. "How's it going?"

"Missy didn't fry me in my sleep," Gabriel said. "Actually I slept well. I drove out to the new space museum."

"You're such a little boy. I'm in a cab. Make me a rum-diet-cola and I'll be there in ten."

He made her drink and a neat whisky for himself. He sat on the concave parlor sofa just as she unlocked the front door.

She walked in, sat across from him, stared balefully. "So."

He took a breath to speak, held it. He felt it was the first time he'd ever spoken. He wanted to do it right.

"I'm a disaster," Gabriel said. "I've been making the wrong moves with my life for decades. It's a wonder anyone talks to me. I'm not blameless, but I think it's part the angels' fault. How do you invite an elephant in your house? You reinforce the floor. They drew us in."

"At least you still talk weird," she said. "Before it happened?"

"I don't know. I feel like a child pulled by an adult, running to keep up. Does that sound like you? Doesn't matter. I was born again in a hotel in Hong Kong, born loving you and with nothing else in my life worth keeping. I saved your life because I love you. Be with me. Be mine. Walk with me into normal."

She sat still, her lips quivering. "I won't make it that far." She hissed.

"You don't mean that," Gabriel said.

"The fuck you know."

"Why else would you square it here? The demon is gone, isn't it? I told you I wanted you if the demon was gone. I meant it. I'm fired. I'm free."

"I'm all you got."

"You're all I want. I'll marry you, Zarabeth."

"That's your idea of a proposal?"

"Those are my *terms*," Gabriel said. "You don't do half-measures either."

"Ha. Marriage. Better or worse."

"Richer and poorer. Younger and older. Be with me."

"You need to know something," Zarabeth said. "The angels killed the Polyglot by remaking me. Like, rewrote me from my DNA. No one else knows. My scars are gone. I've had—periods."

415

"Periods of what?"

"Menstrual periods. I think I can have a kid."

"Do you want to have a kid?" Gabriel said, hoping not to sound eager.

Her eyes as scared as in Hong Kong. "Only with a man. You knock me up, you stay."

"I'll stay regardless. I'll stay for you."

"Is it that easy for you to say?"

He grinned. "You're all I got, remember? I'm not a good man. I saved you for me. OK?"

She made him wait.

"We should at least go buy condoms," she finally said.

* * *

Ten days later the Devereauxs returned, with no warning. Missy inspected the newly-finished parlor, like a prospective buyer annoyed to meet the tenants.

"This turned out well." She held her hands out, thumbs touching index and middle fingers. Missy had gained a few pounds, more than just water-weight. "You both like it too."

"Oh yeah. But we fuck in every room," Zarabeth said. "Except locked ones. In the master we did it on your makeup bench, not your bed. So are you in family mode?"

"Oh poo. I'm just fat. Protein-shake regimen. No food during the Samhain rites. I'll lose it. But I'd like to be pregnant by Yule."

Pregnant. Zarabeth thought of the Smithsonian's glassed-in beehive, fuzzy drones feeding ghost-gray pupae.

Missy yelped, flicked open her fingers. "You seem tense."

"We had a fight," Zarabeth said. "Before you came. We fight a lot. Fight or fuck. If we don't start the day with a quickie, by sunset we're not speaking. Last weekend we went to Annapolis— that went badly. I go to Lincoln three days a week. Coming back is hard. I don't know. It's only been a week."

"What's in Lincoln?" Missy asked.

"This and that. Work."

Gabriel and Waldemar brought beers from the kitchen. Waldemar had lost weight, a better profile but his face gray and desperate, tantalized.

"What's it like to change your name?" Gabriel asked.

"Pain in the ass," Waldemar said. "I haven't really done it. It'll be easier after the handfasting. But I have ID." He handed them business cards that read: *McCauley Foundation, Waldemar Devereaux, President*

"They made you president?" Gabriel asked. "Not very matriarchal."

"They had to," Waldemar said. "It's my foundation."

"What about Alzheimer's?"

"I did my part. I'm more interested in helping the next generation than the last these days. As a larger issue I don't think science funding is working right now in America. Maybe the new foundation can look into that."

"They let you play on your own?"

"It's in their interest," Waldemar said. "If you like your roots ground and boiled, you don't mind bashing Big Pharma. Your tone is hostile."

"You seem docile," Gabriel said.

"Gabriel, chill out," Zarabeth said. "Next time one of your friends forms a company, ask if there's a job for your unemployed ass?"

Gabriel gave back Waldemar's card. "Sorry. I'm going to head up. Welcome back. Thanks for letting us stay."

Waldemar watched him go, looked at Zarabeth, looked at Missy.

"Don't know why he's so tired," Zarabeth said.

The Devereauxs ordered Thai food and went to unpack. Zarabeth went up with them. She found Gabriel in the dark bedroom, his face lit by louvered streetlight. Muffled steps in the ceiling.

"Might be a little while before it's quiet," Gabriel said.

"Good," she said, undressing. "Big dumb guy go down on me."

He peeled off her stockings, kissed her dirty feet, mumbling scents. "Leather. Jerky. Rust." Up her leg. "Coconut." He tasted her sex. "Honeysuckle." He probed with his tongue, found her little spot and lapped at it. She was trembling. She could feel the quivers of his throat, like a panther drinking water.

"I need more," she whispered. He climbed down slowly as if her sex were a cliff, two fingers stroking her. He kissed her ass cheeks, her crack, licked a treble clef around her anus.

"Kiss it," she said.

He kissed her anus, again, snorting hot air on her hotter flesh.

"Tell it you're sorry."

He pressed his lips against it. "I'm sorry," he murmured. "I'm sorry."

A little rocket under her mountain. They moaned together now, one muffled, one sharp. "Sorry again sorry again sorry again sorry—" She came as implosion, her senses coalescing until they burned. He pushed her lava legs apart and curled into her.

* * *

In the kitchen, the Devereauxs stood dressed and neat, watching sleepy, rumpled Gabriel cook. "What is this?" Zarabeth asked. "An intervention?"

"They were up when I was," Gabriel said. "I thought you arranged it."

They discussed the problem over fried rosemary steak, eggs sunny-side up, olive bread. "First, we just had sex and took walks," Zarabeth said. "Then the energy changed. Something would set him off, and my skin would feel hot. I was ovulating."

"Are you fertile now?" Missy asked.

"She means to say, congratulations," Waldemar said.

"Congratulations. You must feel different?"

"She's different," Gabriel muttered.

"I get sad," Zarabeth said. "About things." It welled up in her eyes. She breathed out rapidly. "Only when he's around."

"You rub each other the wrong way," Missy said. "In life, one connects to people, places, lifestyles. Yours are incompatible.

Your bodies mesh but your souls don't."

"What do we do?"

"In my coven, you'd move on." Missy shrugged. "It won't improve on its own. But, you're not in my coven. These Shintos specialize in purification. It's radical. A pedicure for your soul, calluses gone."

"Shintos as in Japan?" Gabriel said. "Any in America?"

"Do it in Japan. Magic conforms to conditions. Japanese magic, best in Japan."

"We can't afford that."

"Then what, Gabriel? This isn't working," Zarabeth said.

"And going to Japan to get chanted over by Shintos will?"

"Yes," Missy said. "You'll be you, but shorn of the thick matted hair full of brambles each of you has. Your new connections will be shared. But that thick hair protected you. You will have to adapt to that. And purification rites are physically demanding."

"We got fried by angels," Zarabeth said.

"For a half-hour."

"We'll treat you," Waldemar said. "Me and Missy. Our wedding present to you."

"Wedding?" Zarabeth said.

"I don't think you quite know what you're suggesting," Missy said.

"Wedding," Waldemar said. "Whatever ritual you choose. You're making a commitment. And you suggested it, Missy."

"I brought it up," Missy said. She worried her mouth a long time. "If you want, we'll help you. He'll pay for it, I'll set it up. A week after Samhain we can go."

"Why?" Gabriel said. "A week after your holiest day, why go to Japan to do something against the tenets of your own mysteries?"

"Because you're friends," Missy said. "It won't be fun."

"I'm in," Zarabeth said. "It could all end tomorrow. Gabriel—no half-measures, remember? Don't punk out." She kissed him and left.

Missy smiled apologetically. It became a stare. Gabriel felt like a bug.

She slapped her hands on her thighs. "What say we go for a walk?"

In Montrose Park they left trails through the silvery dew on the long grass, soaking Gabriel's shoes. Yellow and red leaves on elms and oaks, like matches beginning to light. On the edge of the woods stood two mushroom stems, fire-red with black rot. Gabriel winced at the fecal smell.

"Bugs like it," Missy said. "It invites its own recycling as food. Why is that bad?"

"Are we talking now?" Gabriel said. "I know the difference between foul and wrong."

"Maybe in a whisky glass," Missy said. "In life you lead with your gut, like she does. The gut rivals the brain, in size, in neurons, in complexity. But it doesn't reflect."

They helped each other down the muddy path, Gabriel taking Missy's hand, grasping Waldemar's shoulder.

"I'm not as judgmental as you think," Gabriel said. They stopped on the small wooden bridge over the creek. "But I'm leery of shortcuts. Why can't we just keep trying? Why magic?"

"Because magic is spirit and this is spiritual," Waldemar said. "You get an infection, take toxins from mold. Address the problem at its scale. Missy doesn't like that logic from one side, and you don't from the other. But you use what works."

"It's moot anyway," Gabriel said, his stomach aflutter. "Zarabeth wants it."

"Yes," Missy said. "I was hoping to help you make peace with it."

"Someday it'll be your turn to want something stupid," Waldemar said. "I promise."

NOVEMBER 2009

CHAPTER THIRTY-SEVEN

Tokyo, Kyoto

Minneapolis's white airport had red signs in Japanese and English. Zarabeth stared at the characters hoping to unravel them. Like meeting someone whose name she forgot.

The others were on board from Washington, while she had taken her final flight from Lincoln to join them. Waldemar had treated them to business class seats. They met on the upper deck, fifteen rows of four seats with a central aisle. They navigated hugs and kisses around surly passengers, around chipper flight attendants with trays of sparkling wine and orange juice in stemmed plastic flutes. The high arch of the fuselage, a little chapel for mimosa communion.

"Cheers," she said to Waldemar. "This I like."

"On older planes, upper deck is best," Waldemar said. "Only pairs of seats so no kids, and our own crew and kitchen. Alas new superjumbos have a full-width upper deck. Soon my little treehouse gone. *Sic transit gloria mundi.*" He gulped his sparkling wine and grabbed another from a passing tray.

For takeoff, Zarabeth sat with Missy. She searched Waldemar's phrase. *Thus passes away the glory of the world.*

"What kind of wedding are you having?" Missy asked eagerly.

"I can't talk about such things indoors," Zarabeth said. "Really."

"Please? Mine's all tradition. Can't even pick the flowers. You haven't imagined it?"

"It's Gabriel's idea. I'm happy living in sin."

"You're a bulldog with big dragging balls in a young woman's body. Do you have gum?"

* * *

They walked, all four in wrinkled pants and blazers, from their beaux-arts Shinjuku hotel, through a canyon of empty high-rises, to great pedestrian overpasses below walls of flashing square signs. Children's blocks for giant future atomic children.

"I feel like a kid again," Gabriel said.

"All our childhood cartoons came from here," Waldemar said. "Those crazy animated skylines—voilà. We're superheroes."

Waldemar led them through the tiny smelly streets of Kabukicho, to a restaurant from his work days. A big open room of long low tables, drunk pink salarymen shouting at the servers. Waldemar ordered with single words, waves of his hand. "Four set menus and four liter beers," he explained. "All fugu."

"Isn't that the poison blowfish?" Zarabeth asked.

"It's perfectly safe once they take out the poison sac. Live a little." The server slammed four large beer bottles and glasses on their table.

"Are you sure these people should handle poison?" Gabriel asked.

"That's why we get drunk." Waldemar filled their glasses, put the bottle down. "Don't leave me hanging. I can't pour my own. It's a rule."

Gabriel poured Waldemar's. "In the hotel—"

"They brought the drinks. You pour for others. It's a rule. Japan's full of rules. You'll remember we didn't jaywalk. Only gaijin—foreigners—jaywalk."

"What if no one pours for you?" Zarabeth asked.

"Fill someone else's to the brim. They'll get the hint."

Zarabeth drained her beer. "What's another rule?"

Waldemar poured. "He who loses his cool first, loses. That one's the biggest rule."

The thin translucent sashimi had more texture than taste, a squid's chewiness. A cup of hot sake with a grilled fugu fin, comforting and smoky but the meat still faint. Gabriel drank to wash a citrus-peel tingle off his lips, but it lingered and spread.

"My mouth is going numb," Missy said.

"There's trace amounts of neurotoxin left in the flesh," Walt said. "It's harmless. They say it adds to the flavor."

"You could have warned us."

"Where's the fun in that?" Waldemar laughed.

After dinner they walked around the nightlife areas, past pink perfumed hostess clubs, clouds of beer and yakitori smoke. Zarabeth clung to Gabriel like to shipwreck debris.

Hand-painted movie posters walled a bus roundabout. "The Western actors look Japanese," Gabriel said. "Their eyes. Is that on purpose?"

"I never asked. But, faces have common features," Waldemar said. "Look around. There are local faces we'd call Italian, French, Slavic. But only one kind of eye."

"You know what? I'm actually in Japan," Zarabeth said. She hugged Gabriel tighter. "Thank you for doing this. I was afraid I'd never go overseas again."

"You're welcome," Gabriel said. Poison fish and unseen eyes. He felt endangered by mutual ignorance, like a toddler running in a parking lot.

* * *

Missy woke an hour before local dawn, her rhythms indifferent to jet lag. They had conked out with curtains open, a view of tall white towers along a park with struggling trees. The sky sapphire blue like deep ocean. She felt like Captain Nemo on his submarine. She shook her arms loose and drank in the feeling. Superheroes.

She slid on tight black workout clothing, new pink sneakers. In the empty lobby she found the park entrance. She did cartwheels across a patch of grass, feeling sharp twigs and grit in her hands. A weak sliver of nature, soothing after planes and city.

She came upon a small shrine, with a white concrete torii gate and small, dark brown buildings around a courtyard of square pavers. A priest in a belted white robe swept the porch of a side building. "Good morning," he said in slow British English. He was small-framed with a long face, thick gray hair. "We are not open, but please, walk around."

"Thank you. I thought torii gates had to be wood."

"The city is hard on wood," the priest said. He left his broom on the steps and joined her. "Do you know what this shrine is?"

"A Kumano shrine," Missy said. "Dedicated to three sacred mountains."

"Your study honors us. Sacred mountains. Hongū, Shingū, and Nachi. Not merely dedicated. Their spirits, their *kami* are here. A small piece, a thousandth thousandth, but the kami is indivisible. The mountains are Buddhas also, enlightened beings. Amida Nyorai, who struggles and persists; Senju Kannon, the compassionate; and Yakushi Nyorai, who heals."

"It's strange to me," she said, "that compassion and healing are separate."

"All receive compassion, even those who do not feel it. The healer must choose. Kannon speaks to high and low. Yakushi Nyorai cares for the poor, the sick, the oppressed."

"You're talking about triage," Missy said. "My fiancé tells me that. Better queen than priestess. I like being priestess. I want to be like Kannon."

"Ask Amida Nyorai for guidance, and strength. I must work now. Good morning."

She bowed low at the shrine, for her friends, that they might scrub themselves clean.

* * *

"Shinkansen Nozomi, Shinkansen Nozomi," Zarabeth

repeated autistically. All morning, subjecting herself and everyone to her own total-immersion. It was getting on Missy's last nerve, especially while pushing through the crowds in the airy white-metal concourse strung with banners.

As the bullet train to Kyoto arrived, a stainless steel barrier rose. "Safety first," Gabriel said.

"It prevents suicide attempts," Waldemar said. "Otherwise the train might be late."

The cars and seats were small, Waldemar's head and shoulders drooping to fit. The train trundled past dense square buildings built to the edge of the tracks, sped along narrow inlets with clusters of gray wood homes on rice paddies. Too fast for Missy, the green a blur. She took Waldemar's hand. He squeezed her fingers without looking away from the view.

Kyoto felt like a college town, low buildings and evergreens. They horked down cheap sushi off conveyor belts in a restaurant by the station, a furious eat, like apes but for the chopsticks. Her augmenting phone view found the bus to the Golden Pavilion, a gold and wood temple on stilts above a large pond. It bored Zarabeth immediately, soon bored Missy, but the men kept looking.

"Why?" she asked.

"Because they cared enough to build it," Waldemar said.

They walked the Silver Pavilion's striped sand gardens, admired the apprentice geisha posing in the park, called it a day. In their narrow hotel room Waldemar napped loudly while Missy took another shower, scrubbing hard enough to clean her freckles. When she came out, Waldemar was up, woozy like a tranquilized gorilla, drinking canned coffee.

"Look nice tonight," she told him. "We haven't had a date in a long while."

They met Zarabeth and Gabriel at six o'clock in the hotel's tiny blue-lit bar. Waldemar talked up the restaurant he'd chosen. "It's all tofu, fourteen different courses, from sauces to bricks dense as mushrooms. Ancient Japanese molecular gastronomy. They don't take reservations so the later we get there the longer we wait."

"Can't we just do some barbecue joint?" Zarabeth asked. "Yakitori?" She whistled loudly for the unshaven bartender.

"You're a bad gaijin," Missy said.

When the bartender brought the drinks Zarabeth tossed her card in the tray. "O kaikei onegaishimasu. Drink up," she told Walt. "Fourteen courses of tofu to eat." She drank half her cocktail.

"Marvelous woman," Waldemar said. "I want you with me when the world ends."

"That's just because she'll have pot," Gabriel said.

In the old Gion district they followed Waldemar's phone map through damp alleyways, over gleaming canals. To a dead end. Missy's thumbs pricked painfully.

Waldemar waved his phone around. "I guess we just—"

Blinding white light, hazy green darkness. A grunt, a crack of wood, breaking glass.

She fell, stood. A dim Waldemar walked with arm outstretched. "Can you see?" he asked.

"Some." She looked down at the ground, around. "They're gone."

"Do we—" Waldemar's foot kicked a bag. "Betsy's."

Missy took out Zarabeth's phone. She had learned the security code when Zarabeth turned it on in Tokyo. She called Magda Crane.

"I thought you were on vacation," Crane said.

"Ms. Crane? I'm Missy Devereaux." Surprised to be nervous. "We met once, by telepresence? Zarabeth's been abducted by ninjas. I expect she'll be gone a while. Thought you should know." Missy turned off the phone. "Does the bag go with my dress?"

"It's fine," Waldemar said. "Tofu?"

"Sounds good. You look nice tonight, did I tell you?"

CHAPTER THIRTY-EIGHT

Nowhere, in Japan

They woke in darkness, strapped and gagged with cloth. Zarabeth grunted, Gabriel grunted. Gabriel fought at the gag with tongue and teeth. Not pointless but it would take a long while. Zarabeth stank like wet hot metal, her flesh a foundry.

Zarabeth forced her breath through her clogged nose. Gabriel felt like the crackle of static on an old TV tube. She longed for him. Her arms shook past controlling.

A voice from the dark. "You will purify. It will hurt. We welcome your hatred if it sees you through this alive. You will never know us or find us."

A pinprick. Each was alone. Later they would find they endured the same tortures: padded mallets, bristled brushes, slow hoses in the mouth, the anus. Hosing off with cold water. To know the other was there made it bigger, hard to see as personal. Always the thought, my love feels this too.

In Gabriel's delirium, he was a green cupcake, consumed by molds from inside, endlessly diminishing.

Zarabeth drowned in blue memories. Mages and angels eating her, paralyzing cold venom. "Humble yet?" a spider asked, tap-dancing on talons.

Unbound, ungagged, thrown together on wet stone like fish in a market. His eyes too swollen to see her. He tried to touch her. Boots stomped his hand, kicked his ribs in the thighs. Again and again they cried, for their own pain and each other's, until they were carried apart and held down. Loud voices chanted, weighing them down through the tile, through the ground. Little piranha bites, not just pain but damage. They were cauterizing. It was the worst thing ever, red worms in Gabriel's brain while he shouted no, Zarabeth inert while the blue lights inside her pupated into hairy flies, her back forever honeycombed by their dead chambers.

Hard to forgive each other for this. The first day of three.

CHAPTER THIRTY-NINE

The Ryokan

abriel smelled wood, grass, cotton. A sound of crickets. Daylight behind his eyelids. He opened his eyes. His skin mottled blue and red and black as if tattoos had run.

He bellowed with the last of his anger.

A woman came wearing gray and white Japanese dress, nodded at him and left.

He was in a hospital bed, raised back and lowered legs. Moving his arms felt like a pull-up done drunk. His pain below him on a trading floor, shouting for attention, easy to ignore.

Other than the hospital bed, the room was rustic. White walls, beams of rough-hewn wood, elegant arches curved like shirt collars, vases of furry willow blossoms. He expected doctors, nurses, bustle. Just handicrafts. Five minutes of peace after torture and already he was bored. The thought made him laugh but his chest hurt too much to manage it.

The nurse returned with Waldemar. He wore a billowing collarless black jacket and pants. "You're still in Japan," he said. "On Honshu. A ryokan, a traditional inn, in the Hida mountains. We have the whole place to ourselves. It's Tuesday."

"Four days."

"You were there for three. You were out for one. How do you feel?"

"I'm not sure this isn't a dream. We were brutalized. They beat me. They water boarded me. I hallucinated worse. They chanted—where's Zarabeth?" He felt crazy panic.

"She's still unconscious. She's not here."

Gabriel sat up, yelled at the sharp pain. "I'm going to see her."

"Go right ahead." Waldemar pointed out the window. "Past that tree, across the valley, up the next hill. The staff do it a couple times a day. It would kill you. She's not awake. As soon as you both can, you'll talk by phone. Video in a week."

"Video now."

"You look like a trampled grape. She's just as bad. You're going to sleep and to drink nasty herbal teas to kick your healing into high gear."

"Fuck you. You are smug rich crap." His anger blunted, as imprisoned as in the straps. He panted hotly. "It was hell. Why did they do it?"

"It's like the opposite of yoga. By overwhelming your mind with pain and humiliation you withdraw from the world and your connections wither. Like enslavement. Now we bring you back. You form new connections."

"Did you know?"

"Not when I offered. Later Missy explained what it meant, and that you couldn't know. The disorientation, the betrayal, help break you. She gave me the choice. I did it for you. You said it was for her. But you wanted to be clean too. I paid for your love torture and rehabilitation. In Japan. Be glad the market's up."

"Never thought you'd do this." Gabriel snorted. "My family?"

"They think you were in a car accident. When you're ready you can call."

"You've at least organized it." He sat up a centimeter and hissed at the pain in his ribs. "I think my drugs are wearing off."

"You'll know when they wear off. There's a controller to adjust the bed angle. You're bedpan boy for a while, not that you've eaten."

"I want water."

Waldemar called out in falsetto Japanese. The woman came with a cup and pitcher.

Gabriel held the cup with trembling purple hands. "The only water was from hoses. I made myself swallow it. To survive." He drank, took a deep painful breath. "Tell me more about the stock market."

* * *

Missy and Waldemar kept separate rooms to be nearer their charges, also for their differing schedules. Missy was forbidden on the circle on the star, lest her own magic disturb their friends' recovery, but she woke early to study and to review the day's reports from the staff. Waldemar slept in, hiking in the afternoons, staying up late to look after investments on American business time. They ate dinners together, simple vegetarian meals with cold water and hot sake.

Tonight they shared wake-up stories. "She launched herself at me," Missy said, raising weak bent arms like a Tyrannosaur. "Fell on the floor. Wind knocked out. Her breath came back in this long wail. It was sort of funny."

"Don't tell Gabriel. How is she?"

"A quivering wreck. Gabriel?"

"Outwardly lucid but smaller. I wonder if we'll stay friends."

Missy frowned. "You're very comfortable with this."

"My name change isn't cosmetic. I'm maybe even a little jealous. I was surprised when Gabriel said they were tortured together. I thought they would be isolated."

"The goal was to bring them closer," Missy said.

They drank buckwheat tea by an outdoor fire in the evening. On clear nights they used a twenty-centimeter Dobsonian telescope left behind by a previous guest. Tonight he showed her Jupiter, high in the east, bands of orange and white with three moons like glinting dimples. "It's really there," she said, squeezing his hand. "I feel like Galileo."

"Let's wind up better than he did. Maybe you should go home. It's mostly the staff's job now."

"They can stick it," Missy said. "Every Brigid performs acts of service."

"Then make nice about it. I've been emailing Althee and June about you. Separately."

"I'm not sure I like that."

"You know my password. Read them."

"All right." She kissed him. "I miss you. Make love to me at dawn."

"Yum. See you then."

When she left Waldemar found Jupiter one more time. So massive yet a trick to catch in the telescope. Witches drew strength from nature. Where did nature stop? Missy certainly liked the moon of late. His thoughts disjointed, his eyes heavy.

The sky black and gray, the fire low. Asleep a while. Beside him, two women in traditional dress gave quick bows. "Yamada-san, konbanwa," he told the night manager. "The sake caught up with me."

"Debaro-san, we go inside," the manager said with concern. "Wild dog loose."

"Dog?"

"Several people see."

"Right." Waldemar got up and followed them. "Dog is inu, right?"

"Yes, Debaro-san. Inu."

"Dewa nai inu," the staffer said with alarm. "Ga ookami."

"What is 'ookami'?" Waldemar asked.

The manager looked embarrassed. "Urufu. Like dog but wild and big."

"Wolf. She says it's a wolf?"

The manager shook her head sadly. "Japan urufu dead, Debaro-san. All dead, hundred years. Big dog. Still, very dangerous."

* * *

They talked often, ten times a day, never for long. When Gabriel first brought up their torture Zarabeth shut him down. "When we're face to face and alone," she said, and he gave her that. Two weeks of pleasant nothings, sightings of birds in the bare trees, complaints about the herbal remedies.

They met two weeks after, on the Wednesday before the American Thanksgiving holiday. Zarabeth sported crutches and a cast on her foot, something she hadn't mentioned. Gabriel walked upright in a back brace. They hugged as if the other were a sandcastle, walked away from Waldemar and Missy without a word.

They sat on a worn log, in the sun. "What got you through it?" Gabriel asked.

"Hong Kong," Zarabeth said. "Over and over. Those chants opened me up. Saved me years of nightmares. I know what I can endure." She took his hand. "I should never—"

"It's OK. You did it for us."

"Thank you. What got you through it?"

"I've beaten men and paid nothing. I found love, Bill got lost. I was overdue."

"You're like the Jesus of fair play. Are you really going to stick with me now?"

They kissed, once. It still hurt. "More to come," he said.

They followed the path to a small courtyard. The Devereauxs waited with lunch.

"Japanese food again?" Zarabeth asked.

"And herbal tea. Neither of you are well."

"Let's get married," Gabriel said. "Before we leave." Everyone stared at him. Gabriel carefully went on his knees. "Zarabeth, I love you. Will you marry me?"

She smiled and cried. "Yes. Yes. Yes yes."

Waldemar helped him stand. He kissed her. "Can we get married here?"

Through bright tears, she looked stumped. "It's a lot to get people out here."

"Oh yeah. Guests."

"Not a lot. Family. We can get—" she giggled "—married back in the States."

"We could send them all tablets," Waldemar said. "To do it here. Put up screens here to show them. Formal dress requested. Set menu delivered by a local restaurant."

"I don't—" Gabriel said.

"Perfect," Zarabeth said. "Let's do that. My mom will need on-site support."

"We'll send a guy over," Waldemar said.

"Can you make it a woman? Bilingual English and Portuguese?"

"You're very demanding," Waldemar said.

"No, dear," Missy said, her face lit with joy. "She's a bride."

DECEMBER 2009

CHAPTER FORTY

Osaka

After her weeks in the countryside, Osaka intimidated Zarabeth. She moved slowly on her cane while the city rushed around her. She bought long thin cigarettes to keep the city at bay, her first tobacco since Kyoto. Weak but hard to drag, as if to train her for blowjobs.

Straightforward's office was in a lonely skyscraper in the Umeda district, two dark towers joined at the top like a half-built robot. The offices had white-gray walls, doors, cubicles. The guard stared frankly at her face, as if making sure she was really foreign. She hobbled past quiet women in tan skirt-suits and hair buns. She felt stained with mud.

The telepresence room was the same as in Hong Kong, half-oval, neutral brown. All the same, sameness a prison. She was scatterbrained these days. She pinched her thigh to focus.

The screen woke. Magda wore pinstriped black. "Wonderful to see you. Thanks again for inviting me."

"I'm glad you came. Your dress was dashing."

"My mother's, if you believe it. She wore it to my wedding."

"Did you like your mother?" Zarabeth asked.

"I liked the dress," Magda said. "What the fuck happened to you?"

"I wanted a hug," Zarabeth said. "Janice Goldman said I was the guy in the iron suit. Everyone—What I wanted changed. I had to become less. I'm still pretty good. And more experienced than when you first hired me."

"Look how well that turned out," Magda said. "You're asking to stay on?"

"I have to leave the woo-woo behind. We both do."

"Just as well. Do you know what the Hong Kong data was?"

She shook her head. "I think Gabriel does, but he won't say. His way of leaving it behind. Not like it does us any good. Anyway. I need a job. I can still work for you, on this side of reality. But not much travel. I've got a home life now."

"Are you happy?"

"I put my best in a bottle and threw it in the ocean," Zarabeth said. "Not just I fucked up but I cling to a lie. But I'll keep clinging. Next time you do this, your next trouble magnet? Maybe get someone from their side. It kicked me so hard I flew up."

Magda glowed as if in a sunbeam. "Yes, dear. That's exactly right."

Zarabeth's stupidity hurt like fingers in a car door. Damage to London, to Rome. Double agents. Destroy the firm. Why it hurt to touch her. Magda was—

"You bitch. You *saved* me."

"Ha. I used you as best I could. I'm no expert, but being saved is like being thin. You need to keep at it. And 'bitch' is not a word you'll call me, if you want to work. Are we done?"

"One last question." Zarabeth felt she had swallowed a water balloon. "DJ Elusive said you both shared an 'inconvenient love.' Did you know my father?"

"We didn't travel in the same circles." Magda snorted. "But I know his kind. Whatever happens, we won't speak for some time. Years. Goodbye, my dearest. May your marriage be blessed, and fruitful." The screen went blank.

Zarabeth got up, fell back down. *Fruitful.* Magda knew. Zarabeth crouched as if defending her new womb from rats.

CHAPTER FORTY-ONE

Detroit

The Devereauxs would be in Kentucky until the handfasting on the solstice, and in Argentina after for their honeymoon. Gabriel and Zarabeth had a home until February.

Gabriel shipped three boxes from San Francisco but only opened one, for his sweaters. They kept the convertible, joined a hotel health club, watched TV. He taught Zarabeth to cook. They nuzzled for hours, his chest to her back, saying nothing. She had never been chatty and Gabriel loved silence.

It was golden.

On a Sunday night they were eating Zarabeth's first roast pork with thyme and lemon when her phone rang. She didn't want to answer but calls were rare these days.

A man's voice. "Hello? So you are—Zarabeth, am I right?"

Zarabeth jumped up and down, her brain jammed. The voice from a thousand middle-school afternoons, dependable as a cancer-ward clown. While Mom was out who-knew-where, Joanie Battrie ate shoplifted burritos, watching cheating lovers, changing sexes, sex with mothers and daughters, all presided over by—

"I hear you're looking for a new start," the talk show host said. "Ever consider Detroit?"

"Honestly? No."

"Ever been?"

"On layover."

"Ha. Come visit. Tomorrow. I'll fly you up."

"All right," she said. "See you tomorrow." She hung up and explained it to Gabriel. He didn't completely believe her until the e-tickets came.

* * *

Their breath white sparkling steam in the bitter Detroit cold. Thin snow on the ground, shriveled trees in the distance. They waited on the curb, glove in glove.

"Talk to me here," Zarabeth said. "What do you think?"

"Firms fly up candidates all the time."

"This isn't a firm. This is just—"

"A rich guy with a plan," Gabriel said. "Been there done that."

"What's the plan?"

"Seriously," Gabriel said. "Chill out."

"Fucking chill enough."

A gold minivan drove up. Out stepped the talk show host.

"It's real," Gabriel whispered. "I admit it."

"Great to meet you." He shook their hands winningly as if to sell them real estate. "Nice day for a drive." The talk show host was older, his face thick and drooping behind tortoise-shell glasses. Under a black wool overcoat, he wore a jaunty plaid suit.

Inside the minivan the talk show host passed them each a cup of black coffee from a tray while he gave the driver directions. "So. I'm only here to meet you," the talk show host said. "I have to be in Philly tonight. We've put you up, hotel and dinner. A date night. So, you seem like good kids. I want to know why you were recommended to me."

"Who recommended us?" Gabriel asked.

The talk show host shook his head. "Like any rich fuck, I have a foundation. Gives out money, gets me speaking gigs, lets me bed society dames. But I have a real project. When I meet somebody who's made something, I ask them, you got any crazies? Any misfits? People with potential you can't use? I'm seeding this great American Midwest with the kind of dreamers that came here a hundred years ago, and seeing what they can do again. People with a different perspective, a fresh set of eyes. I don't have to declare it on my taxes, I don't have to manage it. I just seed. You're here because someone thinks you're crazies or misfits. Which is it?"

They looked at each other. "I'm psychic so I had to do security for Empyrean Group," Gabriel said. "I learned to shoot but mostly it sucked. Then I met her."

"I was a corporate spy for Straightforward Consulting," she said. "Had a demon, let me speak all languages. It was cool. Then I met him. We fucked well. We fell in love."

"But her demon didn't like me," Gabriel said. "This led to a misunderstanding, also rooted in fear of commitment."

"I hear that a lot," the talk show host said.

"I ran away. She stole my firm's trade secrets in Hong Kong, and made my boss a rapist."

"He did that on his own," Zarabeth said.

"Two angels attacked her demon. I saved her life. I quit, she quit, we got married."

"We're starting over," Zarabeth said. "We got our souls scrubbed by ninjas."

"There we go." The talk show host reappraised them. "I asked you, Zarabeth. 'Ever think about Detroit?' 'Nah.' Like asking a kid about beans. When I was a boy, Detroit was amazing. Flying cars and tee-vee-watches. You know fifty songs that came from here. The cream of the melting pot, the future city all at once."

"Fat 'n' happy," Zarabeth said.

The talk show host nodded. "A big failure of vision, a lot of complacency. It stopped being about the future, became about now. A total loss of community."

"You think we can help with that?"

"Creative strong people can. You're from DC, right? Great food city now. Organic locavore, all that. When I was in politics,

Washington had this crap steakhouse or that crap steakhouse. French wine if you were lucky. Clinton came in, with college kids who wanted Thai pizza whatever. By the time they impeached him, Washington had good food."

"You were in politics?" Gabriel said.

"You didn't read up on me online?" The talk show host wagged his finger. "These days there's no excuse. I'm a natural politician. I kept my office after a sex scandal. But, it put a ceiling on my career. For the best. If you get bigger without getting better, what's bad in you gets bigger too. Didn't feel like that at the time, of course.

"I went to television to have conversations of substance. Movers and shakers, repeating their lies. Instead I wound up running a sideshow. That was the substance. My fellow Americans were tormented by their inability to be the same inside and out. I changed that. I didn't mock people, I just let them parade across America's consciousness. Think we'd have a transgender man on a prime-time dance contest before my show came along?"

"Dude," Zarabeth protested. "I liked it better when I thought you made fun of them."

"I thought you said—"

"I chose among competing interests. I'm not doing penance."

"Good," the talk show host said. "Penance ends. You do business, right? Short-term versus long-term? I'm thinking long-term. But let's talk short-term."

The minivan pulled over, on a short block of run-down houses and cleared lots. The talk show host jumped out as if to greet fans. They walked along the street, drawing alligator stares from the few people out in the cold. "You see that silver tower in the distance? That's your hotel. How do you go from skyscrapers to this in twenty blocks? You lose half your people. Every other house vacant. They repaint the houses as art projects, grow community gardens. They have to work it out. But they need new dreams."

She could feel Gabriel's interest. A gleam in his eye, one she had forgotten he had.

They drove past an old blue warehouse. "That's a bookstore, you know," the talk show host said. "Five floors. You'll love it. But there's chaff with the wheat. Most of those books are meaningless now. Written for the past. We can write new books. We can't treat people like that. We can't just say they stay out-of-date, they sit idle on the shelf, not while they're alive. Because they're the only ones who have skin in this game. This city has to reshape itself and no one's going to help part-time."

After some blocks the city thinned out to warehouses and snowy hillocks. They drove a narrow curvy road and pulled over at a chain-link fence, by an elegant building with broken leaded-glass windows.

"Once this was a train station," the talk show host said, but Gabriel just got out. He walked along the fence sadly, like a sick kid watching others play.

"They're not working on it," Gabriel said when Zarabeth caught up to him. "Why not fix it?"

"Because they don't need it," Zarabeth said. "'Thus passes the glory of the world.' Who thus? We thus. We get bored with it, break it, throw it away. We're constantly hungry and we'll eat anything that looks like frosting. Everything gets improved."

"Can you improve on this?"

"It's very nice garbage. Turn it back into park. Oh don't wince, Gabriel. You bring tenants out here, middle of nowhere. Why fight the map? This place should be park."

"Or farm," Gabriel said.

"Sure, farm. Open-air produce market," Zarabeth said. "Like in Europe."

"When can you start?" the talk show host said behind them. "Anyone can talk. You stay here, it's because you want to do something." A black town car drove up. "There's my ride. Bernard here will take you to your hotel." The talk show host shook both their hands. "Think about it. This place could use you. Thanks for taking the time."

"What, you're not going to say it?" Zarabeth said.

The talk show host frowned. "Say what?"

"Just say it," Gabriel said. "She's a huge fan."

"Don't bust me in public." Zarabeth frowned, stamped her feet. "But he's right."

The talk show host gave them a small wave. "Take care of yourselves," he said. "And each other."

Zarabeth smiled brighter than the noon sun.

Their hotel was a hollow concrete cylinder spanned by mezzanines with lounges and cafes. They sent up their bags and went out to see the city. On the People Mover monorail they had a worn faded car to themselves for a sobering ride. Despite glass refacings and sandblasted friezes, the city doddered like old people in costume jewelry. What the talk show host said had been, wasn't.

They disembarked in Greektown near gaudy casino signs. The street felt like the Pittsburgh of Zarabeth's youth, all its energy running down to the sewers. Dispiriting if she had something to prove, but she didn't.

They stopped for coffee in a dated lounge that smelled of fry grease.

"Our dollars will go far here," Gabriel said.

"Because there are no jobs."

"Where else can you remake a city? I'm not talking about a couple of blocks. This place wants to work different than it did. I can be useful. Not another office job. Something with my hands, maybe. I want to move here. What do you think?"

"I don't know," Zarabeth said. She didn't see the appeal, save in Gabriel's eyes, but couldn't bring herself to say no.

They dined at a fusion restaurant with curved booths. After the lavish menu, the food itself let them down. "It's fine," Gabriel finally said. "All the ingredients—"

"But," Zarabeth finished. "That'll be Detroit's epitaph. 'But.' Still want to move here?"

"We cook our own food anyway. Let's have more wine. He's buying."

It was too cold to wander by night. Their room had a view of icy river, of Windsor on the far bank, a shadowy skyline with red casino signs. Gabriel was loose and frisky, unburdened. Soon he bossed her around, less than gentle, the strongest sex play since their ordeal. He put her on all fours, slapped her ass, spoke roughly. Tame by her old measures but also fun. Just rough and tumble, a cub's growling play.

She gave into it, all of it. By the red light of Windsor, she was restored.

CHAPTER FORTY-TWO

Detroit

The first week of the new year, they drove their lives to Detroit, each in a car, neither car full. They found a five-bedroom short sale in LaSalle Gardens: crumbling mortar, cracked stone columns, old-people smell, the iron pipes clogged with rust to the width of a drinking straw. It cost less than a year of Zarabeth's old salary. A contact in the talk show host's office got them a local bank manager willing to lend on Gabriel's promise he could fix it up himself. The last of Michelle's wedding present became the down payment. They joined a gym so they could shower.

Zarabeth laundered gemstone euros on networking group memberships. Her talk about swimming self-assemblers and spinal taps at a leadership lecture soon got her an interim position as a city development officer. Martin found her a pot dealer in Lafayette Park, a fey black man named Pettit who favored tight t-shirts and notched-seam gym shorts. After a couple buys she stuck her stash in a jar in the freezer. Cigarettes were harder to give up. She let herself gain a few pounds. Gabriel didn't seem to mind.

Gabriel maintained the cars, did the laundromat trips, and slowly built them a home. By February they could wash their own clothes. In March Zarabeth came home from a two-day trip to Lansing to find a new glassed-in double shower with reclaimed teak. That night she fucked Gabriel as if to make the rest of the finished house pop out of his head.

On a gray April Saturday, Gabriel was driving Shoshana between estate sales, in search of a mantelpiece. He thought of his starlit walk with Bill Thorn, talking about the firm that had become Empyrean Group, adapting to each shift in the economy. Detroit had let transport manufacturing dominate for centuries; shipbuilding begat carriages begat cars, until cars got commoditized. What the city needed wasn't people to bring them new jobs. Detroit needed a sense of readiness, a feeling it could build anything.

He bought gas on Michigan Avenue. Across the street sat an old white building with an ancient for-lease sign. He left his car at the pump and walked around. Standing on a dumpster he wiped the window with his sleeve. Inside a big open floor, trash and chairs and machine parts, an old lathe.

"Can I help you?" The man was short and heavy, with a scruffy face and a knit cap.

Gabriel jumped down and introduced himself. "Do you know the owner?"

"I'm the owner. What d'you want?"

Gabriel's mouth, on its own. "I'm starting a non-profit for training young people to do building work. Renovations, furniture repair. Classes. Ideally, construction apprenticeships, but I think for now just giving kids something to do with their hands would be a big start."

The man's eyes softened. "Do you have a business plan?"

Suddenly, Gabriel had a job.

OCTOBER 2010

CHAPTER FORTY-THREE

Detroit

Strong sunlight through the high eastern windows made the Learn2MakeStuff shop floor a big smelly oven. Between the workbenches sat old sofas, chairs, lamps, fence posts, mildewed crown molding. Floor fans stirred up dust that stuck to Waldemar's sweat-soaked black shirt.

"A doozy of a workshop," Waldemar said. "I expected your house to look like this."

"Once he had this place, our house cleaned up fast," Zarabeth said. "Only reason he started all this was for the lathe."

"It's the one tool that was here when I leased the space," Gabriel said, nimbly darting ahead through the mess. "But I had to rebuild it. Which is how we brought Mr. Henderson in." Gabriel waved to a big jowly black man in denim shirt and jeans, sitting in a folding chair, machine parts on the floor around him.

"Where are the students?" Waldemar asked.

"In school," Gabriel said. "We taught daytime classes in August but we can't promote truancy. Though a few kids always show up before the school bell rings."

"Better here than on the street, Mr. Archer," Mr. Henderson said.

Anthony Dobranski

Under every workbench a tiny server. "Every piece scanned and barcoded," Gabriel said.

"That should make an interesting historical document," Waldemar said. "The Detroit Domesday Book. Ask for a grant for that project alone. Or crowdsource it."

"Ha. Also runs a virtual PBX," Gabriel said, "so no station is far from an emergency call. That alone reduces our insurance enough to cover the data line. We train the kids how to handle accidents. Zarabeth might teach them to script the system."

"Simple stuff," Zarabeth said. "Make all the phones ring in order, that kind of thing."

"Zarabeth's phreaker army," Waldemar said. "Remind me not to use phones in Detroit."

"I know your cell number."

"And a couple for 3-D printing." Gabriel showed them a plastic box like an armored sewing machine, fed by spools of plastic thread. "Melts drops of plastic. Layer by layer, any solid shape. Even moving parts." On a shelf above sat small toys and miniature busts of children. "I just made some replacement gears for an old grandfather clock."

"I need to get back to the hobbyists," Waldemar said. He thought of his own childhood chemistry sets, imagined time with his daughter-to-be, if daughter ever would be. "You are doing a lot of things here. When do you ever go home?"

"For sex," Zarabeth said.

"Just like last year. Maybe we shouldn't have bothered taking you to Japan."

"Fuck you," Gabriel said, his face hot red. He stormed out.

"You better give him some money," Zarabeth said. She ran out after Gabriel.

Mr. Henderson was tightening bolts on a motor housing with a ratcheting socket wrench.

"How do you like working here, sir?" Waldemar asked.

"I'm retired, young man, so I volunteer here." Mr. Henderson's wrench kept clicking. "But I love it. I know these boys. They just need a good direction and a skill or two. That's about all we can do."

"Just boys?"

"One girl comes from time to time, and we've had a couple others try it. But, yessir, just boys. The boys need it more."

"Boys these days need a lot more," Waldemar said.

* * *

Gabriel's loan officer got him a meeting with a commercial real estate firm in Hamtramck. Gabriel had left late, after a long talk with Waldemar, and traffic crawled through road work on the I-94. He arrived on time but felt unprepared.

Collins Warton was a red-brick three-story office west of Coleman Young Airport. The receptionist frowned when Gabriel asked for Fred Collins.

"He's home sick. They didn't call you?" She held up a long-nailed finger, picked up the phone. "He had a meeting—uh-huh." She hung up. "Sit down, Tamara's coming."

Gabriel sat on the low sofa. A delicious vanilla smell. Behind it a pretty face, auburn hair, curvy figure.

"Tammy?" They hugged briefly. Her teeth in plastic braces. He held her hand, turned it up. "You still have the ring."

"I still don't say it either." Tammy looked at his hands. "Wait—you're married? And you run—let's go to my uncle's office." She led him past framed pictures of office buildings. "When did you move here?"

"Last January."

"Me too. Tahoe got—well, you know, actually. I was done. You still talk to Walt?"

Explaining that now, he'd lose his pitch. "He's around. I'll connect you."

Her uncle's office was as big as Gabriel's shop floor, blue and silver with Detroit sports flair. They sat by a life-size decal of a Lions running back, under a *Roar of 84* banner. His pitch came effortlessly. "I spent four months renovating our house. Then one day I thought, what if everyone could do this?"

"I think it's great." Tamara's teeth opened and closed, tongue darting out to touch her full lips. "My family's handy. If you need volunteers?"

"Only every day," Gabriel said. "I'll warn you, they have smart mouths. But there's older men, union guys, keep them in line."

"It sounds great. I'd love to meet your wife too."

"Might take a while," Gabriel said. "She travels for work."

They made an appointment for the following week. Tamara walked him out. When they shook hands she dragged her nails along his palm.

In the car he sat waiting on Shoshana's weak air-conditioning. Eyes closed, thoughts of Tammy, of vanilla. He put his hands on the wheel until his arousal faded.

Zarabeth smelled nothing like vanilla.

* * *

The community center had buzzing fluorescent tube lights and a squeaky fan. It had once been a service station, the two garage bays filled with cinder-block to make the main hall. Six people sat in a circle of folding chairs: two tough-looking white women, three middle-aged black men, and a young black woman with florid fingernails. Excellent coffee. She drank a second cup. People smiled shyly, as comfortable as addicts ever seemed. Missy smiled shyly. Inside she snarled.

Jim the facilitator, thin and dark black in a tight t-shirt and old-fashioned athletic shorts, announced the calendar, thanked a man to Missy's left for this evening's cookies. Missy let her attention wander until all eyes were on her.

"On the phone," Jim said, "you said you had to get back to your family. Want to start?"

"Sure. Thank y'all for having me. I'm Artemis. I'm an addict. I'm not from here—you could tell that, right? I'm in town, visiting. And I needed a meeting."

Two singly, the others in ragged unison. "Hi, Artemis."

She was a failure. Irredeemable.

"Friends and family are triggers," the cookie man offered.

"Yes. Triggers. We don't talk about our drugs but—my drug

is always available. In my workplace. I can't say anything. It would be the end of my job. I just have to not-use. It's hard. I know that's the addiction talking, but it only became an addiction because I loved it. The first time I did it. My first new day on Earth. My senses so sharp, my body hair-trigger. In Japan, I hunted Sika deer. Beautiful creature. The meat, raw and bloody and soft, like sucking ketchup from a packet."

They gave her funny looks. She remembered herself.

"I've changed though. I feel like I'm aging faster. My periods are still off. Like a marathon runner. I'm not pregnant, yet. I have to have a child, real soon now, or it will be a real mess, believe me. That's me doing what's expected of me. Which is why I started using. It's made me savage. My husband picked up on it. He's lost twenty pounds, he's starting martial arts. It's like he's drawn to my using self. What if he used too?"

She was crying, a great pinch in her chest. "I'm so scared by what I've done."

Each addict came over to hug her. Squishy buttery pouches around bra straps and belts. Her fingernails tickled, champagne bubbles under her skin, ready to pop into claws. Couldn't she just eat one?

* * *

In the morning Zarabeth brought the Devereauxs coffee. Waldemar packed while Missy lounged.

"You look prim," Missy said.

"Better modest than slutty. VIPs today from Gulf states. Petrochemical conference. It's my crowning glory, getting them here and getting the top floor of the center. Any other day, you know I'd play hooky. You feeling better?"

"Slept poorly. Hormones." Missy frowned, an uncomfortable intimacy. "Too short a visit in any case. Let's all go someplace together. After Samhain. Montreal, maybe, at long last?"

"Maybe next spring. I need to run. When's your flight?"

"Eleven. We'll leave around nine. Is Gabriel up?"

"He was late at the shop. Do you mind letting him sleep in?

Cab number's on the fridge."

"We'll leave a note," Waldemar said, hugging her goodbye.
"Keep calling, OK? She needs non-coven friends."

"She truly does," Missy said.

"I'll do that," Zarabeth said.

Missy had never hugged her tighter.

She caught the downtown bus with plenty of time. The bright
cloudless morning would make for a fantastic view of the city for
her conferees. She hoped it was a good sign.

From the moment she arrived, Zarabeth kept herself and
everyone else busy, from her development colleagues to the
catering staff. Secure wireless, printers, projectors. Full waters,
pots of sweet coffee and mild tea, sesame and cardamom baklava,
one sheik's popcorn-flavored jellybeans. Low-glycemic lunches
on the down low. She pitched in with serving food so her own
people didn't get any airs. She felt like a beekeeper.

In the afternoon she got minutes of free time, lurking in
corridors and backs of rooms. Presentations and worksheets, on
production, opinion polling, alternative energy. Shiny-suited
juniors quoted numbers, old men in kaffiyeh and bisht muttered
florid verse. Zarabeth missed business.

Late in the afternoon, two pale-brown juniors stopped her.
The taller had a full head of hair, the other's comb-over shiny
with gel.

"You work here," the comb-over barked.

She looked down as she nodded. "How may I help you?"

"If you could tell us where to smoke, please?" the taller asked,
in soft British.

"There's a lounge on the mezzanine. I'll show you," she said.
Perhaps she would bum one. Friends, business, addictions. All
her old regrets in one day.

On the elevator, she stood in front of them. A black woman
in a neat pinstripe pantsuit got on one floor down.

"Would you look at that ass?" The comb-over spoke
neutrally, as if he thought his tone could hide the words. "*Slap*
that ass like two melons."

"Two watermelons," the tall one said, the same false tone.

"You love big-hipped girls."

The woman ignored them. Zarabeth admired her self-control.

"That's a fine ass," the comb-over said. "I want some of that tonight."

"I have a phone number for whores."

"All American women are whores. Give that bitch a couple of drinks and slap that ass."

Vacant look, empty cow smile from the woman. Maybe she was deaf. Other people got on. Zarabeth's skin tingled and itched.

"I like our escort," the tall one said.

"So skinny. And no tits, like a boy's body."

"She's pretty. Maybe we can get her out to the casino."

Zarabeth's fingers spread like claws. She turned around. "Thank you for saying I'm pretty," she told the tall one. "As for things like a boy's," she told the comb-over, "why don't I get some lotion and we'll see how you measure up, OK?"

Their eyes wide with gut fear. "Sorry—sorry," the comb-over stammered. "I—sorry." They pushed their way out as if the cabin was on fire, onto the wrong floor.

The others in the elevator chuckled. The woman in the pinstripe suit grinned at her affectionately. "You told them, sister," she said. "Are you Arab too?"

"No, I dated this guy," she said, touching her burning eye-bone. "In high school."

Zarabeth walked across the crowded lobby in a daze, hand over her fire-hot eye. She stared out at the conference buses idling in the breezeway.

The comb-over had said: *Dhaiifa kithiir wa bilaa bizaaz, zay al-walad.*

She'd understood Arabic. She'd understood it all day.

She tried to repeat the insult. "Dhai—kith—" The words powder, making her cough. The pain faded with the Arabic.

Maybe the angels had missed. Maybe she had absorbed the demon's ashes. It didn't matter. She and Gabriel had a compact, forged in agony: only life they could fully share.

She had to tell him. Missy would remove it, some rite somewhere. More pain.

She had to tell him. Of course she'd tell him. Soon.

Not just yet.

Not.

Just.

Yet.

ABOUT THE AUTHOR

Anthony Dobranski is a native of the Washington, DC area and lives in the city now with his family.

After studying English Literature at Yale, he made his first career at the internet company AOL, working in Western Europe and Asia-Pacific.

This is his first novel.

Find Anthony Dobranski online at:
http://anthonydobranski.com

IF YOU LIKED ...

If you liked *The Demon in Business Class*, you might also enjoy:

Enter the Janitor
The Love-Haight Casefiles
Working Stiff

OTHER WORDFIRE PRESS TITLES

Our list of other WordFire Press authors and titles is always growing. To find out more and to see our selection of titles, visit us at:

wordfirepress.com